An Anthology of Jewish Mystery & Detective Fiction

Lawrence W. Raphael

For People of All Faiths, All Backgrounds

JEWISH LIGHTS PUBLISHING

Woodstock, Vermont

To my wife, Terrie, without whom this book
would not have happened.

—L.W.R.

Mystery Midrash:
An Anthology of Jewish Mystery & Detective Fiction

2001 Third Printing
2000 Second Printing
Copyright © 1999 by Lawrence W. Raphael

Library of Congress Cataloging-in-Publication Data
Mystery midrash : an anthology of Jewish mystery and detective fiction / edited by
    Lawrence W. Raphael
        p.   cm.
    ISBN 1-58023-055-5
    1. Detective and mystery stories, American. 2. American fiction—Jewish authors.
3. Jews Fiction. I. Raphael, Lawrence W.
PS648.D4M94   1999
813'.0872088924—dc21   99–30222
                                                        CIP

Page 300 constitutes a continuation of this copyright information.

First Edition

10 9 8 7 6 5 4 3

Manufactured in the United States of America

Cover design: Bronwen Battaglia
Text design: Chelsea Dippel

For People of All Faiths, All Backgrounds
Published by Jewish Lights Publishing
A Division of LongHill Partners, Inc.
Sunset Farm Offices, Route 4, P.O. Box 237
Woodstock, VT 05091
Tel: (802) 457-4000
Fax: (802) 457-4004
www.jewishlights.com

Contents

▼   ▼   ▼   ▼   ▼   ▼

Preface *Joel Siegel* 4

Introduction *Lawrence W. Raphael* 7

O! Little Town of Bedlam *Toni Brill* 15

The Reading *Howard Engel* 48

A Final Midrash *Richard Fliegel* 65

The Bread of Affliction *Michael A. Kahn* 87

Confession *Stuart M. Kaminsky* 110

Holy Water *Faye Kellerman* 124

Jacob's Voice *Ronald Levitsky* 148

Poison *Ellen Rawlings* 173

Lost Polars *Shelley Singer* 198

The Good Rabbi *Bob Sloan* 217

Wailing Reed *Janice Steinberg* 236

Mom Remembers *James Yaffe* 254

Kaddish *Batya Swift Yasgur* 290

Preface

▼　　▼　　▼　　▼　　▼

JOEL SIEGEL

I THOUGHT *CASABLANCA* WAS FOR SISSIES and when Lauren Bacall said, "You know how to whistle, don't you?" I was sure she really was talking about whistling, so it couldn't have been *To Have and Have Not*. I must have been nine or ten and the movie was *The Maltese Falcon* that made me decide I wanted to be Humphrey Bogart when I grew up, to be a private eye, wear a trench coat, and talk tough and without moving my lips.

I had role models, but none of them were Jewish role models. There's a line in Neil Simon's *Brighton Beach Memoirs* where the kid wants to be a ballplayer, but "all the great Yankees are Italian. Lazerri, Crossetti, DiMaggio. My mom makes spaghetti sauce with ketchup. What chance do I have?"

He had a better chance than I did. I grew up with *They Are All Jews* on our bookshelf. And these days, when I really do have trouble remembering what I had for breakfast or where I have to be for dinner, I have no trouble remembering Siegfried Marcus who invented an internal combustion engine or Otto Lilenthal who flew before the Wright Brothers or Daniel Mendoza who was once heavyweight champion of the world. I also grew up with *Jews in Sports,* an even thinner book in those days before Sandy Koufax and the wrestler who we're now calling just by his last name, Goldberg. But Hank Greenberg was in both books. And his mom probably made spaghetti sauce with chicken schmaltz and *gribbenes*. But there was not one word in these books about a Jewish cop or a Jewish detective or, God forbid, a Jewish crook.

I did know about Jewish crooks. That other Siegel—Bugsy—was one, for instance. Not to mention our landlord, Mr. Cooperstitch. But no Jewish cops and no Jewish detectives.

Even the movie actors who I knew were Jewish—Paul Muni and Kirk Douglas—almost never played characters who were. Louis Pasteur? Vincent Van Gogh? Were they Jewish? I don't think so.

When Edward G. Robinson played a crook, it was an Italian crook. In *Brother Orchard,* he played an Italian crook who repented, entered a monastery, and became a monk. Even when I was a kid and had no idea what a tonsure was called, I knew one thing: it sure wasn't *payess.*

When Edward G. Robinson finally did play the guy who solved the crime, in *Double Indemnity,* he was an insurance actuary. There's a life of glamour and excitement, a real role model.

I've since learned there were reasons why there were so few Jewish cops. In Eastern Europe, our families typically didn't come under civil law until the late nineteenth or early twentieth century. The police or soldiers we did come in contact with were inevitably the enemy; the best we could hope for was that, like Tevye's friend in *Fiddler on the Roof,* they'd warn us a few hours before the pogrom happened. Even in America, this was not a job for a Jewish boy, let alone a *maidel.* Besides, we Jews wrestle with bigger mysteries every *Montag* and *Donnerstag.* Saturdays, too.

It took two generations in America for us to be free enough not just to tackle the mystery genre (haven't we always been puzzle-solvers and problem-solvers?), not just to want to be part of it, but to feel comfortable enough to be part of it. Moses Wine (Roger Simon's Jewish half-hippie law-school dropout) would not have been a credible character in the forties or fifties. The same for Kinky Friedman and for Faye Kellerman's Peter Decker, who might have been an LA cop a generation ago, but who certainly would have hid his Jewishness instead of exploring it.

(When I read Faye Kellerman's first Peter Decker novel, *Murder at the Ritual Bath,* I was sure the original title had been Murder at the Mikveh and the publisher had changed it, thinking "who knows what a mikveh is?" But when her husband, Jonathan, was on *Good Morning America* selling one of his novels—and why isn't Alex Delaware Jewish?—I asked him about the title. He said, "No, that was always the title." The moral? Never ask. Nothing can ruin a good story like the truth.)

True, there is still some apologizing and equivocating in this collection. Among the protagonists you'll find are two reporters, a novelist, an attorney, and a rabbi who just "happen" to solve mysteries on the side.

But in this first-ever collection of Jewish-themed mysteries, you'll also find some terrific stories; dialogue that will make you smile, if not laugh out loud; mysteries that will make you marvel at their neat solutions; and, in the attribute I most appreciated, situations that force the characters to deal with their own Jewish identities. Of course, that forces us into thinking about our own Jewish identities, which, I'd bet, was Larry Raphael's motivation for collecting these stories in the first place. At any rate, he has certainly chosen well. It's been a long time since I've read through collections from *Black Mask,* and these stories reminded me how the short-story form and the mystery genre make a perfect *shiddach.*

If you already know these authors, you will want to read their original stories that appear here for the first time. If there are authors here who you don't know, you will want to go on to their novels after you read the stories here since their characters are that compelling and their stories are that much fun.

And we shouldn't be surprised. After all, remember memorizing your Haftorah? We invented the short story. And though we may not have invented the Mystery with a capital "M," we came up with the idea first that the Mystery might have a solution. And aren't we the people who raise our voices, point a finger, and use the word "Enjoy!" as a command?

So what are you waiting for? Turn the page, already.

Introduction

▼   ▼   ▼   ▼   ▼   ▼   ▼

LAWRENCE W. RAPHAEL

AS A RABBINIC STUDENT at Hebrew Union College–Jewish Institute of Religion in 1972, I was anxious while preparing for my semester's final exams. Seeking a relief from the pressure, I picked up my first mystery novel. Fascinated by the plot and the rich character development of Ross MacDonald, I was hooked. I did manage to complete my exams and papers, and I did pretty well at them, but in the next few months I devoured mystery novels at a faster and faster pace.

Shortly after being initiated into this genre, my wife, Terrie, suggested that I combine my passion for mysteries with my interest in Jewish studies. So my hunt for a good mystery now revolved around seeking Jewish mysteries that featured Jewish characters. That journey was primarily responsible for this book. It was easy to find the mysteries of Harry Kemelman, which had begun to define this sub-genre, but the real research began after I'd read all of his popular Rabbi Small stories.

Rabbi David Small first appeared in 1964 in Kemelman's *Friday the Rabbi Slept Late*. Thirty-two years later, his last book, *The Day the Rabbi Left Town*, was published. It appeared shortly before his death, and it featured the now-retired Rabbi Small who had by now moved out of Barnard's Crossing (a Boston Back-Bay suburb). In all of these novels, Small solved cases by using skills he had honed in his Talmudic studies. In all of them, he had his pulpit in a very accurately described suburban congregation.

Throughout the 1970s and the early 1980s, my quest for Jewish detectives, police officers, and private eyes netted a modest return. Since that time, there have been an increasing number of mysteries with Jews who are detectives by profession or by accident, and whose Jewishness may be peripheral or central to their lives and the plot. In fact, since 1986, more than 150 Jewish mystery novels have been published. Here are a few things I have learned over time about mysteries and about Jewish identity.

First, as the Jewish educator Steven Steinbock has noted, there is something essentially Jewish about mystery fiction. Like the story of Creation, a mystery begins with chaos and ends with everything solved and in its place. The Bible also flows with whodunits. In its earliest tales, God plays detective, such as when asking Eve how she came to eat the fruit and when asking Cain about his brother. The mystery is all about right and wrong, crime and punishment, justice and mercy. And isn't every gumshoe in some sense a rabbi, scouring the mean streets or the sacred texts to get to the truth?

Second, the detective novel is an invention of the nineteenth century, when it sprang up nearly simultaneously in England and America. Couple basic human curiosity, fondness for puzzles, and interest in violence with a growing need for police forces to maintain order and prevent violence during the social and economic changes of the nineteenth century, and the result was an ideal atmosphere for the beginning of the detective novel. Prior to that, tales of outlaws appeared, but they were usually romanticized stories of attractive rogues, or allegedly true accounts of villains who met bad ends and whose punishments served as warnings to readers. These stories emphasized the villain. Whether romanticized or demonized, the robber or murderer was always the centerpiece of the story, not the person who caught the villain.

For my understanding of how these stories shifted their focus to the detective, I am indebted to Natalie Kaufman and Carol Kay, two scholars who have written about mystery fiction. They explain that the word "detective" did not appear in the English language until 1842, when its first recorded use was in the name of a new department of the Metropolitan Police Force in London: The Detective Division. The word "detected" had been in existence as far back as the fourteenth century, when it meant "disclosed," "open," or "exposed."

During the Medieval and Renaissance periods, crime was often solved by confession, which was usually obtained by torture, or by the testimony of a witness or an informant, also frequently obtained by torture. For centuries, self-confession was the basic method of solving a crime.

Transformation of the adjective "detected" into the noun "detective" indicates the nineteenth-century recognition that there was a new method of solving crime. This new method centered on the abilities of someone to think through the details of the crime and rationally conclude the identity of the criminal. Exposure of the criminal was done by the detective, not the criminal. This new method, which seems obvious to us today, was a radical consequence of a great modern shift in popular thinking about the way in which the world operated and how it could be understood.

The shift began in the eighteenth century with the Enlightenment and its reliance on rational thought instead of divine revelation as a way to understand the universe. People came to believe that they were not merely passive receptacles of divine knowledge, but were also capable of generating knowledge.

This increased awareness meant that a single human being could observe the natural world, postulate a theory to explain a phenomenon, and prove that theory through experimentation and analysis. This methodology had many antecedents, including the Jewish philosopher Baruch Spinoza in the seventeenth century. There were many other heroes along the way, but this scientific method reached an important point with the publication of Charles Darwin's *On the Origin of Species* in 1859.

This phenomenon found its way into the Jewish world with the early reformers of Judaism in Germany and later the United States. They understood that their senses and their rational understandings of the world around them had some merit and some basis for dealing with the world of religious revelation.

In recent years, the ever-increasing interest in mystery novels has witnessed an absolute onslaught of detective novel series. Why has this happened?

During this same period, there has been a growing sense of isolation and loneliness in our lives. This loss of a sense of community is attributed to many forces, including a number of initiatives that seemed innately good at first.

What happened can be blamed on the "Law of Unforeseen Circumstances." For example, the widespread introduction of air-conditioning was certainly welcome, but it moved entire families from the front porch or from the fire escape, where they had talked with neighbors. Now they are sealed in the privacy of their homes, or they use a computer as a way of being connected with others. The loss of opportunity for human interaction is very real and quite serious. We all need human contact in order to be emotionally healthy, and most of us figure out some way to get it.

So, at the same time that bookstores are packed with such titles as *How to Be Your Own Best Friend* or *Making Your Spouse Your Friend,* we also devour mysteries, and we welcome the familiarity of their characters. The warmth and connection with which readers talk about their favorite detectives reveals the importance of these characters in their lives. These characters meet a need for friendship and relationships in our lives.

I want to make a far-out claim for a parallel in our religious realm: one result of the Jewish tradition of returning each year to the Biblical characters and their stories as we read the weekly *parashah* is that once again, we are able to relate and connect with the real-life characters, with all their faults and their mistakes, like our patriarchs and matriarchs Abraham, Sarah, Isaac and Rebecca, Jacob, Leah and Rachel. We read them again and again as they come to life each year, and we see parts of ourselves in them each time in slightly different ways.

What do we derive from these crime-solvers? Again Kaufman and Kay explain by using an example from the popular series that Sue Grafton (who is not Jewish) has written. Grafton is the best-selling author of a series about the private investigator Kinsey Millhone, who is featured in "the alphabet books." Grafton has written 14 of them, including *A Is for Alibi* and *B Is for Burglary.*

As Kaufman and Kay write,

> Grafton's ability to defeat the enemy in a terrifying final confrontation encourages us to think that someone might actually be able to clean up the mess we see all around us in the late twentieth century. At the same time, the personal struggles she goes through in order to do that clean-up reassure us that our own fears and phobias are both normal and manageable. If Kinsey is scared of getting an injection from a nurse yet is also capable of running after a murderer and tackling him to the ground, then maybe we can gather up our nerve to ask the boss for a raise, or hold our teenagers to a curfew, or perform whatever bit of daily living is a challenge for us. Things gone wrong can be corrected, at least to some extent, and, equally important, they can be corrected by someone who has foibles much like our own.

Much of the appeal of these novels, then, lies in the dual appeal of escape from our daily lives and of reassurance that we can cope with our daily lives.

While most of us don't chase scam artists into Mexico or become the target of a contract killer, we do know the fears of being the next person to be downsized at the office, or being mugged on downtown streets, or finding drug paraphernalia in our child's room. The best of the mystery novels allow us to confront those fears by fictionalizing and exaggerating the bogeyman into the worst possible situation—murder—and offering the detective as the knight who slays the dragon for us. We get the thrill of the big scare but all in the safety of our comfortable chair (or wherever we like to read), plus we have the reassurance that the dragon can be slain—and by someone not all that different from us.

So, one of the key reasons for the popularity of good mystery writers is their ability to give voice to our contemporary feelings, while at the same time giving us the reassurance of a credible central figure who can hold back the darkness for one more day. The hard-boiled private eye represents clarity and vigor, the immediacy of justice no longer evident in the courts, an antidote to our confusion and our fearfulness. In a country where violence is out of control, the private eye exemplifies order and hope, with the continuing, unspoken assertion that the individual can still make a difference. The private eye novel is still the classic struggle between good and evil played out against the backdrop of our social interactions.

This is how mystery writer Jody Jaffe explains it to us:

> But just like you don't buy the first horse you look at, unless you're stupid like I am, you don't usually catch your killer first time out. After finding two of them myself, I can attest to that. What I've learned in my brief career as a fashion-writing detective of sorts is that solving murders is a metaphor for living life; both are full of curveballs, red herrings, wrong turns, missed opportunities, and, most of all, foolish assumptions. But if you're lucky, you work hard, say your prayers, and your karma's right, the guy in the white hat kicks butt.

What can this literature illustrate about Jewish identity?

To the popular division of mysteries into private eye, police procedural, and armchair detective can be added three sub-categories based on Jewish identity and the role of Judaism in each mystery. First is the Assimilated Jewish Mystery. While Jewish protagonists are in dozens of mystery novels, they are often highly assimilated and sometimes intermarried. Many of them express their identity thinly in cultural and ethnic forms. However, that thread, which binds many Jews to their ancestors and to their co-religionists, has not entirely disappeared. Sometimes it may appear very tenuous, other times it may be knotted and even quite twisted. But nonetheless, it still connects the protagonist with other Jews and with Judaism. Often the God of their ancestors has been abandoned, but the cooking of their mothers has been remembered. And when the cooking of their mothers has been forsaken, our protagonists invent alternative lives and stories that can be tasted, smelled, or hinted at in these pages. The wider body of this detective literature is one more example of how we now appreciate and celebrate ethnic differences in America.

The second category is the Acculturated Jewish Mystery. In this category, the protagonist is acculturated, and some aspect of the character's or the plot's development is related to their sense of Jewishness. These Jewish heroes and heroines of detective fiction mirror in many ways the 2.5 percent of the American population that Jews comprise. They behave in ways similar to what we have learned about the contemporary American Jewish community. Like other Jews, acculturation may have blurred distinctions between them and their gentile neighbors, but a sense of peoplehood has not been entirely lost. They often reflect that wide group of Jews who marry non-Jews (presently at the rate of approximately 50 percent), whose commitment to Jewish education is minimal, whose Jewish identity is often marginal, and whose Jewish attachments are peripheral. Yet they remain clearly Jewish, even if Judaism plays no role in furthering the plot of these mysteries.

There is a third category of novels that I call Affirmed Jewish Mysteries. In these books, the Jewish characters are clearly identified as Jews, and the Jewish religion or tradition helps advance the plot. These mystery novels are those that are most often commercially popular. There are a handful of Jewish mystery writers who have merged their interest in solving a crime with their desire to illuminate some aspect of Judaism and the Jewish community. Perhaps these books owe their popularity to the interests of some Jews who are turning to some form of Jewish tradition. For them, it is nice to have your exposure to tradition reinforced by a fictionalized account of Jewish heroes.

Much can be learned from these books. Here is one excerpt from Stuart Kaminsky's *Lieberman's Folly*. The context is that Abe Lieberman has avoided being elected president of his Conservative *shul*, and Bess, his wife, has been given the honor instead. As Kaminsky writes:

The services were, as always, the major meditation of Abe Lieberman's week. He had, in his life, gone through the usual range of emotions about religious services. For ten years, through his twenties, he had been a silent atheist, boycotting the services his father had made him attend as a boy. For another ten years, after he was married, he had toyed with becoming a Buddhist, a secret Buddhist but a Buddhist nonetheless. When Bess insisted that Lisa have religious training and tradition, Leiberman had gone to services when he couldn't avoid it. The constant thanks to God were at first an irritant. Then, on Yom Kippur, he had had an insight. The services, he discovered, were a meditation, something he could get lost in, not greatly different from Buddhist meditation. The Hebrew words of praise, said by the congregation and the rabbi and sung by the cantor, were a mantra.

Having made this discovery at the age of fifty, Lieberman had stopped fighting his tradition, though he was still not sure about what he made of the universe. But he was not only comfortable with services, he looked forward to them, to being lost in prayer, to sharing the ritual with others. He wasn't sure whether he attributed this to his age or wisdom. He did not choose or need to explore the questions. That it was comforting was sufficient.

Presented in this small segment of the world of popular detective fiction is a vast array of characters, plots, sub-plots, and circumstances that give us ourselves—contemporary American Jews.

Worth noting is the scarce mention of Israel in almost all of American Jewish detective fiction, in spite of the masterful writings of the Israeli writer, Batya Gur, and the American-born Robert Rosenberg (who moved to Israel in the 1970s). Detective novels are a recent phenomenon in a country that saw its greatest danger from external threats, not from internal crime. As Israel comes of age, the popularity of Israeli detectives seems to have increased.

Mystery readers of any of the sub-genres (mysteries about sports, animals, foreign locales, British cozys, to name a few), as well as those who read any mysteries, know that this leisure-time experience is not just reading escapist literature. If you want to learn about the expectations and the synagogue politics of the Jewish community, take a walk with one of the rabbis in these stories. If you are interested in the modern police department, then you can squeeze into the unmarked cars with one of the police lieutenants. If you are interested in Jews in contemporary music and pop culture, then try to keep up with Kinky Friedman. If you want to spend time with a Jewish female attorney who is single and anguishes over her career, her love life, her search for decent Chinese take-out, her relationship with her mother, and what the Upper West Side of Manhattan has become, then you want to hunt down murderers with Nina Fischman. If you are fascinated by the seductive pull of Jewish crime bosses, you must tag along with the journalist William Goldin in Zev Chafetz's mystery novel.

Detective fiction offers us modern heroes who don't kid themselves that they can restore order to an ungovernable universe. They represent the third generation of American Jews. Not many of them are interested in returning to tradition, and not many are interested in demonstrating their religious or ethnic identity, but they do want to resolve conflict and ambiguity. The Jewish ones agonize over this task a little bit more than the others. But they are bona fide literary heroes nonetheless.

With all this in mind, I approached a number of my favorite Jewish mystery writers and asked them to contribute to this book. I was looking for stories in which Jewish characters solved a mystery, and in which some aspect of their Jewish identity or a Jewish theme is developed. They responded with enthusiasm, and as you can tell when you read this book, they went about this task in decidedly different and creative ways.

Enjoy detecting with some of the best Jewish mystery writers!

TONI BRILL, otherwise known as Anthony Olcott, teaches literature at Colgate University in upstate New York. Olcott lives in Syracuse and has written two Midge Cohen novels. In this story, Midge ventures away from her Brooklyn home and encounters a murder in upstate New York.

O! Little Town of Bedlam

▼　▼　▼　▼　▼　▼　▼　▼　▼　▼　▼

TONI BRILL

IT HAD SNOWED EARLIER IN THE EVENING, but now the sky was a black cupola of emptiness above us, the stars like glinting chips of ice. There was only about an inch of new snow, but it squeaked as we walked, the grass and weeds that poked through it crunching like broken glass.

"Jesus," Russo muttered, his voice tense. "It's cold . . . even if we do find Angie . . ."

The flashlight beams bobbed along the towpath ahead of us, following the wobbling, weaving bicycle tracks.

I shivered and tried to pull my parka tighter about me. "It's nearly 4 A.M.," I said to Russo's back, ahead of me. "Why on earth would she go out on her bike now?"

Distracted, because he was only half listening to me, Russo said over his shoulder, "She's a kid . . ."

"Fifteen, you said . . . isn't bike-riding kind of like . . . well, babyish?"

"That's what I'm trying . . ." Mike turned back toward me, starting to explain something, but just then there was a shout from the group up ahead of us, and the flashlight beams all converged on something off to our right. Toward the canal. "Jesus," Russo snapped, turning toward the canal so fast that he slipped on the new snow.

I wasn't much better, the smooth leather soles of my new boots like butter on the snow, but we made our way to the group on the bank, who were trying to figure out how to hold onto each other, to keep from sliding down the short steep bank onto the ice.

15

That the ice wasn't strong enough to support a person's weight was made more than obvious by the jagged patch of black water that sat like punctuation at the end of the wobbling bicycle tracks. Still, the water in this remnant of the Erie Canal couldn't have been so deep, since every time the flashlight beams passed across that gaping hole we could see the pale blur of Angelina's face, wreathed Ophelia-like in her long blonde hair.

I gasped, and hid my face against Russo's chest. He held me, but only after a moment, like he had been too shocked even to move. I could hear his breath, catching in his throat. "Santa brought that damn bike . . ." he spoke, sounding dazed. "It wouldn't have been there, when Angie went to bed . . . she must have got up, there it was under the tree . . ."

Then he stiffened, took me by the elbows, held me at arm's length. "Santa, damn it! The poor kid still believed in Santa Claus!" Mike's face was imploring, strangled with an urgency to explain . . . what? That this kid shouldn't be dead at the bottom of a canal? His gaze searched hard for something in my face, but must not have found it, for Mike dropped my arms, and ran down to the water's edge and to the other men. They had found some scrap lumber and were laying it on the ice, arguing about who was the lightest of them, to try to slither out towards Angie on his belly.

I shivered on the bank, feeling powerless. It wasn't until they actually had Angelina laid on the towpath for a pointless attempt at mouth-to-mouth, that I noticed the fresh sneaker tracks which continued down along the towpath and vanished in the blackness.

Two days before that, the worst thing I might have thought could come from this trip to the country were the credit card bills I ran up while getting ready for it.

"Corduroy skirt, new oxblood boots, parka the color of Liz Taylor's eyes, with a dyed-to-match fox ruff on the hood, no less?" My mother peeked into the overnight bag—also new—that I was packing on my bed. "This is maybe Bing Crosby that's taking you for Christmas in the country? Egg nog, roasting chestnuts, Christmas carols . . . and the warm glow of an old flame?"

"This is not 'Christmas in the country', Mother," I snapped, too sharply. That "old flame" had hurt. "Russo's just an old friend now, and he asked me to do him this favor. It's a huge family wedding, his mother can't make it, and somebody's got to represent Mike's side of the family. He says he doesn't know these people all that well, but he can't bear the way, when he does see them, that everyone teases him about being 36 and not even married yet." I made my stare severe, even a little pointed. "You should know how insufferable families can get about that sort of stuff, am I right? Anyhow, the way you're always fixing me up with the losers you meet at the dentist's office, I've been getting the vague idea that you want me to marry again!"

I was fighting dirty, I know; Pearl swears that she took her job as office manager of the dental practice on the ground floor of her building because it was driving her crazy to sit alone all day doing nothing, and not because she thought it was a good way to find me a nice man to date, even if he had gingivitis. My mother surprised me though. Rather than continue to quarrel, she suddenly perched on the edge of my bed like some sparrow of motherhood, hands in her lap, left one twisting the widow's rings on her right. Looking up at me with big round eyes, her voice soft with worry, she said, "Oh, Midge, I know your detective beau is as good-looking as a real-life person can possibly get, and this trying-to-be-a-writer business has to be terribly lonely, sitting in this dinky apartment all day staring at that computer, but . . ."

"But he's a Catholic and I'm a Jew and that's why it's better that I should stay in this apartment until I wrinkle up like Aunt Doris and they cart me off to be Midwood's entry in the Miss Sunkist Prune contest, correct?" I snarled, then snatched up one of my new silk turtlenecks, to make it clear this conversation was through. "Anyway, he's not my beau and I'm not trying to be a writer, I *am* a writer . . . just not exactly a very published writer. Yet."

Clear to me, maybe. Not to Pearl. "What wrinkles? You know plump women keep their skin taut longer. But if you want to walk out on a perfectly acceptable husband so you can move to the big city and solve mysteries like that Angela Lansbury, who am I to say anything? It's your life, so . . ."

"Oh, mother, please don't bring Paul into this, not again!" I snapped, startled to feel tear salt stinging my eyes and the inside of my nose. It could have been the "plump" —Pearl drew the first tear from me on that subject when I was four, and I was a lot rounder in my half of our new mother-and-daughter outfits than she was in hers. However, I have also had 31 years since that first tear to get used to the idea that, even if God in His infinite mercy suddenly made me a size 2, Pearl would probably still say it was a pity, because all the really nice stuff is 2 Petite. So I was inclined to think those sudden tears also had something to do with the fact that, through that long rainy autumn and into the dark of early winter, the suspicion had increasingly been forcing itself upon me that maybe, in fact, walking out on my schleppy now ex-husband Paul in order to move back to Brooklyn so I could chase my dream of becoming a novelist was not the smartest thing I had ever done.

Angry—with me for having second thoughts, and with my mother for being there to see me have them—I ground my knuckles just under my eyes, careful not to smudge my underliner or knock loose my lenses. Then I said, "Besides, Russo . . . okay, maybe I was a little nuts for the guy last year, but that's over now. We broke up, all summer we didn't see each other, but what does that mean, we can't still be friends? He needs a favor, I said I'd do it for him. And going to a big Sicilian wedding, that might be kind of fun, right?"

My mother sat perfectly still for a half-beat, then shrugged and stood up, cool and slightly distant. Lauren Bacall, in three-quarter scale. She picked up my new bra—old ivory silk, imported lace trim, front clasp—looked at the price tag, then handed it to me, her eyebrows neatly sketched arches of skepticism. "Just friends? For just friends you now pay retail?"

"Hey, so *this* is your lady Sherlock Holmes, Mikey? The one ya took to the old country? *Che berda!* . . . How's about a kiss for Mike's Zio Pietro?" I giggled as the man's sweat-slick, beard-grizzled round cheeks and bootbrush mustache sailed at me on a cloud of oregano and chianti fumes, but I couldn't squirm out of the way of the incoming lips, since this Uncle Pietro had me clutched tight by both wrists.

Luckily, Nonna Donna was pretty quick with her purse. "You old goat!" The big-boned woman just past Pietro slapped her brocade pocketbook down on his balding head, then leaned around her husband to shout above the all-brass version of "Hark the Herald Angels" oomphing from the ceiling speakers, "You gotta excuse him. Sixty-two years old next February, and the man would try to kiss an elephant if one came through that door in a skirt! I'm Donna, Mrs. Cippoletti . . ."

"Right, Midge, this is the uh, Cippolettis, he's the brother of Sal . . . Salvatore, that you met over by the dessert tray?" Mike Russo looked embarrassed and flustered, cute enough that I might have kissed him, but not before I first broke over his head one of the dozens of straw-bottomed wine bottles from the table, for telling everybody at this pre-wedding dinner that

I was the one he had gone to Sicily with last year. I was famous, it turned out; I just wasn't sure for what.

Flustered from wondering if that elephant crack was a hint that my new sheath in grey lambs wool was too tight, I just smiled, nodded, and mumbled something, then dug my nails into Russo's arm. "Lady Sherlock Holmes?" I hissed in his ear. "You told them that too?"

Mike grinned sheepishly, "I kind of, you know . . . had to tell 'em something about you. They kept asking, wanting to know about you. Where we met, how we know each other . . . so Sicily and things with the doctor and that publisher guy, they just sorta came out." He shrugged. "They kinda think we work together."

"You told them I'm a cop?" Horrified, I dug my nails in tighter. "Hark the Herald Angels" segued into "The Little Drummer Boy." "Jesus, isn't that illegal?"

"Hey, ouch! Only if you tell 'em you're a cop. Anyway, come on . . . I hadda tell them you do something for a living. What else was I gonna tell them? You write books? You think any of these people read? Hey, Enzo! *Com' stai!*" Russo snatched his punctured arm from me, to fling it around the guy who now stood up, just beyond Nonna Donna. He looked a lot like Mike, except fifty pounds heavier, and with a black wiry pelt peeking out past his loosened, sweaty collar. Enzo and Mike thumped each other on the back three or four times, and then, still hugging Mike with his left arm, Enzo started pumping my hand too, with his right, like he was hoping to shake the cubic zirconias out of my tennis bracelet. "Glad you could come, you know?! A pleasure, a pleasure . . . so you're the big city detective, hey?" He wheezed slightly, sweat beaded like little pickled onions on his long-ago receded hairline.

"She's a lady detective, for real? Like on 'Homicide'?" squealed the woman just past Enzo—permed ropes of flax-from-a-bottle hair, three-inch plastic nails, faint brown mustache above Ferrari red lipstick. Also taking my hand, which her husband hadn't released yet, she repeated her question, "You're a detective? What, you come to solve a murder or something?" She laughed so hard she started to hiccup.

"Naw, you stupid woman," Enzo let go of both me and Russo to turn on his wife. "She's Mikey's girl, you idiot, from the city. 'Homicide,' that's set in Baltimore or some damned place. This is Canastota. What murders we got up here? This is Canastota, for christsakes. They come for Gina and Tommy's wedding, right? Miss—Miss—"

Maybe it was the floor-to-ceiling tinfoil Christmas tree in the far corner, lit from two directions by spotlights which had three-colored gels revolving in front of them, or maybe it was the garlands of plastic fir and holly that looped here and there beneath the acoustic tiles, or maybe it was the three-foot tall golden angels that stood among the meatballs, gnocchi, and Chianti bottles on the table, blowing their golden trumpets, but I just didn't feel totally comfortable blurting out the word "Cohen."

So I smiled, trying to flex some life back into my numbed hand and doing my best not to hear Nonna Donna behind me, confiding to someone across the table, "Nice girl! Good wide hips!" The muzak now seemed to be doing "Frosty the Snowman." "Midge," I said, "just call me Midge."

Or better yet, I thought, realizing now just how long a weekend I had put myself in for, just call me a cab.

It's easy to make fun of big family events like that, of course. But, to be honest, I can't really say that the thirty-five or so couples there in the Seneca Room of Isadore's Venezia-by-the-Thruway looked or acted a whole lot different than most of the 107 couples, plus children, that my second cousin Simcha had for her Rachel's bas mitzvah, or the crowd at the bris they threw when Sam's boy Bernie and his wife finally managed a son, after four daughters. Sure the food was different, because these were Italians—not many Jewish functions serve octopus, for example—but big ethnic families are big ethnic families. Okay, maybe if it was one of those WASP family gatherings where everyone is so repressed and refined that you understand immediately why there's hardly any WASPs left anymore, maybe then you don't have all the sweaty guys with their big round faces, guffawing through wide mouthfuls of half-chewed food at each other's smutty jokes, and the women, some of them too skinny but most of them too fat, their hair dyed and permed too often and their dresses a little too tight and flouncy for them to be able to sit comfortably. But Greeks, Jews, Italians, Armenians, Poles, maybe even Germans, and Russians—for sure, you're going to have all that, and their kids too. The kids! Chubby-kneed toddlers in sugar-white dresses and frilly rubber underpants, their ears already pierced with little gold studs and their fingers in their mouths as they gape at the older kids. The four-year-old boys in clip-on ties, their shirttails now out and their flapping ties grubby with spilled sauce, all of them yelling and galloping around after the eight- and ten-year-old boys, who were trying to put bits of *casserta* and *tiramisu* in the hair or down the backs of the twelve-year-old girls, three of them plump enough to look like Disney's pigs in party dresses and the rest of them so skinny that they looked like jackstraws in taffeta, their brand-new nylon pantyhose hanging baggy on them like even my schleppiest pair of Levis don't on me. I mean, one of these families even had what I swear is the same maiden aunt that one of my cousin's in-laws has, a perfectly proper-looking woman who, three glasses of wine into the dancing, she starts begging the band to play something loud and bouncy, so she can flip up her hems and show everyone her lacy, racy bloomers. The only difference here was the song was a tarantella, not "Hava Nagila," and this crazy aunt's *gotkes* were green, not flame-red. More Christmassy, I suppose.

"Kind of a freak show, isn't it?" Mike shout-whispered in my ear sometime later, when we were already full of broccoli and ziti and manicotti and stuffed shells, sweaty and foot-sore ourselves from dancing. The rehearsal dinner was moving towards its conclusion; the band—really just two old guys, one with a mandolin, the other with an accordion, a young guy who had the hair and the face of a rock guitarist looking bored as he filled in goomba chords behind them, and a zaftig blonde who had seen better days carrying the words of old standards up and down the scales in a sturdy but serviceable voice—was playing its last set, the youngest kids were bawling on the floor or lying in their mothers' arms, sucking pacifiers or bottles and making sleepy circles in their hair with their chubby, sticky fingers. One of the little boys, who had fallen on a chair and split his lip, was howling and dripping his shirt with blood, and most of the older boys, who had been sneaking sips of wine all evening, had long ago shrieked themselves hoarse.

I caught myself starting to lean back again Mike's shoulder, then straightened, and turned to give him a big "just-friends" smile. "I don't know, it's just people having a good time with family, isn't it? It's actually kinda nice . . ."

Mike watched me for a second, his green-yellow eyes reminding me, as they always did, of sunlight shining through shallow water onto a sandy beach. "Sure it's a good time." I thought I could feel him wanting to put his arms around me, but instead he drew himself up, like his back was stiff, then glanced around the room, before pointing his chin at the bride- and groom-to-be. "Look at 'em, not two years out of high school, and they both know each other all their lives already. What's left for them to discover?"

The couple in question, whom custom had kept seated with their respective families for the first part of the evening—this being only the rehearsal dinner, not the wedding banquet; that would come the day after Christmas—were now dancing. As oblivious to the crowd as they were to the beat of the music, she clung to his neck like he was all that kept her from plunging from a cliff into the dark cold sea, while he bent over her as if looking for loose change in the back pockets of her dress.

"I don't know," I said, for want of anything better to say, "they look kind of sweet."

Russo sniffed and shook his head. "There'll be a baby in, what do you figure, six months? And then another next year? Him sorting onions at Rapasadi's Warehouse and her dreaming about getting to be maybe the receptionist at the Boxing Hall of Fame, if she can just manage to finish the secretarial program at Mohawk Valley Community College? Kinda of . . . I don't know . . . blighted, isn't it?"

I turned, to stare at him. "Pretty big word, isn't it?"

"For a dumb detective, you mean?" he bristled, but only a little. We had left from my building in Brooklyn about ten that morning, but the roads had been bad, icy in spots, and jammed with people headed for Christmas at Grandma's, so we barely had time to dress before the dinner, and even then we had come in late. Then dancing, eating, drinking . . . it was nearly eleven, and we were both weary.

"No, I meant to describe these people . . . Sure, I mean, this isn't the Bloomsbury Group, but, I don't know . . . Isn't it nice to think about how the great-grandparents of those kids probably had parties just about like this one when they married, and their great-grandparents before them? I mean, probably even Dante and Macchiavelli had to go the parties their cousins threw, when their kids got married, right?" As I talked, I could suddenly picture a rustic table set beneath the sweet dappled shade of a grape arbor, the stacks of crusty breads, bits of wood ash clinging to their bottoms, the inky home-made wine still cool from terra cotta storage vats, buried to the neck in the ground, and, in the distance, a slow procession coming from the church, snatches of music just audible above the intervening fields of golden wheat and scarlet poppies . . .

Mike looked skeptical, staring at the room and poking idly at his teeth with a toothpick. "I guess, like tradition, you mean? But it just seems . . . I don't know . . . sort of 'in-grown' is maybe the word."

It dawned on me then that Mike was not staring idly, but rather was intently watching one particular girl.

I could see why, because this same girl had caught my eye on and off through the evening, the way a butterfly might in a jar full of moths. She was tall, nearly six feet, and slender, with a figure that was already clearly female. Her hair was the color of clover honey and worn long, parted simply in the middle, but then falling away in curves—too loose to be curls, but too tight to be mere waves—that were hard to describe as anything other than sensuous. Her dress was high-waisted and A-cut, with choirboy sleeves, in a flowing blue rayon the color of a May sky. Her face was an oval, kept from mathematical perfection by a deep dimple on the left cheek which somehow left her even prettier than perfection.

"She's a beautiful girl, Mike," I finally said.

Mike blushed a little, sat up, nodded. "Angelina . . . good name for her, right?"

I looked again. It was true. She might have been an angel painted by a Florentine master of the Renaissance, right down to the distant, almost other-worldly expression on her face. The other girls darted and clucked, laughing and giggling, while Angelina seemed out of synch, laughing alone, or not at all. "She from your family, or the bride's side?"

Mike laughed. "Meaning am I gonna ask her to dance and make a big fool of my middle-age self?"

"I didn't mean . . ." I said quickly, because I probably *had* meant. "Anyway, if you're middle-age, then . . ."

"You're young, Midge, young . . ." Mike laughed, then patted my shoulder. "We're gonna be 18 forever, you and me."

"18? Can I pick a different year? 22 maybe? No, wait . . . 24? 24 was okay. Kind of . . ."

"Whatever," Mike flipped that discussion away with an indolent wave of his hand, then pointed his toothpick in the direction of a plump woman with dyed red hair at the far corner of the table, who was just licking the last of the ricotta from a *cornetto*. "Angie's Linda's kid. My mom's cousin, so I've known Angie, phew, since she was a baby, I guess." For a quick fraction of a second, Russo's face gripped dark and angry, as if a high thin cloud had passed between him and the sun. Then, a blink later, that icy fury was gone. "Don't look much like a baby now, does she?"

I stretched, then yawned, which I tried to transform into a nod. "What I don't understand though is how come she doesn't have all the boys over there, showing off like horses' asses to get her attention?"

Mike stretched too, looked around the room with what seemed to me to be curious care, before he said enigmatically, "Oh, Linda keeps the boys well away from Angie, believe me . . ." Then, more energetically, he slapped my knee. "Come on, don't go nodding off on me! We've still got things we got to do tonight!"

It took me a while to remember to breathe, while I thought about possible activities we might still have yet to do tonight.

There was an out-of-town crowd for this wedding, plus other Christmas traffic, so Mike's family had had to put us in one motel room. With two beds. In a hurry because we had arrived so late, Mike had changed his shirt, put on a tie, and then gone down to the lobby while I changed my dress, trying not to look at the two beds.

Mike and I had . . . well, a year or so ago we had gone to Sicily together . . . dark slats of the shutters, with the white-hot sun of siesta time beyond, Mike's ribs, like something Michelangelo might have carved, if the artist had worked in suntanned and shower-beaded human flesh, instead of cold Carrera marble, the slender gold chain and tiny cross around Mike's neck catching on his leonine chest hair as he leaned toward the linen sheets, cool with violet-scented talc . . .

But we had broken up. So we couldn't . . . I mean, I had come on this weekend as a friend, not as easy recreation . . . but if what Mike had in mind was procreation . . . including everything that comes afterwards, especially the part twenty years from now when we sit eating bran flakes, arguing about where the kid should go to law school and wondering where the last twenty years have gone to, well, then . . .

"Mike," I began weakly, "I think maybe we ought to talk . . ."

He looked confused for a moment, then laughed. He stood up and held out his hand. "No, no, not that . . . it's Christmas, remember? We got to go to Midnight Mass!"

I felt relieved, foolish . . . and deeply disappointed. Trying to gather my wits, I fumbled around for my purse and shoes, stalling until I could manage a bright smile. When I could, I stood too, holding his hand as I put on my heels. "We're going to Midnight Mass too? Okay, but I'll warn you right now, I'm not taking communion!" I told Mike severely.

Mike's face went terribly serious, the approximate color of milk of magnesia. "Midge, you can't take communion!"

"I just said that, didn't I?" I pushed him in the direction of the door. "After this meal, another bite and I'd burst!"

It was a candlelight service. Pink, red, and white poinsettias carpeted the altar, and balsam fir was garlanded along the pews. Little blonde kids with kitchen towels for *keffiyehs* imitated Palestinian shepherds, a teenager in a rope beard and bathrobe that didn't go far enough down to cover his bright red Chuck Taylors stood woodenly by as Joseph, gazing adoringly but awkwardly down at Angelina, who was a radiant, luminescent Madonna. "Adeste Fideles, O Little Town of Bethlehem," and, as the church bells tolled midnight, "Silent Night."

To tell the truth, the whole thing made me a little homesick, like I was a tourist in a country whose language I only knew a few phrases of. All that solemnity, the mothers fearfully trying to hush their cranky kids, everyone scared to breathe as the priest elevates the cup for the Transfiguration, like if they do something wrong, God's going to backhand them across the mouth, or maybe stalk out of the room in a huff. In that deep reverent silence, I found myself missing the comfort of temple. Even at our most solemn, on the Days of Awe, when the ark is open and we're standing in what the rabbi tell us is *shechina,* the presence of God, we're still scratching and murmuring to our neighbors about how well the cantor looks after his operation and we're handing the little kids toy trucks down where they're sprawled under the pews and trying to decide whether to break the fast with the whitefish first, or maybe treat ourselves with a piece of the *ruggelach,* and then do the whitefish.

The few church services I've been to, it's like Christians haven't been married so very long, and the bride is afraid of saying or doing something wrong, always all tensed up from wondering whether He's going to forget the big anniversary they've got coming up.

Us, we've been with God almost six millennia now. We're both of us pretty used to each other's little idiosyncrasies, so if one party or the other sometimes gets a little out of line, well . . . the marriage can stand it.

After we had shuffled out with the crowd into the ice-crystal sharp night, where the many wishes of "Merry Christmas!" lingered on as white puffs of vapor, Mike shook the priest's hand firmly, then took me by the arm and guided me to his car. Before unlocking my door for me, Mike looked up at the vast expanse of night, sighed deeply, and then, with a tenderness that turned my knees to egg nog, he kissed me. "Merry Christmas, Midge . . ."

I was still replaying drowsy variations on that kiss three hours later, when someone knocked urgently at our door. I jumped up to shake the snoring

Mike—who was in the other bed—and then went to the door to whisper, "Who is it?"

It was Mike's cousins, to tell us that Angelina was missing.

That her new bicycle was not under the Christmas tree and her coat was missing from the hall closet had given the search urgency from the beginning. But once the bike tracks were discovered wobbling toward the canal's towpath, everyone got truly frantic. Angie, as everybody kept repeating, was absolutely forbidden to go anywhere near the canal.

Fifteen minutes later, we had found her body, proving the frenzy justified.

"How many times did I tell her, don't go near that canal!" Angie's mother wailed. "She was a good girl. She knew it wasn't safe . . ."

"It's that canal! It's a crime that that canal is there!" another woman started in hotly, while two others comforted Angie's mother, now sobbing into her hands. "They shoulda filled it in years ago!"

We were in the living room. The tree, the decorations, and the mounds of gaily wrapped presents looking almost like an obscene mockery in front of the grim clusters of family, some in their pajamas and robes, some in outdoor gear. The house was small, and the furnishings—or at least what could be seen of them under the Christmas decorations—were inexpensive. Someone had put on coffee back in the kitchenette, and people stood about awkwardly, clinging to their mugs. Special Christmas mugs, with jolly drawings of Santa Claus riding a bicycle.

There wasn't much any of us could do, but no one thought to leave. Outside it was still black, but one or two of the houses visible from the living room window were already lit up. Relatives of the dead girl? I wondered, or maybe families with small children, already ripping at their mounds of presents?

"Are there . . . other kids?" I asked Mike softly. He looked dazed, his hair standing up in lumps and tufts, his eyes hollow, with a black-green cast beneath them. He turned his head slowly to my question, his expression blank. "Did Ang . . . did she have brothers and sisters that will be waking up, wanting to open presents? It'll be . . . hard on them," I trailed off, knowing I sounded like an idiot.

Mike was too upset even to react to the foolishness of my question.

"No . . . no, she's . . . she was Linda's only kid . . . Jesus God, it just isn't fair!" His features suddenly focused for a second, making him look both brutal and desperate. "The way she fought . . . fought to take care of that girl! Hung over her like a hawk that nothing else should happen to poor little Angie, and nobody ever around to help her . . ."

The fire of his fury sagged back into weary fatigue, and Mike fell silent. Then he shook his head, squeezed my hand, and mumbled something about having to talk to somebody. He ambled off, leaving me to feel even more of an intruder and a stranger than I had before.

I couldn't just go back to the motel, and there was little I could say to Angie's mother, beyond what I had already said several times, that her daughter had been a beautiful girl, and I was very sorry about her terrible loss. After a moment of indecision, I wandered back into the kitchen, to see whether I could find some way to make myself useful out there.

"Some Christmas, huh? Mikey taking it hard?"

The woman who asked me this was slicing a frosted bread ring, laying pieces out on a paper tray, printed with poinsettias. She was my age, more or less, but was even shorter than I am, and trimmer too, with the sparkly eyes and brisk movements of a fox terrier. A taller and older woman stood with her back to us, preparing some food. She didn't turn when I entered the tiny kitchen, but just glanced dourly over her shoulder.

"Yeah, I guess he is," I said. "I'm, uh, Midge . . . is there something I can do to help? I mean, I feel a little . . ."

"Out of it?" the woman smiled. "I know who you are. We met at the dinner. You probably forgot me though, I'm Penny Jo." She held out her hand, white sugar frosting on her thumb.

"Penny Jo?" I shook her hand then, automatically, licked the frosting which was now on the back of my hand.

"Oh hey, I'm sorry 'bout that. Here . . ." she handed me a Christmas towel. "Trailer trash name, right? Penny Jo, Ruby May, Loretta Bob . . ." she said in an exaggerated Dogpatch accent, then shrugged. "I've thought about changing my name maybe to something like Courtney, or one of those TV names that used to be for guys . . . Randy maybe? But then I figured, what the hey, a name like Penny Jo Priaputnewicz, people aren't likely to forget I was in the room, are they? Not that they can get within a city block of spelling it!"

I found myself liking this chirpy little woman, especially after all the effort of staying solemn about a tragedy that I could understand but not feel. "You have an extra apron? Priaputnewicz? So you're not . . . one of the family?"

"Hey, you done real good with my name! Most people, they just mumble it around like a mouthful of carpet tacks! Oh yeah, I'm part of this circus they call a family . . ."

"Family would have a better sense of how to behave at a time like this," the other woman suddenly growled, glowered at me, and then picked up the tray of frosted bread. "Go see to those cheeses and meats, the men will be wanting to eat. I'll take this out to the others . . ." She paused in the doorway, her face dull. She was obviously trying to think of something to say, but in the end contented herself with the vague, "And remember where you are . . ."

Penny Jo grinned at me. "Patsy there never did much approve of me. She thinks I've always been fast," she said the word in a tone of mock horror, then handed me a thick cylinder of sausage.

"Here, you slice this, and make it thin, mind, or we'll be hearing about it! The men just can't be eating thick slices, ya know?"

Glad to have a job, I tied on the apron, found a knife, and for a moment concentrated on curling translucent wafers away from the rosy Hungarian salami. The tiny kitchen crammed with food, the smell of the coffee machine gurgling away, the closeness of the other woman working at the other counter, all these made it hard to stay silent.

"I used to teach Russian. In college, over in Ithaca."

"Oh my goodness, a college teacher," Penny Jo sounded enthusiastic, but amused too, like she was mocking me a little. "*And* a policewoman? My, my!"

I pushed back a lock of hair and laughed. "I'm not a policewoman, that was just Mike. No, all I mean is, that's why I could say your name. Russian, Polish . . . I'm used to long names."

"Damn name is like an elephant sneezing itself to death or something. If it wasn't for the two boys having the name, I swear I'd go back to my maiden name . . . excepting that 'Penny Jo Paterno' sounds like something you'd yell at a football game!"

Penny Jo's good humor was infectious. I laughed, then looked guiltily at the door, knowing the depth of the misery just beyond it. "So you're . . . uh, single too?"

"Divorced," Penny Jo said matter-of-factly.

"Me too," I confided, surprised that I was enjoying this chat, probably because I almost never had ones like this when I was in New York.

"Oh yeah?" Penny Jo was surprised and looked me over for a minute. "I had you figured for one of those . . . you know, big city career gals."

"Full-time police work, right?" Penny Jo laughed, so I added, "No, really, he was a vet, and we had a big house outside Dryden, some acreage even.

I had this big old flower and vegetable garden . . . no kids though, thank God." For a second, I remembered the big kitchen in that house and the extravagant dinners I used to try to make there. Even made my own ketchup, for goodness sake. Then I remembered also the long empty evenings, feeling the chill winds nibbling their way through the authentic original—and very drafty—window panes, as I waited for Paul to come back from a calving somewhere or from seeing to a colicky horse. "Irreconcilable differences, and I refused to take any alimony, so the whole thing was pretty painless really," I concluded, concentrating on the last nub of salami.

"Me and the Polack, we had them differences too," Penny Jo said arch- ly as she took the tray of sliced meat from me, then handed me a smoked provolone to work on. "Like that he just loved beating on me, but I didn't care for it one little bit!" Then, her expression more thoughtful, Penny Jo looked at me inquisitively, tapping her paring knife on the cutting board before she asked, "Mike ever slap you around?"

Feeling grateful that I hadn't confided to Penny Jo that I had left my hus- band simply because he bored me, it took me a second to understand her question. When I did, I was flustered. "Oh, Mike and me, it's not like that, I mean, we're just friends. This was a favor. He asked me to . . . We're not . . . but . . . no, he never, you know . . . I doubt that he'd ever hit anybody. Outside of his work, I mean. If he had to," I dribbled on, lamely.

"Maybe now . . ." Penny said, still tapping the paring knife against the white plastic cutting board.

"But years ago, when he was in high school, and even in college some I guess, he used to spend a lot of the summers up here. He was pretty quick with the fists then, believe me."

"Oh, come on," I snapped, with more heat than I would have thought possible, "Mike a woman beater? I don't believe that for a second."

Penny laughed. "No, no, not women. That's what I mean, he was like, you know, some kind of knight in shining armor or something. One of the guys around here would try to push on a girl, rough house with us a little too much or something, and wham! There was Mikey, two-fisted hero from the big city." Penny Jo wiped her hands on her apron, then looked around the kitchen, hefted the coffee pot to see whether she should make more. "There was a lot of fights, because it made the boys from around here mad, him butting in like the priest had put him in charge of the town's morals for the summer or something. Not that we didn't do what we wanted to when Mikey wasn't around, you know?" She smiled, then said, much more softly, "He proposed to Linda, you know." She cocked her head at me, like a little kid who has poked something with a stick and is now waiting to see what happens.

I nodded, biting on my lower lip, because I wasn't sure what to say, or even what I felt. Through the little window above the sink, I could see the first pink-gray slash of day coming. I barely recalled Linda from last night, and this morning, of course, she had looked terrible. That automatic thing women have, somewhere down where the mitochondrial DNA reproduces itself, it immediately set to work trying to decide whether Linda was more attractive than I was. My more civilized brain cells knew, of course, that Mike and I were nothing to one another anymore, even if such questions weren't totally out of place today in any event, because of what had happened to poor Angie. But I had to ask anyway. "But she's a lot older than him, isn't she? And a cousin too?"

"Kissing cousins. Linda's a couple of years older than Mike, maybe, but what she looked like fifteen years ago?" Penny Jo shook her right hand, as if she had burned herself. "Boy-bait number one around this town. Angie was her natural daughter, you know what I mean?"

I tried to imagine the sobbing silo of a woman in the front room as a willowy, golden-haired angel, but another thought intruded—Mike staring intently at Angie at the party, his fury as she was pulled from the canal, his caged, restless pacing ever since.

"Oh my God," I managed after a second, gripping the counter because my stomach had turned into a cold slush of dread. "You're not trying to tell me that Mike was that girl's father?!"

Penny Jo chuckled and shook her head. "Naw, like I just told ya, back then, Mikey was real religious, always trying to keep the rest of us from sins of the flesh . . . The 'Altarboy,' we called him."

I smiled, oddly relieved. Whether Linda had been "boy-bait" fifteen years before, I could not say, but what this Penny Jo might have been like in those long-ago summer evenings was simplicity to picture now. A face like a grinning cat and—I did not doubt—tiny cut-offs and a halter top, or maybe better yet just a boob tube, this Penny Jo must have given more than one Canastota teen-age boy some hot, sweaty summer dreams. Back in high school, as I was rushing from Student Council to Senior Chorus, or from AP Calculus to French, I would stare with open disgust—and secret envy—at those minx-like Penny Jos—who in Brooklyn were usually named Donna—always at the center of a cluster of goofy, jostling boys, whom those girls seemed to control as tightly and nonchalantly as the Coney Island pony-ride man did his herd of little ponies.

But Penny Jo wasn't telling me this just to gossip. "You and Mike . . . are you two really serious about each other, or . . . ?" She asked, studying me intently. To forestall the objection that had leapt towards the tip of my tongue, she added, "I know that's a personal question, but . . . it's just that, well, I'm worried that Mike might try to play Friend to Jesus again here, and maybe do something real stupid . . ."

"Like what stupid? Mike's a detective on the New York City police force, for God's sake! It's not like he's going to charge around punching out people because of this Angie! Besides, who's to punch? The girl rode her bike into the canal, that's an accident, not a crime!"

Penny Jo shook her head and smiled ironically. "That poor little girl's whole life was an accident . . . but after a while, it's hard not to wonder whether that don't make it a crime . . . and if there's a crime, stands to reason there's got to be a criminal, right?"

"Look, maybe you better just tell me what it is that's worrying you, because I'm really not understanding . . ."

Penny Jo didn't get the chance to answer, however, for the low murmur of voices beyond the swinging kitchen door suddenly grew louder. What sounded like several people were shouting at once, and even some furniture was being slammed about.

Penny Jo paled, put her hand to her mouth, and said, "Oh my God, he can't have been jackass enough to show up here!"

There were so many people jammed into the small living room that I barely could squeeze myself through the swinging door after Penny Jo. Around me, near the wall, most of the action was chorus, people babbling angry commentary to one another. But up closer, at the front door, several of the men were shouting at another man who stood with his back against the door. They were shoving at him a little, and he was shoving back, like just before a fist fight. After what Penny Jo had started to tell me in the kitchen, I was disturbed to see that Mike was one of the half-circle of pushers.

The newcomer still had on his coat, a red and black woolen hunter's plaid, stiff in spots with grease, thrown over what looked like a dirty sweatshirt with the collar ripped off. He wore a battered Russian-style hat; the string on top had come undone, so that the ears flapped and bounced as he scuffled, a cartoon-like touch that was of a piece with his heavy sac of loose chin, baggy bloodhound eyes, and florid, flaccid cheeks. His tongue kept flicking out, to wallow in the livid sores at the corners of his lips, while the networks of purple veins across his nose and cheeks looked like the map to Skid Row.

He was a big man, but not well kept. Underneath the torn sweat shirt a hairy white belly occasionally flopped into view, and his belt was worn low enough beneath it that I hoped he wouldn't turn around, to offer us the working man's Vertical Smile.

The general outline of the argument that was raging was easy enough to make out, even if the details were a mystery. Roger, the big guy, had heard about Angie and had come to tell Linda how sorry he was. Enzo, Mike, and some of the other cousins, not only thought this wasn't a good idea, but thought maybe Roger should better go off someplace by himself and die.

The cacophony would have exploded into a fight for certain, had Linda not suddenly levered herself from her recliner chair and pushed through the knot of men who were arguing with Roger. Startled, they stepped away to let her approach the newcomer. This also let me see Mike more clearly; he was glaring at the newcomer with an expression as calm and as deadly as a pitbull's. I shivered.

Her face puffy from weeping and the pockets of her robe lumpy with wet tissues, Linda managed to exude an extraordinary dignity as she drew herself up full length in front of Roger.

"I'll accept your sympathy now, I guess," she said in a flat voice. "You got a right to give that. But I've told you time enough, Roger Caputo, I do not want you 'round this house, not ever."

Roger was probably a half foot taller than Linda, and certainly a hundred pounds heavier, but he folded and curled in front of her, like a puppy expecting to be whipped. "God damn it, Linda, the girl's gone, and I sure as hell didn't have nothing to do with that! It's a terrible thing for sure, but you can't be going to hold this over me for the rest of my life, are you? How many times can a man say he's sorry, for Christ's sake?"

Linda's voice dropped to a harsh whisper, which only made her sound the more thunderous. "Roger, I can't tell you right now what I'm going to do. But I know this . . . every day of her life, my Angie had it over her. I told you just last week and I'll tell you again right now, because I don't see how this changes a thing . . . I don't want you around here."

"Ah, God damn it, Linda, can't you have some forgiveness in your heart?" Roger seemed almost to wail, twisting the cap, which now was in his hands. Tears made their way through the rough stubble of his floppy cheeks.

"You're my big sister and it's Christmas fucking morning . . ."

With an energy I wouldn't have thought her capable of, Linda threw open her front door, letting a blast of icy air rush into the overheated living room. The sun was the width of a finger above the horizon, making its slow way upward through ragged gray clouds, and the steam from the chimney opposite was standing straight as a stick in the gelid air.

"You're no family of mine!" Linda shrieked, yanking at Roger's coat sleeve, so that he sort of stumbled out the door and fell down the icy steps, his heavy galoshes sticking straight up in the air. "Angie was my family and she's dead! You've done my family all the harm you're ever gonna do it!"

Then she slammed the door, with a force that seemed to rattle forever through the collection of china horses that stood on a plastic *étagère* between the front door and the closet door. As the tinkling finally fell toward silence, in a voice that made the hairs along my spine stand on end, Mike asked, "Linda, what's this about Roger sniffing around Angie again?"

The State Police headquarters was in a small bungalow, made over to be offices, at the foot of the steep hill where Route 20 tried to climb its way out of Morrisville. Mike had driven the eighteen slippery miles from Canastota because he wanted to see whether he could get any more information about Angie. I had come along, because I didn't know what else to do with myself. Stay in the motel room and watch holiday specials on the Cartoon Network? Instead I looked at the empty, icy fields, the trailers strung with colored bulbs, the farmhouses that had been built big and proud in the prosperous nineteenth century, which now looked syphilitic in their poverty, their barns caved in or their siding peeling away like shell off an egg.

Mike hadn't said five words to me since Linda's house, and it was beginning to get on my nerves. There was a single dispatcher on duty in Morrisville, a slender black man in a trooper's uniform. He had examined Mike's badge and identification carefully, then explained that there wasn't anything he could tell Mike, even as a professional courtesy. It was Christmas, after all. I knew Mike was trying to sound neutral and professional, but something was churning away inside of him with intensity enough that apparently even the dispatcher felt it, because the man finally agreed to go make some calls, but he sure wasn't promising any results.

That was fifteen minutes ago, and we were still sitting in the tiny reception area, with nothing to look at but a back issue of the local newspaper, a weekly. Having Mike next to me was like sitting next to a steam radiator that badly needed to be bled. Wondering whether I might be about to find out if Mike was a hitter or not, I touched his arm, and said, "If you can get me on a bus or something, I'd be glad to go back to the city."

Mike started, and I probably cringed, because he took a deep breath, and tried to smile. When that failed, he rubbed his hair hard, with both hands, like he was shampooing, and then looked at me again, his eye meeting mine for the first time in what seemed ages. "Hey, look, Midge, I'm sorry about . . . all this. I really am. I thought I was taking you up for, you know, a big party. This morning, I figured we'd be sitting around watching the little cousins open their presents, then there'd be a big breakfast, everybody all happy and stuff. Instead . . ."

I patted his hand. "It's not your fault. I said I'd be glad to go back to the city on my own. I'm only in the way here, it feels like . . ."

"No, God, it's . . ." he waved his hands, then tried again. "I don't know, this is . . . anyway, I couldn't send you back to the city on a bus. It's Christmas!"

"A plane ticket would bankrupt both of us, buying it at the last minute like this. But even though I can't claim that eight hours on a Greyhound would thrill me to death any day, I don't know why today would be any worse. I mean, at least it isn't hot. The last time I had to ride a bus for that long was coming home from summer camp in the Berkshires when I was eleven, we got stuck in a huge pile-up in Harriman, and Howie Silverman, who always tried to sit next to me, he hadn't changed his tee-shirt since he spilled ketchup on his other one, at the July 4th cookout."

Mike didn't say anything, so I went on, "That was supposed to be funny, Mike. If you won't let me go back to Brooklyn, and you aren't going to let me cheer you up, even a little, then maybe you should at least tell me what in the world is going on. Why is everyone so . . ."

Mike came around on me so fast that I couldn't move, but instead sat blinking like a bunny in the headlights, waiting to get run over. Rather than even think of hitting me though, Mike clubbed his own knees hard enough to make himself wince, then hissed, "Upset?! Why is everyone so upset? Angelina rides . . ."

I held up my hand, trying to look calm and superior, like Pearl does to me when I am about to start a tantrum. "The death of that beautiful girl is a tragedy, Mike. A terrible, genuine tragedy. But unless I'm missing something real big here, her death was an accident."

"That's what I'm down here trying to be sure about," Mike said darkly and looked at the dispatcher's desk, which was still empty.

"You think she was pushed? Or hit or . . . ?" I whispered, clutching his elbow.

"Or molested?" Mike added insinuatingly, then pointed at where the absent officer wasn't. "When he comes back, maybe I can answer that for you."

Lurid scenarios leapt through my mind . . . dark shadows, leering rapists, the fragile beauty of Angelina's face shattered by terror . . . then I remembered something.

"Mike, it was three in the morning and forty below zero! A pervert's a pervert, but that would be nuts!"

Mike had the same look on his face that Penny Jo had had, trying to decide whether or not to tell me something. Like Penny Jo, Mike seemed to be on the verge of deciding against it. So I turned to face him as square on as the plastic bucket seats in the waiting area permitted, put my hand under his chin so that he had to look into my face, and said, "There's something you people aren't telling me, isn't there? You can tell me it's none of my business and I'll accept that, because it probably isn't. But I'm not going to stay up here and have all of you keep talking around me like I'm some kind of damaged shipment. Fill me in or send me home, Mike."

After just a moment more hesitation, Mike sighed and looked at my knees, as if unable to tell the story directly. "You're not the damaged one. Angie was. She was, well, like I told you, sort of stuck in being a kid. Developmentally retarded. The county welfare people kept trying to get Linda to send her away to a special school, but Linda wouldn't stand the idea of being separated from her daughter, even if taking care of her made it hard for her to have a job. Linda made the town keep taking Angie in school, even though she hardly ever could get promoted. She was only a fourth grader."

Mike smiled sadly, then added, "'Course, she was that last year too, and the year before that, I think. The school board was going to try to force her out after this year, because she was going to turn 16 in August. They've been saying it isn't fair to the other kids in the fourth grade, that it was getting distracting as she matured . . . you know, physically. The older boys were . . . well, you know how boys are. Linda did her best to keep them away, but . . . well, Angie was interested too. You don't need a brain to have hormones. And Linda couldn't explain anything to Angie . . . about what she shouldn't do, you know. So she was starting to wonder whether she shouldn't get Angie an operation . . . Can you figure what that must be like? Trying to decide whether to have your own kid spayed?" Mike's attempt at a smile was a lot closer to being a grimace of pain.

"Jeez, she couldn't get past the fourth grade? Was she trainable? Like for some kind of industry job?" I didn't want to say what else was on my mind, that impossible calculus of whether someone like Angie was better blessed to have her life's cord snipped short, or to have it stretched out to the fullest extent of life's long twilight, in decade after decade of the fourth grade.

"I suppose maybe some kind of work, but she had some muscular problems, control kind of things. That's why the bike was such a victory for her, when she finally learned to ride it. She could get around better, kinda keep up with the other kids . . . but that's also why Linda wouldn't ever let her go near that canal. She was afraid she might . . . fall in . . ."

Mike trailed off: He had a quarter in his right hand that he kept turning over and over between his thumb and two forefingers, as if he was trying to decide something. "The thing of it is . . ." he began, paused, then began again. "The thing of it is : . . Angie was born normal. A totally normal, completely beautiful little thing. That's why Linda chose the name for her she did. She and her scumbag husband had a house up north of the Thruway someplace, near Vernon Downs, I think. Been married about a year when the baby came. He was working for Carrier, over in Syracuse, making good money, and then Angie coming seemed to make things perfect . . ."

I waited out the long silence that followed, because I knew now I was going to get the rest of the story.

"Linda's about the oldest of our generation of cousins, so this was like a special thing, the first baby. The christening was a big deal, all the whole family came. My mom even brought us up from the city, and she hates to come up for these kinda things. Angie had this special long dress, all white lace, and Linda had got Jack into a tie. He still looked like a scumbag, of course, but at least he was a scumbag in a tie and jacket. There was a party afterwards, everyone hugging and kissing the baby . . . and then the first sore showed up on Angie about three weeks later."

Suddenly a whole lot more of today made sense to me. "Oh my God!" I put my hands to my mouth in horror. "Roger?! You don't mean to say those sores . . ."

"Genital herpes," Mike confirmed, after looking mildly startled that I had guessed his family's big dark secret so quickly. "Herpes had just started going around up here, and nobody knew very much about it, or what it could do. Roger had picked up a case of it somewhere . . . I've heard his story enough times to make me puke, and to this day I don't know for sure where he got it. By now he's just about convinced himself he had nothing to do with it, that a bunch of hookers raped him or something. But however he got it, he was ashamed enough about it not to tell anyone. And her uncle, he wasn't gonna be the only one who didn't kiss Angie . . .. Even after the doctor told Linda what those sores were, and the whole family was ripping itself to shreds, everyone pointing fingers at everyone else, Roger didn't say anything about him being the one until he had a big blow-out of sores, so there wasn't much question about it being him. Of course with an adult like him, it was just sores, but what the specialists finally told Linda, herpes in an infant, if it gets into the nervous system, it can play all kinds of hell. Which it surely did with Angie. She was four or so before she really learned to walk, and the toilet training was even later. Six, maybe? Just getting her even so she'd sleep all the way through the night nearly killed Linda with exhaustion."

"And her husband?"

"Scumbag? He took off after about a year. Said Angie's crying all the time got on his nerves, plus he was afraid the baby would somehow pass the herpes to Linda or him, screw up his sex life . . . Not much of a loss to have him go, actually, but I always have been kinda sorry he didn't take Roger with him."

And sweet, gentle, considerate Altarboy Mike had felt so sorry for Linda and the hole that life had dumped her and her baby into that he offered to marry his cousin.

A rush of affection made me jump up, plop into his lap, and throw both arms around Mike. He stiffened in surprise for a moment, but then let me hold him. It was awkward, the two of us on one of those slippery blue plastic bucket seats, but for the moment I didn't care, because I was too pleased to have Mike's head cradled against my breast, to run my fingers through his uncombed hair.

We both nearly fell to the floor when the trooper came back into the room.

He gave us a weird look as Mike and I straightened ourselves and tried to quit blushing. "Detective Russo, I called everybody I could think of, but there's not a blessed thing I can tell you today. The body's still in storage over at the hospital in Oneida, waiting for the medical examiner, because he's off on one of those Disney cruises with his family down in the

Caribbean. There's nobody at the offices, of course, but the answering machine says the office will re-open on the 28th."

"And it also took you a while to find anybody down in the city who could vouch for me, right?" Mike zipped up his leather coat.

The trooper didn't bat an eye. "When we pull 'em over out on the road is the time most guys claim to be cops. There aren't so many wander in here with that story. But we always check 'em, buddy, we always check 'em."

"And so you should," Mike stuck out his hand. "Thanks for trying, anyway . . . and Merry Christmas to you."

Outside some of my fatigue sloughed off in the cold air, which now was acrid with woodsmoke, as the people of Morrisville stoked up their stoves. Beyond the town the horizon was tinged with pink, and the tires of the infrequent cars thunked like cement blocks as they hit the town's potholes. Shivering while I waited for Mike to open the car door and let me in, I realized that there was still one piece of this story that didn't make any sense.

"Where does Roger fit into all this, Mike? I mean I know he was the one who gave her the herpes, but . . . well, you looked like you were about to kill him, back there at Linda's. It's not like he could make the herpes go away, once he'd given them to her. I'm not saying the whole thing's not a tragedy, but . . ." I stopped talking, since I couldn't think of a nice way to say that fifteen years seemed like time enough that everyone should have gotten used to Roger's sin.

"Roger couldn't live with the guilt," Mike said, as we settled into the car seats; I stamped my feet to try to bring some feeling to them. My new boots made my feet look pretty, but right now I would have happily traded them for Roger's fleece-lined hunting galoshes. "Once he had to admit it was him had ruined Angie, he was always trying to find some way to get people to forgive him, I guess because, hard as he looked, he still couldn't find forgiveness in the bottom of a bottle. But as bad as she needed help, Linda wouldn't take anything from him, and wouldn't even let him get anywhere near her and the baby, if she could help it. Later on, when Angie got to be more like a person herself, Roger got so he'd try to catch Angie directly. Sweet kid like that, of course she'd say she forgave him, 'cause for all she understood it was like he had spilled Kool-Aid on her, not put a pox on her for life. But even having her say she forgave him didn't seem to do too much for Roger, because a couple of weeks later, there he'd be again, waiting for Angie after school or coming down the alley behind the house, trying to catch her out in the backyard . . . even Linda didn't make too big a deal about it, until Angie started to, you know . . . fill out. Then people got to wondering whether Roger maybe didn't want . . . something more than forgiveness."

"You really think that's true?" I murmured, for lack of anything else to say.

"Tell you what," Mike said with a forced calmness, which was obviously belied by the way he was pushing his car, screeching around the turns and bounding over the bumps, "if I find out it's true . . . I'll put Roger in the ground myself."

It was a very constrained and brittle group that gathered at yet another cousin's house that afternoon for Christmas dinner and, I was told, an exchange of gifts. While Mike and I had been off at the state troopers' office in Morrisville there had apparently been elaborate telephone negotiations about whether to soldier on with the festivities or to cancel the celebration entirely. I was losing track of Mike's relatives, but what it seemed was gathered here was a compromise selection of those more distant from the actual tragedy, or perhaps simply those with kids too young to understand why it was that the opening of presents was not going to happen this year. The table was not nearly as crowded as I knew it could have been, but I had no idea who wasn't there, other than Linda and, of course, Roger.

The food at lunch was elaborate, hearty, and festive, but nobody had much appetite, and the children fussed and whined with impatience, tempted all too urgently by the mound of bright packages that were heaped about halfway up the decorated balsam fir visible through the arch that divided the dining room from the living room. The adults tried to banter, but they were clearly pre-occupied. The men especially seemed increasingly to pull together, muttering among themselves, then looking around to see whether anyone had noticed. Certainly the kids hadn't; as soon as the word was given that presents might be opened, they began ripping through the packages like a tornado through a trailer park.

I was getting distinctly uncomfortable, however. Finally I couldn't stand it anymore and went out into the kitchen, where I found my new friend Penny Jo smoking on the back porch.

"Oh, hey there!" she said brightly, pinching the tip off the cigarette and waving her hand in a vain effort to dispel the smoke.

"Don't stop smoking because of me," I stepped out into the chill of the glassed-in porch, and leaned against the washing machine. "In fact, if I did-n't know for certain it would make me feel even worse than I do, I'd prob-ably bum one from you."

Penny Jo took her hidden pack out of some inner pocket in her long vel-vet vest and held it out. "Farrah here, she don't allow smoking in her fine new house, on account of little Heather. Having landed herself an x-ray tech-nician for a husband, she figures that makes her about royalty in our bunch."

I almost took a cigarette anyway, seduced by the momentary notion that maybe lighting up now would somehow give me a past like Penny Jo's here, or one of the girls like her back at Midwood High, who smoked and rode in cars with boys, sitting right snug up against them, and who did all those other things that plump little girls in the Leadership Council like me never did. Then Penny Jo and I would stand here and share worldly-wise confi-dences . . .

But I shook my head, because I knew that all I really wanted was to be home. All the weariness and stress of the last 24 hours felt draped over me like so many sweaty gym socks.

"You know, I don't recognize Mike at all," I confessed, after a few min-utes of oddly companionable silence.

"I told you, I'm worried about him. He always took the Angie situation close to the bone. Offering to marry Linda like that, and him not even 21 yet? It's no wonder his mother got a bunch of the Pasquales to toss him on the next train back to New York."

I smiled, thinking of Mike's mother, her face set firm and thin-lipped, her eyes hard with dislike whenever we bumped into each other on the stairs down into Mike's apartment in the basement of his mother's house.

"You know her?" Penny Jo leaned against the dryer, alongside me. It was arctic on that porch, but somehow the chilly peace was pleasant, after the food and the tension and the shouting. Standing shoulder to shoulder, we each had our arms wrapped tight across our chests to keep the body warmth in.

I suppose it was the sense of companionship that led me to say, "Ah, I just remembered, when you said that, Mike had this big crucifix on the wall above his fold-out couch, one of those really real looking ones, with blood and thorns and the face all screwed up like this. It gave me the creeps, when . . . when I'd stay over, so I'd make him take it down. And then, next time I was over there, back it would be on the wall again. It was his mother always putting it back up, Mike said."

Penny Jo puffed on her cigarette, then exhaled toward the door to the backyard. "More likely Mike himself put it back, would be my guess," she said, then studied me for a minute. "He must really like you, you know."

I blushed and tried to push away the wild surge of elation those words suddenly released in me, exploding upwards like a flock of startled snowy doves. I shrugged. "Maybe . . . but there was a lot of problems, so . . ."

"Like that you're not Catholic?"

"For one," I said, after a while, trying to let my tone of voice make it clear that I wasn't going to let our conversation go any further down that avenue. "But also Mike can be very stubborn about things too, you know?"

Penny Jo wasn't going to give up so easily. "Like having kids raised in the faith, you mean? Or being married in the church?" She turned towards me now, her expression sharper as she studied my face.

"Oh, I don't know . . . I suppose so, but things between us never got that far, really," I lied. "No, I meant this thing today, how much he seems to hate that poor Roger."

"Poor Roger is a miserable two-legged piece of human garbage," Penny Jo said as calmly and matter-of-factly as if she were reciting his age.

"Yeah, okay, so maybe he is but what on earth is it going to help, the things Mike and the others are muttering out there? How they want to take him on a one-way deer hunt, or go ice-fishing, with Roger as bait?"

"Well, somebody got Angelina to come out of her house in the middle of the night!" Penny Jo shot back. "Maybe whoever it was didn't even lay a finger on her, but what does that matter? Rape her, beat her up, and throw her in the canal, or just watch her lose control of her bike and fall in, and then walk away. Either way Angie's just as dead, isn't she? So yeah, I can see why those guys would get all muscle-bound and hormoned up that whoever did something like that shouldn't be able to just walk off and forget about it!"

"So you're saying, that's right, let's all go hang Roger from the door like a hunk of mistletoe?!"

"No, I'm saying that those bone-headed little boys out there are likely to *think* they should do something to Roger."

"But Mike's a cop!" I objected. "He's probably the most honest person I ever met! He won't even let me jaywalk when I'm with him, and you're worried about him maybe lynching somebody? No, wait, not just lynching somebody, lynching a cousin? And over what? Santa brings this simple-minded little girl a new bike, why is it so strange that she's gonna take it for a ride, even if it was the middle of the night? Why is everyone so all-fired determined to take all of this out on Roger?"

Except Penny Jo wasn't listening to me anymore, but was staring over my shoulder. "Listen, sugar," she said, "why don't you just ask Mike that yourself, hmm? Tell you what, you two kids have a little chat out here and I'll go put figs in the pudding or jingle some bells, some Christmassy kinda thing like that, okay?"

I turned around to find Mike, of course, standing on the jamb, partway through the door into the kitchen. He let Penny Lo slip past him, then let himself be pushed far enough onto the back porch for her to be able to shut the door, leaving us alone.

I was embarrassed, but only to a point. "Well, how long were you standing there?"

"Just, oh . . . a couple of . . ." He waved his left hand, but kept his right hand behind his back, for some reason. He looked weary, but then his features came into sharper focus. "Because one way or another, what happened to Angie was Roger's fault, that's why!"

"This is like original sin? The wife offers Adam a bite of her midafternoon snack, and for the rest of time we're expelled from paradise? What happened to forgiveness? I thought the whole thing with you people was forgiveness of sin?"

"There's such a thing as expiation of sin, you know," Mike said darkly. "You think it's enough just to say, hey, I'm sorry I gave the pox to your baby, tough break? Sin is something you have to cleanse yourself, by suffering."

"When did you get put in charge of deciding what's enough suffering? Mike, I can't argue Catholic theology with you because, for one thing, the last time I read the New Testament was when I was eight years old, and the next day I fell jumping rope and fractured my wrist, which I figured was God's way of telling me to mind my own business. But even the little I know, it's enough to know that you aren't the one who decides whether Roger goes to hell!"

"Why are you defending Roger? It was because of Roger that that child never had a chance in this life!"

"Mike, none of us have a chance in life! The only way out of this world is to die. But by the time we've figured that out, it's already too late! The trick's been played, we're *here*! Cancer, car wreck, drown in a canal, or live to be so old that you just kinda constipate to death, we're all gonna be tragedies one way or another! Even Pamela Harriman dropping dead after swimming laps at the Paris Ritz, or my Great-Uncle Arthur having a massive coronary just after he holes out from the sand trap on the fifth hole at his country club—the nicest, sweetest deaths I've ever heard. I bet if you could ask them, even they didn't want to go! I'm not defending Roger! I just can't for the life of me understand why you've all made life such hell for the poor schlub. It's not enough he's got to live with himself?"

Mike inhaled and raised both his hands, like he was going to yell something back at me. There was a small parcel in his left hand, the one he had been keeping behind his back. Scarlet foil wrapping, white ribbon bow. Mike dropped his hands and shook his head, like he wasn't going to argue anymore. He laughed, very weakly. "Cheerful talk, but kinda goes with the rest of the weekend, I guess. Jeez, Midge, this weekend hasn't gone anything like it was supposed to."

"What do you mean, how it was supposed to go?" I could sense strange fears suddenly beginning to lift their heads in alarm, somewhere in the dark, back corners of my heart.

Mike cleared his throat, cleared it again, then looked at me. "I missed you this fall, Midge. I thought about you, the things we did, the way you make me laugh, how smart you are. So, when they told me about Gina and Tommy's wedding, I thought maybe . . . maybe if you came up here with me and saw what Christmas was really like . . . like the spirit of the holiday, you'd . . ." he stopped, blushed, and then thrust forward the box. "And then I was gonna give you this . . ."

My hands were trembling so badly I was afraid to take the box. Instead I just stared at him, unable to understand why a moment I had longed for and thought about so much was now making me feel like I wanted to vomit from tension.

"It's not an engagement ring, if that's what you're afraid of," Mike said, when I didn't reach for the box. He reached down, picked up my right hand, and put the box in it.

"Afraid?" I croaked, my mouth parched. "I just . . . I didn't . . . get you a pres—"

"Open it," Mike commanded, helping me fumble open the paper. His hands felt hot and rough against the ice of mine. A velvet-covered box. Mike flipped back the lid, to expose a ring of heavy silver. A heart with a crown over it, cradled in two hands.

"It's an Irish friendship ring, Midge," Mike took my two elbows and pulled me toward him. "To tell you . . . well, I guess to tell you that I'd like to start with friendship again, and see if we can't build from there."

To say I was speechless would be mild. My brain, though, was headed for Warp Drive. The "friendly favor" that turns out to be a pretext to get me up to Christmas-land, where I am supposed to be so moved that I, what, ask the priest to baptize me in eggnog? And the ring that is supposed to be for friendship but looks like the flaming heart of Jesus, like you see on stickers in the windows of bakeries along Atlantic Avenue? And if Mike wanted to be friends again, why didn't he just ask me, instead of setting up this whole thing to lure me? Like a long line of dominoes, each knocking into the next, luring made me think of Linda, who drove the boys away from Angie like a mother bear, and of Angie, whom ancient urges were driving towards boys just as urgently, and of Roger, who wore big insulated hunting boots . . .

Mike had my elbows. Now I grabbed the front of his sweater. "Quick, Mike, who was Joseph?"

"Joseph who?" Mike was confused, this not being a response he had anticipated.

"Mary's husband! Who was he?"

"You mean like Mary and Joseph? Jesus' parents?"

"No, no, not in real life! I mean, not in the story, I mean at the church! Who was the kid who played Joseph?"

Mike gave me a truly queer look, as if perhaps I had just changed colors, and then his eyes suddenly narrowed, as comprehension dawned. "You've got an idea, haven't you, Midge?"

"It was the boots," I said, nearly smugly, "Roger wears big heavy boots! If he was waiting for Angelina out by the canal, those boots would have left tracks we'd have seen, even the way you and your posse were tromping around. But the only tracks I saw headed the other way along the canal, they were tennis shoes. And Joseph wore tennis shoes!"

Patrick Garvey was seventeen. He knew that Linda Williams defended her lovely daughter fiercely, and he knew too that Angelina was still in the fourth grade, likely perhaps to remain there forever.

But more than anything Patrick knew that Angelina was the loveliest creature he had ever laid eyes on. That was why he had resolved to give her, as a Christmas present, another of God's fair creations—two silvery dolphins, embracing an opalescent glass marble. A pendant, a gift, a clumsy attempt to express the awe Patrick felt when he contemplated Angelina's beauty.

He had no further motive. He was a good boy. Would the priest have let him play Joseph in the pageant if he weren't?

The canal at 3 A.M. was much colder than Patrick had expected it to be and much less romantic than the idea had seemed back at the pageant, where he used the intimacy of the crèche scene to persuade Angelina to promise to meet him, out along the canal, halfway between his house and hers.

And . . . if he had but known how poorly Angelina could tell time . . . if he had but known how badly she rode a bicycle, especially a new, taller bicycle . . . if he had but known why the ice in the canal was broken in the spot near where he waited as long as he could endure the cold . . .

If, if, if . . .

Mike said that, after they talked, late in the evening of Christmas Day, poor Patrick was in tears.

Gina and Tommy talked about postponing their wedding, set for the next day, but the food was ordered, the family was there, and most important, probably, they were young and anxious to get on with life.

Mike and I left right after the ceremony. I had had enough rich food that weekend, and I think Mike was feeling kind of overloaded, too.

We chatted easily enough on the Thruway, but the nearer we got to Brooklyn, the more that ring sat between us, like some kind of chaperone. When Mike pulled into the No Parking zone in front of my building, I knew we were going to have to talk about it.

"Is it because of the dumb stuff I said about Roger you won't take the ring? I admit, I was wrong about him and Angie. This time. But that still doesn't make me want to sit the guy down at my table, make him my friend."

"No, I can see that I wouldn't want him for a friend either."

"So, what, it's the religion, plain and simple?"

"I guess . . ."

"See, that's the thing I can't get, Midge, I just can't get. You don't even practice your religion. You don't keep kosher, you don't go to the synagogue . . ."

"I go sometimes," I interrupted.

"Yeah, and sometimes you have a ham and cheese sandwich," Mike shot back sharply. "But me, I believe, or I try to. My faith means something to me. But you aren't willing even to think about maybe doing things differently. Not even if it meant . . . I don't know, marriage, kids, us spending our lives together. Getting old together."

The tears were starting to flow freely now. "Don't talk like this, Mike, please . . ."

Mike slapped the steering wheel, impatiently, his jaw set in anger. "So what is it then? You're a Jew and that just plain makes you too damn good to become a Catholic?"

I turned sharply in the bucket seat, angry. "No! Not too good, but not so bad that I have to become something, either, just so I can be good enough to be your wife! I'm not Roger, infected with some pox that I have to go beg the priest to wash off me, so that the church will let me be the mother to your children!"

"Midge, that isn't what . . ."

"I know that's not what you're saying! But it is, you know? And I'll tell you something else, Mike Russo. I used to think that it was enough that I knew I would be a good mother to your children, and a good wife to you, if you were ever to ask me to become those things. I wouldn't ask you to become a Jew, and you wouldn't ask me to be a Catholic. We'd be just people, and we'd love each other, and that would be enough. Because, I thought, religions are just something that people made up, since none of us—not you, not me, not the Pope, and not even my mother—understands the tiniest little part of who God is, or what He was thinking when He put all this together . . ." I threw my hands up, indicating us two, Brooklyn, the world, the universe. "Or even, I hate to say it, but maybe there isn't even anything out there at all, just some twisty little molecules that want to keep making copies of themselves . . ."

"Midge . . ."

"No, Mike, let me finish. After this weekend, I don't think that anymore. Every December 25th from now 'til you die, you're gonna figure the world should like hold its breath, that the day should be something shiny and special and new. And me, even if I never set foot in a temple again, come late September, early October, I'm gonna be thinking about how it's time to clear the books, admit what I did wrong, think about what I should do better. You slap provolone on prosciutto, and that's never gonna be anything more than a good lunch to you. Me? It's gonna be a spiritual crisis, even if I can make my own mouth water right now, talking about it. Mike, this weekend, I can't figure out one blessed thing about who's guilty and who isn't in what happened to Angie. Roger, who didn't know what disease he had, and so didn't know he shouldn't kiss her? That kid, who shouldn't have thought Angie was so beautiful that he asked her to meet him? Linda, who maybe shouldn't have tried so hard to keep the girl around home, if she couldn't handle her?"

"Midge . . ."

"No, Mike, let me finish. What I do know? Life makes things like that. Life is messes like Angie and Linda and Roger and that poor little schmuck Joseph . . ."

"Patrick."

"Whatever. What I'm saying is those messes we have to deal with them as best we can, with what we are. If we got married, Mike, and there was trouble, God forbid, how would we decide what we are? There'd be kids for sure, because that's why I'd be getting married, and if there's kids, there'd be . . ."

As I talked, Mike smiled gently, then leaned across me to open my door.

"I got the picture, Midge . . ."

Benny Cooperman is the small-town Canadian private investigator who lives slightly north of the American border in Grantham, Ontario. His creator, **HOWARD ENGEL,** has featured his Jewish detective in nine novels beginning with *The Suicide Murders* and most recently in *Getting Away With Murder.* Benny is not your average sleuth. He's klutzy and sickens at the sight of blood. Why he didn't join his father in ladies' ready-to-wear is a mystery. Benny has a passion for tidying the lives of other people. The following is one of his rare appearances in short fiction.

The Reading

▼　　▼　　▼　　▼　　▼　　▼　　▼

HOWARD ENGEL

DUNCAN MCCALLION WAS A GREAT WRITER. There is no question about that. He wrote *From Here to Yesterday, The Choice,* and *The Tale of a Sunday Reformer.* The last won him the Governor General's Award and the Giller Prize. McCallion came from somewhere near the London docks but had banked his original Whitechapel accent with a layer of BBC English, fine-tuned by a few years in Victoria, British Columbia, where even Englishmen need subtitles to understand what the natives are saying.

I know about McCallion because my mother's butcher, Mr. Attos, came from the same street in the East End of London. McCallion's father was a fruit peddler, who doubled as a part-time *shammas* at the *shul.* He sent his son to a private school in Westminster on a scholarship. The kid never came back to the East End after that. Mr. Attos thought Duncan McCallion, whom he called Dovid Mandlebaum, was very funny because he had reinvented himself in such a predictable way as a kind of *BBC Third Programme* Englishman. When McCallion appeared on the radio here, which was more often than I would have liked, his plummy tones were immediately recognizable from coast to coast. When I heard him, I usually reached for the tuning dial.

Left to my own devices, I wouldn't have gone out to hear him that night. But Anna Abraham, who is always trying to improve my mind, got tickets. Personally, I don't think there is anything wrong with my mind. Maybe it wants cultivating a little. What with my high school diploma and a certificate from the Talmud Torah on Calvin Street that announced that I could read a little Hebrew, I felt equipped for most occasions. My mother couldn't understand why, if I *had* to be a policeman, I should choose to be free-lance. A private investigator she couldn't understand.

Anna works at Secord University in the history department and is on good terms with Gordon Palmer, founder of the Writers' Reading Series. I thought as she outlined our evening, at least I would have her company while my mind was being improved.

"Gordon will probably save Duncan McCallion for last," Anna told me, as we came through the lobby. "The icing on the cake. The other readers are Marcantonio Risso, the poet from Brantford; Helen Porter Whitney, the young struggling novelist who married Harry Comfort, the travel-book publisher; and finally Duncan . . ."

"Who needs no introduction but will get one anyway."

In the lobby, giving us a foretaste of the pleasures to come, posters showing the authors gazed down at us. Risso, with his big brown eyes, stood under a tree, reading from a slim volume of verse. Maybe Omar Khayyam. Helen Porter Whitney, in big close-up, stared out at her audience with wide-open eyes that made you think her fingers were pinched in a car door. McCallion was seen at a table signing autographs with the biggest fountain pen I've ever seen. He appeared to be momentarily glancing up at the camera with a look of surprise and delight. Such subversive thoughts began to worry me. Did I really distrust gentile culture to such an extent? Was I nervous, convinced I was a phoney among these culture vultures? Or was I just arming myself for disappointment even though the evening hadn't even started yet? I said nothing to Anna.

The Ted Adams' Auditorium was about half full when we got to our seats, and the rest of the place filled quickly during the next fifteen minutes. I turned around in my seat to see who else was being improved. I didn't rec-ognize a soul. The people I knew were playing cards or watching the hock-ey game. Still, Anna rarely misled me. When she said I would like something, I usually did, whether I owned up to it or not. She'd taken me to a show of paintings from the 1920s at the art gallery in Toronto once, and I lived to see the dawn. Movies with subtitles were her specialty. Anna's devotion to improving me, I figured, stemmed from the fact that she was pretty well perfect herself and needed to reach out to the unrefined stuff available to her. I played along with that because I enjoyed her company.

She always came prepared for these evenings. Not only did she carry jellybeans in her pocket, but she had clippings on the readers, which she slipped me for my reading pleasure. I glanced through the news items from the *Globe* and *Star*. Here I learned that Risso had denounced the National Film Board at the annual General Meeting of the Writers' Union; that McCallion had just become an arts czar, taking over the funding of certain Canada Council–supported events; and that Helen Porter Whitney had been featured in *Frank* magazine for trying to break up an all-candidates meeting at the Toronto Skydome.

It was nearly eight-thirty when the lights dimmed, and Gordon Palmer came on stage through the gap in the scarlet curtain.

"Gordon's a wonder at this, Benny," Anna whispered. "But don't try to muscle into his territory. He loves these readings better than his wife."

"She doesn't come?" I asked in all innocence.

"Better that he *loves* his wife. You're not taking this at all seriously." She leaned closer to the portly gentleman on the other side.

Gordon Palmer was a tall skinny man with an Adam's apple that wobbled as he talked. Up close, I remembered that his chin and neck always exhibited tiny razor cuts, as though he attempted to do away with himself on a daily basis. This reading series at Secord University had turned Palmer into a local celebrity, which bought him a few free drinks and canapés at receptions here and in Toronto.

"Ladies and gentlemen," he began, removing the microphone from its stand and moving with the cord to the front of the stage, "I would like to welcome you to the first in this year's series of Writers' Readings at Secord and to remind you that next week Carleton Carp will be reading from his Booker Prize novel, *The Swedish Invalid*. There are still a few tickets left . . ."

Palmer went on and on, more like a politician than a master of ceremonies. We heard all about the highlights of the coming season, his debt to the support of the Canada Council and the local arts council. He even thanked the company that ran the writers to Grantham from Toronto and back again in their grey, stretch limousines. We heard about Palmer's own soon-to-be published book of essays on the celebrities he had encountered in his travels. I had already stifled a yawn behind my hand, receiving an elbow in the ribs from my bluestocking neighbor, when Palmer launched into the introduction of the poet, Marcantonio Risso, who as Anna said earlier, was the light-weight first act. Risso read and read. He droned on for nearly thirty minutes, until Palmer had to interrupt him by coming through the curtains clapping. This cued the audience to clap him into an acknowledgment that his contribution had just been concluded for him. I felt sorry for Risso, who showed his disappointment and anger so generously.

Helen Porter Whitney read from her "work in progress" called, tentatively, *The Disembowelling*. She was a good reader in the tradition of writers who read out loud. It was almost like a chant in *shul*. The emphasis was displaced from where it belonged in order to make every sentence sound like a wail. She could have been reading from *The Book of Lamentations* as far as I was concerned.

At last, the lights came up and it was Intermission. Fifty percent of the evening was over. Only an hour to go, I thought. I followed Anna up the aisle and into the lobby, where the Perrier began to flow like water.

"What did you think?" Anna asked.

"I got lost in that last reading," I admitted. "She was in a boat or something, wasn't she?"

"It was the raft of the *Medusa*, Benny. You know the Guerricault painting?"

"I do not," I said. "You mean her book is about a *picture?*"

"No, not *about* a picture, but an *homage* to the picture."

"A *what?*" Anna gave me a look and I set about looking for the men's room. While waiting my turn there, I overheard the news that the second act might not be over until ten-thirty. I thought of McCallion's rolling cadences from my last hearing of him on the radio. I thought of England and unzipped.

Behind me, somebody was saying that he couldn't wait to see McCallion after the reading, if just to poke him in the eye.

"Why?" his companion wanted to know.

"Because he wrecked the sale of my book in the States," he said. "He told Ezra Segal at Harvest House that I was a nine-day wonder. I can show you the letter. The son of a bitch!"

I glanced around to see the speaker. He was short, balding, and bearded. I didn't think he was local, so he might have come from Toronto or Buffalo to blacken McCallion's eye.

"You're not the only enemy in the house," his friend replied. "I've seen a few who wouldn't mind reading his obituary in the morning paper. If he reads from that autobiography he's been working on, he's going to put some noses out of joint."

"You can add my name to that list," offered a third voice. "That bastard broke up my last marriage." The other two looked at the newcomer hoping for more, but it didn't come. The speaker was a heavy-set man with curly, golden hair going grey and bald all at once. I recognized him as a writer of detective stories but I couldn't just then recall his name.

A bell sounded, warning that the Intermission was coming to an end. I could stall no longer where I was, so I re-zipped and made way for the short bearded writer with the itchy fists.

Gordon Palmer came through the curtains again and again rehearsed the names of his sponsors. When he had accounted for the restaurant that served meals to the visiting readers, he slipped his notes back in his pocket. Now back at the lectern, he picked up his prepared introduction to the main reader of the evening. I couldn't help comparing Palmer to a ringmaster announcing the next bout of the evening from the middle of a boxing ring: "Duncan McCallion, at two hundred and sixty pounds and still champ-een wordsmith in a blue Savile Row suit . . ."

To do him justice, Palmer had done his homework on McCallion. We heard about his origins—those he admitted to, about his early journalistic forays, about his struggles to be published twenty-five years ago. "And now," Palmer announced, extending his hand in the direction of the right-hand-side of the stage, "I give you a man who has more than paid his dues in the paper wars, who has come to us directly from London, England, where he is working on the film-script of his latest novel . . ."

We didn't get to hear the name of the film or the details of who was making it. We didn't even get to hear Duncan McCallion, for at that moment a noise, which could only have been a gunshot, was heard throughout the auditorium. Palmer stopped mid-hyperbole. He glanced at the proscenium arch where he had expected McCallion to come from. For the next thirty seconds, Palmer gaped at the audience. We gaped back. Then there was a rising buzz in the hall. Anna turned to me and asked what I thought happened. I told her that in books it was never a car backfiring. It was a gun. In real life, I had no more information than the next guy. I checked my watch. It was nine-fifty-three.

Without another word, Palmer withdrew behind the curtain. One of the lighting men followed him, hopping up on the stage. I hadn't intended to move, but I found myself in the aisle heading for the door leading backstage.

I wasn't alone in this. We were quite a crowd. As I came up a short flight of steps and rounded a corner, I arrived at the exact moment when Palmer and three stagehands broke through the door leading to one of the dressing rooms. I heard the wood protest as the bolt was ripped from its fastenings. Through the doorway all I could see were four backs protecting me from whatever horror lay beyond. I pushed two of them aside and took a look. Duncan McCallion was sprawled in a leather chair facing himself in a mirror that almost ran the length of the counter on that side of the small room. It never occurred to me that he might still be alive. The greyness of his face, the blood, the weapon lying on the floor just below his dangling hand, all suggested the only possible conclusion.

"Hamish, call 911!" Palmer yelled. "We have to get out of here. Back up, everybody. There's nothing we can do for him." I backed up with difficulty; there were twenty people behind me. Together, we all retreated to our seats to tell our companions what we had seen.

"But, Benny," demanded Anna, "why would McCallion shoot himself?"

"Would *you* like to face this mob? I wouldn't."

"Yes, but you wouldn't kill yourself. Stop trying to be funny. This is serious." Anna was flushed and breathing like she'd just run up a hill. "What do you make of it?"

"All I saw was the body of a dead man. There was a gun on the floor. Draw your own conclusions."

The level of noise in the auditorium had slowly risen as three hundred opinions about what had happened were exchanged. I went over what I had seen again and again to Anna, who quizzed me like I was one of her doctoral candidates at an oral examination. "What about the door?" she asked.

"It was locked on the inside by an old-fashioned bolt lock. It was pulled off when they forced the door."

"Did he leave a note?"

"Maybe. But I didn't see one."

At this point, Gordon Palmer again appeared on stage. He looked frightened and disorganized. One of the stagehands followed him and while they talked hurriedly, Palmer kept his hand over the microphone. When the stagehand disappeared behind the curtain again, Palmer again called us to attention. "Ladies and gentlemen. There has been the most terrible accident. Duncan McCallion appears to have shot himself. The police have been called and I ask you all to remain calm. I'm sure that none of you will be detained, but, just so that we don't make any mistakes, I'm asking you to please remain in your seats. It won't be for long."

At this point, shouts came up to Palmer across the footlights: "Are you sure he's dead?" "Is there a doctor in the house?" "Is this some kind of trick?"

A fleshy man with an Irish fisherman's sweater got up from his seat and began making his way down the aisle. "I'm a doctor!" he shouted. "I'm a doctor!" God knows I didn't doubt him. He moved to the front and awkwardly responded to Palmer's directions for getting backstage. When he was gone, our attention slipped back to the lectern, where Palmer was still trying to answer questions.

"No, I don't think it's a good idea for any of us to leave the auditorium. Not just yet. The police will be here in a minute."

In fact, they came in just over seven minutes. There were four of them, all in uniform. I recognized my old friend, Staff Sergeant Pete Staziak. He didn't see me in the crowd, but I was glad that he was in charge. Pete is no genius, but he's a good police officer: tidy, methodical, and fair. Gordon Palmer went behind the curtain again, leaving us alone, all three hundred of us, with our speculations. After another quarter of an hour, another medical man—this time from Niagara Regional, I suspect—arrived with a metal suitcase and vanished like his predecessor behind the scenes. Shortly after that, one of the uniforms appeared at the microphone and announced that the evening was over and that, after giving our names to his brother officer at the door, we could all go home. In spite of the closeness of death, a light burst of applause broke out. I suspect that there were still some of us who reacted as though it was one of Palmer's publicity stunts.

I gathered Anna's coat around her shoulders and slipped into my own. A perfect stranger behind me grinned at me. McCallion's death had turned us into something other than perfect strangers. We were fellow witnesses, even here in the hall, cut off from the real drama. We were witnesses and would remain tied together by what we had seen from then onward. The gathering of names at the door was a slow process, and before we were more than halfway up the aisle, one of the uniforms tugged me by the sleeve: "Sergeant Staziak would like a word, Mr. Cooperman."

"I'll catch a ride home with somebody," I told Anna. "This might take a minute and it might take an hour. I'll catch you up later."

"I've got classes in the morning anyway, Benny. You can give me a full report over dinner tomorrow night. Deal?"

"Deal," I said, and, after only two backward glances, where I saw Anna smiling at the uniform taking her name, I followed the policeman down the aisle and through the door leading back to the dead man.

Here the scene was as busy as it had been when I saw it first, only now a police photographer was taking shots of everything in sight, from the autographed picture of the writer Michael Ondaatje on one wall to the poster of Gwendolyn MacEwen, the poet, facing it. He pointed his camera at the body from time to time, which reassured me that his snapshots of the black and yellow ghetto-blaster on the counter and the box of greasy make-up were not just personal amusements that he had devised to get him through the tough close-ups of the corpse with its dead eyes turned into the mirror. While this was going on, the coroner was checking out the body with instruments from his suitcase, which lay open on the counter top. Supervising all this from the doorway, Pete Staziak was holding a fingerprint expert in check: the room was too small for three experts to work efficiently. He turned when he saw me come up behind him.

"Benny!" he said in a husky voice. "What brings you out on a hockey night to a place like this. You a big fan of the dear departed?"

"I got enough of him on the radio, Pete. Anna's to blame. I let her drag me here. I owed her for standing her up last Thursday because of that used Ferrari scam I told you about."

"Yeah, I remember." Pete mimed the actions of someone reaching for a pack of cigarettes in his pocket. Instead of cigarettes, he found a package of gum. He looked glumly at the wrapper and offered me a stick. I accepted. I'm a reformed smoker too, and like it as little as Pete does. "What do you make of this thing, Benny. A big-deal writer shoots himself rather than face an audience of three hundred fans?"

"They weren't all fans, Pete. I heard a couple of people who wanted to take a poke at him."

"You think they scared him into wasting himself. Come on!"

"All I meant was that McCallion had history with some of these people. That's all. I don't know anything that would change this into a murder. Except . . ."

"Except. Except what?"

"Well, this door for one thing. It was locked with this bolt. Nobody still believes that a locked bolt makes for a locked-room mystery." We were standing in the doorway and could see where the light bolt had been torn from its moorings, leaving the wood-screws still clinging to the hardware. Pete looked at the lock and then down at me.

"Hello, Benny! This isn't one of your paperback mysteries. The body of Duncan McCallion isn't going to disappear when you get to the last page. This is a suicide. It smells like a suicide; it looks like a suicide. Why shouldn't it be a suicide?"

"I didn't say it wasn't. I only said that the locked room didn't on its own make it one. With a piece of string, you and I could bolt any door in town behind us. It was in one of those Saturday matinee serials when we were kids."

"Yeah, I remember."

The coroner came out of the room. I could see that he was wearing pajamas under his sweater. In English mysteries made for TV, coroners are always wearing dinner jackets just to show that they have lives beyond supplying the time of death for the convenience of Poirot or Morse. This guy, whose name was Morton Seligman, was a classmate of my brother Sam.

"Well?" asked Pete.

"Can't really tell anything until I get him on the table." He shook his head, indicating the unplumbed difficulties of his job. "Hi, Benny. What do you know for sure?" I grinned an answer, which even I didn't understand. "You know, Pete, I was at university with Benny's big brother."

"Yeah, I know. You told me a million times. Tell me what you can about the man in the leather chair, Mort."

"I got contact marks on the right temple, Pete, and a gun on the floor under his right hand. You're going to tell me that there is a single shot missing from the chamber of this—what is it?—a .38 Smith & Wesson, maybe."

"Close enough. Yeah, there's only one shot gone from a full chamber."

"As to the time of death . . ."

"Mort, the shot was heard by three hundred witnesses. So don't be giving me time of death."

"Yeah, I know that. But from what I saw when I got here, your customer in there looks a little well done for—what was the time of the shot?"

"I haven't quizzed the three hundred witnesses yet, so, Benny, tell me what time it was."

"It was nine-fifty-three by my imitation Seiko."

"So, let's see: I got here about half past ten and that makes him dead less than half an hour. You're not going to get big changes in that short time, Pete. It's too soon for rigor, too soon for lividity. What else can I give you for nothing. I can tell you he's pretty fresh, but you know that already."

"Thanks, Mort. Just spare a thought for the ones that aren't this easy. I like a case with a hard bottom once in a while. What are you looking so gloomy about, Benny?"

"Nothing."

"Nothing. Why does nothing put an expression like that on your face?"

"Pete, I hate to say this."

"Then don't say it. It's that easy." Here he turned to Mort and began to talk to him in tones low enough for me to feel excluded. Mort nodded and grinned as he was expected to, but he kept his eyes on me for some reason.

"Benny," he said, interrupting Staziak in mid-witticism. "What's the matter? Tell me."

"Mort, when you were turning the body over, I saw his belt. The point of the belt was pointing right."

"So what?" This from Staziak. "Is that a Masonic message of some kind?"

"And outside, in the lobby, there's a poster showing him signing books," I said.

"So?"

"Well, I hate to screw things up for you, Pete, but he's signing those books with a pen held in his left hand. I thought they might have flipped the negative for some reason, but they didn't: the printing isn't backwards. McCallion was left handed. Now, tell me, why does a left-handed man shoot himself in the right temple with his right hand?"

Pete Staziak's face looked puzzled, as though he was searching for a solution to the puzzle that wouldn't keep him up all night. Mort Seligman went back to the body and turned it so that he could see his belt. Then he picked up McCallion's left hand and sniffed it. "Ink on his fingers, Pete, and no smell of burned powder. Read 'em and weep. He's right about the belt too, damn it."

Pete ran his hand over his face. When he put his hand back in his pocket, he said, without looking at me, "I'll have to talk to those other two writers. They were backstage at least part of the time, except when they were reading. Or what else would you suggest, Benny?" This was no friendly request for help. Pete was angry and I'd made it happen. "Better still, who was back here when the gun went off?"

"Talk to the production crew," I suggested. "Get a fix on where everybody was when the gunshot was heard. And there may be more ways backstage than the one we've used. There were people breaking in the door when I got here. I don't know where they came from."

"Okay. That's a beginning. Meanwhile," he said, raising his voice so that the two uniformed men leaning against the walls of the hallway could hear, "nobody else leaves the auditorium. We're looking for a murderer: someone smart enough to think of the suicide gimmick, but not bright enough to remember that McCallion was a lefty."

Twenty minutes later, the body had been removed from the dressing room and Mort Seligman had left with it. Pete Staziak was interviewing the backstage crew on the stage under the work lights, the curtains having been pulled open. Also on stage sat Marcantonio Risso and Helen Whitney. Both looked like waxworks in a museum as they waited their turn. Pete enjoyed letting them dangle while he filled in his sketch map of the area in his notebook with information from the stage crew.

To kill time, since I hadn't been dismissed, I went down a set of stairs that led from the end of the dressing room corridor and through a fire door to the main lobby, which led in one direction to a double set of doors opening on to one of a dozen parking lots. In the opposite direction, the corridor led to the main entrance of Nesbitt Hall, the entrance that Anna and I had used only two hours earlier. The fire door had a bar only on the inside. Once outside, I had to re-enter the auditorium in the normal way, past the box office and the wall with its posters: McCallion's picture now looking oddly changed from when I had first seen it. At least, he was holding his pen in his left hand. Thank God I got that right.

Once back in the Ted Adams' Auditorium, I could see Pete Staziak questioning the two writers. They sat in straight-backed chairs. With the stagehands watching, it looked like a rehearsal for a play that needed a lot of work before opening night. I walked up the middle aisle and listened. Risso was saying that he had not seen McCallion at all, that the door had been shut when he arrived, and it was still closed when he went out to give his reading. Then Helen Whitney said that she hadn't seen the door open at any time. A lighting man volunteered that he had seen Ms. Whitney knock on McCallion's door while Risso was reading.

"I was concerned for him," she said, defensively. "It's not easy waiting, Sergeant. It's like waiting your turn for the firing squad. I thought that we could pass the time more happily together."

"And?"

"Well, I knocked and he chose not to let me in. The light was off, so I thought he might be resting."

"How did you know about the light?"

"Under the door, dear boy. I spoke through the door and identified myself, but he obviously preferred to be alone. I don't question that. It was his choice."

"Did you try the door?"

"Certainly not!" Ms. Whitney said with a great show of propriety. Then she added: "Sergeant Staziak, I must confess to something that may not be generally known." Here she lowered her voice and spoke reverently of the dead writer. "I knew Duncan from earlier in our lives."

"Oh. How's that?"

"Well, you'll find this out anyway. Duncan and I lived together in New York for six months in 1987. West 46th Street. We were both young and, as I thought, very much in love. But it ended, and we have been friends ever since."

Marcantonio Risso giggled but stopped at once when he saw Staziak's eye on him. He shrugged.

"What's that trying to tell us?" he asked.

"Well," Risso said, rolling his large eyes. "You don't want me to repeat gossip, Sergeant?"

"Let me be judge of that," said Pete, clutching at a straw. "Let's have it."

"I heard—and I know that this is hearsay, but all the same—I heard that McCallion had to have a court order to get her off his back. A court order! She wouldn't leave him alone."

"And what about you, you venomous fishwife. You tried to compromise him after the lecture he gave in Buffalo last May. Didn't the police question you after that, darling?"

"The man was living a lie! Ask anyone you like. He insists on denying his nature."

"Come again?"

"The man was gay, but he refused to come out."

"As is his right!" added Ms. Whitney. "He wasn't gay when I knew him, I'll tell you that for nothing."

Now it was Pete's turn to roll his eyes. I couldn't think of anything to do to help him out. I went quietly back through the door leading backstage. The room where the body had been was empty now. Tell-tale powdering on flat surfaces showed where the fingerprint man had been prospecting for evidence. The room was still in disarray with a uniformed officer, Corporal Bedrosian, standing outside making sure that I didn't pinch anything. There wasn't much to take, actually. Except the ghetto-blaster. "Do you know who owns this?" I asked the officer.

"Uh, that goes with the theatre. The manager, Mr. Palmer, says that he put it in here along with the kettle and tea things this morning. Said he was a little nervous of McCallion, because he had a reputation for being a prickly kind of guy."

"What was he listening to? *Ideas* on CBC?"

"It wasn't on. I mean the radio wasn't turned on. I thought he might be listening to a tape. There's a cassette in there. But it's blank."

"Maybe he was going to record his reading?"

"No way. Palmer—I mean, Mr. Palmer—won't allow it. This isn't a union hall, but he doesn't let anyone but the theatre sound man record the readings."

"Are you sure there's nothing on the tape?"

"I checked it myself. The machine was switched off but plugged in. It's the sort of recorder that turns itself off when the cassette comes to the end. When I tried to play it, I got that grinding noise you get when the cassette won't move any more in that direction. I turned it around and spot checked it: blank. A brand new cassette. I tested it back to the beginning. Totally unused. I turned it over again and tried it for fifteen minutes. Nothing on it on either side. Best quality tape. Thirty minutes per side."

"What about the tea stuff. I see there's a dirty cup and a plate with crumbs on it. Cookies."

"Yeah, funny about that. Looks like he made himself a cuppa before he was shot. Drank most of it. Lapsang Sushong. Must have brought the bags himself because Palmer says that they only supply Red Rose. Finished off the cookies, too."

"Did anybody see or talk to McCallion when he got here tonight?"

"Palmer said that he had phoned to say that he was coming early because he wanted to make some adjustments to his reading. Got here just after 7:00. He didn't go out to eat with Palmer and the rest of the writers across the street at that new Italian restaurant. Palmer's assistant, Veronica Le Pan, herded them over the highway, and Palmer joined them as soon as he'd made McCallion comfortable."

"Anybody else see him?"

"Not that I know of." Corporal Bedrosian began to attach one end of a roll of yellow police tape across the doorway.

"What about the stage crew. When did they arrive?"

"They had an afternoon concert in here today. So they did their set-up before they went over to the pub. They didn't get back here until around 8:00."

I had to bend down to climb under the tape. He'd taped me in with the evidence as we'd talked. He'd attached the tape to convenient outcroppings in the corridor: a doorknob and the ring in a grey fusebox. I took a look inside the box: each of the dressing rooms was on a separate circuit breaker. I guess that prevents wide-scale disruption when somebody plugs in a kettle and an iron at the same time. I closed the fuse box and went back on stage, where Ms. Whitney and Risso were still sparring. Palmer was there too, looking embarrassed on behalf of the entire arts community as the pot continued blackening the kettle.

"You've no right to suggest that I harbor any . . ."

"Duncan warmed you over in his autobiography. Gave you an eye-popping roasting. Too bad he can't read it."

"You likely fixed it so he can't!"

"Sergeant, do I have to listen to this?"

"Please try to talk one at a time," Pete suggested and then sighed when the suggestion was ignored. He looked to Palmer for help.

"Look, you two," Palmer said. "Sergeant Staziak could take you both downtown right now and question you formally and separately. He's trying to be reasonable. He is asking for your voluntary assistance. You are not under arrest. You are not being charged with anything. To hear you talk, you'd think they'd brought back the third degree. This is the stage of the Ted Adams' Auditorium, not the Star Chamber." Risso looked slightly chastened; Whitney pouted with her lower lip extended petulantly. Palmer had done the trick, though. I took a chair and sat down.

When Pete asked me what I could contribute, I told him about what I'd heard in the men's room earlier.

"Hmmmm." said Pete when I'd done. He rubbed his chin.

"One of those people was Michael Harrington. His threats are not to be ignored," said Risso. "He once threatened me with libel after I'd lampooned his lamentable record with the Canada Council."

"He the one with the broken marriage or the queered booksale?" asked Pete.

"Oh, Quentin Heller is not to be feared. That marriage was condemned. Anyway, he wouldn't harm a fly," offered Ms. Whitney. "But I agree. Harrington's a cornered rat now that Ezra has tried to drop him."

"Never mind Ezra!" shouted Pete, exasperated. "Unless he was here tonight. Somebody here shot Duncan McCallion tonight, and it wasn't an agent in New York, and it wasn't anybody sitting out there in the hall either. Somebody might have propped the door from the outer lobby open and done the job, but nobody saw him or her. It could have been one of the stagehands, but none of them saw anyone go near the door except Ms. Whitney. Palmer was on stage talking. Risso and you, Ms. Whitney, were in your dressing rooms. But nobody saw you at the moment the shot went off. McCallion had a parcel of enemies, God knows, but nobody appears to have come calling on him with that gun."

"What about that gun?" I asked.

"Too early to tell anything. It was a Smith & Wesson .38 clone by the look of it. But we'll have to wait to see what the numbers on it will tell us. I don't suppose that you saw the weapon on him when you saw him early this evening, Mr. Palmer?"

"I wish I could help, but no I didn't. Duncan came in by taxi. He was upset and wasn't inclined to talk. I showed him the way to his dressing room, and he told me to call him when it was five minutes to go."

"And did you?" I asked.

"I . . . I don't think I did. Backstage commotion, you know?"

"The commotion started when the shot was heard," I suggested. "Things were relatively peaceful before you began your introduction?"

"Yes, I suppose so. I was thinking of what I was going to say. You perhaps don't know what a prickly character Duncan was. One word wrong, and you'd never hear the end of it."

"But he didn't hear whether your introduction was sufficiently flattering, did he?"

"No. He was still in his room." Palmer examined me from where he was sitting, giving a glance at Staziak, who looked about to resume the questioning himself. That didn't stop me.

"No, the reason he didn't hear your introduction was because he was already dead."

"What?" This from everyone on stage. "Benny, what are you talking about?" said Staziak.

Then everybody was talking at once and I had to wait until they quieted down before I could go on.

"You shot McCallion," I said looking straight across the stage to Palmer.

"You're crazy! Three hundred people saw me right here on stage when the gun went off!"

"They heard the recording of the shot that went off two and a half hours before you began your introduction. The shot was recorded on that ghetto-blaster in his dressing room. It was on the last bit of tape at the end of the side. The rest was blank. Then you rewound the tape, left it switched on and playing, set up your pretend suicide, and bolted the door behind you with a bit of string. Next you turned off the circuit breaker in McCallion's dressing room. The lights went out in McCallion's room and the tape stopped. That done, you followed the other readers across the street and ate your dinner with them. Somewhere between 9:15 and 9:30, when Ms. Whitney was reading, you fixed the fuse. Lights in the dressing room went on and the tape continued to play. It was a few minutes before the Intermission. You'd turned the volume on the ghetto-blaster up to the top, so that we'd all hear the noise of that gunshot. A moment later, the tape ended and the machine shut itself off."

"Save that for a book, Mr. Cooperman. That's where it belongs," shouted Palmer. He looked towards Staziak for support. But Pete was being careful. He knew me well enough to know that I wasn't making this up. But there was a good deal of data to be absorbed, and it took a minute before he was able to speak.

"Bedrosian?"

"Sir?"

"You checked that tape like I asked?"

"Uh, I spot-checked it. I didn't listen all the way through. That would have taken an hour. Uh, but he's right: I didn't hear the very last part of the side that was up on the machine."

"I see," Pete said, nodding sadly. "I see. Well, Mr. Palmer, what do you say to Mr. Cooperman's accusation?"

"Why, it's absurd, of course. Anybody could make up such a story. That doesn't make it true. Why would I want to kill Duncan?"

"Because of this," I said and pulled Anna's clipping from the *Globe*. "You were very comfortable here at Secord with your reading empire. But Duncan McCallion was trying to cut Canada Council funding for readings like this. And he could do it, too. So, it was time for him to do away with himself. Yes, we mustn't forget that you wanted it to be seen as a suicide. But, once that didn't work, murder would do just as well. You had the perfect alibi. Three hundred people were looking at you when the gun shot was heard and you weren't holding a gun."

Pete asked Palmer to accompany him downtown. To soften the blow, he invited the other two readers to come along. He didn't say a word to me, but I could read his face. I drove with Bedrosian, who also didn't say a word. The car crept down the corkscrew turns of the escarpment and drove steadily through the night city. Television sets, glimpsed through carelessly drawn curtains, told me that the third period was still being played somewhere.

Pete wasn't finished with me until nearly two in the morning. When I left, the two writers left with me. Palmer was being detained for further questioning. As I walked back to the flat, I wondered what was it that whispered the truth to me. I was going up the stairs when I remembered. Palmer hadn't knocked on McCallion's door like any good assistant stage manager would have. It was impractical. McCallion couldn't hear. He was already dead.

It was too late for anything but a shower and bed. So I did that.

RICHARD FLIEGEL has published seven Shelly Lowenkopf mysteries. He otherwise occupies himself writing screenplays, and as a professor and administrator at the University of Southern California in Los Angeles. In this story, Fliegel has created New York City Police Lieutenant David Lehman, who ingeniously solves a crime after a thorough exploration of many more obvious alternatives.

A Final Midrash

▼   ▼   ▼   ▼   ▼   ▼   ▼   ▼

RICHARD FLIEGEL

LIEUTENANT DAVID OWEN LEHMAN knew enough about politics in the Robbery Homicide Division to know there was no point in complaining about his sudden change of assignment. And he understood enough of the stentorian tones of his captain, Marcus Freeman, to suspect that the call had been made in the lofty heights of the New York City Police Department's top drawer, so there was probably nothing Marcus could have done, even if he wanted to help. From the way the big man sprawled in his chair, rubbing his grizzly stubble, David saw plainly he stood no chance at all. But it was two o'clock in the morning. His hand-tailored suit bagged at his elbows, his tact had slipped with his necktie, and he couldn't resist making one final report on the search for the Westside Strangler.

"We're close to him, Marcus—I can feel it. We've got two decent leads, finally, and a good team on the ground, so it's just a matter of persistence. And shoe leather. We'll nab him any time now. If you just let us stick to it."

"Can't help it, Dave," said the captain with a soft shrug that seemed to encompass every frustration in this vale of tears. He was only too familiar with Lehman's feelings, having soothed them, resented them, and counted on them for much of the last two years. Marcus was wearing a woolen coat with the collar turned up and the top button closed. At his sleeves flashed the cuffs of flannel pajamas, green with grey elephants. Having been roused from his bed by the late-night call, he was eager to climb back into it. He wanted the

Westside Strangler as much as David did. But he wasn't about to succumb to any means of persuasion tonight. "They'll have to nab him without you. Or you can get back to it just as soon as you settle this other little thing."

There was no point in arguing further. But Lehman hadn't made lieutenant at thirty-three by giving up easily. What he needed was another line of argument. He crossed one rumpled knee over the other and tamped an imported cigarette against the edge of Freeman's desk. His own cuff was grey, and his nails cried out for a clipping. He fished a porcelain baseball from the sea of paper overflowing the trays and flicked the copper wheel on its top.

"Slovenly habit," said Marcus. "You shouldn't smoke."

"I agree." The pressed tobacco made a nice crackle as he sucked the unfiltered end. "Why does it have to be me?"

"Because you dress so nicely, for one reason."

Lehman plucked his baggy jacket sleeve. "This old thing?"

"You went to the right schools. Fieldston and Princeton, wasn't it?"

"Only Brandeis."

"Uh huh. And you come from a good family. Your daddy knew Einstein, I hear."

"He once went to a dinner honoring the man. There were two hundred other people there."

"Well, my daddy wasn't one of them. And look at you!" He waved a hand, taking in David's clear blue eyes and sardonic mouth, the fine black curls of his hair. "You're so damned presentable, the chief asked for you by name."

"Oh, sure."

"He did. He said, 'Give it to your hotshot—Layman. That's Jewish, right?' I said, 'Not the way you pronounce it, Bob.'"

Lehman groaned. "He's got to be kidding. All I know about being Jewish would fit on one page of my notepad. With margins to spare."

"Hey," said the Captain and waited out a yawn, "you have any idea how many dumb details yours truly drew just because I happened to be black?"

"Still are, Marcus, aren't you?"

Freeman raised his hand in proof. "Want to check anything of yours?"

Lehman grinned, despite himself. "No, thanks."

"Personnel calls it 'special sensitivity to the community.' Just take the assignment as a commendation, David, and show a little grace under pressure groups. Not to mention team spirit, for the Chief. With your luck, the

Westside Strangler will still be crawling up drainpipes when you make the collar at the synagogue."

"A synagogue? Jesus. I haven't been in one of those in years."

"Time to brush up your *brachas,* Bubbie."

"That's a Jewish grandma."

"You see? You knew that. I didn't. You're the man."

The evening was still young. David leafed through the file Marcus had given him, drank half a cup of coffee from the machine, and talked to the desk sergeant who had taken the call, an hour and a half earlier. He went into the bathroom, splashed cold water on his neck and straightened his tie, although nothing could be done about the suit without stopping off at his place on Bank and Greenwich Avenue. He could have shaved there, too, but decided what-the-hell, he had customers waiting.

Lehman bid goodnight to Warnecke, the detective sergeant who had driven him down to headquarters when the call came in from Freeman, and gave him some final instructions for the next shift of decoys. He hated to pull even one unmarked car off the Strangler's favorite prowl. The cabbie dropped him off in the east sixties, in front of a wrought iron fence that circled three sides of a stone edifice and the oak-shaded lawn of its fourth. As soon as it did, he felt a certain ambivalence that always crept over him at the gates of a synagogue.

Except for weddings and b'nai mitzvah, he rarely stepped inside a synagogue. His sister Hannah usually went once a year on Yom Kippur to say a blessing for their dead parents at the Yiskor service, and David imagined uncomfortably she was saying it for him, too. He was a rational man, who had committed his life to the rational pursuit of justice, and he could have made his peace with the humanistic reforms of post-Enlightenment Judaism. He couldn't stand most of the traditional mumbo-jumbo and especially despised Orthodox attitudes toward women and gentiles. Yet, something about the mystery of the older rituals made them feel awe-fully authentic. Old men in prayer shawls, swaying back and forth as they mumbled blessings he couldn't understand—that was what Judaism should be like. Though not, of course, for him. Rather than struggling to resolve these feelings, he dismissed the whole question of his Jewishness whenever it arose. A forgiving God would forgive him for his lack of blind faith and who wanted to believe in any other kind of divinity?

But now here he was again, outside a synagogue, whose black iron gates were open, a little, to admit him, if he chose. A bush-lined lane disappeared into the oak shade. David followed it and passed into a place that set his unshaved cheeks tingling. The path was fragrant and led past a bench under a streetlamp, to a few broad steps climbing to the entranceway, an arch hewn out of a pile of purplish stones, shot with pink. It looked as if it had been erected to front a private townhouse in the early years of the century. Its street doors were made of dark wood with brass fittings: studs and a handle with a latch instead of a knob, and a plate that supported the doorbell and a peephole. David inspected the brass, saw no sign of tampering or forced entry, and pushed the bell. It made no sound that he could hear, and no one came to the peephole. He pushed it again.

"Lieutenant Lehman?"

It was a tiny voice, nearly lost in the wind. David turned to the bushes on his left, from which it seemed to have emanated.

"Yes? Here I am—"

"Thank heaven," said the voice again, and this time it sounded closer at hand. Lehman heard a clang of iron and the shuffle of shoes among the leaves on the windswept lane. He turned and saw Officer Doreen Taglia struggling with the weight of the black iron gate, which had swung free and now threatened to slam shut, perhaps sealing both of them inside. Taglia mastered it, forcing it back against the side of the iron fence and binding it there with a twisted wire that had once been a clothes hanger. She twisted to face the lieutenant, who was waiting out her battle with the gate.

"Officer Taglia?"

"Yes, sir. We aren't using the front door, Lieutenant. It leads to a reception area and then the sanctuary. They're waiting for you upstairs, in the rabbi's study, which is reached most quickly by a staircase around the side."

"No sign of any break-in here."

"No, sir. The crime scene unit is still working on the second floor, but they tell me there's no evidence of forced entrance or lock-picking anywhere downstairs."

"So our killer was admitted to the building."

"Looks like it."

"Or came in with a key."

"Only three keys, Lieutenant, and the rabbi had one still in his pocket. The second one belongs to the janitor, who spent the night with his daughter in the Bronx. She's an attorney and swears he hasn't been out of her house since seven o'clock tonight. The third key belongs to the cantor, who's been laid up in Mount Sinai for over a week with a broken right hip. I asked the night nurse on his floor to check his pockets, and the key was still on his ring."

Lehman considered Taglia, who must have been twenty-two or -three, with quick green eyes in an eager face. "You've been busy."

"I hope you don't mind, sir. My getting the jump on your arrival."

"I'm grateful for whatever information I can get, Taglia. It's more than I usually expect from the officer on the scene."

"You mean from a uniform, Lieutenant. I aim to be a detective."

"You have the initiative for it."

"Thank you, sir. I appreciate your saying so. It's up these stairs and to your right. Watch the clearance."

Officer Taglia stepped aside and let Lehman lead the way through a side door and up a staircase that wound behind the back of the sanctuary stage and climbed steeply to the second floor. David had to duck twice to avoid hitting his head when the ceiling of the staircase dropped low, concealing an airshaft or some other utility added to the building after its original construction.

The staircase ended at a narrow door that issued onto a hallway hardly less narrow. It was dense with carpeting, and hanging lamps, and wooden picture frames that held diplomas and commendations and official-looking documents, stamped and ribboned and inscribed in Hebrew.

Lehman found himself at the very end of the hall, with a closed door ahead on his left and an open one further down on his right. From the latter door came muffled voices, and though he could not make out any words, he recognized the murmur of grief.

Taglia appeared behind him in the doorway. "We've asked them all to wait in the rabbi's study. Until we knew what you wanted us to do."

The closed door on the left opened and a man crawled out on his hands and knees, following the molding that ran along the base of the wall at the carpet-line. He did not look up, and Lehman chose not to distract him. He would need all the results of the crime scene unit at the earliest possible moment. The least he could do was allow them time to work uninterrupted.

"The study is fine," said Lehman.

"It's just to the right."

Taglia managed to get ahead of him again despite the narrow hallway, so that she could lead the way and then stand aside at the doorway to the study, announcing, "Here you are, Lieutenant."

David would have preferred a less ostentatious entrance, but it had its effect: a blond patrolman inside the door looked up laconically, and three witnesses, seated around a coffee table, raised guilty faces toward him.

"Hello," said David, with charm.

"That's my partner," Taglia informed him, still in the hall. "Officer Healy. Brian, this is David O. Lehman."

"O'Leeman?" Healy blinked, rousing himself from the doorjamb.

"Lieutenant *Leh*-man," said Taglia, with a frown.

The blond mouthed a silent "Oh" when he realized the lieutenant was Jewish, and that made David uneasy for a moment, though he couldn't have said exactly why. The approval of the others present hardly reassured him.

The room called the "study" seemed more like a reception room, with a sofa facing the door, and two armchairs facing the sofa across an inlaid coffee table. The nearest armchair was empty, but the one to its right was occupied by a wiry old man, sipping tea from a plastic cup. He sipped it noisily, upending the cup, and then set it down on the coffee table in front of him, where a sudden spastic clenching of his fist crushed it entirely. Across from him, on the sofa, an upright figure edged uneasily forward. Beside him, a bearlike man held his face in his hands, weeping profusely.

Both men on the couch looked to be in their forties; the man in the chair, nearly twice that. On the coffee table between them stood a bottle of Schnapps, half-emptied, and a three-shot glass. At the far end of the room was a narrow stained glass window. Both of the side walls were lined with cedar bookshelves, organized by language, with English and Hebrew closer to the door, French, German, Spanish, and Russian nearer the window. The volumes were neatly arranged in size places and the shelves were dusted cleanly. It did not look to David like a place anyone could get any work done.

The bearlike man dropped his hands from his face and started at once for Lehman. To reach him, he had to step around the coffee table and over the old man's legs, but he nonetheless managed to offer his hand before anyone else had moved. His handshake was large and powerful, warm and dry.

"Thank you for coming, at this hour," he said, as if David had been a pediatrician on a late-night house call. "My name is Samuelson—Rabbi Ezra Samuelson. This is not my study nor my synagogue. And yet I feel a ridiculous obligation to serve as host here, since poor Hershel—" He shook his head and trailed off, overcome by emotion. He raised a hand, refusing help Lehman hadn't offered.

The old man in the armchair looked silently from Samuelson to the detective and adjusted the *kepa* on his head. It was the plainest of the three, hand-sewn from black silk. From its edge long wisps of thin hair escaped, trailing down his cheeks.

"We are now apparently guests of the lieutenant," said the pale man on the couch. He wore a forest green suit with a lime green tie and green-and-gold argyle socks. His shoes were brown wing-tips, one bouncing over the other in midair, until he uncrossed his legs and leaned forward to declare, "Emil Shechter."

"*Rabbi* Shechter," said Samuelson.

Lehman accepted his outstretched hand. "Another rabbi?"

"Three of us," explained Shechter, gesturing to include all of the witnesses. "Four, originally. But of course you know that." He sat down again on the sofa and faced the old man in the armchair, whose eyes were cast on the table, where his hands lay folded in front of him, one palm over the other. They shook slightly as he studied them, and his lips trembled as if he were about to speak. These movements shook the fine hairs on his upper lip and the sparse growth on his cheeks. His eyebrows and lashes were gone, burned away by whatever spiritual fire had left its light burning in his grey eyes.

"Rav Gershom Levin," said Samuelson, with resonant reverence.

The old man lifted his eyes heavenward.

"This is Lieutenant Lehman," Samuelson went on, raising his voice, although it seemed to David that Rabbi Levin had shown no trouble hearing his own name said aloud. "He's here to solve the mystery of poor Hershel's murder."

"*Olav ha'sholom*," said Levin.

"May he rest in peace," echoed Samuelson.

Shechter mumbled under his breath.

For an instant David wondered if they were expecting some words from him, but the old rabbi made clear that they didn't. He fixed one eye on Lehman, while his other wandered slightly afield. "Shouldn't you be asking us questions, then, peering through a magnifying glass. You are, in fact, the one chosen to see through this terrible deed to the truth that lies hidden behind it?"

"I suppose," said Lehman, taken aback. "I thought I'd meet you all first, take a quick look at the scene, and then interview each of you alone."

"So we can't work out our stories together, is that it?" The old man smiled, a thin, crooked line that nearly cracked his face. "To catch us when we slip up, face to face? That makes sense to me. Why don't you use the office here?"—waving in the direction of an adjacent room, the dead man's private retreat—"so we don't have too far to walk in confronting our destinies?"

Lehman turned to Taglia, who shrugged. "The crime scene boys are done in there. No sign of a clue, is what they told me."

Lehman nodded. "All right. Rabbi Levin, why don't you start heading in, then? By the time you're settled inside, I'll be back."

Emil Shechter made a sour face as Levin pushed out his chair. "Wait, Gershom. I'll help you."

The old man scowled. "If I have to wait, why do I need your help?"

"All right, don't wait, then."

"I'm waiting."

Lehman drew a deep breath and murmured to Taglia, "Cute, aren't they?"

"They're just more thoughtful than most folks. And sensitive."

He shook his head. "Where's the body?"

"Down the hall."

"This way?"

Doreen led the lieutenant to the right, where a door had been propped open with a wastepaper basket. Inside was the bathroom, one stall and a urinal, and a tile floor checked in black and white. A sallow man from the crime scene unit was leaning over the sink, picking his teeth in the mirror. When Lehman arrived, his pinkie nail was still stuck between his molars, and it took him a moment to extract it—which did not, however, delay him from talking.

"Lieutenant!" he said, glad to see him, "There you are! We're finished in here with pictures and prints, blood samples and evidence bags." The last of these were lined up on the cracked windowshelf in front of a frosted window. David looked them over. The usual collection of junk from the corners: an old comb and a dirty penny, paper clip and a pen cap, a wad of tissue stained with yellow urine, and the empty cardboard core of a roll of toilet paper.

"Any blood on this?" asked Lehman, about the cardboard roll.

The sallow criminalist shook his head. "Not to the naked eye. It was over by the sink, with the rest. So we bagged it."

David approved. You had one chance to collect what you needed before a crime scene was contaminated. The smart way to go was to take anything that could possibly prove helpful later. As a result, the crime scene unit did a better job of cleaning than most professional cleaning services. Except, of course, for the powder, traces of which often clung to glass and metal surfaces afterwards.

Doreen peered at the toilet paper roll through its plastic bag. "It makes you think differently about this stuff, doesn't it?"

Between the window and the back of the stall, a young man in a white coat knelt on the tiles. In front of him, a body lay sprawled. Lehman knew this deputy coroner, whose name he thought might be Dr. Stone—and for the first time he wondered if it hadn't once been Stein or Stern, for him or someone else in his family. He had rolled the dead man on his stomach and made an incision to take the body temperature, which would give them a time of death. But David already knew the time of death, from the captain's file. Rabbi Hershel Goodman had been in the study at eleven fifty-five, when his colleagues had closed their eyes. They noticed he was missing about twelve-twenty and found him shortly thereafter. He had been speaking to them for ten or fifteen minutes—ten minutes, at least. Sometime between twelve-oh-five and twelve-twenty he had slipped out and met his doom in the bathroom. The question was, who else did he meet in the bathroom?

"What can you tell me?" he asked Stone.

The deputy coroner rolled the body on its side, exposing its belly. Plenty of brown blood had soaked through the white button-down shirt and onto the stiff, paisley tie. Stone stuck two fingers between the buttons over the solar plexus and opened a space between them.

"From what I've seen thus far, the cause of death was an incision here, from a relatively blunt sharp instrument. One stab, upwards, right through the space between the buttons, piercing the undershirt beneath. There's a wound to the head as well, but from what I can tell here, that seems to have followed the stabbing. He took the jab to the solar plexus, grabbed his stomach, fell and hit his head. Death came pretty quickly."

Lehman said, "On the sink?"

"Or the urinal. There was a brown hair in the drain."

"We bagged it," said the criminalist.

Though darkened with clotted blood, the dead man's hair was brown.

The deputy coroner set down the body gently and stood, brushing off his knees. "I need to get the fellows from the wagon to haul the corpse out of here. You might want to check out those numbers he wrote."

Lehman knelt and lay his face on the cold tiles alongside the dead man. The floor was sticky with his blood. There was lots of it around and beneath him, seeping through his clothes—and it must have come fast enough for the deceased to have poked his middle finger into it and scrawled a final message on the tiles. A bloody finger is not a smooth writing implement, and the character lines were broken, having pooled in spots and given out in others, but to Lehman's professional eye it seemed to read: 6:1

"What do you make of that, Taglia?" David asked.

"I don't know, sir. A citation?"

"Looks like it."

"I'm ashamed to say I don't know the Good Book well enough to place it."

"Neither do I," said Lehman. He did *not* feel ashamed, and he wondered about that for a minute. Why should Doreen feel worse about not knowing the Torah than he did? *The Old Testament* she would have called it and considered it half of her Bible. Shouldn't he think of it as least as much his own? But David had a job at hand, and he pushed the question out of his mind. "Fortunately, there are people in this house who do."

Doreen gave him a doubtful glance. One of them might be a murderer, it was true. But that meant two at least probably weren't. David resolved to present the dead man's final message to each of them and see what they could suggest. After all, who better than a panel of rabbis to interpret another rabbi's text? The criminalist had fourteen Polaroids of the bloody numbers, and Lehman stuck one in his pocket.

Doreen was on her knees, studying the scrawled message. She sighed. "I wish he had left us a straightforward clue."

"He might have," said David. "We'll see."

The first rabbi he had to confront was Gershom Levin, who was waiting for him in Goodman's office, off the larger study. This room looked more like David's idea of what a rabbi's study should be. There was a desk with two chairs at one end and a small window at the other. The rest of the space was crowded with books, which overhung them on all sides and in no apparent order, most of them in Hebrew, interspersed with an occasional text in English on *Double Marriage,* or *Conversion,* and Tolstoy's *Anna Karenina.* There were two chairs in the office. Behind the desk was a springy, high-back executive's chair and beside the desk was a low, stationary chair with wooden arms and legs and a leather seat. Levin was established in Goodman's chair, so Lehman dropped in as his visitor.

"I could have done it," said Rabbi Levin.

"Of course," replied Lehman, stretching his legs. "But what possible motive could you have had for such an awful act?"

"What possible motive?" asked Levin, stroking his cheek with the flat of his hand. "That's difficult to answer. All motives are possible, aren't they? I could have hated Hershel, or feared him. Or envied him, I suppose."

"Did you?"

"No. But those are the usual three, aren't they?"

"You could have loved him, too."

"Is that so? Do people actually kill each other out of love?"

"Every day! Jealousy is a kind of love, isn't it? And unrequited desire. Pride is self-love, really. And its twisted sister, shame, will also do. Any cause of anger can lead to violence. Avarice is your biggest motive, especially among strangers. But there doesn't seem to be a financial side to this particular case, so . . ."

"Love, then. Well, I did love Hershel. If that gives me a motive, I had one."

"The means we haven't found yet."

"The means?"

"The murder weapon. A sharp object, apparently, blunted at the tip. But, to be fair about it, you did have the opportunity."

"I did?"

"You had a chance to kill Goodman. You were here when he died. You could've followed him into the bathroom while the other two had their eyes closed. Why exactly did you have your eyes closed, by the way?"

"We are a study group, the four of us; we meet every week on this night for study and prayer. The three of them were all my students, once. Hershel was leading us in a special sort of prayer, a meditation he believed could transcend the limits of this world and bring us closer to the divine. There is a story which recalls how four ancient rabbis were able to do so, you see. They entered into *Pardes,* the Orchard, which is to say, the Garden of Eden. It comes from the same root as the English word, 'Paradise.' Together they passed over the border of this world and came face to face with God. It was, alas, costly for them. One of them died; the second went mad; the third became a heretic; and only Rabbi Akiba survived."

"Rough night," said Lehman.

"The word *Pardes* is interesting in itself. If you take the word apart, its letters make an anagram for ways to read the Torah. The first letter, *peh,* the 'p' sound, stands for *pshat,* the plain meaning of the words. The 'r' sound refers to *remez*, a second sort of reading in which one makes connections to other parts of the text. The third letter stands for *drash*, related to *midrash*, the telling of stories and other interpretations based on details of the passage. And the fourth letter, *samech*, refers to *sod*, the secret meaning of the text."

"*Sod*," repeated Lehman. "That's what I'm after. The Truth."

"All the meanings are true," said the rabbi. "Kabbalah reveals the most profound. But sometimes the simplest reading is the best. It depends on the text."

"There is a text I could use your help in interpreting," Lehman suddenly recalled. He fished the Polaroid from his jacket pocket and set it on the desk in front of Levin. "Any idea what that refers to?"

The old rabbi studied the picture. "This is what Hershel wrote before he died? On the floor in his own blood?"

"That's right. Any idea what it means?"

"Chapter six, verse one," Levin mumbled, "might refer to the Book of Genesis: 'And it came to pass, when men began to multiply on the face of the earth, and daughters were born unto them.'" He thought about it for a moment. "Now, it has been asked, who were these men who had daughters born unto them? From the next verse, Rashi, our greatest Biblical scholar, has answered, '*B'nai ha-elohim*,' 'the sons of princes and rulers.' Now a logical person might ask, what does this have to do with Hershel's final message?"

David considered himself a logical man. "You see a connection?"

Levin found a scrap of paper on the desk, took a fountain pen from his own jacket, and drew triangles and circles to represent the text. "On the purely interpretive level, the connection is clear. First, we have daughters born. Second, we have their fathers." Pen lines snaked from the triangles to the circles. "So then, who is this master to whom daughters are born?"

"I give up," replied Lehman.

"My wife, of blessed memory, bore no children. Ezra never married. But Emil Shechter is the father of four daughters and no sons." Levin glanced over significantly. David did not consider that enough of a reason to have killed anybody, but the old rabbi evidently did. "Among his many distractions, he plays chess. You'll see him in the park, in the afternoon, pushing wooden pieces around the cardboard squares! Often enough to achieve the rank of master."

"Shechter? You mean he's . . . ?"

"A master to whom daughters are born."

"Would he have any motive to murder Hershel Goodman?"

"Again, with a motive?"

"Any reason to have wanted him dead?"

"Reason? We're not talking about reasons here, Mr. Lehman. As you say, Emil could have loved him or hated him, it makes no difference. Both of them could be a motive. We've been talking about interpretation here—isn't that what you asked me for? So, now I've given you one. You'll have to ask Emil for the rest." He stuck the pen back in his jacket and handed David the diagram. The old man's broken lines and blotted geometry expanded into the paper.

Emil Shechter laughed when he saw it and heard what his teacher had said. "A brilliant exposition! Except he sometimes forgets these passages refer to people. I am a vegetarian, who cannot stomach the taking of a life, even from a beast of the field. Not fish nor fowl nor alcohol passes these lips. Do you imagine I could have stabbed Hershel like that," he snapped his fingers, "in cold blood?"

Lehman had trouble imagining that. "But then how would you interpret his final message? Who else has a daughter, Rabbi Shechter?"

He tapped his lips in thought. "We must remember, Lieutenant, that Hershel was a teacher. Does a teacher write only for himself? Of course not! Hershel was writing his message for us to find."

And he turned the Polaroid upside down so that the scarlet scribble read: 1:9.

"Now what does it signify? Chapter one, verse nine. That wouldn't be Genesis—there were no people created yet. And it's a number, isn't it, without a reference text? Then let's think Numbers." He took down a volume off a shelf and opened it to the page. "Ah yes, here we are. This is very good! A listing of people's names. Moses has been commanded to take a census of the people of Israel, and from each house a man is named to assist him. Chapter one, verse nine refers to the tribe of Zebulon. Now, what do we know of Zebulon? At the very end of Genesis, on his deathbed, Jacob blesses his sons and tells each of them what to expect from the future. Jacob says, 'Zebulon shall dwell at the shore of the sea; he shall become a haven for ships, and his border shall be at Sidon.'" Shechter arched one eyebrow significantly.

"Do any of you live at Sidon?" Lehman inquired.

"No, but one of us has a *shul* at the southern end of Brooklyn. At Coney Island, where the ships used to dock."

"That would be Ezra Samuelson? He seems a little high strung."

"Do you think so? You should have seen him six years ago, screaming out the window of his study at two or three in the morning! He spent a couple of weeks in a quiet place resting up after that episode."

"A breakdown?"

Emil nodded. "Don't you think in his final moments Hershel would've remembered Jacob on his deathbed, rather than some verse on marriage and families?"

"But why would Ezra Samuelson have murdered Hershel Goodman? They were lifelong friends and colleagues, weren't they?"

Shechter leaned in closer. "Lifelong rivals, maybe. Ezra is like a teddy bear, full of emotion, always ready to wrap you in a hug. His connection to Gershom is mainly through the heart. Hershel was a thinker, like the rabbi himself—a scholar who followed in his footsteps. So Ezra probably loves Levin more than I do, even more than Hershel was capable of. But Levin in all likelihood preferred Hershel."

"And you?"

"Me?" Shechter smiled bitterly. "I'm just the third son. I never stood a chance. You've heard of Cain and Abel, haven't you? How about Seth?"

Ezra Samuelson was not amused when he learned what Shechter had suggested. "Zebulon?" he demanded. "Is that what he thinks of me?" He glared at the office door, as if his resentment might burn right through to the study. "Ridiculous. In the first place, it's obvious that my dear colleague hasn't read a word of Hershel's scholarship lately. Because if he had, he would recall that Goodman's attention was focused on the numerological meanings of texts, rather than the textual meanings of numbers."

Lehman held up his hand. "Slowly."

Samuelson's brown eyes darkened as he struggled for control of his emotions.

"What you have to keep in mind is that Hershel was a scholar. He devoted himself to it, and never let go of an insight until he had tracked down its last secret meaning. Most of his thinking follows Levin's, of course, as the student should follow his teacher. He did some research into the rabbi's early life, which was amazing, really. He hid for two years in a root cellar with a Russian partisan's son. They never had enough for both to eat, so Levin often went without. And yet, he was the one who survived." Samuelson shook his head. "But lately Hershel had been paying attention to numbers, as they signify hidden meanings in all things. And Emil has overlooked the most obvious question. Why should Hershel have failed to indicate which book of the Torah he was citing?"

"Perhaps he didn't have time."

"To scrawl a single letter before the chapter and verse? Instead of leaving us to guess which book he meant for his last, essential message? Does that make any sense? No! But there is an answer." Samuelson ran a hand along the spines on the bookshelves, until it settled on a worn volume.

"Aha! Here we have it: Gematria. If you can spare me one moment, I'll show you what I mean."

David could spare a moment. "Please. Take your time."

Samuelson leafed through the pages of columns and numbers and held up his hand. "Emil was partially right, it seems. The number is not 61 but 19—written for us to read. Each letter is given its numerical value. Now listen to all of the citations in which the total of the letters equal nineteen." He cleared his throat and read aloud in a commanding voice: "and void the gold and he brought his father Eve my brother shall come and he came and the father of brother of my brethren and you go good, in the best Teb'ah her hand the brother of garments of she shall come, shall come in the sinew unawares, surely, unresisted, in safety a nation and one a slaughtered Ehi surrounded with thorns the hand the enemy of garments of and one will be brought for good is the hand? of the valley Haggidgad nation and on the feast beloved do trust."

Samuelson looked up happily, as if his point had been proven. Lehman looked over his shoulder. The words were printed on the page in columns, each line pointing to a different place in the Torah. Samuelson had read them all together, as if they were a poem by Jerome Rothenberg. David said, "Want to run that by me again?"

Samuelson began, "And void the gold . . ."

"No, I heard the list," said Lehman, "or the poem, or whatever it is you're reading. What I didn't hear was any connection to Hershel Goodman's murder."

"You have to listen with an open ear," Samuelson explained. "Let me ask you this: what do you remember from listening, just now? Without trying to piece it all together, what words stick in your memory?"

"Something about brothers. And garments. Someone slaughtered by the hand of an enemy. And someone else coming."

"Who?"

"I don't know. Eve? A female."

"You see? You do know. A female—exactly! You were perfectly capable of rendering the significance. 'Slaughter at the hand of an enemy' must refer to Hershel's last moments of life. The brethren in garments refer to us, of course, or collectively, to the rabbinate. Now then, who is this female coming upon us? Would it help if I told you that Emil Shechter . . ."

"Is the father of four daughters?"

"And that one of them—Eva—is intent on becoming a rabbi? Gilbert has talked to the girl, explaining that she might as well aspire to marry a gentile . . ."

Lehman interrupted. "Who's Gilbert?"

"Rabbi Levin."

"Isn't his first name Gershom?"

"That's his Hebrew name. Mine is Ezra, just like my English name, because *Ezra* is a Hebrew name, from the Bible. But there is no reason why a Hebrew name has to be even similar to an English one. Hershel's was *Heshel*, of course. But Emil's Hebrew name is actually *Mordechai*."

"You knew them both pretty well, didn't you?"

"Better than their families."

"And you can't think of a reason Emil might want to murder Hershel?"

"A reason? No, there couldn't have been one."

"But there had to be a reason. Because somebody did it."

Samuelson's face reddened again, and his brow furrowed darkly. He looked away from Lehman, first at the bookshelves over their heads, finally at the window against the far wall. David could see he was choking back a grief that had stuck in his throat. But the emotion was winning.

Samuelson stood from his chair and walked over to the window, peering out. "Twenty years together, the three of us, and now what? I hardly know how to be a rabbi without Hershel to disagree." His voice thickened, and he stopped whatever it was he planned to say next. Then he scraped open the window and breathed, filling his lungs with the cold morning air. But instead of exhaling in the same way, he stuck his head out through the open window and hollered, "All right, so we cannot know Your will! Why should it be Hershel, the Good Man himself, struck down in the prime of his life? In this brutal fashion! While I . . ."

He paused mid-sentence and turned to Lehman. "I'm sorry," he said. "I shouldn't be shouting. People are sleeping at this hour. But for twenty years . . ."

Again his eyes filled with tears. This time David did reach toward him, offering a tissue from Hershel's desk, which Samuelson used to wipe his eyelashes.

"I'm sorry. I'm a little *meshugah* tonight, myself. I loved him like a brother."

"It's perfectly understandable," said Lehman.

Samuelson sighed. He dropped into his seat behind the desk, and the chair sighed beneath him. "Is there anything else I can tell you?"

Lehman thought for a moment and shook his head. "No—except I'd like to use the phone. If you'd wait in the study with the others, I'll be out soon. And we can wrap up this business tonight."

There was a grey light in the sky. Emotionally exhausted, the rabbi yawned. "It is getting early. And you've made a good start on the case."

"Oh, more than that. It's solved."

Samuelson stared. "You've worked everything out?"

"Not everything yet. Just who killed Hershel Goodman. Please shut the door as you go. Thanks," said David, tugging a dirty cuff out of his jacket sleeve. He dialed the precinct number and as it rang he ruminated on death, madness, renunciation, and a peace that passeth understanding.

Could the answer possibly be so simple? He saw a need to be wary of wishful thinking. And yet his thoughts drifted back to the Westside.

They were gathered in their places in the rabbi's study when Lehman emerged from his office. It had taken thirty minutes, somewhat longer than he had expected, and the suspects were losing patience. It had been a long night for them, after all, filled with death and suspicion and endless waiting. The boredom was over for all of them now. But he had to handle it properly.

The scene was just as he had first found it: Shechter and Samuelson sitting on the sofa, facing the door and the two armchairs, one of which was empty, while in the other slumped Gershom Levin.

The two uniformed patrolmen were at the door, Brian Healy on the threshold and Doreen Taglia out in the hall, talking to the sallow criminalist. David cleared his throat. "Is this the way you people were seated? During the meditation Rabbi Goodman was leading?"

Shechter spoke for all of them. "Yes, I believe it is. Except Hershel, of course, was in the chair by the door. He was leading, speaking words and phrases aloud."

"Like the recitation you did for me?" Lehman asked Samuelson.

"I was just reading some *Gematria*," Samuelson said, mostly to his colleagues. "Hershel was reciting his own text, from memory."

"And did it work?"

Emil glanced doubtfully at the other two. "Yes," he told David, "it did work, for me. I wouldn't say I visited Paradise, precisely, unless that word is understood as an experience of our own souls. But Hershel's guided meditation did produce a state in me of extraordinary peace and contentment."

Samuelson nodded, and Levin raised his grey eyes to Lehman. "What's your point, exactly? My bladder won't hold out forever."

"I was thinking of that story," David said, "the one you called *Pardes*. Didn't you tell me that of the four rabbis, only one survived the experience?"

"Rabbi Akiba survived, but Ben Azzai died. Ben Zoma went mad. And Elisha ben Abuyah, who was afterwards called Aher, renounced his faith. Of course, some say he was a Christian all along."

Lehman nodded. "In this case, Goodman died. And from what I've seen, Rabbi Samuelson is pretty close to the end of his tether." The others turned to Ezra, whose brows furrowed and cheeks once again flushed.

"Which leaves what?" asked Shechter caustically, glancing toward Rabbi Levin. "One of us to renounce our faith? Or both to survive, like Akiba?"

"You tell me," said David.

"The answer to that is simple. Gershom and I were born Jews and we'll die Jews. And that's the end of that line of questioning."

"Not quite yet," said Lehman. "Your daughter Eva is determined to be a rabbi, isn't she? But she can't do that in any Orthodox seminary. She won't give it up. Why should she? And you love her very much. So what's a father to do, except maybe counsel his daughter to consider Conservative or Reform schools?"

Shechter turned the color of kosher wine. "That doesn't make me an apostate."

Levin grumbled, "It doesn't make you the Baal Shem Tov, either."

Lehman was watching the old rabbi closely. "Don't be too hard on him. People renounce all sorts of orthodoxies."

"I haven't renounced anything—" Shechter began.

"Doreen," said David to Officer Taglia, who stuck her head in the room, "have you seen the books in the office? They're in half a dozen languages. I studied some French in high school and a little Latin in college, but the only one inside that I remember reading was written in Russian. *Anna Karenina*."

"I read that," said Taglia. "In English."

"Me too," said Lehman. "Do you happen to remember the characters?"

"There was Anna," said Taglia. "And her boyfriend Bronsky."

"Vronsky."

"Right. Her husband had almost the same name . . ."

"Karenin," said Lehman, "without the final 'a.' Do you remember the other story? About Anna's sister-in-law, Kitty? She marries a man who experiments with ways to manage his estate to help the peasants who work for him?"

"Oh, yeah. What was his name?"

"Levin," said David.

"I repeat," broke in the old rabbi. "What exactly is your point?"

"Listening to you people got me wondering," said Lehman, "what a book like that was doing on Goodman's shelves—a book Doreen and I have read. I don't see a lot of novels, you know, even out here, and the office is crammed with books used for his work. It made me start to consider what he might have found in it. Until the character of Levin made the obvious connection."

The real-life Gershom Levin sat stonily.

"Mostly because the name *Levin* appears in the book at all," continued Lehman. "The character wasn't even Jewish, was he?"

Shechter replied carefully, "*Levin* is not always a Jewish name."

"That's what occurred to me," said Lehman, "and I wondered if it hadn't occurred to Hershel Goodman as well. Rabbi Samuelson told me that Hershel had been doing a great deal of research on Gershom Levin's early life in Russia, before and during the war. I wondered if Goodman hadn't learned something that somebody else didn't want learned. I then discovered that Gershom's first name isn't really Gershom. I called the precinct, who had to wake up the clerk at home. It took her twenty minutes, but at last she found on the Federal downlink an immigration record for one Gilbert Levin, who sailed from Gdansk in 1946. He was seventeen years old. That would make him sixty-eight, today, wouldn't it?"

Shechter turned to Rabbi Levin, who didn't say a word.

David squatted down beside the old man's armchair. "Do you want to tell us the religion he marked on his immigration form? Sworn before the Almighty?"

"Russian Orthodox," said Levin, turning away his head.

There was a shocked silence in the room. Ezra Samuelson blinked, but that was the best he could muster. David waited.

Finally Emil Shechter said, "But a convert to Judaism is accepted by the faith as equal to a natural-born Jew. Conversion is nothing to be ashamed of."

"If he did," said Lehman.

"Of course he converted," Shechter insisted. "Didn't you?"

Levin stared at him with gravity. "What do you believe, in your heart?"

Shechter didn't want to rely on that. "He must have," he said. "They wouldn't have ordained him a rabbi without it."

"Only if they checked," Lehman replied. "He came from a D.P. camp, didn't he? Orphaned by the war? How many questions do you think they would have asked him about his parents? He spent two years in a root cellar, Samuelson told me. A yeshiva boy and the son of a Russian partisan, alone together for all that time. One of them came out speaking Yiddish and Hebrew. But which one was it?"

He directed the question at Levin, who gave him only a nasty look in response, and the Lieutenant had to answer it himself.

"My guess is Gilbert Levin went into the root cellar as a partisan's son. Alone in the dark for two years, what else did the boys have to do but talk? Levin was a quick study, with a sharp mind. By the end of the war, he had learned enough Yiddish to obtain a share of the aid that came pouring into Eastern Europe for survivors of the Holocaust. He heard about America and wanted to go. The Jewish agencies in the West would never have taken a Russian boy, so he walked into a relief camp speaking halting Yiddish, and no one had the heart to press him further."

"But," Shechter stammered, "how could Hershel have known?"

"He probably didn't, for sure," said Lehman. "But he might have found something that made him question Levin's early family history. A birth record, even, if he was as sharp a researcher as you claim."

"He was persistent as a mole," Samuelson swore.

"It must've posed a terrible problem for him," observed Lehman. "He must have doubted his research methods. So he would have checked again, digging deeper, and found even more evidence. A baptismal date, say. There was no way he could question Levin, of course, without gravely insulting his teacher. So he kept the horror to himself. Until last night, after midnight, when the two of you were deep in meditation. All three of his guests had listened, of course, during his recitation. All three closed their eyes. But only one of you went to the men's room afterwards, while the others were deep in reverie, or asleep. It wasn't Emil, I suspect, who'd had nothing to drink. It wasn't Ezra either, because as I saw when I first arrived here, Ezra had to crawl around the coffee table and climb over Levin's legs, in order to shake my hand. He couldn't have slipped out of the room without the others knowing."

"Which leaves only me," said Levin finally.

"Which leaves you," agreed Lehman. "Your bladder, of course, was the reason. You went to the bathroom, to do as you needed. But Goodman had been waiting for that opportunity. He followed you, didn't he? Out of the study and down the hall, sneaking into the john behind you. Did he tap you on the shoulder at the urinal? Or surprise you in the stall? Either way, he looked down and saw something which convinced him that his research had indeed been correct—undeniable evidence of a non-Jewish birth. What did you do when he confronted you? There was no way to argue false evidence, or faulty reasoning, was there?"

"I urinated on his shoes."

"But that's not all you did, was it?" Lehman reached for the old man's jacket and held it open—where a dark blue blotch stained the inside pocket. With a handkerchief from his own, the Lieutenant drew out of the rabbi's jacket a fountain pen, nose down. "This was the weapon you used, wasn't it? The instrument close at hand. What happened to the cap, Rabbi Levin? It wouldn't by any chance be the one we found on the floor of the bathroom, by the sink?"

Levin raised himself from his chair and glanced toward the exit, but there were two young police people blocking his path and his legs buckled beneath him. He sank down into his armchair and covered his face with his hands. Ezra Samuelson rushed over and knelt in front of him, brown eyes brimming with tears. Emil Shechter, still on the sofa, gripped his own knees but could not suppress a sniffle. David Lehman surveyed the scene and felt awful about it. He wished that he had never been called on this case and thought wistfully of the Strangler.

Taglia tugged at his elbow, her face a study in pity. "It's horrible."

Lehman shrugged. "That's what it takes to drive a good man to murder. What you need to find is the particular twist of horror."

Doreen shivered. "How did you know where to look?"

David reached into the side pocket of his jacket and again produced the Polaroid.

"Remember the message in blood on the tiles? You know what it means?"

She hesitated. "Some kind of Biblical verse, isn't it?"

"Look again, Officer. You wished for a straightforward clue. Just read it."

"Six point one?"

"Where did you get the 'point'?"

"I didn't know how to pronounce the middle mark. The colon."

"The middle mark isn't a colon—it's a dotted letter 'i.' Together they spell, 'G-i-l.' Gershom Levin's given name is Gilbert." Doreen's eyes widened, but David shrugged. "Like he said: sometimes the simplest reading is best."

In this story, **MICHAEL KAHN** takes some familiar
imagery from the Passover Seder and weaves a mystery tale around it. Kahn told me that some years ago
while teaching in the public schools, his "dark side"
took over and he enrolled in law school. He is now a
trial attorney in St. Louis and has written five mysteries starring Rachel Gold, a former teacher who is
now an attorney. The most recent mystery is *Sheer
Gall* (Dutton, 1996). This story originally appeared
in *Ellery Queen Magazine.*

The Bread of Affliction

▼   ▼   ▼   ▼   ▼   ▼   ▼   ▼   ▼   ▼   ▼

MICHAEL A. KAHN

*Michael dedicates this story to Ann
and Morris Lenga, with love and respect.*

I KNOW A FORMER TRIAL LAWYER who gave it up to write courtroom
thrillers. He claims he prefers the fictional kind because he gets to control
the judge, the lawyers, the witnesses, and, best of all, the outcome. I think of
him with envy whenever I have to deal with *In re: the Estate of Mendel Sofer.*
It's definitely real, and I've long since lost control.

Back in the beginning, back when all I knew was that an 82-year-old
widower named Mendel Sofer had died of a heart attack, it had seemed a
simple case. Indeed, those were the very words that Phil Rosenberg used
when he called.

"It's a simple case, Rachel," he assured me. "Even better, you'll be doing
a *mitzvah.*"

Phil and I had been classmates at Harvard and teammates on the Equitable
Estoppels, a law school co-ed softball team. Phil had grown up in New York
and moved back after graduation to join a midtown firm. I moved to Chicago, started as an associate at Abbott & Windsor, and eventually left that
LaSalle Street sweatshop to go solo. Two years ago, shortly after my father

died, I returned home to St. Louis and opened the Law Offices of Rachel Gold on the first floor of a renovated Victorian in the Central West End.

"A *mitzvah*?" I repeated. "Who was this guy, Phil?"

"A Holocaust survivor. Real tragedy. Lost his family in the concentration camps—mother, father, two brothers, a wife, two kids. All killed. Came to this country in 1948. Married again in '56. She died of cancer eleven years ago. No children. He lived alone in an apartment downtown."

"Where do I fit in?"

"You'll represent Shalom Aliyah. It's an international organization that helps Jews emigrate to Israel. They've resettled thousands of black Jews from Ethiopia. They've helped Jews get out of Iran and Iraq and Red China and Bosnia. They also give financial assistance to hundreds of impoverished Jews in America who want to move to Israel. It's a great outfit. We're their general counsel."

"What's the connection with Mr. Sofer?"

"He left his entire estate to Shalom Aliyah—all but a hundred grand."

"How much are we talking about?"

"Seven figures. The guy was a cobbler. Literally. Shoe repair. Never made much, but whatever he had he put into stocks. One share here, one share there—it adds up. Guy died a millionaire."

Phil explained that after Mendel Sofer's death the public administrator conducted a search of his apartment and found a copy of the will in his desk. He contacted Shalom Aliyah, Shalom Aliyah contacted Phil's firm, and Phil contacted me. Tinkers to Evers to Chance. I was Chance, and my role was to get the will admitted to probate and expedite the distribution of the assets.

"I don't do much probate work, Phil."

"No problem, Rachel. This one's a no-brainer."

And so it had seemed back when I sketched the outline of the petition. A simple but compelling story. The document itself was extraordinary. Mr. Sofer's last will and testament dispensed with the usual legal gobbledygook for an impassioned style exemplified by the first sentence:

I, Mendel Sofer, born into this world of grief and horror on the 15th day of *Nisan*, have tasted the Bread of Affliction.

In the Jewish calendar, the 15th day of *Nisan* is the first day of Passover, the festival of freedom celebrating the deliverance of the Jews from their oppression under Pharaoh.

The Bread of Affliction is the unleavened bread known as *matzah* that the

Jews eat throughout the holiday to remind us that our ancestors, in their hasty exodus from Egypt, hadn't had time to let their bread dough rise. The Passover allusions in Mr. Sofer's will added another layer of poignancy to the story of a man who had suffered the atrocities of a modern pharaoh named Adolf Hitler, who'd lost his loved ones in the ovens of Auschwitz as his ancestors had lost theirs in the misery of bondage. The link between the ancient and the modern seemed to transform his gift to Shalom Aliyah into a sacred bequest.

"Who's the other beneficiary, Phil?"

"A cleaning lady named Pearl Jefferson. Apparently, she cleaned his apartment for years."

That bequest seemed a wonderful final touch and even more so after I met her. Pearl Jefferson was a heavyset black woman in her early forties who cleaned homes six days a week and lived in a tiny, dilapidated house in north St. Louis with her three adolescent sons and her husband Earl. Earl was on complete disability from a forklift accident; he spent his days in a wheelchair reading the Bible and doing needlepoint. Pearl almost fainted when I explained Mendel Sofer's bequest. One hundred thousand dollars was more than five times her annual income. Afterwards, I strolled down her front walk feeling like a fairy godmother.

Unfortunately, I'd forgotten what happens to gifts from fairy godmothers when the clock strikes midnight.

The chimes began sounding the following week when Mendel Sofer's bank opened his safe deposit box. Among his various personal papers were two sheets of bond paper. They were the original pages one and two of his will. Although stapled together, there was an additional pair of staple holes in the upper left corner of each page. Those additional holes confirmed what was already obvious: we had a significant problem.

Mendel Sofer's will was six pages long. The last four pages of the original were missing. They weren't in his safe deposit box and they weren't in his apartment, which the landlord had kept secured since the morning that Pearl Jefferson had found Mr. Sofer's corpse facedown on the bedroom floor. Three days after she discovered his body, the public administrator performed an official search of the apartment and prepared a meticulous inventory of its contents, right down to the trash in the trash cans. I did my own search the day after I learned of the missing pages. I found plenty of documents in the apartment—all duly noted on the public administrator's inventory—but no sign of pages three through six of his will.

Those missing pages were a potential disaster. Although I had a copy of the entire will in mint condition, there are certain rules of law that predate the era of high-speed photocopiers, one of which states that if the testator had custody of his will before his death and it cannot be found among his belongings after his death, he is presumed to have destroyed the will with the intent to revoke it. If that rule governed here, Mr. Sofer would be deemed to have died without a will, which would void his bequests to my client and to Pearl Jefferson. Instead, his estate would be distributed according to the ancient laws of descent—assuming that any blood heirs could be found. That was a big if, since all of the family on Mr. Sofer's side had perished in the concentration camps. As for his second wife, she had been the only child of two only children—now all deceased. Unfortunately, though, the lack of heirs would not resurrect the bequests in his will; instead, the money would go to the State of Missouri.

Nevertheless, the absence of heirs gave me some hope, since it also meant an absence of adversaries. Our judicial system operates on the adversary process. Just as inadmissible hearsay will be allowed if no one objects, my petition for admission of the will to probate might be allowed if no one opposed it. Accordingly, I was guardedly optimistic as the hearing date approached.

And that's when more midnight chimes sounded. Specifically, the Grubbs appeared. All twelve of them—residents of Montana and distant blood relatives of Mendel Sofer's second wife on her father's side. Her father had not been Jewish, and neither were the Grubbs. Even worse, two of them were members of the Aryan Jesus Regiment, a white supremacist militia outfit headquartered in Montana. None of the Grubbs had ever heard of Mendel Sofer, or his second wife, or her parents. They learned of his estate the old fashioned way: through an heir tracer. Heir tracers make their living by spotting lucrative estates with no known heirs. They go out and locate potential heirs and offer to help them pursue an undisclosed inheritance somewhere in America in exchange for a piece of the action. Here, if the judge upheld the presumption that Mr. Sofer revoked his will, the Grubbs would net approximately $1 million after paying the tracer. Needless to say, they jumped at the deal, and the tracer quickly retained an attorney to challenge the will.

That attorney was Myron Dathan, and as far as I was concerned his appearance in the case was the final stroke of midnight. Dathan was one of the creepiest lawyers in St. Louis—cuddly as a tarantula, affable as a moray eel. Unfortunately, he was also one of the best lawyers in town—a brilliant litigator with an uncanny ability to detect his opponent's pressure points. Among Dathan's many unpleasant qualities was the way he exploited his religion for strategic advantage. He used his encyclopedic knowledge of Jewish law to cancel hearings, halt depositions, terminate meetings, and otherwise refuse to cooperate; when challenged, he would curtly cite an obscure Jewish holiday or custom that purportedly created the scheduling conflict. It was a technique that incapacitated gentiles. Although he generally wore a *yarmulke,* many fellow Jews questioned the depth of his convictions. He could, for example, be spotted at the trendier restaurants in town, usually in the company of one of his series of blond, leggy *shiksas,* and generally dining on meals that were no more kosher than a Big Mac and milkshake. So, too, he often observed the Jewish sabbath aboard one of the riverboat casinos.

"Rachel," Dathan said, shaking his head in amusement, "the man tore up his will. You're in denial here. Face it: your claim is *dreck.*"

We were meeting in his sleek office—chrome-and-glass furniture, contemporary leather chairs, huge abstract paintings on the walls. Dathan gazed at me with an expression that hovered somewhere between pity and disdain—it was hard to tell which because his eyes were veiled behind the tinted lenses of his aviator glasses. The tint also made it hard to tell which part of my anatomy he was inspecting at the moment—although with Dathan you could safely narrow it to a few specific locations. The way he lounged in his chair and languidly stroked his goatee made me feel as if I were in a carnivore's lair.

"Wrong, Myron," I told him. "Mr. Sofer simply made an innocent mistake. Don't forget that he grew up in an era of *carbon* copies. Carbon copies *look* like copies. Photocopies look like originals."

"Ah, but they feel like copies."

"Doesn't matter. He signed the photocopy in original ink. I'll argue that he thought he was signing the original of the will."

He chuckled. "You don't need me to tell you that one's a loser, Rachel. You already know it yourself."

He was right, but I'd never let on. "You're overconfident, Myron."

"No, I'm simply confident, and with excellent reason. But I'm also practical." He leaned back in his chair and steepled his hands beneath his goateed chin. "The hearing is in two weeks. If we can settle this now, we can both save ourselves and our clients the time and expense of trial preparations. Let's talk some reality here, okay?"

"I'm listening."

"Under the will, your client will get about $1.5 million. The rest goes to the *schvartza*."

I stiffened. "Her name is Pearl Jefferson."

He waved his hand dismissively. "Whatever. The point is: when the will gets revoked, you both get *bupkes*." He glanced at his watch. "Whoops, I'll make this short. We'll have to leave soon."

I checked my watch. 3:20 P.M. I gave him a puzzled look. "Why?"

"Come, come, Rachel. It's the thirteenth day of *Nisan*."

"So?"

He gave me a patronizing look. "Tonight is *bedikat chametz*, remember?"

It took a moment to connect the words with the fuzzy memory from childhood. "Oh, right."

Tomorrow was Passover eve. In traditional Jewish homes (as I confirmed later that night by checking the *Guide for the Jewish Homemaker* that my Aunt Becky gave me when I graduated law school), an important preparation for the holiday is to eliminate all *chametz* (leaven) from the home. The ceremony is known as the *bedikat chametz* (search for leaven) and takes place immediately after sunset on the night before Passover eve. The head of the house searches for *chametz* while carrying a wooden spoon, a feather, and a lighted candle. I remember as a child following my father around the kitchen and breakfast room. He let me carry the feather. When he found some *chametz*— bread crumbs, for example—we used the feather to sweep them into the spoon while reciting a special blessing. The crumbs, along with the feather and spoon, were burned the following morning. Frankly, I had trouble envisioning Myron Dathan playing "Hide the *Chametz*" with his current main squeeze, a giggly St. Louis Rams cheerleader with big hair and bigger boobs.

He stroked his goatee. "Here's our proposal: seventy-five grand to your client, seventy-five grand to the *schvart*—to the cleaning lady. I've already taken the liberty of conveying the offer to her. After all, she isn't represented by counsel." He paused and gave me a wink. "I was gratified by her reaction. She agrees that seventy-five thousand dollars is a lavish offer. She's quite eager to accept it. Unfortunately, I had to explain that the offer is contingent upon your client's acceptance. We either settle with both of you or we settle with neither of you." He glanced at his watch and stood up. "I have to leave. Perhaps you do, too."

When I returned to my office there were two urgent phone messages from Pearl Jefferson, the frantic and unwitting pawn in Myron Dathan's sadistic strategy. She was, as Dathan knew, his best settlement leverage over me.

"Oh, Miss Gold, you just got to help my family," she begged when I returned her call. I listened with my eyes shut as she told me what that money would mean to her family: physical therapy for her husband, a home in a gang-free part of town with better schools for her sons, a cataract operation for her mother. She was sobbing at the end of the call, and my stomach was in knots. I told her I would talk it over with my client but that I couldn't promise anything.

"Oh, please, Miss Gold, you just got to help my family."

I talked it over with Phil, who talked it over with the client. They reached the same painful conclusion that I'd already reached: we couldn't give in. To accede to a settlement that would make the Grubbs—a clan with neo-Nazi ties—the principal beneficiaries of the estate of a Holocaust survivor was too appalling to contemplate. If we were going down, we were going down fighting. We owed that much to the memory of Mendel Sofer.

Later that night I went on a long jog with Ozzie, my golden retriever. He trotted along at my side as I obsessed over the case, sifting through the facts for the hundredth time, struggling to come up with a more compelling legal theory than the one I tried on Myron Dathan. I came up empty. Every possible scenario crashed into the same obstacle, namely, the mystery of the missing pages. If there'd been no original pages, I could at least argue that Mr. Sofer mistook the photocopy for the original. I'd prevailed before on weaker grounds than that. But with two pages of the original will in his safe deposit box, the "mistake" argument was futile.

I could come up with no rational explanation for why Mr. Sofer would have torn off the last four pages of his will but saved the first two. Although the pages he kept included his bequests to Shalom Aliyah and Pearl Jefferson, surely he knew that they were meaningless without the rest of the will—especially page six, which contained his notarized signature and the signatures of the two witnesses. Why discard that crucial page but save the first two?

As I passed the two-mile mark and turned back toward the house, I said, "*Lahma Anya.*"

Ozzie looked at me, his head tilted curiously.

I glanced down at him with a smile and shook my head. "Never mind, Oz."

Lahma Anya. That's what Mr. Sofer had scrawled on the back of page two of the will. I thought at first it might be someone's name—perhaps an important person in his life. I searched for such a connection in his other papers—especially the ones from the safe deposit box—but found none. Same with the phone book. I wondered whether *Lahma Anya* was a Polish or Hebrew phrase; after all, he grew up in Poland and attended a yeshiva. But upon checking with a professor of Slavic languages at Washington University and an Israeli friend, I learned that the phrase was neither Polish nor Hebrew.

We gathered the following night at my sister Ann's house for the seder. Once upon a time, when I was a child at the seders conducted by my father, there'd been a magical quality to the evening, especially when my father reached the ten plagues. I used to imagine the original Passover, more than 3,000 years ago—that terrifying night when the angel of death stalked the Egyptian firstborn while the Hebrew slave families gathered in silence to eat the lamb that each had killed for the blood to smear on their doorposts as a sign to the angel to "pass over" their home.

But over the years, the magic had faded. My expectations were especially low this year, mainly because I assumed that my brother-in-law, Richie the orthodontist, would conduct the seder. Richie was a thoroughly assimilated Jew. He observed Yom Kippur with a round of golf at his country club, knew absolutely no Hebrew, and seemed to believe that the traditional dance at a Jewish wedding was the Electric Slide. Richie bragged that he conducted a Jiffy Lube seder—"In and out in ten minutes or your money back."

But this year, Richie's plans were foiled by the surprise arrival of his Uncle Al from New Jersey. While hardly a *chasid,* Uncle Al was still a firm believer in what he called the "cover-to-cover bilingual seder," which meant that the evening would include both the original Hebrew and the English translations in the Haggadah. And thus it was Uncle Al, bald head gleaming as if he'd buffed it in honor of Passover, who solved the first mystery.

We had finished the opening blessing over the wine, the traditional washing of the hands, and the blessing over the greens—all according to the *seder* sequence. As Richie glumly looked on, Uncle Al pulled the middle *matzah* out of the covered pile of three. Breaking the *matzah* in two, he studied the two pieces for a moment and then held up the smaller one.

Pausing to gaze around the table, he said, "Now we say the *Ha Lahma Anya.*" He looked down at the Haggadah and recited, "*Ha lahma anya di a-khalu a-vahatana b'ar'a d'Mitzrayim.*"

In the background Uncle Al's voice droned on, but I was no longer listening. I was staring down at the Hebrew letters that spelled out the words *Lahma anya.* I glanced at the English translation. *Bread of affliction?* I remembered enough Hebrew from my bat mitzvah to know that *lechem* meant "bread."

"Wait," I said, looking up with a frown. "What language is this?"

Uncle Al stopped. "Pardon, Rachel?"

"*Lahma anya*," I said. "Is that Hebrew?"

He reread the text and looked up with a smile. "It's actually Aramaic."

"It means 'bread of affliction'?" I asked.

"It certainly does."

And then he turned to the children with an impish grin, put down the smaller half of the broken *matzah* and held up the other piece. "And who knows what this is?"

I sat back in wonder as two of the children shouted, "The *afikoman*!"

It was as if Mendel Sofer himself had whispered the answer to me from his grave. The smaller piece of the broken *matzah* is the *Lahma Anya*, the Bread of Affliction. But as every Jewish child knows, the larger piece, known as the *afikoman*, is the important half. It's the half that's worth money. The leader has to hide the *afikoman* during the first half of the seder. When dinner is over, the children are allowed to search for it. The one who finds it can hold it hostage until the leader pays a ransom.

Some commentators believe that the *afikoman* is symbolic of the Paschal lamb that was sacrificed at the time of the Temple in Jerusalem. Others believe that it evokes the forty years wandering in the desert in search of the Promised Land. And still others believe that its principal function is to keep the children alert during the long first half of the seder. Whatever its traditional purpose, its very existence that night filled me with hope, an emotion I hadn't felt since the arrival of those awful Grubbs. Maybe Mendel Sofer hadn't destroyed those missing pages. Maybe they were his *afikoman*.

I hate those brainteaser games—the ones that start with a weird scenario: "A man lives on the 12th floor and rides the elevator to the lobby each morning but when he comes home from work he rides only to the 8th floor unless someone else is on the elevator with him." You're supposed to solve the mystery by asking astute yes-or-no questions. Well, I'm terrible at it. I can never think of the right thing to ask and quickly lose patience. "Just tell me the answer," I finally grumble.

That's exactly how I felt: "A Holocaust survivor born on the first day of Passover prepares a new will a month after his second wife dies. He later labels the front part the Bread of Affliction, tears off the back pages and—maybe, hopefully—hides it before he dies. Why, and where?" "Just tell me the answer," I grumbled, exasperated.

Unfortunately, Mendel Sofer wasn't telling and neither were his personal

papers. I'd searched through them again the morning after the seder, looking for a clue. Nothing. I'd visited Pearl Jefferson to find out whether she
knew anything about the missing pages.

Mainly what I learned from Pearl—sandwiched between her pleas to settle with Dathan—was that the *afikoman* routine was out of character for
Mendel Sofer. He was not a light-hearted man, and he was certainly not
the type who enjoyed practical jokes or puzzles. Pearl Jefferson claimed she
never saw him smile during the years she cleaned his apartment. He was a
bitter, suspicious man who even refused to apply for his social security pension because, as he told Pearl, the government would use it as a way to spy
on him and steal his money if he went to the hospital.

He used to tell her that she was in his will, but she dismissed it as one of
his ploys to keep her in line because the only time he brought it up was when
he was angry with her.

"That man would rush over to his desk and root around in them drawers and pull out some papers and wave 'em at me, all the while yelling if I
didn't do what he told me he gonna tear it up and leave me out in the cold."
She sighed at the memory. "I never dreamed the man was telling the truth."

"Did you ever look at the document yourself?"

"No, ma'am. Didn't see any reason to 'cause I didn't believe him in the
first place." She paused and shook her head. "He was a troublesome man
to work for, especially after poor Mrs. Sofer passed, bless her soul."

"Why did you stay on?"

She studied me for a moment. "Because of that tattoo."

"What tattoo?"

"Those numbers. On his arm." She placed her hand upon her ample
bosom. "Every time I saw those numbers, I recalled how much Mr. Sofer
had already suffered, how much the Lord had already taken away from him,
and I said to myself if he wants me to stay on—well." She paused and
shrugged. "How could I say no to that man?"

"Let her out, Myron."

I could hear him snicker on the other end of the line. "You're asking the
wrong person, Rachel. Look in the mirror. You're the only one with the
power to put real cash in her hands. Convince your client to accept the settlement, and the cleaning lady gets her money. If not, not. By the way, the
offer is about to change. After all, the trial is less than a week away. Begin-

ning tomorrow, it drops ten grand per person per day. Sixty-five/sixty-five tomorrow. Fifty-five/fifty-five the day after."

"You're a jerk, Myron."

He chuckled. "Actually, I'm a fool. I shouldn't offer you a penny. It must be my weakness for pretty attorneys with sexy legs. Your claim isn't worth seventy-five grand, Rachel. Nowhere close. You have absolutely no leverage here. Your people may want to roll the dice, but make sure they understand they're gambling with the *schvartza*'s money, too."

Harriet Weinberger shook her head sadly. "I'm sorry, dear. I wish I could help. My Irving never told me anything about that."

We were in the lounge of Covenant House, an apartment complex for elderly adults located across the parking lot from the Jewish Community Center. Harriet Weinberger had moved there after her husband died a year ago at the age of eighty-seven. Harriet and Irving had been high school sweethearts, she told me. That was a long time ago. She looked every bit her eighty-eight years—even though she'd dyed her thinning hair jet black. There was a slight palsy in her hands and head. It made her voice quiver.

Irving Weinberger had drafted Mendel Sofer's will eleven years ago. He'd also signed it as one of the witnesses. Unfortunately, Harriet knew nothing about Mendel Sofer, about his will, or about any missing pages. Indeed, she knew very little about her husband's career.

"Did he sell his law practice when he retired?" I asked.

She shook her head. "No. He just closed the door one day and came home and never returned."

"What about his clients?"

Harriet gazed at me with sad blue eyes, her head shaking slightly. "I don't think there were many clients toward the end. You see, my Irving had Alzheimer's disease." She paused and sighed. "He started forgetting things. It caused problems for some clients." Her eyes suddenly welled up with tears. "Poor thing."

I leaned forward and squeezed her hand. A wave of despair washed over me at the thought that Mr. Sofer might have hidden the back half of his will with his ailing attorney. If so, the prospect of finding the missing pages became even more remote.

"What about client files?" I asked, by now clutching at the proverbial straws. Maybe Weinberger had placed the missing pages in his Mendel Sofer file. I certainly had plenty of odds and ends in my client files.

Harriet shook her head helplessly. "I wouldn't know, dear."

"Would anyone?"

She mulled it over. "Perhaps Elsa."

"Elsa Kemper?"

She sat back with surprise. "Why, yes."

"She was your husband's secretary?"

"My goodness, you know Elsa?"

"Just her name." I showed her my copy of the last page of the will. "She signed as the other witness. I assumed that she was your husband's secretary."

I assumed correctly. Better yet, Elsa Kemper had been Irving Weinberger's secretary for almost forty years. And best of all, she was alive and—as that odd expression goes—still in full possession of her faculties. Her only concession to the aging process—she, too, was in her eighties—was a cane. We met in the sitting room of the immaculate bungalow in south St. Louis that she shared with her sister, Mary.

Elsa nodded her head, remembering. "Oh, yes. Mr. Sofer. He was one of Mr. Weinberger's greenhorns." She paused and smiled at me. "That's what he called the newcomers. Greenhorns."

She explained that her boss had volunteered his legal services with the St. Louis Jewish Family and Children's Service after World War II. He was actively involved in the resettlement of Holocaust survivors, helping them navigate through landlord-tenant laws, employment policies, union rules, insurance regulations, and the like. Some of his greenhorns adapted quite well to their new country, eventually numbering among Weinberger's wealthiest clients. But for most, his services remained *pro bono*. Mendel Sofer fell somewhere in the middle: he insisted upon paying for the occasional legal service he required.

"Oh, but such a gloomy man," Elsa said, shaking her head. "And so distrustful. He was always nervous around me."

"Why?"

"My family came from Germany. It didn't matter that my parents moved here in 1924. He was convinced that anyone from Germany was a secret Nazi." She sighed. "Poor man."

"Do you recall that he changed his will after his second wife died?" I showed her my copy, pointing out where she had signed as a witness.

"Oh, yes, I typed it." She turned back to the first page and read the opening paragraph. "'Bread of Affliction.' I remember this one."

I explained the problem of the missing pages.

She shrugged. "I have no idea."

"Is it possible that he gave those pages to Mr. Weinberger to hide for him?"

She mulled it over. "I suppose anything's possible."

"Did your boss have a safe in his office?"

She nodded. "He did. A big black one. He kept it in the corner of his office. My heavens, it must have weighed five hundred pounds."

I felt a glimmer of hope. "What happened to it after he retired?"

"It was sold, along with all the office furniture." She smiled sadly and shook her head. "I took all the papers out and made sure they were sent back to the clients."

My shoulders sagged. "And there was nothing of Mr. Sofer's in there?"

"Nothing, dear."

"What about a file?"

She gave me a puzzled look. "A file?"

"You said that Mr. Weinberger did some legal work for Mr. Sofer over the years. Did he keep a client file for him?"

She nodded. "Oh, yes. I maintained one on every client."

"Do you have any idea where they would be today?"

She leaned forward on her cane as she frowned in thought. I waited.

"The bar association," she finally said. "When we closed the practice, I arranged for delivery of all closed files to the bar association. They promised to put them in storage in case a former client needed his file. You might check with them."

I did.

It took the bar association three teeth-gnashing days to locate the storage warehouse where they'd sent Irving Weinberger's files, and then it took another full day for me to obtain permission to look through them. By then it was forty-eight hours before the trial and roughly forty-five minutes after Myron Dathan had called with his final offer: five thousand for my client, five thousand for Pearl Jefferson. With great effort I resisted the urge to tell Dathan just exactly where he could insert every one of those dollars, bill by bill. Instead, I declined his offer and gently hung up the phone. I wasn't about to let him get any perverse jollies from thinking that he'd finally gotten to me. Nor would I give him any new material for his creepy repertoire of women-lawyer-with-PMS anecdotes.

I'd brought a change of clothes to work that morning, having already confirmed what the warehouse address seemed to suggest: Irving Weinberger's client files were stored under conditions somewhat less hygienic than a hospital operating room. I called my mother before changing into jeans and sneakers.

"They finally gave me permission."

"It's about time," she said, thoroughly annoyed with them. "You leaving now?"

"Five minutes."

"I'll meet you there."

"You're sure you want to do this, Mom?"

"Absolutely, sweetie."

And sure enough, there she was, standing on the sidewalk in front of the seedy warehouse. I waved at her as I pulled into a parking space. I had to smile. Sarah Gold to the rescue. My mother is the most determined, resourceful, and exasperating woman I know. Life trained her well. She came to America from Lithuania at the age of three, having escaped with her mother and baby sister after the Nazis killed her father and the rest of his family. Fate remained cruel. My mother—a woman who reveres books and learning—was forced to drop out of high school and go to work when her mother (after whom I'm named) was diagnosed with terminal cancer. My grandmother Rachel died six months later, leaving her two daughters, Sarah and Becky, orphans at the ages of seventeen and fifteen. Two years later, at the age of nineteen, my mother married a gentle, shy bookkeeper ten years her senior named Seymour Gold. My sweet father was totally smitten by his beautiful, spirited wife and remained so until his death from a heart attack two years ago on the morning after Thanksgiving. Given her own link to the Holocaust, my mother had followed *In re Sofer* with great interest.

Her outfit today was a Sarah Gold classic: thick hiking boots, a faded pair of black Guess jeans, a blue chambray workshirt, and, of all things, an aluminum hard hat.

"Where in the world did you get that hat?"

"Your father had it in the basement. What for I don't know." She gestured toward the warehouse. "I should have brought one for you, too."

I was smiling. "You look like one of the Village People."

"Who?"

"Never mind." I gave her a kiss. "You look great, Mom."

And she did. My mother worked out regularly these days, including a weightlifting class that met twice a week at the JCC. With her high cheekbones, trim figure, and curly red hair (colored these days to cover the gray),

Sarah Gold was still a striking woman at the age of fifty-six. I called her my Red Hot Mama.

Once inside the building, we followed a warehouse employee up the stairs to the second floor. It was a cavernous area lined with row after row of floor-to-ceiling metal shelves on which were stacked hundreds—maybe thousands—of cardboard boxes. Motes of dust revolved slowly in the beams of light coming through cracks in the translucent windows.

The worker led us down one of the aisles and stopped midway. He checked his sheet, squinted up at the boxes, and nodded. "That's them."

Irving Weinberger's client files were stored in thirty-two moldy boxes stacked in two columns. The worker pointed to a rolling ladder at the end of the aisle before he departed. My mother and I stood there in silence staring up at the boxes.

"Well," she finally said, "let's get busy."

It took us two hours and twenty-two boxes to find the manila file folder labeled *Mendel Sofer.* I carried it down the ladder and took it over to the rickety wooden table at the end of the aisle. Inside the folder were about seventy-five pages of documents. There were letters to Mr. Sofer's landlords, to his employers, and to a local department store (over a disputed charge account bill). There was correspondence with the German government regarding reparations. There were a few contracts, drafts of his prior wills (there had been two of them), and a copy of his final will. But no *afikoman.*

Tired and disappointed, I sat down on the floor and rested my back against a stack of boxes. My mother was leaning over the table, her back to me, scrutinizing the file. My mind felt numb as I watched her page through the documents. I tried to imagine where else he could have hidden the missing pages. I tilted my head back and stared at the cobwebs wafting from the light fixtures overhead. Nothing.

"Interesting," my mother said.

I lowered my gaze as she turned to me, holding a one-page document in her hand.

"What?" I asked dully.

"It's a memo he dictated after his first meeting with Mendel Sofer. Back on March 8th, 1948."

"And?"

My mother pursed her lips as she reread a portion of the memo. "I thought he was at Auschwitz."

I frowned. "He wasn't?"

She shook her head. "Mauthausen."

"What was that?"

She explained that Mauthausen was a concentration camp where the prisoners worked in rock quarries. Mr. Sofer was the only member of his family sent there. The Nazis shipped the rest of his family off to Auschwitz. After two years in Mauthausen, he somehow escaped. He hid in the forests of eastern Europe until he was discovered, starving and nearly delirious from fever, by a courageous Catholic priest named Herman Groszek. Father Groszek hid Sofer in the church attic until the war ended and then arranged for him to come to America. Groszek had a sister in St. Louis named Maria. She and her husband Edgar agreed to be Mendel Sofer's sponsors.

"What are sponsors?"

My mother explained that the U.S. government required that each Jewish immigrant have a sponsor in the city where he was to reside. The sponsor guaranteed that the new American wouldn't be a financial burden on the government. The Jewish philanthropic organizations found wealthy families to serve as nominal sponsors for the many Holocaust survivors who knew no one in America. Most of those immigrants rarely met their sponsors; instead, the local Jewish agency arranged for their housing and employment. In fact, as my mother explained, she and my grandmother had never met their sponsor.

But Mendel Sofer had real sponsors: Maria and Edgar Juskievicz. Although the Jewish Family and Children's Service helped secure him an apartment and a job, Mr. Sofer not only met the Juskieviczes but became close with them.

When my mother finished reading Weinberger's memo aloud, we gazed at each other.

Finally, my mother shrugged, "You have any better idea?"

I shook my head.

Nothing was easy about this case.

There was no telephone listing for Edgar or Maria Juskievicz. It took several tedious hours searching through old newspapers on microfilm to discover why. Edgar had died in 1964, Maria in 1972. According to her obituary, she was survived by a daughter, Hannah, and a son, Edgar, Jr. There was no St. Louis listing for a Juskievicz named Hannah or Edgar, Jr. The library had telephone directories for about thirty other cities around the country. None had a listing for either Hannah or Edgar, Jr.

By the time the library closed that evening at nine, I was completely out of leads. Even worse, it was now thirty-six hours to the trial. I sat alone in my car in the library parking lot staring into the darkness, struggling with my frustration as I tried to concoct a rational litigation plan of attack. But no matter which strategy I considered, I kept returning to Hannah and Edgar, Jr. Finally, I got out of the car with my address book, walked over to the pay phone in front of the library, dropped in a quarter, and dialed the number. He answered on the third ring.

"I need you to find someone, Charlie."

"Jesus, Rachel, it's ten o'clock. Can't this wait 'til tomorrow?"

"No."

A pause. A weary sigh. "Jesus, Rachel."

I smiled. Charlie Ross was an ex-FBI agent special agent and one of the best private investigators I'd ever worked with. Last year, I'd represented his son in a messy paternity lawsuit. Charlie owed me one. It was time to collect.

"Okay," he said. "Tell me what you know so far."

At 5:45 P.M. the following afternoon, I crossed my fingers, said a silent prayer, and rang the doorbell to #83 Chaucer Lane. It was, according to Charlie, the home of Mr. and Mrs. Randall O'Connor—a modest, ranch-style house in Canterbury Trails, a cookie-cutter subdivision in the far south suburbs. I could hear a dog barking out back and the laugh-track of a TV sit-com inside.

The door was opened by a twenty-something woman in white shorts and an untucked pink blouse. She was barefoot and had a diapered toddler perched on her hip. Her straight blond hair was pulled back in a ponytail. Several strands had come loose, and she brushed them away from her face with her free hand.

She registered my lawyer's garb and briefcase in a quick glance. "Yes?"

"Mrs. O'Connor?"

"That's me."

"I'm Rachel Gold."

"Oh, right. Come on in, Miss Gold."

"Call me Rachel," I said as I followed her into the house. "Please."

She turned. "Okay." She smiled. "Call me Miriam."

The following morning we gathered in the courtroom of the Honorable Jeremiah Donohue, Probate Division, Circuit Court of the City of St. Louis. I was alone at the plaintiff's table. Over at the other table sat Myron Dathan and what I presumed to be two members of the Grubbs clan—a man and woman who could have passed for a stout version of the grim farm couple from *American Gothic,* except that he was wearing a leisure suit and a bolo tie. Behind me in the first row of the gallery sat Pearl Jefferson and two of her teenage sons—all dressed in their Sunday best.

Judge Donohue, looking even more florid than usual, entered the courtroom at ten minutes after nine and gaveled things to order.

"Your Honor," I said, moving toward the podium, "we've encountered an unexpected problem this morning that may require a short continuance."

Out of the corner of my eye, I saw Myron Dathan rise angrily to his feet.

"One of my witnesses," I continued, "is Rabbi Robert Abrams. He called me from the hospital an hour ago. Two of his congregants were involved in a serious automobile accident last night and both are in critical condition. Rabbi Abrams has been at the hospital with the victims' families since five this morning. I have the telephone number of the nurse's station on the floor where he is. Your Honor's clerk could call to find out whether he'll be able to come to court today."

"Judge," Dathan snapped with irritation, "I object to any delay. Of what possible relevance is the testimony of a Reform rabbi in a will contest?" He turned to me with disdain. "Was Rabbi Abrams the decedent's rabbi?"

"No, Mr. Dathan." I turned to the judge. "Rabbi Abrams will testify as an expert witness. As Mr. Dathan knows, the descendant's will contains references to the Passover holiday. I intend to have Rabbi Abrams explain certain matters of Jewish law and custom relevant to those references."

Dathan snorted in amusement. "In that case, there's no reason to disturb him. I am quite certain that I can elucidate any Passover references that Ms. Gold deems relevant. Let the rabbi tend to his flock."

The judge studied Dathan for a moment and turned to me. "Counselor?"

I shrugged nonchalantly, trying to hide my pleasure. I'd initially panicked when Rabbi Abrams called—*Another thing gone wrong,* I'd groaned—but all things considered, I'd rather have the Passover testimony come from Dathan's lips.

"I'll accept counsel's offer," I said, "so long as I reserve the right to put Rabbi Abrams on the stand to explain any points of Jewish law or custom on which Mr. Dathan proves to be ignorant."

Judge Donohue nodded. "That seems fair enough. Call your first witness, Ms. Gold."

"We call Myron Dathan."

The judge gestured toward the witness box. "Mr. Dathan, watch your step."

I waited until he was sworn, seated, and ready.

"Mr. Dathan, the opening sentence of Mr. Sofer's will refers to the 15th day of Nisan. Can you explain that reference to the court?"

"Certainly."

Dathan quickly warmed to the task. He gave a concise and, frankly, fascinating exegesis of the Jewish calendar, and from there we moved to the first reference to the Bread of Affliction, which Dathan explained with an interesting blend of Biblical fact and Talmudic rumination. By the time we reached the Aramaic version of Bread of Affliction, Dathan was into his pompous mode full-throttle. He gave the historical explanation for certain Jewish blessings being in Aramaic and then—in what he no doubt believed was an impressive display of Jewish erudition—recited the entire *Ha Lahma Anya* from memory.

I glanced over at his slack-jawed clients, who were watching their attorney as if he were speaking in tongues.

I nodded as he spoke, delighted to have such an eloquent presentation of this crucial point in my case and even more delighted by Dathan's demeanor, which seemed to suggest that he hadn't even considered whether Mr. Sofer's Aramaic scrawl was anything more than an idle doodle.

"And what about the other half of the *matzah*?" I asked.

"You refer, of course, to the *afikoman*."

"The what?" Judge Donohue asked, looking up from his notes.

Dathan turned toward the judge and smiled patiently. "The *afikoman*, Your Honor. Unlike the *Lahma Anya*, which has profound roots in the actual moment of the exodus from Egypt, most scholars believe that *afikoman* comes from the Greek word *epikomoi*, which is generally thought to mean "dessert." Indeed, it is stipulated that the consumption of the *afikoman* is the final act of eating at the seder."

Keeping my tone casual, I said, "Tell the Court what happens to the *afikoman* after it's separated from the Bread of Affliction."

"Certainly." Dathan turned toward the judge, who was taking careful notes. "After the leader recites the *Ha Lahma Anya*, Your Honor, he places that portion of the *matzah* back on his plate. Then he waits until he is confident that no one is watching him, at which point—"

His voice trailed off.

The judge looked up, his pen poised over his notes. "Yes? And then?"

Dathan was glaring at me, his eyes narrow slits.

I gave him a sweet smile. "Please continue, Mr. Dathan."

Dathan was silent.

"Mr. Dathan," the judge said, "what does the leader do with that other half of the *matzah* when no one's watching?"

Dathan scratched his goatee as he considered potential escape routes. There were none. "He hides it."

"Hides it?" the judge asked

"Hides it," I repeated, watching Dathan. "And the goal of the others is to try to find the missing piece and bring it back, correct?"

Dathan stared at me.

"Correct?" I repeated.

After a moment, Dathan said, "Yes."

"No further questions."

The judge looked up with a frown. "Let me make sure I have this right. You start with a whole piece of *matzah,* and then the leader breaks it in half. One part is the . . ." he paused to check his notes—"the *Lahma Anya,* and that stays right there where everyone can see it. But the other half gets hidden, right?"

I nodded "Correct."

The judge turned to Dathan. "What happens when you find it, Mr. Dathan?"

Dathan slowly turned to him. In a barely audible tone, he said, "You can claim the reward."

"Reward? Like money?"

Dathan nodded, his jaws clenched.

The judge nodded. "Fascinating. Just fascinating. Thank you, Counselor. You may step down."

Dathan passed by me without acknowledgment or eye contact.

"Call your next witness, Ms. Gold."

"Miriam O'Connor."

Miriam came forward from the back of the courtroom and took the oath in the witness box. She was holding a manila envelope in her left hand.

I moved her quickly through the preliminaries—name, address, marital status, etc.—and then asked her whether she knew Mendel Sofer.

"I did. I was named after his sister. She was killed in the concentration camps."

"Were you close with Mr. Sofer?"

She nodded. "My entire family was."

"Why, Miriam?"

"My mother's Uncle Herman was a priest in Poland during World War Two. After Mr. Sofer escaped from the concentration camps, Uncle Herman hid him in the church until the war ended."

She told the story of how Mendel Sofer came to America with the priest's sister as his sponsor; of how Maria's daughter Hannah was named after Mendel Sofer's first wife; of how Hannah had stayed close with Mr. Sofer after she became an adult. Miriam was Hannah's daughter, and she too grew to love the lonely man that everyone in her family called Uncle Mendel. Miriam's mother and father died in an automobile crash eight years ago. Mendel Sofer, who detested rabbis and organized religion, nevertheless went to the synagogue every morning for the next eleven months to recite the mourner's *kaddish* for Miriam's parents.

"Did you stay close after that?" I asked softly.

She nodded, daubing her eyes with a handkerchief. "He sent us Christmas gifts each year. We had him over to the house for dinner each year on his birthday. I called him once a week to make sure he was okay." She shook her head, her lips quivering. "He was such an unhappy man. And so alone. He didn't trust the government. He didn't trust his bank. He didn't trust the police. I guess because they'd all betrayed him in Poland. He didn't trust anyone but our family. He called us his blessed trust."

She paused to blow her nose. Her eyes were red. I waited until she regained her self-control.

"Did Mr. Sofer entrust you with anything special?"

She nodded. "Three years ago, he came to visit me on the first day of Passover." She smiled sheepishly. "I didn't know it was Passover until he told me." She brushed back her hair with her hand. "He gave me two manila envelopes. "This one," she said, holding it up, "and another."

"First tell me about the other one."

"He said it was mine but that I shouldn't open it until after he was dead."

"And when he died?"

She nodded, her eyes welling up again.

"What was inside, Miriam?"

"Stock certificates. From different companies. All with assignment forms transferring them from him to me."

"How much are the stocks worth?"

"Almost two hundred thousand dollars."

I heard a gasp from one of the Grubbs.

"That was his gift to you, Miriam?" I asked.

She nodded, wiping her eyes again with the handkerchief. I waited. After a moment, she looked up and took a deep breath.

"Tell us about the other envelope, Miriam," I asked gently. "The one you brought today."

"Uncle Mend—, um, Mr. Sofer told me that it held a secret and that I should never open the envelope. He told me that people might come looking for it after he died but that I could only give it to a certain person."

"Who?"

"He didn't know who the person would be. He said that he'd written a special password in Hebrew on the document. He also wrote it in English on the outside of the envelope so that I'd know what it was. He told me that I could only give the envelope to the person who knew the password. He made me promise."

"What happened after he died?"

"Nothing until yesterday, when you came to see me. You asked me whether Mr. Sofer had hidden any papers with me."

"And what did you say?"

"I asked if you knew the password."

"Did I?"

"Yes."

"Please hand the envelope to the judge, Miriam."

She did. I watched as he turned it over and squinted at the word scrawled just below the flap. He looked up at me, raised his eyebrows, and nodded.

I glanced toward Myron Dathan. He was staring up at the ceiling tiles, his arms crossed over his chest.

I turned back to the witness. "Please tell us the password, Miriam."

"*Afikoman.*"

It took a little over two months for the judgment to become final. Although Dathan filed the usual post-trial motions, he was literally going through the motions, and when the judge denied all of them he didn't even bother filing an appeal. The judgment became final on a Monday in early June, and two days later I arranged for the wire transfer of $1,534,000.00 to Shalom Aliyah's headquarters in Tel Aviv. Later that afternoon, I had the joy of handing Pearl Jefferson a cashier's check for $100,000.

That was Wednesday. Sunday was Father's Day—the second one since my father had died. It was an overcast day, unseasonably cool. I picked up my mother and my sister and drove the three of us to the Chesed Shel Emeth

Cemetery in University City. When we reached my father's grave, we took turns bringing him up to date on all the family news and gossip, and then we each placed a small rock on his headstone. I placed mine right next to the one I'd put there last month. My mother stepped back to the foot of the grave and stared at the headstone. My sister and I waited at her side.

Several minutes passed, and then my mother sighed and turned to me. "So where is he?"

I unfolded the diagram the cemetery worker had drawn for me and studied it. "That way," I said, pointing.

Mendel Sofer was also buried at Chesed Shel Emeth, next to his second wife, Ruth. His grave was as yet unmarked—just a narrow, rectangular mound of earth on which tendrils of new grass had sprouted. As Sunday approached, I'd tried to think of some way to honor Mendel Sofer's memory, to help give closure to my brief but intense sojourn in his life and death. I'd looked at a few Holocaust poems, at a beautiful essay by Elie Weisel, at excerpts from speeches of Dr. Martin Luther King, Jr.—but none felt quite right for Mendel Sofer. Then I'd remembered the language of his will, and suddenly it was obvious.

I took out my Haggadah and opened it to the *Ha Lahma Anya*. I'd practiced this morning to make sure I could read the Hebrew. Clearing my throat, I began:

> *Ha lahma anya di a-khalu a-vahatana b'ar'a d'Mitzrayim.* This is the bread of affliction which our ancestors ate in the land of Egypt. *Kol dikhfin yei'tei v'yeikhul.* For all who are hungry, let them come eat with us. *Kol ditzrikh yei'tei v'yefsah.* For all who are alone, let them come celebrate Passover with us. *Ha-shata hakha.* Now we are here. *Lashanah ha-ba'ah b'ar'a d'Yisrael.* Next year we shall be in the land of Israel. *Ha-shata av'dei.* Now we are enslaved. *Lashana ha-ba'ah b'nei horin.* Next year we shall be free.

Slowly, I closed the book. We stood together in silence at the foot of Mendel Sofer's grave.

"Amen," my mother finally said.

My sister nodded her head. "Amen."

I wiped a tear from the corner of my eye. "Shalom," I whispered to him.

STUART KAMINSKY has written about the weary
Chicago police detective, Abe Lieberman, in six novels. Here, Abe is able to take advantage of the police
usage of the term "rabbi" to his crime-solving advantage. Stuart's mystery writing includes several other
series. In each, the reader is treated to a deft mystery,
as well as insightful commentary on contemporary
social issues. While growing up in Chicago, Kaminsky got to know people like the Liebermans. He
moved to Sarasota, Florida, several years ago.

Confession

▼　　▼　　▼　　▼　　▼　　▼　　▼

STUART M. KAMINSKY

HE SAT ON A POLISHED LIGHT WOOD BENCH in the blue-tiled lobby of Temple Mir Shavot looking at the door. A white-on-black plastic plaque told him
that beyond the door was the rabbi's office. It was a little after eight on a
Thursday morning, and he had been sitting for almost forty minutes.

He knew the rabbi was in. He had seen a modest green Mazda in the
parking spot, and the license plate was marked "clergy." The man had
intended to stride in, find the rabbi, and beg him, if necessary, for an immediate meeting. But when he had seen the door to the rabbi's office, he hesitated, his legs weak and heavy. He made it to the bench and sat looking
first at his shaking hands and then at the door.

From beyond a door to his right, the voices of men came in a low chant.
Occasionally, a voice would rise with determination and even emotion. The
man, who had not been in a house of worship since he was a child, remembered the morning minyans his father and grandfather had taken him to even
before he went to school. There was something plaintive and alien in the
sound of long-forgotten Hebrew and the man, who had regained some control of his legs, now felt as if he might weep.

A few people passed while he was sitting on the bench. Most did not
look at him. One woman, heavy, young, wearing thick glasses and carrying

a stack of yellow flyers gave him a smile he was unable to return.

He was, he knew, not a memorable man. Average height, not overweight, dark face now in need of a shave, very black wavy hair, which he had not combed but had brushed back and down with his fingers. He wore slacks, a sport jacket, and a tie loose at the collar. His clothes were conservative and only memorable if someone looked a little more carefully and noted the wrinkles and the dark irregular splash marks on his jacket and slacks, and marks that were smaller but definitely red on his white shirt.

He sighed deeply, thinking he recognized the ending of the morning prayers. He started to rise, not sure whether he was going to leave or go to the door to the office and knock on it.

He was saved from the decision by the opening of the door. Two men stepped into the lobby. One was large, burly, maybe about fifty, and bearing the look of an ex-athlete whose pink face strongly suggested that he was not Jewish. But the man knew that Jews came in all sizes, faces, and colors. The other man was a study in contrast. He was thin, a bit less than average height, and probably nearing seventy. His hair was curly and white, and he had a little mustache that was equally white. The older man had one of those perpetually sad looks and resembled one of those contrite beagles the waiting man's brother owned.

"Rabbi," said the big man, "I'll be back here with the car in half an hour."

"Make that an hour, Father Murphy," said the smaller man.

The big man looked at his watch, nodded, and said, "That should give me enough time to check on Rabbit."

Both the rabbi and the priest wore little round black *kepahs,* as did the man who watched them. He had remembered to take one out of the box inside the entrance and cover his head in the house of the Lord.

The big priest glanced at the waiting man, walked past him, and went through the door into the morning sunlight. The rabbi turned and started down the hallway.

"Please," called the waiting man.

The rabbi stopped and looked at him.

"Yeah?"

"I . . . can we talk for a few minutes?"

The rabbi looked at his watch and said, "Me?"

"Yes, it's important."

"I know you?"

"No," said the man.

"I've got a meeting in ten minutes," the rabbi said. "What is it?"

The man rose from the bench, touched his forehead, and said, "Someplace a little private?"

The rabbi shrugged and held out his hand toward a white double door across the lobby. The man followed as the rabbi opened the door and stepped into a huge carpeted room with three-story ceilings and stained glass windows. There were wooden benches facing the ark, which the man remembered contained at least one Torah.

It all came back to him. Hebrew words without meaning came rushing into his consciousness from the well of memory. He touched his forehead. He had not slept at all.

Folding chairs were neatly stacked against the back wall. The rabbi motioned for the man to follow him and unfolded two chairs so they faced each other in the back of the room. They sat. The rabbi put his hands in his lap and waited.

"I was born a Jew," the man said. "When I got married, I converted because my wife is Catholic. I don't know if I'm still a Jew."

"Tough question. As far as I'm concerned, you're born a Jew, you're a Jew forever. Maybe you can be both, like dual citizenship."

"So, I'm in the right place," the man said whispering.

"Depends on what's on your mind."

"Confession," the man said. "Is a rabbi sort of like a priest? I mean, if something is told to a rabbi in confidence, if someone confesses to something, is it protected? Is the rabbi forbidden to tell anyone?"

"Depends on the rabbi."

"What about here? This synagogue?"

"I wouldn't tell anyone."

The man sighed.

"My name is Arnold Sokol. I killed a boy last night."

"Who?"

"I don't know," said Sokol touching his forehead. "Mary, my wife, and I had a fight. The minute I came home from work. I worked late last night. You know the Hollywood Linen Shop in Old Orchard?"

"No."

"That's my family's. Where was I . . . Oh, yes. Mary and I have been having a lot of fights. She wants more children. We've got four. I said, 'No more.' So we fight. No hitting. Nothing like that. Just anger, shouting. You know, I said, I gave up my religion for her and she said she gave up friends and family, and since when had I practiced *any* religion. The kids were in bed but I'm sure they heard the whole thing. Mary got loud. I got loud. The baby cried. I went out."

"Out?"

"For a drive. It was about eleven. We live a few blocks from here. I drove to the lake, in Evanston, near the university. I sat on the rocks, listening to the waves. And then it started."

"It?"

"I guess they spotted me alone. I didn't hear them coming." Sokol went on looking toward the ark.

"How many?"

"Four. Young. White. I don't think any of them was more than seventeen or eighteen. Probably younger. I didn't know they were there until one of them behind me said, 'Hey, you.' I was startled. I turned around and saw them, standing in a line on the grass behind the rocks. They were smiling. I looked around. We were the only ones in sight. I thought about running, jumping into the water, shouting, but I knew none of these would work. And I didn't consider fighting."

"What did they say, or do?"

"One of them said, 'How'd you like to give us your watch and wallet?' Another said, 'And your belt.' And a third one said, 'And anything else you've got in them pockets.' I stood up. The strange thing was that I wasn't afraid. I had fought with Mary. I was depressed. One of them said, 'Come here.' I stayed on the rocks. Maybe deep inside I was afraid to move, but I didn't feel afraid. I didn't even consider calling for the help of God and certainly not of Jesus. This is a confession, right?"

"Sounds like one to me," said the rabbi.

"I've been a lousy Catholic," said Arnold Sokol. "I don't believe in it. I did it to please my wife. Is that a sin? I mean for a Jew?"

"A mistake, not a sin. Least I don't think so. That's between you and God," said the rabbi.

"But I don't believe in God, either. They came toward me. I was wearing these shoes, good shoes for standing all day. Not good for running on rocks. The biggest one came alone. He held out his hand. He was smiling. One of the other boys was looking around to see if anyone was coming. The one in front of me said, 'Give fast, man.' I was frozen. I thought they were going to beat me, probably kill me. When he pushed me in the face, I stumbled backward, almost losing my balance. He came forward. One of the others, I don't know which, said, 'Hurry up Z,' something like that. The big one called 'Z' came at me. I didn't know what was behind. Something happened inside me. I don't know what. Rage, fear, humiliation. I grabbed his arm and pulled. He didn't expect it. I almost fell again. The one called 'Z' went down on his face on the edge of a rock. The others stood frozen for a second. 'Z' got to one knee and grabbed me around the waist. I don't know if he wanted my help or to kill me. His face was bleeding. I can't describe it. He sat back. The other three came forward. One of them slipped on the rocks and tumbled into the water shouting something obscene at me. The last two started to punch me. I doubled over and then came up. I hit the one in front of me in the throat. He made a gargling sound and grabbed his throat. The last one said, 'I'm gonna kill you, mister.'

"I thought I heard the one in the water climbing out. I tried to pull away. He hit me here, on the side of my head. That's when I heard the voices. I think it was a group of Northwestern students going back to campus. The one holding me hit me again, harder. I think the bone under my right eye might be broken. Maybe his knuckles are broken. The one in the water had climbed out and he started for me, hair hanging down, hate in his eyes. 'Take Paulie,' the one who had hit me said. 'Let's go.' And then he looked at me and said, 'We'll find you, mister. We'll kill you.' They went away. The one I had hit in the throat was still trying to catch his breath.

"I looked down at the one called 'Z.' It was hard to tell in the moonlight, but it looked like there was a lot of blood, and he wasn't moving.

"I went over the rocks back to the grass and stood shaking, my hands on my knees. The group that had saved my life passed on the pathway about thirty yards away. They were too busy talking and possibly a little too drunk to see me. I drove around a bit and then came here."

"That it?" asked the rabbi.

"No," said Sokol looking at his hands. "I wanted to kill him. I wanted to kill them all. I want to say I'm sorry for what I did, but I'm not. I feel good. I'm a murderer, God help me, and I feel good about it and bad about it. Am I making sense? Do you understand?"

"I think I understand," said the rabbi.

"I'm not going to the police," Sokol said. "I'm not going to tell Mary. I'm going to think about this. I can kill. Somehow it's made me feel better about myself. I'll keep this secret. I just had to tell someone."

"It's too late," said the rabbi.

Sokol looked up.

"Too late?"

"You've already gone to the police," the rabbi said.

"What?"

"I'm a police officer. Detective Lieberman."

"The priest called you 'rabbi,'" the confused Sokol said.

"He's not a priest. He's a cop, too," said Lieberman. "We call each other 'Rabbi' and 'Father Murphy.'"

"You lied," said Sokol, angrily rising from the folding chair, which clattered back behind him.

"Never told you I was the rabbi," Lieberman said, still sitting.

"You should have told me."

"Maybe," said Lieberman. "I'm not sure what the rules are."

"I could kill you right here," said Sokol, looking around for something to attack the smaller man with. He started for the chair.

"I don't know what the punishment is for killing someone in a synagogue," said Lieberman. "I wouldn't be surprised if God struck you dead. Actually, I would be surprised. On the other hand, I don't know what He would do to me if I had to shoot you."

Sokol had his back turned to Lieberman. He had one hand on the fallen chair when he looked over his shoulder and saw the detective aiming a gun in his direction.

Sokol took his hand away from the chair, faced the detective, and began to cry.

"I'm putting the gun away," said Lieberman. "Shouldn't have brought it in here anyway. You going to give me trouble?"

Sokol shook his head "no."

"You want to see Rabbi Wass?"

Again, Sokol shook his head "no" and tried to keep the tears back.

"Cheer up," said Lieberman standing. "I'm not sure your confession is admissible."

Someone came through the doors, a youngish man in a suit, wearing glasses.

"Lieberman . . . ," he began and then saw the crying man, the overturned chair, and the detective.

"Irving," Lieberman said. "I can't make the meeting. It's all yours."

The man in the glasses and designer suit and tie looked as if he were going to speak, changed his mind, and left the room. Lieberman shook his head wearily and turned toward the ark. He stood silently for about a minute.

"Are you praying?" asked Sokol.

"Something like that," said Lieberman.

"For me?"

"Not sure," said Lieberman. "Maybe. Maybe for both of us. Maybe that Irving Hammel, who just burst in here, doesn't screw up the meeting. Maybe . . . I don't use words very well. I don't know if God is listening. Sometimes I think God created the world and everything on it including us and then left us, on our own, went to some other world, tried again. Maybe He comes back to look in on what He left behind. Maybe He doesn't. I like to think He doesn't. If I thought He did, I'd be a little angry that He doesn't say 'stop.'"

"You understand?"

"I don't know," said Sokol.

"Good. Neither do I. Let's go make some phone calls."

The secretary, Mrs. Gold, had been with Temple Mir Shavot since it was located in Albany Park and old Rabbi Wass was still a young man. Now Mrs. Gold, a solid citizen of seventy who liked to reminisce with anyone who would listen about the good old days on the West Side, considered herself the protector of the young Rabbi Wass, who was, at 45, no longer quite young.

Mrs. Gold was short and plump. Her hair was short and dyed black, and her glasses hung professorially at the end of her nose. She had perfected the art of looking over her glasses at strangers in a way that told them she had some doubts about their intentions and origin.

"Can I use the phone in Rachel's office?" asked Lieberman, as Mrs. Gold looked at the disheveled, blood-stained Arnold Sokol.

"Why not?" asked Mrs. Gold. "Aren't you supposed to be in a meeting?"

"Something came up," said Lieberman.

"You know what'll happen if you're not in that meeting?"

"Chaos," said Lieberman. "The sky will fall and it will be up to me to set it right."

"Shakespeare?" she said shaking her head.

"Comes from years of insomnia and reading in the bathtub," said Lieberman, motioning for Sokol to follow him into a small office. Lieberman pointed to a chair next to the desk. Sokol sat while Lieberman stood making calls and taking notes.

A resigned calm had taken over Arnold Sokol. Events would carry him.

He would drift. Others would take care of him, possibly send him to prison. He had experienced his moment. He was complete. He tried to remember every moment of the night before. It came in small jerking bits in which he stood triumphant. Sokol heard almost nothing of what the detective said, and when Lieberman hung up after taking notes, Sokol had trouble concentrating on what he was being told.

"His name is Zembinsky, Melvin Zembinsky," said Lieberman. "Notice I said 'is.' You didn't kill him. At least he's not dead yet. He's in Evanston Hospital. Let's go see him."

"He's not dead?" asked Sokol. "This is a trick. I killed him. He attacked me. I killed him."

Lieberman looked at the seated man, who looked as if he were going to panic.

"And you want him dead?"

"Yes," said Sokol, pounding the desk. "Yes, yes, yes."

The door to the office opened, and a man in a white shirt and dark slacks held up by suspenders stepped in, leaving the door open behind him.

The man was thin, wore glasses and a *kepah*. He looked at Sokol and then at Lieberman.

"Abraham, what's going on?"

"Rabbi Wass, this is Arnold Sokol. He thought I was you. He confessed to a murder, but the victim isn't dead, and Mr. Sokol is disappointed."

Rabbi Wass looked confused. He took off his glasses, which he often did to make momentary sense of the immediate world, put them on again, and looked at Sokol.

"I was working on my sermon," Rabbi Wass said.

Both Sokol and Lieberman failed to see the relevance of the statement.

"Never mind," said the rabbi. "Who did you try to kill? Why? Why are you disappointed that he isn't dead? And, forgive me, but I don't recognize you. You're not a member of this congregation."

"I'm a Catholic," said Sokol.

"He's a Jew," said Lieberman.

"I thought I killed a young man who was trying to rob me," said Sokol. "Him and his gang, four of them. I fought them off. Then I wanted to confess, to tell someone."

"You were proud of what you had done?" asked the rabbi.

"Yes."

"Why didn't you go to a priest?"

"I . . ."

"He's a convert to Catholicism," said Lieberman. "He's as confused as Jerry Slattery."

Slattery was a convert from Catholicism to Judaism. It had come to Slattery when he was 50. He was a postal worker, a reader, a bachelor with recurrent stomach problems. Then he had become a pain in the behind. No one is more Jewish than a convert. Slattery spoke out, decried the lack of religious discipline in the congregation. He had been to Israel twice, spoke Hebrew almost fluently, and argued with Rabbi Wass about just about everything. And then, suddenly, Slattery had second thoughts about his conversion, went to see a priest, and dropped out of religious life of all kind. He sat at home in his small apartment at night, watching television and playing Tetris on a Game Boy.

Rabbi Wass and the priest, Father Sutton, had joined forces to save Slattery, had visited him at home, taken him to dinner, tried to argue, persuade, threaten, cajole. So far, nothing had worked, and Lieberman, to tell the truth, was happy that Slattery wasn't around to correct everyone on ritual procedure and rail against the Arab world.

Sokol wasn't a member of the congregation. Sokol was a Catholic.

What was Rabbi Wass's duty? Find the name of the man's priest? Was this another Slattery situation?

"We're going to the hospital," said Lieberman, motioning for Sokol to rise.

"I'll go with you," said Rabbi Wass. "I'll get my jacket."

"No," said Sokol.

The rabbi paused at the door.

"I would like to go," said the rabbi.

"You can't save my soul," said Sokol. "I don't want it saved, and I don't want clichés and simple-minded advice."

"You'd be surprised at how many people find solace in simple truths," said Rabbi Wass.

"Not me," said Sokol.

"Fine, whatever conversation we have, I'll try to make it dense, metaphysical, and difficult to follow. Will that satisfy you?"

Sokol looked at the rabbi, who was serious and without expression. The rabbi left to get his jacket.

Ten minutes later, Lieberman's partner returned, was briefed, and the four men got into the car and headed for the hospital.

"I checked with your friend Bryant in Evanston," Lieberman said in the front seat, while Hanrahan drove. "Our victim is 18, has a long list of arrests for robbery and assault. Did six months as a juvenile offender. Father's a probation officer. Mother's on a state juvenile crime commission."

Hanrahan looked into the rear-view mirror. Rabbi Wass was speaking softly to Sokol, who seemed galaxies away.

"What're we doing, Abe? Why not turn him over to Bryant and get to the station before Kearney puts us on report."

"I called Kearney. He was in one of his moods. Doesn't care what we do," said Lieberman.

"It would be a comfort, though a small one, if I had some idea of what we were doing," said Hanrahan as they drove down the road between the parking structure and the rear of the hospital. Hanrahan parked near the Emergency Room and put down his visor with the Chicago police card clipped to it.

"I think we're trying to save a man's soul, whatever that is," said Lieberman.

"We'd be better off out catching a few bad guys," said Hanrahan.

"I called his wife."

"You got a lot done fast, Rabbi."

"She's coming here. Kids are in school except for a baby."

Hanrahan looked in the mirror again.

"Looks like a true believer in nothing," said Hanrahan.

"Maybe," said Lieberman. "Let's go."

They got out of the car, the two policemen ahead, the rabbi and Sokol behind.

There were about a dozen people in the waiting room, none of them Sokol's wife. They had beaten her there, which was fine with Lieberman.

Identification was shown, and the woman behind the counter told them how to get to the room of Melvin Zembinsky.

At the nursing station, a thin, pretty black nurse with her hair in a bun said that Zembinsky had suffered no serious injury other than facial contusions, a concussion that had knocked him out and a cut in his head that required thirty-two stitches. There was no reason they couldn't see him, especially since he was a suspect in a crime.

There were two men in the other beds in the room with Zembinsky. Neither man was in any condition to notice the quartet that moved toward the bed of the bandaged young man whose eyes were closed. Hanrahan pulled the curtain around the bed to give them some sense of privacy.

"Melvin," said Lieberman.

Nothing.

"Z," Lieberman said, and the young man's eyes struggled and opened.

"I'm Detective Lieberman. This is my partner, Detective Hanrahan, and this is Rabbi Wass. I think you know this man."

Zembinsky's eyes turned to Sokol without recognition.

"He's the one who put you in here," said Lieberman. "Wanna just shake hands and be friends?"

Zembinsky's eyes now turned to the thin little detective.

"I didn't think so," said Lieberman. "You're a Jew."

"I'm nothing," Zembinsky whispered. "Religion sucks."

"Sokol," said Lieberman. "It sounds like you and your victim have a lot in common."

"Why didn't you die?" asked Sokol with resignation.

"So I could get out of this bed, find you, and punch a hole in your stomach," said Zembinsky, so softly that the four men could hardly hear him. Zembinsky's eyes closed, and he seemed exhausted.

"We're gonna get you, man," Zembinsky went on, eyes still closed. "We're gonna get you at home or on the street when you don't know we're coming. And if you've got a family . . ."

Lieberman was at the foot of the bed facing the battered young man. Rabbi Wass stood next to the bed with Hanrahan at his side. Sokol stood next to Lieberman.

And it happened. Arnold Sokol let out an animal snort of rage, pushed Lieberman against the bed, and grabbed the detective's weapon from his holster. Lieberman's hip had caught a metal bar. Pain shot through his side.

"No," said Rabbi Wass, as Sokol aimed the weapon at the young man on the bed who opened his eyes, looked at Arnold and smiled.

"Put it down, Mr. Sokol," said Hanrahan whose weapon was out and pointed at the shaking man with the gun in his hand.

"No," said Sokol. "I'm going to finish this."

"Go ahead," said the man in the bed. "I don't give a crap. You'll make the headlines. My friends won't have any trouble finding you. Shoot. You'll probably miss and screw it up again."

"You ever fire a weapon, Arnold?" Lieberman said.

"I'm just going to pull the trigger," said Sokol. "Pull it and pull it till it's empty, or the other policeman shoots me. You don't understand. It has to be or I'm nothing."

"First the synagogue, now the hospital," said Lieberman. "And who the hell knows what you've done to my hip. And let's not forget that if you shoot him with my gun, I'm in big trouble. I've got a wife, daughter, two grandchildren, and I'm near a retirement pension. Shoot him and who knows what I lose. All you lose is your life."

Sokol looked at the three men around the bed and hesitated.

"I have to," he said. "Don't you see?"

"Be quiet will you, for Christ's sake," came the voice of a man in another bed beyond the curtain. "I'm supposed to be here to get some rest."

"Sorry," said Lieberman.

Sokol aimed the gun at the young man in the bed before him. Hanrahan leveled his weapon. Before he could move, Rabbi Wass leaned over the man on the bed and covered him with his body, his back to Sokol.

"Get out of the way," Sokol cried.

The rabbi was eye-to-eye with the battered man on the bed. The pain of the rabbi's weight was off-set by the rabbi's attempt at a reassuring smile.

"No," said Rabbi Wass. "Arnold, give Detective Lieberman his gun back. No lives will be lost here with the possible exception of yours and mine."

Sokol screamed, "Get the hell off of him."

"I would like to get the hell off of him," said the rabbi, "but at the moment, one step at a time."

"You people are all crazy," said Sokol. "I'm crazy."

"And I'm calling the damn nurse," came the voice from the other bed.

Lieberman held out his hand. Sokol hesitated and handed him the weapon. Hanrahan slowly put his gun away.

"He did it," croaked Zembinsky, looking into the rabbi's eyes.

Rabbi Wass closed his eyes and stood up on less than firm legs.

"You've got balls," said the young man in the bed, struggling for air.

"I'll take that as a compliment," said the rabbi, adjusting his glasses. "Now, if you want to repay me and God for saving your life, promise that when this is all ended, that you will not seek revenge. You don't deserve revenge."

The pretty black nurse came in and saw that Zembinsky was having trouble breathing.

"What happened?" she asked, looking at Lieberman and then at her patient who was breathing loud and heavily.

"I fell upon him," said Rabbi Wass.

The nurse leaned over the heavily breathing young man and said, "You people have some damn weird rituals."

"We do," said Lieberman.

Zembinsky's eyes met those of Arnold Sokol, and he spoke as the nurse listened to his chest with the stethoscope that hung around her neck.

"Okay," said the young man gasped. "I owe you one. I leave the bastard alone. He doesn't bring any charges."

"Be quiet," the nurse said.

Sokol shook his head "yes," and Zembinsky nodded and closed his eyes. The nurse stood up.

"He'll be all right," she said. "I'd say this visit is over."

"Amen," said Lieberman.

"You believe the little bugger?" asked Hanrahan, in the corridor outside the room.

"Yes," said Rabbi Wass.

"I think so," said Sokol.

"Yes," said Lieberman, but kept to himself the knowledge gained from more than thirty years on the street, a knowledge that one's word was only as good as the person who gave it and rage walked the streets.

"Go downstairs, Mr. Sokol," said Rabbi Wass. "Your wife should be there. Go home. I'll call you if you wish, to see how you're doing."

"That would be fine."

"Maybe you could come back for a Friday night? I think you'll be the subject of my sermon. I don't know what I'll say. Maybe I'll surprise us both. God often gives me words I didn't expect. Sometimes they're not so bad."

"I'll think about it," said Sokol, shaking hands with the two policemen.

"I'd say you owe the rabbi," said Hanrahan.

"Yes," said Sokol, looking at his watch. "I could still take a shower, change clothes, and get to work."

"The baby's name?" asked Lieberman, as Sokol started to turn toward the elevator. "What's your baby's name?"

"Luke," said Sokol. "Did I tell you my wife's name is Mary?"

"You did," said Lieberman. "They're waiting for you downstairs."

The three men stood in the hospital corridor while Sokol got in the elevator.

"You're a hero, Rabbi," said Lieberman.

"I'm a man, that's all," said Rabbi Wass.

"So," said Lieberman. "What does it mean? What happened this morning?"

"I don't know," said the rabbi. "But it feels right."

When the three men got down to the lobby, the tattered Arnold Sokol was standing in the corner near the window arguing with a plump woman with disheveled hair and a baby over her shoulder.

"Doesn't look promising," said Hanrahan.

"They're talking," said Rabbi Wass, adjusting his glasses. "It's a start."

"Time for coffee?" asked Lieberman.

"Why not?" said Rabbi Wass, who walked ahead of them, lost in his thoughts.

"Abe," Hanrahan said softly. "You load your weapon yet this morning?"

"Nope," said Lieberman. "Father Murph, you know I don't load 'til I get to the squad room."

"Yeah," said Hanrahan, as the automatic doors opened in front of the hospital. "How about you paying for the coffee?"

"How about Rabbi Wass paying for the coffee and Danish?" Lieberman said as the rabbi stood waiting for them.

"That'll be fine with me," said Hanrahan. "Just fine."

FAYE KELLERMAN has written ten best-selling mystery novels starring the characters Peter Decker and Rina Lazarus. These mysteries have taught a great deal about traditional Judaism while entertaining the reader with a good whodunit. This story was originally published in *Deadly Allies II,* an anthology of mystery stories.

Holy Water

▾　　▾　　▾　　▾　　▾　　▾　　▾

Faye Kellerman

UNTIL HE FELT THE GUN IN HIS BACK, Rabbi Feinermann thought it was a joke: somebody's idea of a silly pre-Purim schtick. After all, the men who flanked him wore costume masks. The Marx fellows—Groucho and Karl. Two old Jewish troublemakers, but at least one of them had been funny. The revelers spoke in such trite dialogue it had to be a hoax.

"Don't move, old man, and you won't get hurt."

Although he was fasting, Feinermann was always one to join in the festivities—though this prank was on the early side. So he played along, adjusting his hat, then holding up his hands.

"Don't shoot," Feinermann said. "I'll give you my *humantash*. I'll even give you a shot of Schnapps. But first, my two Marxes, we must wait until we've heard the *megilla* before we can break our fasts."

Then as he tried to turn around, Groucho held him tightly, kept him facing forward, pressing his arm uncomfortably into his back. At that moment, Feinermann felt the gun. Had he seen it when the two masked men made their initial approach? Maybe. But to Feinermann's naive eyes, the pistol seemed like a toy.

"We're not fooling around here, Rabbi," Karl said. "I want you to walk slowly to the gray car straight ahead."

Feinermann looked around the *shul's* parking lot. It was located in the back alley on a little-used dead-end side street. He was alone with these hoodlums, but he had grown up in New York. Hoodlums were nothing new, although the masks were a little different. In his day, a stocking over the face was sufficient. In the "old days," no one had ski masks.

But times change. The old man had grown up in neighborhoods where ethnic groups competed for turf—the Irish, the Italian, the Germans, the Poles, then later on, the Puerto Ricans. Each nationality fighting to prove who was the mightiest. Of course, they all tormented the Jews. Pious old men and women had been no match for angry energy and youthful indignation.

No, hoodlums were nothing new. But the gun in the back was something different. When he was young, the weapon of choice had been fists. If the altercation grew very nasty, a pen knife would glint in the moonlight. But not revolvers. Revolvers were for bank robbers, not street fighters. Had mankind really progressed?, the rabbi mused.

"Come on, Rabbi," Karl said. "Don't make this difficult on us or on yourself."

"Which car do you mean, Mr. Marx?" Feinermann asked. "The '84 Electra?"

"The '90 Seville," Groucho answered.

"Oooo, a Cadillac," Feinermann said. "A good car for abduction. May I ask what this is all about?"

"Just shut up and keep going," Karl said.

"No need for a sharp tongue, Mr. Marx," the rabbi said.

"Why do you keep calling me 'Marx'?" Karl asked. He pointed to Groucho. "He's the Marx guy."

"Your mask is Karl Marx," Feinermann said.

"No it's not," Karl protested. "I'm Albert Einstein."

"I hate to say this, young man, but you're no Einstein."

"Will both of you just *shut* up?" Groucho snarled.

"Then who am I?" Karl plowed on.

"Karl Marx," Feinermann declared. "The founder of Communism . . . which isn't doing too well these days."

"You mean, I'm a *pinko* instead of a genius?" Karl was aghast.

"Just shut up!" Groucho yelled. To Feinermann, he said. "You can scream your head off, Rabbi. No one will hear you. We're all alone."

"Besides," Karl added, "you do want to see your wife again, don't you?"

Feinermann paused. "I'm not so sure. Nevertheless, I will cooperate. You haven't shot me yet. You haven't robbed me. I assume what you want from me is more complex than a wallet or a watch."

Groucho pushed the gun deeper into Feinermann's spine. "Get a move on it, Rabbi."

Feinermann said. "Watch my backbone, Mister Jeffrey T. Spaulding. I had disk surgery not more than a year ago. Why cause an old man needless pain?"

Instantly, the rabbi felt relief as the pressure eased off his back. "So you're not without compassion."

"Just keep walking, Rabbi," Groucho said.

"Who's Jeffrey T. Spaulding?" Karl asked.

"Shut up!" Groucho said. "Just cooperate, Rabbi, and no one will get hurt."

"Mr. Hugo Z. Hackenbush, I have no doubt that you will not get hurt," Feinermann said. "It's me I'm concerned about."

"Hugo Hack . . ." Karl scratched his face under his mask. "Who are all these kooks?"

"C'mon!" Groucho pushed the rabbi forward. "Step on it."

As the Marxes sequestered him in the back seat of the Seville, Feinermann tried to figure out why he was being kidnapped. He wasn't a wealthy man, not in possession of any items of great value. His estate—a small, two bedroom house in the Fairfax district of Los Angeles—would be left to Sarah upon his demise. He and his wife had had their differences, but he couldn't imagine her hiring people to kill him for his paltry insurance policy. Sarah was a *kvetch* and a *yente*, but basically a good, pious woman. And a practical woman as well. The cost of the hit would greatly exceed any monetary gain she'd receive from the policy.

Karl kept him company in the back seat as Groucho gunned the motor. Then they were off. The men were good-sized, capable of doing major physical damage. And they seemed very nervous. Perhaps this was their very first kidnapping, Feinermann thought. It is always difficult to do something for the first time. As the old man thought about it, he felt it might have been better to be in the hands of professional abductors. True, it would be harder to escape, but novice kidnappers could do something rash. It wouldn't necessarily be their fault, just lack of experience.

It was then and there that Feinermann decided to make his abductors feel welcome.

"A nice shirt you have on, Karl Marx," he said. "Is it silk?"

Karl looked at his buttercup chemise. "Yeah. You really like it?"

The old man fingered the fabric. "Very good quality. I grew up in New York, had many a friend in the *shmatah* business. This is an impressive shirt."

"The silk's washable," Karl said. "Pain in the ass to dryclean your stuff all the time." He paused. "Excuse my language . . . me saying ass and all."

"No problem," Feinermann said.

"Quiet back there," Groucho said.

The old man pressed his lips together. At least, his discussion with Karl had produced the desired effects. Feinermann could see the man in the buttercup shirt visibly relax, his shoulders unbunching, his feet burying deep into the Caddy's plush carpeting. The Seville, with its cushy gray leather upholstery and its black-tinted windows, had lots of leg room. It was good that Karl felt at home. He shouldn't be nervous holding a gun.

Groucho, on the other hand, was a different story. His body language was hidden from Feinermann's view. The only thing the rabbi could make out was a pair of dark eyes peeking through a mask with the bushy eyebrows—a reflection in the rear view mirror. The eyes gave Feinermann no hint as to who was the man behind them.

The old man sat stiffly and hunched forward, his elbows resting on his knees. Karl reached into his pocket and pulled out a handkerchief.

"Sorry to have to do this to you, old man."

"Do what?" Feinermann felt his heart skip a beat. "You are going to tie me up?"

"Nah, you're not much of a threat." Karl said. "I'm gonna have to blind-fold you. Don't want to you to see where we're taking you. Be a good man and hold still."

"I always cooperate with people carrying revolvers."

"Good thinking."

Feinermann closed his eyes as they were covered with a soft cloth, the ends of the kerchief secured tightly around his head. Quality silk—very soft and smooth. His abductors had spared him no expense. It made the old man feel important.

"May I now ask what this is all about?"

"Soon enough," Karl answered. "Don't worry. No one wants to hurt you. They just want a little information from you."

"Information?"

Groucho barked, "Keep your trap shut, for christsakes!"

"Are you talking to me, Mr. Rufus T. Firefly?" Feinermann asked.

"No, not you, Rabbi. I would never talk to a man of the cloth like that." Groucho paused. "Well, maybe I did tell you to shut up. Sorry about that. I was nervous."

"First time as a kidnapper?"

"You can tell, huh?"

"You don't seem like the hardened criminal type."

"I owed someone a favor."

"It must have been a pretty big favor."

"Ain't they all. Just relax, old man. We're gonna be in the car for a while."

"Then maybe I'll take a little rest." Feinermann took off his hat, exposing the black skullcap underneath and unbuttoned his jacket. "Is this your first kidnapping as well, Karl?"

"Yep." Karl lowered his voice. "I owed him a favor."

Feinermann took the "him" to be Groucho and pondered, "Groucho owed someone a favor, you owed Groucho a favor."

"Yeah," Karl said. "It's kinda like a bad chain letter."

A Hebrew proverb came to Feinermann's mind: "From righteous deeds comes righteous deeds. From sin comes sin."

The rabbi opened his eyes only to find them still encased in darkness. He was not surprised that he had fallen asleep. The car was comfortable, the ride was rhythmic, and he was temporarily bathed in artificial darkness. What else was there to do? He heard the motor die, heard the slamming of a car door.

"We're here, old man."

Karl. By now, Feinermann could distinguish between the two Marxes.

"And where is here?"

"Never mind." Groucho helped him out of the car, making sure both he and Feinermann had their balance before they began walking. "Watch your step."

Feinermann thought he'd watch his step if he could see where he was walking.

They brought him indoors, eased him onto a baby-smooth leather chair, and propped his feet up on an ottoman. Such service, Feinermann thought. After the Marxes had made him comfortable, they removed the blindfold, then left.

The old man found himself in a magnificent library. The room was about the size of the *shul's* dining hall, but much more fancy. The paneling and bookcases were fashioned from rich, deep mahogany, so smooth and shiny the wood seemed to be plastic. The brass pulls on the cases gleamed—not a scratch dared mar the mirror polish. The furniture consisted of burnt almond leather sofas and chairs, with a couple of tapestry wing-backs thrown in for color. The parquet floor was covered in several places by what looked to be original Persian rugs.

Directly in front of Feinermann's view was a U-shaped desk made out of rosewood with ebony trim. The man behind the desk appeared to be of slight frame, around 35, but bald except for a well-trimmed cocoa-colored fringe outlining his nude crown. Across his eyes sat an updated version of the old-fashioned wire-rimmed, round spectacles. except these weren't the heavy kind that left a red mark on the bridge of the nose. Mr. Baldy was attired in a black suit, his pocket handkerchief matching the mandarin ascot draped around his neck. He held a crystal highball glass filled with ice, a carbonated beverage, and two swizzle sticks.

"May I offer you something to drink, Rabbi?" The bald man stirred his drink. His voice was surprisingly deep. "I'm drinking KingCola—the only beverage considered worthy of the Benton's finest imported Bavarian crystal. But we have a full bar—Chivas aged some twenty-five years—if you're so inclined."

"Thank you, sir," said Feinermann, "but I shall be obliged to pass. Today is fast day in my religion—the fast of Esther. Eating and drinking are prohibited until tonight's holiday."

The bald man stirred his KingCola. "Interesting. And what holiday is tonight, if I may ask?"

"You may ask and I'll tell you. Tonight is *Purim*—the festival of lots—when one righteous woman foiled the plans to annihilate the Jews of Persia."

"And you fast on such a day?"

"First came the fasting and praying, then came the celebration. Makes more sense to feast when you're really hungry. Not to mention it's good for weight control." Feinermann adjusted his hat. "Are you Benton of the famous Benton's crystal?"

The bald man looked up and chuckled. "No, Rabbi, I am not Mr. Benton."

The old man stroked his beard. "I am trying to figure out why his name rings a bell."

The bald man said, "Perhaps you'd recognize the name in a different form. Benton Hall at the university. Or perhaps you've been to the Benton Civic Light Opera Company. Or read about the new Benton Library downtown."

"Ah . . ."

"Mr. Patrick W. Benton is quite the philanthropist."

"Apparently."

"Not apparently. Definitely."

"So what does a rich philanthropist need with a rabbi who has a herniated disk?"

"You are not just a rabbi. You are *the* rabbi."

"I don't understand."

"I realize that. But before we begin, I want you to know that bringing you here was my idea, not Mr. Benton's. I work for Mr. Benton, formulating his . . . covert operations."

"Sounds mysterious. Perhaps you're a student of the *Zohar*?"

"Who?"

"Not important. Nu, so what do you want with me?"

"All will be explained in good time."

"Now seems like a perfectly good time."

The bald man chuckled once again. Feinermann found the laugh irritating. "Do you have a name, Mr. Sharp Dresser?"

"Sharp dress—you've noticed my *couture*?"

"I like the touch of orange with the black suit." Actually Feinermann thought the man looked like a Jack-O-Lantern. But hurling insults was not the old man's style. And now was not the time for insults anyway.

The bald man nodded in approval. "Well, I thought it made rather a bold statement."

The rabbi said nothing. To him, a bold statement was splitting the Red Sea. "So, Mr. . . . ."

"You may call me Philip."

"Philip it is. Exactly what does your Mr. Benton want from me?"

"It is *I* who want something from you, Rabbi Feinermann. I want something not for myself, but for Mr. Benton. You see he is more than my boss. He is my mentor, my sage."

"If he is your sage, what do you need with an old rabbi?"

"Because you, Rabbi Feinermann, are the only one who can help Mr. Benton continue his course of philanthropy."

"Me?"

"Only you."

"How so?"

"First, I need to explain a few things to you."

The old man stroked his beard. "I knew this wasn't going to be simple. Kidnappings are never simple affairs."

Again, Philip let go with his pesky chuckle. "Come, come, Rabbi. Surely you don't think we intend for any harm to befall you."

"To tell you the truth, with a gun in my back, I wasn't so sure, Philip."

"Merely a display to show you our seriousness of intent. To get your attention."

"You have my attention."

"Rabbi Feinermann, you may wonder why a man like me would go to such extreme . . . measures to help out Mr. Benton. It's because I truly believe in his work and in what he does."

"And what does he do besides erect buildings with his name on them?"

"He cares, Rabbi. He has built his empire on caring. His multi-billion dollar corporation was one of the first to include the human side of business. One of the first to offer complete major medical and dental care. And if that was not enough, he included in his medical package—free of charge— optometry, orthodonture, and podiatry services. Do you know how many of his employees have availed themselves of braces, eyeglasses, and bunion removal at Mr. Benton's expense?"

"I have no idea."

"Thousands."

"A lot of bunions, Philip."

"Corns are no laughing matter, Rabbi."

"Not at all, Philip."

"It's not just in medical services where Mr. Benton has taken the social lead. It's in other fields. Loans for his employees—for new houses, for vacations, for cars, for education of his workers' children. Mr. Benton provides these loans at market price with no points. His was one of the first major corporations to provide on-site day care, flexible shifts for working mothers, and free turkeys on Thanksgiving, Christmas and Easter." Philip paused. "And kosher turkeys for our kosher-keeping workers, I might add."

"Sounds like a thoughtful man, your Mr. Benton."

"That he is, Rabbi." Philip tensed his body and shook with gravity. "That's why desperate times call for desperate measures. You being here . . . it was a desperate measure that I took. But one that I hope you will truly understand."

"I'm all ears, Philip."

"Do you know how Mr. Benton made his money, Rabbi?"

"I'm afraid I don't."

"I'm not surprised. He is not a grandstander like your ordinary billionaire."

"I'm not a maven on billionaires, Philip. I wouldn't know an ordinary one from an unusual one."

"Well, let me assure you that Mr. Benton is extraordinary."

"I'm assured."

"He made his money right here." Philip held his highball tumbler afloat. "Right in the palm of my hand."

"In Bavarian crystal?"

Philip frowned. "No. In the soft drink industry. KingCola. A 'King,' as it is affectionately known. 'I'll have a hamburger, French fries, and a King.' How many times have you heard that, Rabbi?"

"Not too many. But don't go by me. I don't patronize fast food places because I keep kosher."

"But even you, as insulated as you are from pop culture, have heard of KingCola."

"Certainly."

"But there's so much more to Mr. Benton than KingCola."

Feinermann noticed Philip was shaking again. "We've been over the wonders of Mr. Benton. May I ask what does any of this have to do with me?"

"I can sum that up in two words."

Feinermann waited. Philip waited. Obviously, the Jack-O-Lantern wanted the rabbi to ask. So Feinermann obliged.

"What are those two words?"

"Cola Gold."

"Cola Gold?"

"Exactly."

"Your chief competitor."

"Our *enemy,* Rabbi!' Philip started foaming at the mouth. "Not just our enemy in the War of the Soft Drinks, oh no, Rabbi. It's deeper than that. Much, much deeper. If it was only money, do you think Mr. Benton would waste his time on them?"

Feinermann thought maybe Mr. Benton would bother wasting his time. From his scant knowledge of billionaires, the old man was under the impression that billionaires—and maybe millionaires as well—spent a great deal of time on the subject of money. But he was silent.

Philip went on, "It's the whole CeeGee mentality, rabbi. CeeGee—that's our code word for Cola Gold."

Feinermann nodded.

"CeeGee's attitude is a Machiavellian—only the product counts, not the people behind the product. Do you know that last year alone, CeeGee laid off over 200 people?"

"Hard times are upon us."

"It wasn't that they were not needed, Rabbi. They were replaced! And do you know who replaced them?"

"Who?"

"Not a who, it was a what!" Philip spat out. "Machines! Machines took over jobs that had once put bread on the table of families. You have a family, Rabbi. How would you feel if a machine took over your job?"

"Not too good."

"Exactly!" Philip pulled an orange handkerchief from his pocket and wiped his face and forehead. "We're not talking about ordinary business competition, rabbi. We're not just talking about sugar, flavoring, and water. We are talking sugar, flavoring, and holy water, Rabbi. What KingCola and Cola Gold have going is an all out holy war."

"I see your point, Philip."

"So you will help, won't you rabbi?"

Feinermann stroked his beard, then held his finger up in the air. "Yes, I shall help. Call up Cola Gold and ask for the list of those who've been laid off. I could use an extra man to clean up the *shul* after Friday night *kiddush*."

Philip bristled. "That's not what I had in mind!"

"So if you have an alternative plan, tell me."

Philip pointed a finger at the old man. "It rests entirely in your hands."

Feinermann looked at his hands. All he saw was air.

Philip said, "It has to do with CeeGee's new formula. The one they use to appeal to the youth?"

"Ah, yes," the old man said. "I'm aware of it. What is the slogan? 'The new cola for the now generation.'"

"Don't utter those words!" Philip held his ears and began to pant.

Feinermann stood and quickly handed Philip his glass of KingCola. By now the ice had melted, and the drink looked watered down. But it looked pretty good nonetheless because his mouth was dry from fasting. "Philip, calm down and drink."

Philip slurped up the remains of his soft drink.

"I beg your pardon," the rabbi said. "I didn't realize it would cause such a reaction. I won't say another word."

Philip took a deep breath and let it out slowly. "It's not your fault, Rabbi. You couldn't have known."

Feinermann said, "I take it by your reaction that the new . . . youthful formula has been successful."

"Youth!" Philip despaired. "What do they know of Mr. Benton's greatness and humanism?"

"Why don't you tell them?"

"As if they'd listen. As if this generation cares about humanism. Did you know that soft drinks is a $48 billion industry? Did you know that colas—both caffeinated and decaffeinated—comprise a forty percent market share? And who do you think drinks cola?"

"Who?"

"Youth!" Philip exclaimed. "Youth, youth, youth! Those rats at CeeGee have not only exploited the workers, they've exploited our youth! Did you know that they've have signed DeJon Jonson to a $20 million ad contract?"

"He's the fellow with a lamé glove?"

"He's the hottest thing in the recording industry, Rabbi. And CeeGee's got him under contract."

"Twenty million is a lot to pay for a fellow with just one glove. Surely you can find a chap with two gloves for a cheaper price."

Philip glared at him.

"What do you want from me, Philip?" Feinermann asked.

"I've tried everything, Rabbi. This is my last desperate attempt to give a victory for our side—the side of truth and justice. The key is in your hands because . . ." Philip paused for dramatic effect. "Because you are one of the handful of people who knows Cola Gold's secret formula."

The rabbi's eyes widened. "Me?"

"There's no use in denying it, Rabbi," Philip stated. "You are one of the privileged who knows every single ingredient, additive, and flavoring, artificial or otherwise, that gives CeeGee's new formula its unique taste."

"Philip—"

"You, Rabbi, have personally checked the formula in an official capacity in order to give sanction to the kosher-keeping world that the new formula is as kosher as their original formula. Don't deny it, Rabbi, don't deny it."

"A minute, Philip. Give an old man a minute. Two would even be preferable."

Feinermann needed to collect his thoughts.

He had to think back, because the job had not been part of his regular duties. The assignment had been given to him because Rav Gottlieb, the *mashgiach* for Cola Gold, had come down with a flu named after one of the continents—Asian or African. Feinermann hadn't thought much about it at the time. Gottlieb had been certifying all Cola Gold Inc. beverages as kosher for over twenty years. Still the corporate wheels hadn't wanted to wait for an old man's recuperation. Gottlieb had suggested Rav Morris Feinermann as a substitute.

As Feinermann recalled it, the CeeGee people hadn't been happy to deal with him. Only reluctantly had they parted with the formula, and then they'd sworn him to secrecy. At the time, Feinermann had thought the management overly dramatic.

He stroked his beard—a mistake on his part to underestimate the competition.

Philip couldn't contain himself. "I want that formula and you will give it to me. You will give it to me because you, like Mr. Benton, are a humanitarian and have the best interest of people utmost in your mind! If we lose our market share, Rabbi, our sales will go down. If our sales decrease, it will be necessary to lay people off from work. And why? Because a cold, heartless manufacturer prefers to use robots rather than people. You're a humanist, Rabbi. You will help."

"But I can't give you the formula, Philip. It would be unethical. And there's also a very practical reason. I gave the company *hashgacha* over a year ago. I don't remember it. All the Latin-sounding chemical names they used for flavoring. Very confusing. Perhaps if you had kidnapped me earlier . . ."

"Had we have known the precipitous rise in their market share, believe me, Rabbi, we wouldn't have waited so long. Still, it's never too late."

Philip pounded the table.

"I'll help you, Rabbi. I have lists and lists of chemicals, the finest hypnotists to help you with memory recall. We will work day and night if we have to. I will go without food or sleep. I will not rest until I discover their secret ingredients. I will do anything within my power, sacrifice myself, because I believe in Mr. Benton."

"I was never a big student of sacrifices, Philip. The bottom line, my young friend, is I will not divulge anything that was given to me in confidence."

Philip's face turned crimson, his eyes becoming steely and cold. Then his lips turned into a mean smile. "I can see you'll need a bit of convincing." He rang a bell. In walked the Marxes. Red-faced Philip turned to him and with his irritating chuckle said, "Take Rabbi Feinermann to the dungeon!"

The Marxes gasped.

"Not the dungeon," Karl exclaimed. "Not the dungeon, Mr. P. Not for a rabbi!"

"To the dungeon!" Philip ordered. "And no food and water for him."

That part was acceptable, Feinermann thought. He was fasting anyway.

The old man told them to walk slowly. His back was sore from the car ride, and he was a little light in the head from not having eaten. Then he said, "And just what is this dungeon?"

"Corporate torture, Rabbi," Groucho responded solemnly "It's better if you don't know."

The rabbi sighed. "I'll survive. Our people have experienced all sorts of adversity."

"Yeah, you guys have sure had some hard knocks," Karl added.

"If you got any personal role models, Rabbi," Groucho said. "You know, people you admire cause they're strong. Maybe now's the time to start thinking about them."

"There are no shortage of Jewish martyrs," Feinermann said. "Take for example, Channah and her ten sons. A bit of a zealot Channah was, but righteous nonetheless. She instructed her ten sons to die rather than give themselves over to the Hellenistic ways."

"Did they listen to her?" Karl asked.

"Yes, indeed they did. The youngest was only six, yet he accepted death rather than bow down to the Greek gods and goddesses."

"That's terrible," Groucho said. "A six-year-old kid, what does he know?"

"They were probably more mature in those days," Karl said. "After all, didn't most people kick the bucket around thirty?"

"Still, the kid was only six," Groucho said.

"Surely your corporate torture could not be as terrible as that," Feinermann piped in.

Karl said. "If thinking of this broad helps you along, Rabbi, then more power to you."

"Then I shall think about Channah. And I shall also think about the ten martyrs our people read about on Yom Kippur. Our holiest rabbis were tortured to death by the Romans because of their beliefs. One was decapitated, one was burnt, one was flayed, and one of the most famous of our sages, Rabbi Akiva, had his flesh raked with hot combs."

"Those Romans were surely uncivilized people!" Groucho exclaimed. "Gladiators, lion pits, and torturing men of the cloth. Even Mr. P wouldn't do that."

"Comforting," Feinermann said.

"Yeah, Rabbi, that's the spirit!" Karl cheered on.

Feinermann thought: so maybe this was his chance to show his faith, like the ten martyrs. Always the little Jew against someone of might—the Persians, the Romans, the Spanish of the Inquisition, the Cossacks, and, most deadly the Nazis. Not to mention Tommy Hoolihan who beat Feinermann up every day for two years, as the small boy of ten with the big, black *kippah* walked home from *heder*. Telling his questioning, worried mother that the bruises he'd sustained were from falls. She must have thought he was the clumsiest kid in New York.

Twenty-five hundred years of persecution.

Yet the Jews as a nation refused to die. Could he, like Rabbi Akiva, die with the words *Sh'ma Yisroel* on his lips and mean it?

He thought about that as the two masked men led him to his destiny.

Perhaps he could die a true martyr, perhaps not. But if he couldn't, he wouldn't worry about it too much. After all, how many Rabbi Akivas were there in a lifetime?

He expected darkness and filth, chains and nooses hanging from the ceiling. And some red-eyed, emaciated rats ready to eat his *kishkas* out. Instead Feinermann was brought into a semi-circular projection room. The auditorium consisted of a wide-angled screen and a half-dozen rows of plush chairs, maybe seating for fifty in all.

Not so bad for a dungeon, Feinermann thought.

They placed him in the center row and shackled his feet and hands to the chair. Was he about to be shocked or gassed? Frightened, he couldn't help thinking about the newsreels of the concentration camp victims—his brothers and sisters slaughtered, burned, and asphyxiated by the Nazis. Imagine if this was going to happen to him. Imagine such a torture in America.

No, Feinermann said to himself. No, it just can't be. Corporate America may be inhumane, but surely they are not Nazis. Even capital punishment is prohibited from being cruel and unusual. He watched fearfully as Karl took out some masking tape. But all Marx did was tape the old man's eyes open. Not tight enough as to prevent him from clearing his eyes of debris, but firmly enough to prevent him from pressing his lids together.

"Scream when you can't take it anymore." Karl stood up. "Nothing personal, Rabbi. I'd like to help you, but I can't." He moved closer to the old man's ear and whispered, "I'm into Elvis for a lot of bread."

"Elvis?" Feinermann said.

Karl swore and hit his face mask, whispering, "That's Groucho's real name. Don't say nothing or we'll both be in deep water."

"Come on," Groucho/Elvis shouted as he dimmed the lights. "Let's get this over with. Buck up, old man. And give us a yell when you're willing to cooperate."

Feinermann waited solemnly, wondering why Elvis didn't hide under an Elvis Presley mask. It would have seemed like a natural disguise.

Soon, the old man was sitting in total darkness. All he could hear and feel were the sensations his own body provided—the whooshing of blood coursing through his head, his heartbeat, the quick steps of his nervous breathing.

Then the first outside stimulus. A motor running. The room slowly beginning to brighten as shadowy shapes illuminated the movie screen. Sound . . . music . . . bad music. Not only was it sappy but old and distorted. It sounded as if it had come from an ancient, irrelevant documentary—the kind they show frequently on PBS.

On screen was a fuzzy, sienna image of a young man digging up potatoes. A voice-over with a reedy mid-Atlantic accent explained that this man was Patrick Benton, Sr., the potato farmer. The shack in the background was Benton's house in Cork County. The film went on to explain the hardships of Irish potato farming, including the great famine in the late eighteen hundreds.

A little history lesson never hurt anyone, the rabbi thought. Still, he wished he could blink in earnest. Next on the screen he saw a boat stuffed with Irish immigrants approaching Ellis Island. He wondered if Tommy Hoolihan's parents were aboard.

Then a cut to a tenement house, not far from where Feinermann grew up. He recognized old buildings that had been razed decades ago. The old clothing, the pushcarts, faces of men and women who still believed in the American dream. Nostalgia gripped his chest. The film switched to an indoor shot—a frame of a woman with a plump face holding a baby in her arms. She looked like Feinermann's mother. In fact, she could have been any one of a thousand immigrant mothers. Eyes watering, Feinermann knew it wasn't because he couldn't blink. The moisture in his eyes represented something deeper.

The baby had been christened Patrick Junior. Feinermann didn't know Mr. Benton's forename, but he was pretty certain he was looking at the great philanthropist himself. As the film progressed, it was clear to the old man that what he was watching was Patrick Junior's rags-to-riches story. From the son of a potato farmer to the CEO of one of the biggest corporations in the world.

Only in America.

The old man watched with rapt attention.

Philip said to Groucho, "How long has he been in there now?"

"Close to six hours, sir."

"Incredible." Philip paced. "Simply incredible. Most ordinary men would have cracked hours ago. Seeing that same story over and over. Are you sure he didn't puke? Puking is usually the first sign that they're coming around."

"No sign of puke anywhere," Karl said. "It's really amazing. That thing is so corny, I almost puked. And I only had to sit through it once."

"Maybe it's because he hasn't eaten," Groucho suggested.

Philip thought about that for a moment. "Did he retch at all?"

"Not even a single gag," Karl said.

"I just don't understand." Philip pulled out his kerchief and wiped his face. "If psychological torture isn't bringing him around, we'll have to take sterner measures."

Groucho said, "Surely you're not suggestin' physical torture?"

"Our market share in the industry is plummeting." Philip wrung his hands. "CeeGee's new formula is wiping us off the map. I've got a five-figure monthly mortgage and a Range Rover owned by B of A. I'm gonna crack that old geezer somehow!"

Over the intercom came Feinermann's voice. "Marxes, can you hear me?"

"Rabbi, it's Philip. We can hear you. What do you want."

"I think we should talk."

"Are you going to help us with the formula, Rabbi?" Philip inquired.

"I didn't say that. I just said I think we can talk."

"It's no good, Rabbi. Either you give us your word that you will help us or you must remain inside the projection room and continue to watch Mr. Benton's life story."

"I will help you, I will help you," Feinermann said.

Philip broke into a wide smile and whispered to his henchmen, "I knew it, I knew it. No one can sit through that much hokey drivel and come out sane." Into the intercom, he said, "I have your word that you will help me, Rabbi?"

"Absolutely, but first I must have your help."

"What do you require from me?"

"I want a few things. First, you must call my wife and tell her I will be delayed. She should go hear the *megillah* without me, and she shouldn't worry. I'll be home in time to deliver our *shalach manos*—our gift baskets—and our charity to the poor."

"What do I say if she asks questions?"

"Sarah's a practical woman. As long as I can make deliveries tomorrow, she won't care. Next, you must get me a *Megillas Esther*. It's night time, and I need to read it before I can eat."

Philip didn't answer.

Feinermann said, "No *megillah,* no help."

"All right. I shall find you this . . . *megillah.*"

"Be sure it's a *Megillas Esther.* There are five *megillos.*"

"Rabbi, I assure you you'll get the whole *megillah,*" Philip said. "Anything else?"

"I'd like to eat after I read. A kosher meal."

"Done."

"Not so fast, Philip. It is not enough to have a kosher meal. I must have a *se'udah*—a feast. Not a feast in terms of food. I must have a feast in terms of a party, a gathering." The rabbi thought a moment. "I want to have a feast and I want it to be in your honor, Philip. You have shown me the light."

"Why, Rabbi, I'm so honored."

"The Marxes can come, too. That will make it quite a deal. And also, you must invite your Mr. Benton as the guest of honor."

Philip didn't like that idea at all. "I don't know if I can do that, Rabbi."

"You want the help?" Feinermann asked.

Philip thought of his five-figure monthly mortgage. "He'll be there under one condition."

"What's that?"

"That I have your word that you will not tell him you were strongly convinced to come here."

"Strongly convinced? I was kidnapped, Philip. But I'm willing to let bygones be bygones. I won't mention the abduction. I'm not even angry about it. I think it was the Almighty's way of telling me something."

"You are a remarkable man, Rabbi," Philip said.

"So you will call up our Mr. Benton?"

"Yes," Philip said. "And we will have a feast—to celebrate our new partnership, shall we say?"

"I don't know if partnership is the right word, but if you meet my conditions, I will help you. That's all for now."

Feinermann stopped talking, wondering if his idea would work out. The part about the banquet he'd cribbed straight out of the *megilla*. But he didn't feel too guilty about it. If it worked once, maybe it would work again.

Left alone in the library, Feinermann read the *megilla* aloud. What they had brought him was a book that contained the text of the scroll. He would have preferred an actual scroll of Esther, but that was too much to ask. He read each word with precision, stomping his foot loudly whenever he came to the name of the evil Haman. According to Jewish law, Haman was so wicked that one's ears were not even supposed to hear his name. And also according to Jewish law, one was required to hear every word of the *megillah,* including the name of Haman. A difficult dilemma, Feinermann thought.

When he was done, he closed the Hebrew text, imbued with sense of purpose. He buzzed Philip, and the bald man came in, a grin slapped upon his face.

"We have prepared a most sumptuous kosher meal for you, Rabbi Feinermann. I've phoned Mr. Benton and he can't wait to meet the man who will bring KingCola back to its rightful number one position."

The bald man rubbed his hands together.

"Now don't worry if it takes a little time to recall the formula in its entirety. We have an excellent staff who'll be at your beck and call. Tell me the truth, Rabbi. Did they indeed use Trichlrobenzodroate? I'm not a taste expert, but I swear I detect a little Trichlor in their new formula."

"I don't remember, Philip. And even if I did, I couldn't tell you."

"What!" Philip exclaimed.

"I said, I'd help you. I never said I'd give you the formula—"

"B-b-b . . . but you swore," Philip stammered.

"I swore I wouldn't tell Mr. Benton that you abducted me—a big concession on my part."

"But—"

"And I swore to help you. I will help you. But I will not give you Cola Gold's formula!"

A buzz came over the intercom. The secretary said, "Mr. Benton's limo has just pulled up, Mr. P."

The bald man began to sweat. Out came the kerchief. Feinermann noticed it was a new one—white linen, starched and ironed. Philip said,

"So help me God, if I hadn't asked Mr. Benton to come personally, I'd tear you limb from limb."

"Not a smart idea, Philip. And against religious law as well."

"Banquet in my honor! This was just a ruse, wasn't it!"

"It worked for Queen Esther—"

"Shut up!"

"Are you going to let me help you or are you going to sit there like a lump and sweat like a pig?"

Philip glared at him. For the first time, he realized he was working with a formidable opponent. "Just what do I tell Mr. Benton?"

Feinermann held up his hand. "You let me handle your Mr. Benton." He stood. "First, we will eat."

The meal started with cabbage soup. The main course was boiled chicken with vegetables, kasha and farfel stuffing, and a salad of chopped onions, tomatoes, and cucumbers. Dessert consisted of apple strudel, tea, and coffee.

Philip thought the food dreadful. He could see he wasn't alone. Elvis and his plant-brained friend had hardly touched their plates. Yet Mr. Benton ate as heartily as the rabbi. It appeared that both men had been fasting.

Feinermann wiped his mouth with satisfaction while studying the faces of the men who had abducted him, who were introduced to Benton as chauffeurs. Elvis and Donnie were in their thirties, both had bad skin and little ponytails. Without the masks and the guns, they were not impressive as thugs. But Philip had gotten them for free. You buy cheap, you get cheap. The old man also noticed that the food was not to their liking. He expected that. He also noticed that Benton had cleaned his plate.

So everything was going according to plan.

The rabbi asked for a moment to say grace after meals. While he gave benedictions to the Almighty, he sneaked side-long glances at the great industrialist/philanthropist.

Patrick Benton had been a tall man in his youth. From the film, Feinermann remembered a strapping man of thirty whose frame easily topped those around him. But now with the hunched shoulders and the curved spine, he didn't seem so tall. His eyes were watery blue, his skin as translucent as tracing paper. What was left of his hair was white. The rabbi noted with pride most of his own hair was still brown.

Finishing up the last of his prayers, Feinermann sat with his hands folded and smiled at Benton. KingCola's CEO smiled back.

"I don't know when I've eaten such tasty nostalgic food. All these exclusive restaurants I go to, where everyone knows my name and kisses my keyster." He waved his hand in the air. "Food that doesn't look like food and the portions aren't big enough to feed a flea. Damn fine grub, Feinermann." He turned to his assistant. "Philip, make a note of where the chow came from. This is the kind of cooking I like."

The bald man quickly pulled out a notepad and began to scribble.

"So," Benton hurrumphed. "I understand you have a way to help out KingCola. Philip was sketchy with the details. Give me your ideas, Rabbi."

"Mr. Benton, first I want to say what an honor it is to meet you, even though this was not my idea."

Philip turned pale.

"Not your idea?" Benton questioned.

"Not at all," the rabbi said. "I'll be honest. I didn't know you from any of the other philanthropists with names on buildings until Philip here convinced me to come and meet you. Even so, I wasn't so crazy about the prospect. His idea of help and my idea of help weren't exactly the same thing."

Benton looked intrigued. "How so?"

"You see, Mr. Benton, I worked with Cola Gold in a very tangential way. Even so, it was necessary for me to learn the formula of their new line of Cola—"

"Good God, Rabbi! You know the formula? That would be worth millions to me!"

"I take it you'd pass a few million to me in the process. But that's not the point. I can't give you the formula. That would be unethical."

Benton sat back in his seat. "Yes, of course." He ran his hand through thin strands of white hair. "However, there's nothing unethical about you making suggestions for additives in our competing brand of new generation cola."

"The problem is, Mr. Benton, I don't know anything about new generations—period. I am from an old generation."

"What I mean, Rabbi, is—"

"I know what you mean, Mr. Benton. You want me to suggest ingredients, some of which might be in Cola Gold's formula. With all due respect, that isn't the way I was brought up to do business."

Benton turned to Philip. "So this is why you interrupted me at the clubhouse?"

"Hold on, Mr. Benton," Feinermann said. "Don't be so rude to Philip. The man is not my best friend, but he does have your interest at heart. I don't have any suggestions for your new generation drinks. But I have a lot of suggestions with your old generation drinks."

"What old generation drinks?" Benton asked.

"That's the problem," the rabbi said. "There are none. Mr. Benton, I watched your life story, many, many times. Not my doing, but be that as it may, I feel I know you quite well. We have a lot in common. We both had immigrant parents, grew up dirt poor in New York, the first generation of Americans in our family. We were the dreams and hopes of our parents who sacrificed everything so we could have it a little better, nu? We lived through the Depression, fought in World War II, gritted our teeth as our hippy children lived through the sixties. And now, in the waning years of our lives, we sit with a sense of pride in our lives and maybe bask a little in our grandchildren. Am I not correct?"

Benton stared at Feinermann. "Exactly!"

Elvis/Groucho said, "You are a very wise man, Rabbi."

Benton looked at the "chauffeurs." "Who are these jokers, Philip?"

The bald man blushed. Feinermann said, "They are my guests." He turned to his abductors.

"Gentlemen, please. We are having a very important discussion."

Elvis/Groucho apologized and looked very humble.

Benton said, "Actually, I do see you as a man with vision! Philip, hire this man on as a consultant. Start him at—"

"Wait, wait," Feinermann interjected. "Thank you for the offer, but I already have a job. And I'm not so wise. How do I know how you feel? Because we're from the same generation. I saw your mother, Mr. Benton. She looked like my mother. She probably knocked herself out chopping meat by hand and scrubbing floors with a sponge."

"Her hands were as rough as sandpaper, poor woman."

"And I bet she always had a pitcher of iced tea in the ice box when you came home from school. Maybe some *shpritz* from a bottle with the cee-oh-two pellets?"

Benton smiled. "You've got that one down."

"No cans of cola in her refrigerator."

"Just where is all this leading?" Philip asked.

"Shut up!" Benton replied. "We're reminiscing."

Again, Feinermann wiped his mouth. "I'll tell you where this is leading, Philip. Pay attention because it has to do with this business."

The bald man wiped his forehead. "I'm listening."

Feinermann said, "You have a multi-billion dollar business that provides beverages to America. And all of your products are aimed at the young or the ones who wish they were young. Not that I have anything against the new generation, but I can't relate to them. And I don't drink the same things they drink. I want my glass of tea with a lemon. I want my old-fashioned *shpritz* without essences of this flavor or that flavor. What ever happened to tonic water and ginger ale for goodness sakes?"

"We have ginger ale," Philip protested. "King Ginger."

"Ach!" The rabbi gave him a disgusted look. "Relegated to the back of the cooler. The young people think it's a drink for stomach maladies."

"You have to realize that New Age drinks comprise a measly $327 million of market sales," Philip said. "Ginger ale's a drink with no appeal."

"It appeals to me," Feinermann insisted.

"The rabbi's got a point," Benton said. "The New Age drinks do appeal to the older set. And let's not forget the growth rate, Philip—15 percent, as compared to 2 percent in the industry as a whole."

"There you go," Feinermann stated. "When are you companies going to wake up and realize there is a whole generation out there waiting for you to appeal to them?" He turned to Benton. "You gobbled up dinner tonight because it reminded you of your mother's cooking."

Benton bit his lip. "I see what you're saying. But Rabbi, you have to realize that carbonated beverages is still a youth-oriented market."

"Because you choose to woo the youth. What about me?"

"The elderly market is tricky," Benton said.

"Even if you convert them to your product, they're just going to keel over anyway," Philip said.

Benton glared at his assistant. "I beg your pardon."

"No . . . I mean . . . not you, Mr. Benton—"

"Calm down, Philip," Feinermann said with little patience. "Yes, we're all going to die. Even your Mr. Benton here. But I see your point. So don't market the old-fashioned drinks as a drink solely for the elderly. Make them family drinks. Seltzer, tonic water, ginger ale. Promote them as new lighter, less sugary drinks, with a history of America. Show teenagers and grandfathers drinking them at the family barbecues. What could be better? And then there's the health food angle. Lighter, clearer beverages are easier on the stomach. We all know that."

Philip said, "I've got the hook, sir—a 'New Age' drink with a touch of nostalgia."

"I like it, Philip," Benton said.

"And what about iced teas?" Feinermann said.

Philip said, "Only a $400 million share of the market."

Feinermann said, "But combine it with your $327 million New Age share, Philip. That's almost a billion dollars."

"Man's got a point, Philip."

"Tenser's has a lock on tea, sir," Philip said. "Besides, I heard Heavenly Brew is coming out with a new line. Lots of teas for such a little market share."

"Ah, Heavenly Brew. That's not tea. Not tea the way Mr. Benton and I remember it."

Benton nodded. "True. We had tea that ratted the guts. How about a new full-flavored tea drink, Philip?"

Philip thought—or pretended to. "It just might work, sir, especially if we get a decaf version."

Feinermann said, "We're a lost generation, Mr. Benton, just waiting for someone to sing our tunes. Stop regurgitating old cola recipes and expand your horizons."

Benton exclaimed, "Glad you brought all this to my attention, Rabbi. Philip, make a note to bring all this crap to the board's attention this Thursday. And, Rabbi, you will join us at the meeting, won't you?"

"Thursday, I have a funeral to preside over. I'm afraid I must pass."

"Then next Thursday?" Benton tried.

"No, I don't think so. I've stated my piece. Perhaps now, your Philip will leave me in peace?"

"Absolutely! Philip, stop pestering the rabbi." Philip nodded like a kewpie doll.

Feinermann stood. "If you don't mind, I'd like to take my leave."

"Certainly, rabbi," Benton responded. "And anytime you need anything, just ask."

"Thank you, Mr. Benton." The old man shook hands with the philanthropist and bade him good-bye. As he was accompanied back to the car, walking in the cool March air, he reflected on how much he missed his childhood. Not the part about being beaten up by Tommy Hoolihan and he didn't miss the cholera and polio, either. But he did miss his youth—a generation that grew up without TV. And that had a good glass of ginger ale. Corporations do forget about the elderly—a reflection of society, he supposed.

Ah well, at least he'd sleep in his own bed tonight.

When they arrived at the Cadillac, Feinermann said to Philip, "You don't have to come back with me. The Marxes know the way."

"The Marxes?" Philip said.

"Private joke, Mr. P," Donnie/Karl said.

Philip shook hands with the rabbi. "I'm sorry if I inconvenienced you."

"No problem," Feinermann said. "I'll integrate the experience into next week's sermon." He opened the door to the back seat. "By the way, Marxes, what did you do with the face masks?"

"They're in the trunk," Elvis/Groucho said. "Why?"

"Unless you're planning another abduction, give them to me," Feinermann said. "I'll use them in the Purim festivities! Why let them go to waste?"

RONALD LEVITSKY has written four mystery novels featuring the civil liberties lawyer Nate Rosen. Here Nate faces a challenge that is not a First Amendment controversy like the ones he has seen in the novels. When he is not writing mysteries, Ronald Levitsky teaches social studies at a junior high school in Northfield, Illinois.

Jacob's Voice

▼   ▼   ▼   ▼   ▼   ▼   ▼

RONALD LEVITSKY

"TELL ME, ROSEN, DO YOU BELIEVE IN GHOSTS?"

The words hung as heavy in the air as the smoke from Max Samuels' cigar. The question, which would have sounded foolish if spoken anywhere else among the glass and metal cubicles that occupied the building's top floor, resonated within Samuels' private office. Between the two men, an old walnut desk with a glass top contained a brass lamp, a humidor, and a pile of papers stuck on a spindle. Along the walls, dozens of books, many in worn leather bindings, were encased in cabinets with glass doors.

Behind the desk, where Samuels sat, the window was open a crack, and Rosen felt a little of what made Chicago the windy city. But instead of fresh air, he smelled the mustiness of old parchment, as he gazed at the faces on the wall. Photos of men in black suits and women wearing babushkas and long dresses. Faces of the *shtetl*, cut from stone that hadn't weathered over time.

Max Samuels had such a face. Broad with dark predator eyes, a wide nose, and iron gray hair combed straight back, it had the "fearful symmetry" of William Blake's tiger. In his late sixties, Samuels was a big man, but his yellowish skin, loose around the neck, suggested that he'd once been even bigger and stronger.

"Well, do you?" Samuels' voice was hoarse and tinged with a Yiddish accent.

Rosen shrugged. "You mean something in a white sheet rattling chains?"

148

"I mean something not from flesh, yet of the flesh. Something from the blood that speaks the truth, that chills the soul."

Samuels' eyes burned behind the smoke. They seemed like those of a prophet. Or of a madman.

Rosen cleared his throat. "You wanted to see me on a legal matter?"

"It's about my niece, Judith Arens. Her husband has taken her to court. He wants guardianship of her business."

"On what grounds?"

"He says she's crazy. Claims she tried to kill him."

"'Claims'? You think he's lying?"

"He's a *mamzer*—no good from the day she met him. The hearing's next Wednesday. A week's not much time to prepare, so you'll have to work fast."

"I'm a civil liberties attorney. What you're talking about is an adjudication of disability, which isn't my expertise. That's probate."

"I had a probate lawyer do all the preliminary work. I want you for the hearing."

"Why?"

Samuels' eyes narrowed. "Do you know what a *dybbuk* is?"

Rosen hadn't heard that word since he was a little boy. It belonged to people long since dead, like those whose photographs hung from Samuels' wall. "It's an evil spirit that enters the body of a living person."

"Not only an evil spirit. It can be the soul of a dead person that has yet to enter heaven."

"What does this have to do with your niece?"

"Judith has been possessed by a *dybbuk*. I want you to defend her on that basis."

"I don't understand."

"Then you're not much of a lawyer."

"You want me to take this case as a First Amendment issue? That the *dybbuk* is real and part of her religious belief?"

"That's right."

"How can your niece believe something like that?"

Samuels broke into a coughing jab, his face growing pale. After swallowing a pill, he held still a few seconds, then snubbed out his cigar in an ashtray.

Rosen asked, "You all right?"

The old man waved away Rosen's concern. "If you want to know how Judith can believe this, you have to understand my family. We got out of

Poland just before the war. My father studied Talmud all his life. Even a little *kabbala*. Judith first heard about *dybbukim* in the bedtime stories he
told her."

"Your family was devout?"

"Yes. God always came first, then work. My younger brother Harry and
I sold auto parts out of broken crates on Maxwell Street. We both had a
good head for business. We eventually went into selling used cars and buying up buildings.

"In the late Fifties, we split the business. Harry took over the car dealerships, and I got the real estate. Harry and his wife had two children, Jacob
and Judith. Both parents died a few years ago in a car accident. Harry was . . .

"What?"

Samuels shook his head. "Afterwards, I watched over my niece and
nephew as best I could. Never got married myself.

"My niece and nephew were very close. They even made up their own
play language of Yiddish and English. Kind of a secret world. Later, Jacob
got pretty wild—ran through his share of the inheritance and didn't get
along with Judith's husband, who managed the car dealerships. Couldn't
hold a job, so I took the kid into my business. Kid—he was thirty-six."
Samuels' voice softened. "I was just trying to help."

"What happened?"

"I was angry with Jacob because he hadn't taken care of his accounts, so
I sent him to the West Side to collect some back rent. It was a dangerous
neighborhood. I should have known better."

Samuels leaned forward, his elbows on the desk, and rocked back and
forth as if in prayer. "Some punks killed him. Eight times they stabbed him.
For what? The $85 in his wallet? For being the landlord's nephew? For me
being stupid enough to send him down there alone."

Rosen waited, until the old man leaned back heavily in his chair, then
asked, "When was this?"

"About a year ago. Now Judith has only me to turn to. She hasn't been
too strong. Her children—she has a boy and a girl—they're away at school,
thank God."

"What about her husband?"

"Mickey Arens married Judith out of high school. He was one of those
fast talkers with slick hair and a smile to match. My brother took him into the
car business. Three dealerships. When Harry died, Mickey became manager. Only now, that's not enough. Everything's in Judith's name, and he

wants it all. He complains about the money she gives to charity, but I bet that *gonif* is stealing her blind."

"Do you have any evidence of that?"

"In my business dealings, I come across my share of gamblers, con men, and thieves. I can smell them. Mickey Arens stinks the worst of all. Why do you think he's so eager to take control of the dealerships? He wants to sell them, take the money, and run all the way to Vegas. Judith won't agree to sell. That's what it's all about. He's a *gonif* all right."

"But if your niece tried to kill him—"

"Judith didn't do anything. It was the *dybbuk*."

Rosen was about to speak, then hesitated. He should simply have said "no" and walked out. The longer he stayed, the more he gave credence to this crazy talk.

Something made him stay, something made him ask, "Who is this *dybbuk* supposed to be?"

"Her brother Jacob."

It was ridiculous, yet the look on Samuels' face was one of belief. The kind of belief shown by those who studied the Torah so deeply, they forgot to eat and sleep.

Rosen asked, "Has Judith had a psychiatric evaluation?"

"When Mickey brought suit, the court appointed a shrink to examine her."

"The guardian *ad litem*."

"That's right. He said Judith couldn't be responsible for making business decisions. He determined that from talking to her two times. The quack."

"We have a right to have our own psychiatrist examine her."

Samuels tapped his fingers on the humidor. "After her brother died, Judith went into a deep depression. A psychiatrist named Gilliam helped her. She's continued to see him. I've arranged for you to meet them both tomorrow afternoon. Judith lives in Highland Park, not far from Michael Jordan's house."

"I still don't think I'm the right person to represent your niece."

Samuels scribbled the address on a slip of paper, which he handed to Rosen. "I don't want some hot shot probate or litigation lawyer. I want somebody who believes in Judith as much as I do."

"And you think I will?"

"I got your name from your ex-wife's husband, Shelly Gold. He told me about your upbringing—that you were a yeshiva boy. A real Talmud-Torah man."

"That was a long time ago. I'm not like that anymore."

Walking to the window, Samuels pushed up the sash. The cold November wind rushed in.

"When I bought this building, a maintenance man told me all the windows had to be sealed for the heating and air conditioning to work properly. I took a hammer and smashed the glass in this window, put in a new frame that slid up and down." He breathed deeply. "Sealing a building is like trying to keep out God. Fresh air, wind, rain. That's God. The *goyim* think of Jesus as love and forgiveness. Some Jews think of God that way too, but we know better.

"Our God calls for justice, no matter what the cost. As it says in Genesis, '. . . life for life, eye for eye, tooth for tooth, hand for hand, foot for foot, burn for burn, wound for wound, bruise for bruise.' Sometimes God's justice is beyond our understanding, but it's justice all the same. For God came out of the whirlwind, told Job to gird his loins like a man, and take it. 'Have you an arm like God's?'"

Rosen heard himself reply, "'Can you thunder with a voice like His?'"

Samuels' eyes widened. "So you do understand."

The next afternoon Rosen drove north from Chicago to the suburb of Highland Park. He hadn't had much sleep the night before. He'd kept thinking about the three old widows, refugees from Lithuania, who lived in the apartment building where he'd grown up. Many afternoons, they would sit in his kitchen, with him on his mother's lap, and tell in Yiddish the same stories that, as little girls, they'd heard from old women. Stories far older than the oldest woman could remember and, therefore, true.

Stories like that of the strangled thief whose soul, cursed by thousands of other condemned souls, wandered the earth and entered first a doe, then a righteous man, and finally a woman who had called out angrily to the devil. A tormented soul—a *dybbuk*.

So long ago, yet still from time to time, over the years, came the nightmare of a lost soul calling him. A soul that resembled a little boy. Why had he taken the case? Did he want the nightmare to end? Or did he want to know what the lost soul was saying?

Judith Arens' estate was located a few blocks from Lake Michigan and was set back from the street by a wide expanse of lawn, where ancient black oak raised their barren branches as if trying to frighten him. Like the three old women who had sat at his mother's table.

Two cars were parked in the circular driveway—a white Lexus and an older green Lincoln Continental, chipped and mottled with rust.

Rosen pressed the door bell, which sounded like chimes. The housekeeper led him through a long hallway into the living room, which opened two stories to a crystal chandelier. Light gleamed from the hardwood floors. In the center of the room, on a blue and gold Persian rug, a white leather sectional and matching chairs were arranged around an ornately carved coffee table.

Two other men were in the room. One, who walked toward Rosen, wore a Chicago Bears tee shirt, jeans, and sandals. About forty, he was medium height with a racquetball player's body—broad shoulders, large forearms, and the beginning of a belly.

The man shook Rosen's hand. He wore a cologne surprisingly delicate for his rugged frame. "I'm Judith's husband, Mickey Arens."

"I'm Nate Rosen. I'll be representing—"

"Yeah, Judith's new lawyer. This is her shrink, Dr. Gilliam."

The psychiatrist nodded from one of chairs. In his mid-fifties—tall, thin, and wearing wire-rimmed glasses—he had the long serious face of a corporation executive. But his silk tie had faded, and the elbows of his gray suit coat were shiny.

"Sit down, Rosen," Arens said, returning to the couch. "Not that you're gonna be here long. Judith ain't here."

"We had an appointment," Gilliam said. His voice had a soft, soothing quality, like water lapping over sand.

"Well, she stood the both of you up. But, then, that's Judith."

Rosen said, "Mr. Arens, you seem pretty calm for a man who claims his wife tried to kill him."

"It happened all right."

"Why haven't you had her arrested?"

"What kind of schmuck do you think I am? I sell cars. What's the public's perception of car dealers?"

"I suppose about the same as it is of politicians."

"Right. All I need is to let everybody in Chicago know my wife tried to kill me. That'd really be good for business. Besides, I've got two kids to protect."

"But you are taking her to court."

"A nice quiet disability hearing. Judith would continue to get the help she needs but, in the meantime, couldn't screw up the company."

Rosen said, "Tell me about the alleged attack."

"Alleged, my ass. I walked out of my room at two A.M. She was standing in the hall, and she went at me with a knife."

"You and your wife sleep separately?"

"She sleeps in one of the kids' rooms. No secret our marriage ain't so good. I wish it could be better, but a wife trying to cut your heart out kind of kills the romance. Of course, now I keep my door locked."

"You say she attacked you at two in the morning. Why did you go out in the hall that late at night?"

"I heard something ringing. At first I thought it was my alarm. Maybe it was the doorbell or one of the kids' phones or maybe just my imagination. When I got in the hall, Judith was just coming out of her room. I thought she was sleepwalking, but when I went to stop her, she went at me. I got the knife away—that snapped her out of it. Scared the hell out of me, but worse . . . that voice."

Rosen asked, "What voice?"

"Not her voice. It was deeper and the wise ass way it spoke. I'd swear it was her dead brother Jake."

From somewhere in the house, the telephone rang. Rosen almost jumped. Sweat formed under his collar. "Do you believe your wife could be possessed by a *dybbuk*?"

"When her head starts spinning around, maybe I'll believe. Until then, I think she's just freaking nuts."

A young woman walked into the room. Dressed in a white turtleneck, gray blazer, and matching skirt, she gave the no-nonsense appearance of a serious young businesswoman. She sat beside Arens. Her hair was honey blond, and her eyes were blue steel. Her square jaw made her less than beautiful, but stronger and somehow even more desirable.

Arens said, "Kathy, this is Judith's new lawyer. Rosen, this is my business manager, Katherine Ericson."

She nodded. "Mickey, that was your wife on the phone. She's at the synagogue."

"Didn't she remember her appointment with these guys?"

"Some sort of emergency with a benefit she's working on."

"Another benefit. I don't mind a little charity—it's a good tax write-off. But it's giving away the store."

Rosen said, "I understand you two have a difference of opinion regarding the future of your business."

"What the hell does that mean?"

"You want to sell it, and she won't let you."

"She wouldn't know a good deal if it smacked her in the face. In fact, I ought to—"

"Mickey," Ericson said, "we have that report to finish, and I'm sure these gentlemen have busy schedules as well."

As they stood, Dr. Gilliam said to Arens, "I'm afraid I'll have to bill your wife for this appointment."

"Yeah, well that's her problem."

"Perhaps you could advance me the cost of the session."

"Hell, no. If you stayed away from the ponies, maybe you wouldn't need—" Arens suddenly stopped, as Ericson gave a slight shake of her head.

Rosen said, "Perhaps I could see your wife at the synagogue."

"Why not. Go east to the lake, then two blocks north. You can't miss it."

Ericson opened the door for the two men. Dr. Gilliam looked miserable as he passed.

Rosen said, "Tell me, Miss Ericson, what's your read on this? Do you think Judith Arens is possessed or psychologically disturbed?"

"Neither. I think Judith is faking."

"Why?"

"So she can kill Mickey and plead insanity. That's one way of getting away with murder, isn't it?"

"Why would Mrs. Arens want to do that?"

She smiled, as if that was the stupidest question on earth.

Rosen asked, "That Lexus in the driveway—yours?"

"Mickey's a very generous employer. It was nice meeting you."

When Rosen took her hand, he inhaled a delicate fragrance. He'd been wrong. The cologne hadn't been Arens'.

Dr. Gilliam was already in his car. Rosen knocked on the window, which the psychiatrist rolled down.

Rosen asked, "Are you going to the synagogue?"

"No, I'll have to reschedule with Judith."

"Isn't it a little strange to have a session in your client's home as opposed to your office?"

"I'm . . . uh . . . between offices at the moment. Mrs. Arens has a room that is quite private. I'll send my report to you tomorrow."

"How about a quick overview now?"

Gilliam drummed his fingers on the dashboard, as if he wanted to get away from the house as quickly as possible. "It's complex."

"Hasn't Mrs. Arens given permission for you to speak to me?"

"Very well. You know I've seen Judith before, when her brother was killed. I've come to believe that she suffers from dissociative behavior characterized by multiple personalities."

"So she's imagining this *dybbuk*?"

"It's actually an independent, alternate personality. Under extreme stress, often occurring during early childhood, a person may create a new personality completely cut off from the victimization she suffered."

"Judith Arens was a victim? Of what?"

"I don't know yet. I sense that the relationship between Judith and her late father was not good, and that she formed a very close relationship with her brother."

"Her uncle said they even had their own secret language. In other words, you're saying they were so close that she couldn't accept Jacob's death, so she recreated him in her mind?"

"Perhaps. There may be other possibilities."

"Such as?"

"That Judith feels responsible for Jacob's death and therefore will not let him go. I've learned a great deal about their relationship, not so much from her, but by talking to the personality representing her brother. Of course, there's still—"

"Wait—you've actually talked to Jacob? How?"

"I've put Judith under hypnosis. Multiples are excellent hypnotic subjects. That's how Jacob and I met. After two more sessions, I simply said to Judith, 'May I speak with Jacob?' She'd close her eyes, and a moment later he would appear."

"Mickey Arens said that Judith sounded just like her brother when she tried to stab him. Could he be telling the truth?"

"It's possible. Now, I really must be going."

As the psychiatrist drove away, Rosen shook his head. On the one hand, he felt better hearing a scientific explanation for Judith's behavior. On the other, he had enough problems dealing with one client, let alone two occupying the same body.

The synagogue was a modern building of brick and glass, with two sections of the roof swept back to resemble wings. Inside, the wide entrance hall was painted white with dark oak trim. Two metal sculptures hung opposite each other—a menorah and Moses holding the Ten Commandments. The area resembled an art gallery. Not like the house of worship of Rosen's youth, a small dark room crowded with the heavy smells of books and bodies, the men and boys deep in prayer with the breath of God on the back of their necks.

Rosen walked down a long corridor toward the sounds of voices. A multipurpose room was crowded like a flea market, with rows of tables where women filled boxes with canned goods and clothing. Most women, on the younger side of forty, dressed smartly, but several older ones, speaking Yiddish, wore long shapeless dresses and babushkas.

A tall redhead in a green jogging suit asked, "May I help you?"

"I'm looking for Judith Arens."

She pointed to a door at the far end. "Judith's in the next room doing the addresses."

He walked into the room, where a young woman, surrounded by an island of boxes, was talking on the phone. Hanging up the receiver, she turned as he approached. Judith Arens was beautiful like a porcelain statue, her complexion, even whiter, framed by jet black hair. Her delicate nose and lips seemed to have been sketched by an artist's brush. Energy burned in her dark eyes.

"Mrs. Arens, I'm your new attorney, Nate Rosen. Your uncle asked me to help you get ready for the hearing."

"We don't need help." Her voice was almost a whisper.

"We?"

She smiled but said nothing.

"Is it true you believe you've been possessed by a *dybbuk*?"

"A *dybbuk* is an evil soul. My brother Jacob wasn't evil."

"But your uncle—"

"You wouldn't understand."

"Try me."

"You wouldn't . . . all right. Do you know what the Hebrew term *ibbur* means?"

"To make pregnant. But you don't mean a normal pregnancy. You're talking about a soul entering another person."

Head cocked, she stared at him. "That's right. The *ibbur* of a good man's soul into the body of another. There are 613 commandments to fulfill on this earth. If during his life, a good man fulfilled all but one, his soul can enter someone else to complete that last commandment."

Rosen remembered hearing the story when he was a boy in yeshiva. But nobody believed that really. Not here in America.

He asked, "How can you be sure it's your brother, Jacob?"

"I know my brother."

"Which commandment is your brother to fulfill through you?"

She shook her head. "I don't know. Jacob won't tell me."

"As I remember, a soul entering another's body happens at random. It never possesses the body of a relative."

"Who can fathom the will of God?"

"Was it God's will that you almost stabbed your husband?"

"Mickey thinks I spend too much money on charity. He doesn't understand that *tzedaka* is a commandment. He wants to see me as crazy. You believe me though. Don't you?"

A simple question, spoken with a child's innocence. Yet the one question he had spent most of his life avoiding. And now, what could he say—that in his soul remained one small corner of belief?

"I want to help," he answered.

Her smile was small, almost mocking.

Rosen said, "You know that Dr. Gilliam considers you a multiple. Don't you think maybe he's right? That what you need is therapy to see this so-called *ibbur* for what it really is?"

"No!" She stamped her foot, again like a child.

He was afraid of agitating her but had to continue. There wasn't much time until the hearing.

"Your uncle wants me to argue your case on the First Amendment. Don't you see how dangerous a freedom of religion defense is? Believing you're possessed sounds crazy to most people."

"I don't care."

"Won't you drop this idea of *ibbur*?"

Judith's cheeks reddened. "No, I won't lie! I won't abandon my brother! I won't!"

Two older women, jabbering in Yiddish, carried a heavy box into the room. As Rosen helped them lift it on top of several others, the telephone rang. He watched the women leave, still kibbitzing, while the phone kept ringing.

When he turned, Judith stared at him, her arms crossed and feet spread apart like a man.

"Get out of the way," Judith said. Only the voice wasn't Judith's. It was lower, more forceful, and came from somewhere deep inside her.

Rosen couldn't break her gaze. "Who are you?"

"You know who I am."

"Jacob."

A short hard laugh. "Yes, Jacob. Now get out of my way."

Rosen lay his hand on a box to steady himself. It was one thing to hear stories of a *dybbuk*. One thing to be frightened by them as a child. Easy to be frightened as a child. But Rosen was no longer a child, and it was no longer just a story. It was something real, as Samuels had said, "not from flesh, yet of the flesh." Something he could reach out and touch.

He asked, "Why can't you stay and talk?"

"I have something to do."

"Which commandment do you need to fulfill?"

A shake of the head. "Judith doesn't know. Only I know."

"What is it?"

"A secret."

"You want to hurt Mickey. Why? What's he done to Judith?"

"This isn't about her. It's about me."

"You know there's going to be a disability hearing. Judith could lose control of your father's business."

"You speak of man's law. No, this will be settled in God's house."

"'God's house.' I don't understand."

"I don't expect you to. Now get out of my way!"

When Rosen grabbed Judith, the fist that struck his jaw was a man's, and when Rosen struck back, it was as if he'd hit a man.

Falling to the floor, Judith wiped the blood disdainfully from her lower lip and said in that cold voice of a stranger, "Get out of my way, or I'll kill you too."

Rosen leaned against the podium, but standing before the judge felt as unreal as when he'd met Jacob. Four days had passed, yet still he trembled remembering how they had continued to struggle for several minutes, until Judith suddenly snapped out of it. After trying unsuccessfully to locate Dr. Gilliam, he'd called Max Samuels, who took Judith home. She'd been silent—strangely calm, as if unaware of her "brother's" actions.

She told Rosen nothing, nor did he learn anything more from the guardian *ad litem*'s report or that of Dr. Gilliam. Both dealt with psychiatry, a mundane science that addressed what ordinary people regarded as normalcy. Even his cross-examination of Mickey Arens, which showed Judith's husband as a greedy businessman and more than hinted at an affair with Katherine Ericson, was meaningless in the context of what he had been ordered to do. As was, at that moment, cross-examining Dr. Moretti, the guardian *ad litem*.

Dr. Moretti said, "Mrs. Arens' behavior indicates that she lacks the ability to manage her financial affairs. As for the possibility that she is a multiple, certainly further examination is needed."

"You misunderstand me," Rosen replied. "I don't object to your calling Judith Arens a multiple—from a medical standpoint."

"What other standpoint is there?"

"Suppose you were asked to examine a man who claimed to have seen God sitting on a throne surrounded by angels. That because the man was unclean beholding God, an angel burned his tongue with a hot coal. Would you diagnose him as mentally ill?"

"I'd have to speak with him, but I think it safe to say that I would have concerns regarding his view of reality."

"Doctor, the man I'm speaking about was Isaiah, one of the great Hebrew prophets. 'I saw the Lord sitting upon a throne, high and lifted up; and His train filled the temple.' Was Isaiah mentally ill?"

"I don't understand your point."

"Or if a man suddenly abandoned wealth, social position, a beautiful wife and baby, because he had an overpowering sense of unhappiness. Finding a great truth, he spent the rest of his years in abject poverty, wandering the countryside to spread that truth. That, of course, was Buddha. Was he insane?"

Arens' attorney said, "This is ridiculous."

The judge asked, "Mr. Rosen, do you consider this adjudication of disability a freedom of religion issue?"

"Yes, your Honor. The joining of Jacob Samuels' soul with his sister is a recognized religious experience by those who believe in Jewish mysticism."

Arens' attorney repeated, "That's ridiculous!"

"Would you say the same about those Catholics who go to Lourdes to be cured of cancer?"

"Your Honor!"

"No more questions."

When the judge recessed for lunch, Rosen remained in his seat. All around him were snatches of conversations, indistinct mutterings, soft seductive murmurs. Were the folk tales of his people true? Were there really millions of lost souls, cursed for their wickedness, who wandered the earth looking for the shelter of an unsuspecting body?

He was trembling as when, a young boy years before, the three old crones had frightened him with their *shtetl* tales. And like a young boy, he had to be led from court by the firm hand of Max Samuels.

He sat in the cafeteria with Samuels and Judith, a few tables from Mickey Arens and Katherine Ericson. He barely touched his lunch. Samuels sipped hot tea from a glass, another old custom that once again pulled Rosen back to his childhood.

"You did well," the old man said.

"Did I?" It wouldn't do any good, but he had to try once more. "This is a civil action, not a rabbinical court. If you insist on treating this as a religious issue, we'll lose."

Samuels said, "You forget why I chose you."

Rosen wished the two of them would just disappear, or that he had never met them. What did they really want from him?

Samuels said, "I'm going for more tea."

As the old man left the table, Rosen turned to Judith. The toast on her plate had been nibbled around the edges like a mouse might have done. She seemed so vulnerable, but at the synagogue she'd struggled with him as strong as a man, and that voice. Jacob's voice. Realizing Rosen wouldn't let go, Jacob had retreated back inside Judith, yet remained just behind her eyes.

Rosen stared at her. Whose eyes was he seeing?

He asked, "Are you sure about this?"

She seemed not to hear.

"Judith?"

He touched her arm. She blinked, then looked into his face.

"Judith, do you want me to speak in court about *ibbur*?"

"Oh yes."

"Even though it might jeopardize winning the case?"

"Is winning the case so important?"

"If it means so little to you, why fight your husband?"

"Fighting seems to be the only thing the two of us can do together."

"You're not very happy, are you?"

She stared at her plate. "I suppose not. I don't know if I've ever been really happy."

"It must have been tough losing both your parents in a car accident. Your uncle must have been very close to your father to—"

"I don't want to talk about my father," she said, shivering.

"Sorry. I didn't mean to upset you."

After a few seconds, she said, "It's all right. You were asking about my husband."

"Yes."

"It wasn't always so bad between Mickey and me. It was fun for a little while at least."

"What happened?"

"His idea of fun usually meant being involved with more than one woman at a time. I didn't mind so much, at least when Jacob was around. We were always so close. I know he was stubborn with other people—he and Mickey never got along, but he could always make me laugh, as far back as I can remember."

Judith closed her eyes for a moment, and in that same instance Rosen panicked, thinking that Jacob might return. But she smiled and said, "You're a strange man, Nate."

"Me? Why do you think that?"

"Well, you say you don't believe in anything I say, yet you know about *ibbur* and *dybbuk*."

"I told you, that was a long time ago."

"You're not so old. It can't be that long ago. What happened—if you don't mind me asking?"

He shrugged. It was an old scar he'd gotten used to showing. "There's not much to tell. I was raised according to Halakhah."

"God's law."

"So I thought, but it was my father who administered the law, and he was a hard man."

"In what way? Did he . . . ?"

"Hit me? No, never. But it was his words that cut like flint, or the look in his eyes. No joy, and whatever love he had was hidden away deeper than kabbalah."

Judith put her hand over his. "That's not all."

"What do you mean?"

"You took the case, and you spoke so beautifully this morning."

"That's what a lawyer does." He felt ashamed but still did not draw his hand away.

"You didn't speak as a lawyer. You love God as much as I do. That's why you fight it so much."

"I . . ."

He had to get away from her. He had to think—no, not think. He didn't know what he wanted.

Samuels returned to the table. The old man sat down heavily, the glass of tea nearly hidden in his hand. "You all right, Rosen?"

He felt flushed, his head pounding. Swallowing hard, he managed to reply, "I'm fine. Maybe . . . maybe I'll step outside for a few minutes to get some fresh air."

Someone leaned against him, preventing him from getting up.

"You sounded pretty nutty in court, counselor." Mickey Arens stood over their table. His tie was loose, and he smelled of sweat. "It almost sounded like you believed that crap you were saying."

When Rosen looked away, Arens said to Judith, "It's not too late to stop all this."

"You mean the hearing?"

"I mean everything. You go away for awhile, let them get your head straight, and we can start fresh."

Her face hardening, she nodded toward Arens' table, where Katherine Ericson sat. "How would she feel about that?"

"What does Katherine have to do with this? You don't really think—"

"I don't care about that anymore." She bunched a napkin in her left hand so tightly, the knuckles whitened. "Really, Mickey, I don't care what you do."

"Then why don't you stop all this crap? Jake's dead. Get it through your head, that no good brother of yours—"

"No!"

Her right hand slapped him hard across the face. Rosen tensed, searching Judith's face to see if, once again, Jacob had returned. No—it was a woman who, eyes glassing over with tears, tore the napkin into small pieces.

Rubbing his cheek, Arens glared at Judith. "You bitch. I ought to—"

Samuels said, "You touch her and I'll kill you. You—"

Suddenly the old man began a hacking cough. He pulled out a handkerchief with one hand and a small plastic container with the other. Judith stood over him, holding a glass of water for him to wash down the pill.

Katherine Ericson hurried to the table and took Arens' arm. "Come on, Mickey."

As Samuels labored to regain his breath, Mickey said to his wife, "We'll see you in court. And after I get control of the business, I'm putting you away for a long time. But you won't mind—not with your brother keeping you company."

As the couple walked away, Samuels said hoarsely, "He talks of courts. Fool. Doesn't he understand only God's court is important?"

Judith whispered something so softly, Rosen couldn't understand. Too afraid to lean forward—to even move, he could only wonder for whom the words were spoken. For him, her uncle, or her brother, Jacob?

"J and J Motors North" was one of Judith's car dealerships located in a suburb about ten miles northwest of the Arens home. The dealership was enclosed by a corral fence, and the "J and J" wrought iron sign resembled a rancher's brand. Inside, the salesmen wore ten-gallon hats, and the showroom was decorated with cacti and posters of John Wayne and Clint Eastwood.

"I have an appointment with Mickey Arens," Rosen said.

The salesman lifted a receiver and, after a short conversation, pointed to a hallway behind him. "Go on up. Mr. Arens is expecting you."

On the wall hung several plaques honoring the dealership for community service, sales, and customer satisfaction. A half-dozen photographs chronicled the progress of the business over several decades.

One showed Judith and her brother as young children, standing on either side of a TV announcer in a checkered coat. Judith smiled, a sugar and spice girl of braces, pigtails, and skinny legs. Jacob, however, stood straight and solemn as a palace guard. His eyes stared blankly at the camera.

Rosen walked up the creaking linoleum stairs to a landing, where Katherine Ericson stood in front of an open door. She wore a gray blazer and skirt over a white turtleneck and sheer stockings. Her outfit was cut to show her figure. An ink smudge on her right cheek, like a beauty mark, highlighted her lips, which parted slowly.

"Please come in."

The office was a large rectangular room, with two picture windows in the long wall overlooking the showroom and a smaller window at the far end. Near Rosen stood a metal desk with computer and fax systems. Past them, a set of old red vinyl chairs and matching couch were arranged around a beat-up coffee table.

Shirt sleeves rolled and tie loosened, Mickey Arens sat on the couch studying a ledger. Rosen took a chair, while Ericson sat next to her boss.

Arens looked up, his eyes etched with dark rings and his curly hair limp and matted. "Yeah, Rosen, thanks for coming."

"I should've worn my spurs."

"A lot of conservative Republicans out here—from station wagon mommies to shit-kicking farmers. They go for the cowboy hats and John Wayne posters. Anything to make the customers happy. You want them to keep coming back. That's something Judith's old man never understood. He'd slam a customer into a car, then worry about the next one. Not like that anymore. It's all CSI—customer satisfaction index. The place has got to be *haimish*. Know what I mean?"

He used the Yiddish word for a warm, friendly feeling. Rosen nodded.

"Anyway, this cowboy thing seems to be working. Sales have been picking up. It was Katherine's idea. She's real smart for a college girl."

"Yes. It's really busy downstairs."

"You want to see where we really make our money?"

Rosen followed him behind the couch to the smaller window overlooking the service area. There were fifteen or twenty stations, where a team of mechanics crawled over each car like ants on a dead beetle.

Arens smiled. "We do good work, and everything's clean. You could eat off the floor. *Haimish.* That and a smile and a Christmas card keeps them coming back."

"Is that why you're so anxious to sell the business?"

"You don't know a thing about cars, do you, Rosen?" Both hands on the window, Arens stared down at the service area. "When I was a kid, I used to fool with cars all the time. I had this '70 Mustang—the girls loved it. It was like the back seat was covered with silk sheets. God, those were the days."

He nodded toward the mechanics. "Think those guys worry about anything? They get a steady paycheck, clock out after eight hours, and walk away from the job. Think they worry about cash flow and sales figures? Think they go home and worry about their wife sticking a knife in them? I'm tired of all this crap. I worked hard all my life. Now I want to play."

From behind them, Ericson said, "Mr. Rosen is a busy man. Why don't we discuss why we asked him up here?"

Arens took one last look at the garage, then both men returned to their seats.

Ericson said, "We'd like to discuss Judith. She's—"

"She's freaking crazy," Arens said. "We all know that."

Rosen shook his head. "We've been over all this before."

Ericson continued, "You've seen what Judith is like, when she purports to be possessed by her brother's spirit."

Of course, she would say "purports." Probably Arens liked her to use big words—it was a turn-on. Of course, she believed that Judith was neither possessed nor a multiple, but simply a fake.

Leaning back in the couch, her legs crossed, Ericson looked so sure of herself. What if . . . ?

The thought flitted through Rosen's head too quickly to be understood, but long enough to leave a vague sense of uneasiness. What if?

She said, "We have an offer to make."

"I don't think Judith will consider anything but your withdrawing your petition. Other than that, we'll see you in court."

Arens almost jumped from the couch. "Court! In court you treated me like John freaking Wayne Gacy. No, you're gonna listen now. I don't know what's wrong with you. Seems like you and Judith are on the same wavelength. Know what I mean?"

Rosen felt his face grow warm. "No I don't."

"That religious crap about being possessed. In court you sounded like you actually believed it."

"It's my duty to follow my client's wishes."

"Your duty—don't make me laugh. All you lawyers are whores."

"What does living off your wife's business make you?"

Rosen thought that Arens was about to go for him. That was all right. That was just fine.

But Ericson, grabbing Arens' arm, said, "Gentlemen, can we get to the point? Mickey is willing to allow Judith to commit herself to a residential treatment center. Judith would get the treatment she needs, far more intense than her weekly one-hour session with Dr. Gilliam."

Rosen asked, "And if she refuses?"

"I'm afraid Mickey's decided, after the trial, to have Judith declared a 'disabled person' and seek guardianship."

"And then have her committed."

"Damn right," Arens said.

"Assuming for a moment that Judith would agree to your request, what's to prevent her from checking herself out in a few days?"

Ericson said, "She'd have to agree to at least six months' residency in the facility."

"Of course, she couldn't oversee her company while inside a treatment center."

"We'd settle for a temporary agreement putting Mickey in charge. The agreement would run for at least six months."

"And if, as a condition of her consent, Judith wished to prohibit any outside investment in or sales of J and J Motors?"

"We couldn't agree to any such condition." Ericson uncrossed her legs and smiled. "We all want what's best for the company."

Her smile was more threatening than Arens' scowl.

Rosen said, "I don't think Judith will find your offer acceptable."

Arens stood. "Then you can both go to hell!" Tossing the ledger onto the floor, he strode past Rosen and out the door.

The room grew quiet. Ericson didn't seem to mind the silence. She used it like Rosen did—to make other people uncomfortable, so that they'd talk. But long ago, he had learned to listen to the silence and, as he watched her watch him, the thought flitted back into this head, hovering so that he could see it, arrogant in its naked revelation.

He asked, "What's this really all about?"

"What do you mean?"

"You're quite the psychologist—the way you handle the customers downstairs. The way you handle Mickey."

"You flatter me."

"You're quite a psychologist, but you don't believe that Judith is a multiple, just as you refuse to believe she's possessed."

Ericson sighed. "I have no idea what you're talking about."

"Dr. Gilliam told me how responsive Judith is to hypnosis. What if she's somehow been made to believe she's possessed?"

"Are you saying I've done that?" This time Rosen didn't reply, and she couldn't help but continue. "How could I accomplish something like that? And even assuming that was possible, what would I gain?"

Rosen shook his head.

Ericson said, "You think I'd get Mickey."

"Mickey and the company."

"But Judith almost killed Mickey."

"We don't know that. She stood over him with a knife, but she didn't actually make an attempt on his life. What we do know is that her actions pushed Mickey even further from his wife and closer to you."

For a moment Ericson's eyes narrowed. Resting a cool hand over Rosen's, she smiled—he thought she was going to laugh. "Even if I were capable, I don't need to hypnotize Judith. I already have her husband and her company."

As he had predicted, Judith wouldn't consider her husband's offer. So during the next two days Rosen continued to represent her religious defense as best he could, while trying to persuade her to abandon it. He'd wanted to look more closely into her husband's financial dealings, which Samuels had insisted weren't above board. But she would have none of it, leaving him the weekend to prepare for putting her on the stand.

But could he do that? How could he risk examining someone whose belief he wasn't sure of? Was she crazy, as her husband believed? Or coldly plotting her husband's murder, as Katherine Ericson contended? Or could the voice really be that of Judith's brother?

Rosen spent Saturday in his apartment with the Holy Scriptures on his lap. He'd kept thumbing through the Torah, looking for the last commandment the voice of Jacob said it had to fulfill. Judith and her uncle no doubt had gone to morning services, as he used to as a boy, wearing his *tallis* and *tefillin,* and *davening.* But that was long ago, before he'd lost his faith. Still, he remembered his favorite prayer upon rising, thanking God "for giving back my soul, which was in Your keeping."

A God who could give and take souls, could that God not place her brother's soul in Judith?

Evening came, but Rosen remained in his chair, still holding the Scriptures and not bothering to turn on the light. He drifted off to sleep, awakened suddenly by the telephone, and lifted the receiver in the darkness.

"Mr. Rosen?"

"Yes."

"I'm Lt. Connelly of the Highland Park Police Force. Have you heard from your client Judith Arens in the last hour or so?"

The illuminated dial on his watch read 1:15. "No. What's this all about?"

"I'm over at the Arens house. About a half hour ago, Mr. Arens tried to stop his wife from leaving. She stabbed him and cut his arm. He'll be all right. But she left, apparently on foot. Both cars are still here. I have my men searching the neighborhood, but they can't find her."

The policeman paused, then continued, "Mr. Arens says his wife is crazy. That right?"

"I really can't comment."

"Well, let me know if you hear from her."

Rosen hung up, hesitating before flipping on the light, half-expecting Judith to materialize before him. He was alone, his hand still clutching the Scriptures. He had to find her.

Rosen arrived in Judith's neighborhood in twenty minutes. He called her house from his car phone, but the police reported that she was still missing. If she were on foot, where could she go? Where would she go?

Yawning, he rubbed his eyes, feeling the uneasy fear as if alone in an old dark house. His left hand still felt the weight of the Bible. Could the answer be there? What had they kept telling him?

"God's house."

"God's court."

Of course.

He turned toward the lake and a few minutes later arrived at Judith's synagogue. After parking beside a lone Cadillac, he walked up the steps. The building was dark, but the door was unlocked. He listened just inside the door. At first nothing, then a low whisper that chilled him. A voice to his right, where soft light leaked through another doorway.

Walking into the sanctuary, Rosen looked toward the front, where lights shone above the dais. The ark was open and empty. A few feet away, Max Samuels sat in a chair and held the Torah scroll against his right shoulder. His face had the yellow pallor of old parchment.

Wearing a man's white shirt hanging over a pair of slacks, Judith stood beside her uncle. Her shoulders thrown back, legs spread apart—Rosen had seen that posture before. And had heard that voice. It was her brother's.

"You know you're going to be punished."

Samuels nodded. "Yes. My fault, all my fault."

"And what punishment do you deserve?"

Judith raised her right hand, which gripped a long knife. She stared down at Samuels, who said, "What God commands—'life for life.'"

Suddenly Rosen understood everything. It had to do with God, but even more with an old man's twisted mind.

"Samuels!" he shouted.

The old man drew himself up in the chair. Coughing hard, he rasped, "So you too, Rosen, are here to bear witness."

"I should've known, but it was just too crazy."

"Crazy? I can understand other people thinking so, but not you. Not the way you were brought up, a real Talmud Torah man. That's why I hired you. I wanted somebody else to understand. You do understand."

"Tell Judith to put the knife down."

"It is Jacob standing over me, and it has to be a knife. The Torah says that a murderer must be slain by the sword. I stand accused of murder, have pled guilty, and await sentence."

"It wasn't your fault."

"It was my fault. I sent Jacob alone into that neighborhood to make a collection. He was killed, and for that, I deserve to die."

"So you conjured up Jacob to carry out the sentence."

"Jacob is real."

"He was made up by you and Dr. Gilliam from bells and whistles. That's all."

"Don't you see, Rosen, what Jacob was sent back to complete? I've been condemned in front of two witnesses, as the Torah commands. My niece and my nephew. Now, Jacob, do God's justice."

Judith raised her knife, while her uncle chanted, "life for life, eye for eye, tooth for tooth, hand for hand, foot for foot, burn for burn, wound for wound, bruise for bruise."

"No!"

As Rosen ran up the dais, Judith plunged the knife into Samuels' chest. The old man slid down, struggling not for himself, but to keep the Torah scrolls from touching the floor. Rosen bent beside him.

Judith blinked and looked around the synagogue, her gaze finally settling on her uncle.

Samuels' face was an ivory mask, his eyes grown large. "Judith forgive . . . Jacob, take me before his throne . . . life for life . . ."

Leaning close, Judith whispered, "Jacob. Jacob?" Then she collapsed against the dying man.

The simple green walls, the straight back wooden chairs, even the stale smell of the police interrogation room comforted Rosen. It was not unlike the small dark room where, as a boy, he'd study and pray with the other boys. Both places were, after all, where one followed the law. But even his old rabbi, as wise as he was, would have had difficulty comprehending what Dr. Gilliam had just confessed to Rosen and police Lt. Connelly.

Samuels had paid the psychiatrist's gambling debts, and in return Gilliam, through hypnosis, had programmed Judith into becoming Jacob.

The two signals would be for Samuels to telephone Judith—the ringing bells—and speak playfully in Yiddish, as sister and brother had once teased each other. Then she would change to her brother, who was instructed to kill his uncle. Mickey had been attacked both times for interrupting Jacob. When Rosen had first met Judith, in the room where she'd been addressing boxes, two women had been chatting in Yiddish, then the phone rang—the two signals—causing Judith to become Jacob.

Gilliam said, "Samuels was obsessed with what he perceived as Old Testament justice. His guilt over what he'd done to his nephew was too great. The old man was ill and didn't want the burden of that guilt when he met his maker."

"It was more than that," Rosen said. "Something about Judith and her father."

"I really can't discuss that. It's privileged communication between physician and client."

"Isn't it a bit late for you to speak of ethics? When we first met, you told me that extreme stress during early childhood caused Judith to dissociate into another personality. Extreme stress—that usually means sexual abuse. Judith's father abused her, didn't he?"

Gilliam hesitated, then nodded. "For years Samuels suspected his brother but refused to believe it. Later, the way Judith reacted whenever her father's name was brought up, he knew. But it was too late. Then Jacob's death put him over the edge."

Lt. Connelly, who stood over the psychiatrist, said, "One thing I don't get. If Samuels was so full of guilt, why didn't he just kill himself?"

Rosen replied, "The injunction from Genesis. 'But for your own life-blood I will require a reckoning.' A devout Jew can't commit suicide."

The psychiatrist shrugged. "Didn't he? I suppose it depends whether you look at it psychologically or legally."

"Yeah, Doc," the policeman said, "and the way the judge looks at it might make you accessory to murder."

Gilliam winced. "I didn't mean it to turn out this way."

"Didn't you?"

"It's just that Samuels threatened to ruin me. I had no choice."

Choice was what it had been all about. Gilliam's choice to sell his profession for a fistful of gambling markers. Samuels' choice to forget the most important tenet of his faith—that man was made to follow God's law and not vice versa.

And Rosen's choice. Judith had been right all along. He had taken this case and spoken of a faith in God in words that only a believer would use. The same faith that made him finally understand, leading him to Samuels and the truth.

Rosen's choice drew him closer to that lost soul of his nightmare, which was not a nightmare after all, but a dream. The dream of a young boy on his way to prayers, singing the same prayer that Rosen heard now: "Thank you, Lord, for giving back my soul which was in your keeping." The prayer whose melody he still felt with every beat of his heart. A prayer for a God Who, despite what Samuels had said, stood not merely for justice, but for love as well.

Perhaps that was the real sin. Samuels had forgotten what love really meant. And now he had left his niece to take the consequences.

Rosen stared at the psychiatrist. "What about Judith? Look what you did to her."

"Yeah," Connelly said. "I hope Mrs. Arens is okay. She seemed pretty bad when I sent her to the psych ward."

Gilliam managed a weak smile. "Don't worry. It's amazing what therapy can do for a person."

ELLEN RAWLINGS is a former editor, management analyst, and college English teacher. She has published five Regency romances and two mysteries (both mysteries with the Jewish heroine Rachel Crowne). This is Rachel's first appearance in a short story, which takes place near the author's home in Columbia, Maryland.

Poison

▼   ▼   ▼   ▼   ▼   ▼

ELLEN RAWLINGS

I GOT A PHONE CALL from a woman named Joanne Koppel. She said she was Meredith Whitney's agent. "I mean ex-agent," she said.

I already knew about that. "Yes?"

"Well, she's been murdered, and I'm afraid people will believe I did it. I thought I might hire you to clear my name."

I knew about the murder, too. "Did you kill her?" I asked. "Meredith thought you might."

I heard her draw in a deep breath. "Maybe I don't want to hire you after all."

"It doesn't matter," I said. "I've already been hired—by the victim before she died."

I first met Meredith Whitney—that was her pen name; her real name was Myrna Weinstein—at the annual Romance Writers of America convention. It was being held in Fairfield, Maryland, which is where I live. Meredith lived there, too.

I don't write romances. I was there because I was doing an article on the convention and some of its stellar attendees. Meredith wasn't just stellar; she was galactic.

I'm not. I'm a freelance writer of little fame. Sometimes, I'm an amateur detective. My name is Rachel Crowne, though Crowne should really be

173

Cohen. When my great-grandfather came over from Russia, having drawn the number "one" in the Tsar's army lottery, and thus free to emigrate, the official at Ellis Island changed the name to Crowne. And that's what it's been since.

"Has a man been in here asking for me?" Meredith said as she seated herself carefully on the barstool next to mine at the Lakeside Hotel. She hadn't told me her name, assuming, I guess, that I'd know who she was. She was right.

She arranged her silk skirt so that its slit opened invitingly along the length of one black, lacy stocking. "He's tall, dark, and handsome—naturally," she added with a giggle.

I shook my head.

"He isn't?" She looked upset.

I was fingering the small gold and blue-enameled *mezzuzah* I wear around my neck. She looked at it, then said, "Ah, a *landsman*. What's your name?"

When I introduced myself, she looked baffled. "Are you anybody? I've never heard of you."

"My family and friends think I am."

Her laugh had an unpleasant edge to it. "Everybody's family and friends think so. At least, that's what I've heard. I mean, are you anybody to the public?"

It was evident from her peacocky air that she thought she was, and, as I've mentioned, she was right. Meredith was probably the most popular romance writer in the world. She'd even managed in the last few years to get herself onto the *New York Times* best-seller list, a place where romance writers don't usually show up.

She looked successful, too: blonde power hairdo, a beautifully made dinner suit, and huge diamonds seeming to weigh down her skinny hands and wrists. I figured her age at the late fifties, with some help from plastic surgeons to make her appear younger.

"Well?" she asked impatiently, then made a complaining remark about the noise in the bar.

Truthfully, it wasn't that noisy. There was some laughter, of course, and clinking of glasses, but, for the most part, the other conventioneers were fairly quiet.

To be amiable, I nodded. Then, getting back to our previous conversation, I said, "I was written up in the *Fairfield Flier*," our local weekly. "I solved some murder cases in the area."

She said, "Oh, yes, I remember reading about that. So that was you."
She smirked. "In other words, essentially, you're nobody special." This was,
I decided, a woman I could dislike intensely with no trouble.

"Wrong," I said. "I'm important." I was lying, out of contrariness, not
to impress her, "and I'd like to interview you for the article I'm doing for
World Magazine."

"An article on me?"

I shook my head. "No, on the convention." As she started to turn away,
I added, again stretching the truth, "but highlighting you."

She swiveled back on her stool and flashed me a big, phony smile that
showed her gorgeous dental work. "I suppose I could give you a little time.
Let's move to a more comfortable spot."

She commandeered the maitre d' and shortly had us seated at a promi-
nently placed table. "What do you need to know about me?" she asked
immediately after ordering a martini. I had a feeling it wasn't her first, maybe
not even her second. "Do you want to ask me why I'm here?"

I knew she was there to receive the award for the best romance writer of
the year, just as she'd received the award the previous year and I don't know
how many years before that. Since I wanted to get her talking, I said yes.

She told me about the award, then added, "I deserve it. This organization
would be no place without me." The fingers of her left hand went around
my wrist, the long, painted thumbnail digging into my skin. "That's off the
record. Write it and I'll sue you."

I pried off her fingers. "I won't write it, but I'd like to know why you
feel that way."

She made a sweeping gesture with a braceleted arm. "Are you kidding?
Look at these people. Almost every one of them is a 'wanna'—wanna have
an agent, wanna be published, wanna stay published. You get the picture.
They have limited abilities, if any, *and* . . . ," she leaned closer to me, "and
they look like the devil. They're fat, most of them, and dowdy, and homely.
Except maybe for Kathryn Reynolds. But she's a dyke. These others, they
don't have a clue. The truth is, Miss Whatever Your Name Is, they don't
deserve success. I do." She laughed again. "But I've gotten off the track,
haven't I? What I meant to say is that I add luster to this group. My presence
attracts editors and agents—and writers like you. Without me, this event
wouldn't be anything."

I nodded as though I agreed with every word. I said, "Tell me how you
became successful."

Again, she laughed. Wow, what a sense of humor! Then she took a big gulp of martini. "Do you mean besides the fact that I'm a wonderful writer?"

I smiled. "Of course."

"Well, look at me. What do you think of when you see me?"

If I told her, she'd scratch my eyes out with those bright red nails. "Tell me," I said.

"You see glamour." She touched her hair. "You see success. This jewelry and Armani suit say importance and accomplishment. Readers buy my dream in part for the reason that I personify it. When I say they can have romance, they believe me. That's because I look as though I know what I'm talking about.

"And don't forget: I'm a fabulous writer."

A minute ago, she'd said she was "wonderful." The self-praise was escalating.

"Are there people here who resent your fame?" I asked.

Her smile wasn't nice. "Aren't there? I'll bet half of them, especially those who think I'm in their way, would love to see me quit writing."

I shook my head. "I don't understand. How can you be in someone else's way?"

"You don't know much about the business, do you?" She stopped and stared at my head.

"What's the matter?"

"Honey," she said, "let me give you some advice. You've got a bad perm and a worse dye job. They make you look old."

"I don't have a perm." My voice came out icy. "My hair is naturally curly. I don't dye it, either. And I'm thirty-five, usually mistaken for twenty-something."

"Oh, well, some people won't take help when it's offered." She sighed as though she really cared. Then she brightened. "Back to publishing. It's like this. My books come out in hardback. They make the best-seller list. A year later, they're issued in paperback and they make the paperback best-seller list. At the same time, the new hardback comes out, etc., etc. These books stay on the list for months. So do reissues. Get it? The more slots I take up, the fewer there are for others. At least, that's what they think."

"And you don't?" I asked tight-lipped. I was still simmering over her hair remarks.

"Honey, they don't have any talent. They're keeping themselves off. If I were to die right now, it wouldn't make any difference to their careers."

Maybe not, I thought, but it might cheer them up a lot. It might give me a temporary lift, too.

Okay, I'm not a saint. I don't even want to be, which is a good thing considering how I feel about being gratuitously attacked. Still, as I stood I thanked her for her time.

"Wait," she said, again getting my wrist in a tight grasp. She pulled me back into my chair. "About dying . . ."

I hoped I wasn't going to have to listen to a drunken speech on her religious and philosophical beliefs. "What about it?"

"It could happen to me."

I was tired of her. "Did you think you were immortal?"

She shook her head impatiently. "That's not what I mean. It's possible someone is trying to kill me. I've received some threats."

The investigative reporter in me was aroused. "Oh? What kind of threats? Who made them?"

"You know, some letters and phone calls from obsessed fans. Also after a fight with a guy I know."

"Fight?"

She frowned. "I don't intend to get any more specific than that, not now."

"So why are you telling me this?"

"Why not? You're a detective, aren't you? You should be interested."

"I'm strictly amateur," I said. "Besides, since Fairfield isn't exactly a killing field, it's doubtful I'll ever be called on to do any detecting again."

She went on as though I hadn't spoken. "And you're a reporter. If I'm killed, you could write about it, keep the pot boiling until my murderer is caught. At least, I'd have that satisfaction."

"What do you mean?"

Her expression hardened. "It's important to me that nobody gets away with messing with me. Ever. I've gotten revenge for every lousy thing that's ever been done to me. I live by that rule. If I can't make it happen, I want to know that there's someone else who can."

"I have a better idea," I said, standing again. "If you're really serious about what you're saying, tell the police."

She rose, too. I noticed the slit in her skirt was skewed, but I didn't say anything—payback for her hair and age remarks. "I don't trust the police. Damn bureaucrats. Give me your card. I'm going to call you if I need you. And you will respond—if you're smart. This could be your big story."

"Yes, sure," I said. I didn't expect to hear from her, of course.

I won't go into detail about the awards dinner, because the only surprise it held, for me, at least, was that Meredith received a new award, named after her, and was gracious when she accepted it. Apparently, she could keep the vitriol under control when she wanted to.

The convention ended with a luncheon the next day. I noticed that Meredith was absent and was told she'd checked out the night before, right after she got her award. That was fine with me.

After lunch I chatted with several people, then headed for home. There were three messages on my answering machine. One was from my friend and next door neighbor, Tom Brant. He's a detective with the Howard County Police. The second was from my boyfriend, Hank Rubin, telling me he missed me. I was glad to hear it. The third was from Meredith Whitney. "Call me," her frantic-sounding voice said. "It's a matter of life and death. I'm not kidding."

I sighed. I figured that like many other writers I knew, she exaggerated. I thought that probably whatever had happened to set her off was something pretty small, like her best buddy getting a good review in the *Baltimore Sun*. Besides, why should I rush to her aid? There's a Jewish saying: when your enemy gets knocked down, don't kick him—but don't rush to help him up, either. Anybody who belittled my coiffure, not to mention my age, so cruelly, was, if not an enemy, not a pal. She could wait. Besides, it was Hank I wanted to talk to.

I had just begun dialing his number when I heard a knock on my door. I put down the phone and looked through the peephole. It was Tom. He's a big, tough-looking guy with a five o'clock shadow no matter how often or how thoroughly he shaves. So if I hadn't known him, I wouldn't even have opened the door with the chain on.

He gave me a hug that possibly cracked three ribs, then allowed himself to be ushered into my untidy, badly furnished townhouse.

"It's about time you're back," he said in his gravelly voice that always makes me think of smoke-filled bars. "Did you enjoy yourself?"

I sat on my saggy green sofa. "Well, yes and no."

"Which is it?" he asked, giving me a shove so that I'd make room for him next to me.

I pointed to first one, then the other of my two ugly chairs. "Can't you sit somewhere else? You're like a cat. If I had a book on my lap, you'd plop on top of the page I was reading." Without waiting for his response, I got up and went over to one of the chairs.

"Surly today, aren't you?" he said. "What set you off?"

I sighed. "At the convention, I interviewed someone I didn't like. Now she wants me to call her."

"You don't have to do it, do you?"

"No, but her message said it was a life and death matter. If nothing else, my curiosity would force me to it."

He looked interested. "Life and death, huh?"

"I doubt it. I figure she's overstating the case."

Tom yawned and stretched. "What don't you like about her?"

"Everything."

He grinned. "You don't waste words, do you?"

"Nope."

He grinned again.

"Okay, you want me to be specific? Did I ever tell you about the Jewish sin of *lashon hara*?"

"God, I hope not. It sounds deadly."

I smiled. "It's not good. It means making malicious talk. This woman must be the hands-down queen of *lashon hara*."

"That bad, huh?"

"The only thing she didn't belittle when I spoke with her was the American flag, but that's probably because the subject never came up."

We discussed her for a short while, then the Romance Writers convention. While we spoke, Tom had a cup of coffee and two chocolate doughnuts. Finally he left, and I went right to the telephone, to put in a call to Hank. He wasn't home, so I decided I might as well phone dear Meredith. She answered on the first ring. "It's about time," she snapped when I identified myself. "Can you come right away?"

"What's this all about?"

"I'm not going to talk about it on the phone. Please get over here." She gave me her address on Druid's Cove Way, then hung up before I could agree to see her at her place.

I was tempted not to show, but, again, curiosity ruled me, that and the thought of a juicy story. I got in my car and drove to her apartment, which was the eighth floor penthouse of a very fancy building near the main mall. Nobody was at the reception desk, so not bothering to sign in, I took the elevator to the top floor. When I knocked at her door, a nervous, wheezy voice said, "Who is it?"

"It's Rachel Crowne."

I heard her fumbling with the locks, then the door swung open. Meredith stood there, swaying. Unless she was ill, she was drunk again. And it wasn't just that she was unsteady on her feet. Her lipstick, put on with such abandonment that smeared it almost to her nose in one place, suggested the work of someone who wasn't in control of her hands. Also, the jacket of her red slack suit was fastened so that there was an empty buttonhole at the top and a holeless button at the bottom.

"Don't just stand there," she said, slurring her words. "Come in here, for God's sake."

Her place was lovely if you like crystal chandeliers, richly carved antique furniture, and magnificent Oriental carpets. I sat on a gorgeous apricot sofa and watched her sink into a brown velvet chair. I sniffed the air, appreciating its floral scent, before saying, a bit impatiently, "What's the problem?"

"Someone is trying to kill me."

"How do you know?"

"Because there were flowers sent here this morning, dozens of them. My fool of a husband accepted the delivery."

"Flowers sound good to me."

"I'm allergic to flowers. Whoever ordered them was trying to make me sick."

"I thought you said someone was trying to kill you."

"That will be next."

"I don't see any flowers now."

"You know," she said, sitting a little straighter, "you're even less astute than you look. I had the super take them out, of course."

I stood up. "Ms. Whitney or Weinstein, I don't care if someone kills you. You're one mean lady. Goodbye."

She started to cry. "You think I'm awful," she said, between sobs.

I wasn't in a diplomatic mood. "I do, and you are."

"Wait! I apologize. Please listen. Maybe you don't believe me, but I'm telling you that everyone who knows me is aware I'm severely allergic."

"Including your husband?"

"Naturally."

This was weird stuff. I said, "Could he have sent them?"

"Why not? Or it could have been my son or Joanne Koppel, my ex-agent. I recently dumped her, and she didn't take it too well. They all hate me."

"Give me some details," I said.

She took a sip from a teacup that had been sitting on a side table. I would have bet that there was liquor in it, not tea. "My husband," she said. "He says I don't treat him with respect. Well, why should I? He doesn't do anything to deserve it. He's got the same lousy shoe salesman's job he had when I married him." She leaned closer. "To tell you the truth, I'm thinking of ditching him, too."

"For the man you were asking about at the convention?"

At first she looked confused. Then her face reddened. "Oh, him. Of course not, although the idea of a new man isn't bad. A clean start, you know." She giggled. "New agent and maybe a new husband. I'm not getting any younger."

"That's certainly true," I said, unable to resist.

If looks could kill—you know the rest.

"And the others?" I said.

She glared at me, then took another swallow from the teacup. Was it my imagination, or was she getting less nervous and more abrasive with each sip? "There's my son, the basket case. At least, that's what he wants me to think, but I know better. He's twenty-one, doesn't go to school, and doesn't work. Not that the job he had was worth anything. He was a taxidermist's assistant. Can you believe it? Jews aren't even supposed to hunt, and my son is helping stuff dead foxes and bears for *goyim*."

I said, "I'm not following you, that is, about the basket case part."

Her laugh was derisive. "He tells me he can't leave the house. If he does, the ghosts of the animals he fixed will gnaw his legs off. Can you believe that?"

"Are you saying he's mentally ill?"

"He's lazy, that's what he is. He wants me to support him." She frowned. "I can tell you that I'm not going to do it much longer. If I work, he can work, too." She sat back as though pleased with her little speech. "And now my ex-agent."

"When did she become your 'ex'?"

"Last week. We had the kind of contract that let us do it verbally if one of us was dissatisfied, so it was easy. She didn't take it kindly, I can tell you."

"I guess you were her cash cow," I said, deliberately being crude.

She sniffed. "If you want to put it like that. I prefer to say I was her premier client."

"Why did you drop her?"

She sprawled more loosely on her seat. In contrast, her voice got harder. "Because I'd outgrown her. Actually I'd done that a long time ago. I only kept her as long as I did out of pity."

Yeah, sure. And Hitler took Jewish money to invest it for his victims so they'd have a nice nest egg when the war was over. I said, "Did she threaten you?"

Meredith finished off the contents of the teacup. "Did she? She called me every name under the sun. She said she'd made me, that without her I would have been nothing. She said she'd see I'd be nothing again. That's a threat."

"And you said?"

Her grin was wide—and malicious. "I said, 'Even if that were true about you making me, which it isn't, so what?' That's when she threw a book at me and said she'd see me in hell. Of course, I walked out of her office after that. I always try to maintain my dignity."

She could have fooled me. I hadn't noticed that she had any. Heroically, I kept my thoughts to myself. I said, "Do you really think she'd be capable of killing you?"

"Sure I do. They all are. Listen, promise me you'll investigate if I meet with foul play."

"Foul play?" I felt like telling her she'd been reading—or writing—too many potboilers.

"Yes."

"Look," I said, "despite what you might have read in the *Fairfield Flier,* I'm not a real detective."

Her chin thrust out stubbornly. "You're real enough for me."

"Nah, I . . ."

She didn't let me finish. "I'll pay you two hundred dollars a day."

"No, you won't. You'll be dead."

She frowned at me. "I'll leave a note to the effect that you're to be paid out of the estate. Why should I care how these *mamzers'* inheritance is squandered!"

"Okay," I said, to stop her pestering me. Why not? I didn't expect her to be murdered.

I got a call from Tom the next day. "I'm at the station house," he said. "You know that woman you told me about yesterday, the one who had *lashon* herring?"

"*Lashon hara.* What about her?"

"She's dead. The Medical Examiner thinks she was poisoned, and, if she was, it was probably cyanide. Her skin was pink and he thought he detected a bitter almond smell."

"And you were assigned the case?" I asked.

"Yep. Anything you can tell me that might help?"

"Besides the fact that to know her was to want to murder her?"

"Right."

I told him I'd seen her the preceding day and what she'd said.

"That's interesting. You think the agent could have done it? Would firing him be a good reason to kill Ms. Weinstein?"

"It's a she," I said, "and if you considered killing an option, it might. Meredith was a money tree, and Joanne Koppel was probably collecting fifteen percent of everything Meredith made. That would come to a great deal of money."

"So Koppel could have been upset about suddenly being out in the cold, huh?"

"Shivering all over," I said.

"Right," he said. "And poison is usually a woman's weapon. I'll get back to you."

After his call, I finally heard from Hank. He's not much of a talker, but I'll bet we spent a whole half hour on the phone, catching up with each other's activities. For Hank, a half hour was equivalent to three for an average person.

That evening, Joanne Koppel phoned me about hiring me to find Meredith's killer. I said, "Are you sure people will think you're a suspect?" I didn't mention that Tom already thought so.

She sounded bitter. "One of the editors I do business with asked me if I'd killed her. She pretended she was joking, but I could tell she was really wondering."

"How did you get to me?"

"I called Meredith's house today and spoke with her son. He told me she'd been murdered and he'd found this note from her saying you should be contacted if she was. He said he didn't know what to do about it."

"So you took over."

"Yes."

"Why did you call her house?"

"I was hoping she'd change her mind about me."

I said, "Are you close with the family?"

"I've never met any of them," she said. "Meredith kept her writing and her home life completely separate. She never even let her husband accompany her to conventions and things like that. She told me he didn't enjoy them, but I think she was ashamed of him and didn't want him around. She thought he'd spoil her image, something like that. She was such a bitch."

There was silence on her end, she said, "I didn't mean that." I didn't respond. "Okay, I did, but I didn't kill her. So, are you going to look into the case?"

"The police . . ."

"I'm like Meredith," she said. "I don't trust them. Listen, if I can arrange it, will you go to her apartment tomorrow afternoon to meet with her husband and son and me to interview us?"

"That will work," I said. "Give me a call when you set this thing up."

Manny Weinstein, Meredith's husband, let me into their apartment and introduced me to his son, Kevin. The younger Weinstein—he looked in his early twenties—was sitting in a corner chair wearing rumpled khaki pants and a yellow pullover sweater. Mr. Weinstein was dressed equally casually, except, I noticed, for his shoes. They were oxblood color, the leather supple-looking, the shine dazzling. Of course, I thought: he was a shoe salesman; wearing well-made footwear was probably important in his job.

The physical resemblance between father and son was strong. They both had pale brown hair and eyes, a high forehead, and a thin nose and mouth. It was a noble-looking face, except that on the father it seemed ravaged. On the son, it appeared demon-ridden.

"I'm sorry for your loss," I said.

Manny Weinstein's eyes filled with tears. Kevin's glance darted about the room, as though watching for hidden "things" to leap out at him.

The bell rang and, again, Manny went to the door; Kevin seemed to shrink in his chair. A blonde who looked very much like Meredith barged in. She squeezed Manny's arm. This time, his tears spilled over.

When order was restored, we moved to the sofa and chairs, except for Kevin, who stayed where he was. Maybe corners seem the safest places for the pursued.

Joanne Koppel got down to business. "It's important to all of us—isn't it?—to find out who killed Meredith. Personally, I think it was another writer."

"Why do you think that?" I asked.

"They all hated her." She put a hand over her mouth, then gave Manny an apologetic look and added, "*Aleha ha-shalom.* I guess I shouldn't have said that about her, but the truth is, they did."

"I know she thought so," I said, "but would they really hate her for being a success?"

Again, she shot Manny the look that asked his forgiveness. "Of course. But that's only part of it. The rest is that she did everything she could to put other romance writers in their place. She talked down to them when she wasn't ignoring them. She insulted them. She boasted a lot. That's not a good idea, you know. Writers don't want to hear about another writer's good fortune. It's a lot easier to feel affection for the other person when you know her manuscripts keep getting rejected."

"Did they dislike hearing it enough to kill her?"

She sat back and stared at her nail polish. It was black. I wondered if that was how she was expressing her mourning. "Writers have strong emotions."

"Any hater in particular?"

"Oh, God, the list would be endless."

"How would such a person have gotten in here?" I said, remembering that I had yet to see a doorman.

Manny said, "She could walk right in. The damn doorman is never around. I think he drinks."

"Have you reported him?"

He looked sheepish. "I spoke to him. He says he needs the job."

"The police think I did it," Kevin said in a toneless voice. I wondered if he was on drugs, prescription or otherwise.

"Don't be silly," Joanne said dismissively. "Why should they?"

"They think I'm crazy. Everyone does. Except my mother. She thinks I'm a faker."

"Well, you're not," his father said, his tone sharp. "You're not crazy or a faker. You're just having a hard time right now."

When his son didn't respond, Manny said, "The police are saying she died of cyanide poisoning."

"Did they say how the poison got into her?" I asked. That was something Tom hadn't mentioned and I hadn't thought to ask.

Manny said, "They think it was in her tea. They took the cup away."

"What kind of tea was it?"

"It must have been oolong," Joanne said. "That's all she drank. Right, Manny?" He nodded.

Remembering that Tom had said that poison is a woman's weapon, I stared at Joanne. She turned her head away.

Manny said, "Why does that matter?"

I said, "According to something I saw on the Internet, oolong is the drink of choice for adding poison. That's because the tea is so strong."

"This is horrible," Manny said. "I don't want to listen any more. Look, Miss, I know my wife said she wanted you to do this, but she's dead now. Suppose I just give you a week's pay and you go home and forget about it."

"I couldn't do that, Mr. Weinstein," I said. "I made Meredith a promise. I have to keep it." I could have added that I wanted to stay involved because I found this group's *mishegoss* fascinating.

I said, "Just one more question. Where were all of you when Mrs. Weinstein was murdered?"

Joanne shuddered; Mr. Weinstein looked shocked; Kevin tried to make himself even smaller. I decided to get him over with first. "Kevin?"

"I was asleep," he said, starting to cry. "The police don't believe me, but I was."

"He sleeps like the dead," Manny said. "It's his medication. An army could have come in here, and he wouldn't have heard."

"Mom always complained about that," Kevin said. "She wanted me to get up early, like her."

"She wanted him to work," Manny said. "She wouldn't believe that he isn't able to right now."

Kevin said, "She didn't believe me about the animals, but I saw them." His voice went up a few notches. "Even if they're not really there, I see them. I get afraid. They're mad at me, you know."

He was either a great actor or he had major emotional problems. I tended to believe the latter even if his mother hadn't.

"Where were you, Mr. Weinstein?"

"I was at work. Listen, I already told the police this."

"Sure, but I can't investigate without information, even if the cops have it first. What did they say?"

"They said they'd check."

He could have walked out of work to race home and poison her, or he could have left her the tea. I'd have to see what I could get out of Tom, my police buddy.

"And you, Ms. Koppel?"

"I was in my office all morning. You can ask my secretary."

"Is there more than one exit from your office?"

"Hey, I don't like your insinuation."

I shrugged.

"I'm convinced it was someone outside," she said to me, reiterating her theme. "What you need to do is search out who. Why don't you look through her letters and stuff, and see if you can find anything threatening? That would be a start."

"I could do that," I said.

"There you go." She looked more relaxed than at any time since she'd come in. "Somebody else did it. That's got to be the answer. I just know it couldn't have been one of us."

When had the three of them become an "us"? I was beginning to wonder if these people had known each other previously. I had only Joanne's word for it that they'd been strangers to each other. But if she was lying, what was her motive?

I said. "Did the police find any evidence of a break-in?"

Manny's thin eyebrows quirked. "What do you mean?"

"Well, how would an outsider gain access to this apartment?"

"Meredith could have let the person in," Joanne said eagerly, maybe a little too eagerly. I wanted to think about that and about her knowing what kind of tea the poison had been in.

I let it drop. It was something I needed to talk to Tom about, also. I had a lot of other questions, too. Unfortunately, I didn't have any answers yet.

I had to finish two articles that had been due the day before, so I couldn't check Meredith's computer then. I did try to get in touch with Tom, though, as soon as I got to my house. He wasn't at home or at work, so I left him a message both places.

He got back to me the next morning. "Come over to my house," he said on the phone. "I have something to tell you."

When I stepped outside, I saw that his door was wide open. This was unusual for a cop who trusted no one and always expected the worst of people. Except me, of course.

He was pacing the length of his living room. "What took you so long?" he asked in his gravelly voice.

"For heaven's sake. I came right away. What's this stuff you have to tell me that can't wait?"

He stopped pacing. "Let's go in the kitchen and have some coffee first.

I've got cookies, too. My partner's wife made them."

"If I kill you on the spot," I said, "it will be justifiable homicide."

He managed to look innocent, a really incredible feat for him. "What's the matter?"

"You sound like your house is on fire to get me here, and then you tell me to have coffee first."

"Okay, don't have coffee, but come in the kitchen anyway."

I stormed in and roughly grabbed a cup, which I filled from a gorgeous black coffeemaker. It was the only decent-looking object in the room. Everything else appeared as though it had been willed to him by an ancient, impoverished peasant. I could see this because practically every item in there was in the sink or on the drainboard, waiting to be washed. "Look at this mess," I said. "You're disgusting. What's the news?"

"We found a bottle of cyanide in the Weinstein house. It was in a stack of computer paper."

I thought about the three people I'd been with not that many hours before. I can't say I felt concern for Joanne Koppel; she was too hard-edged to elicit such a feeling from me. I did feel sorry for the remaining Weinsteins, though. I said, "Whose is it?"

Tom sneered. "The kid said he brought it home from work because they had bugs or something they wanted to get rid of."

I said, "Someone else could have gotten in and brought his own cyanide. It didn't have to be that cyanide, did it?"

"Yeah, sure, people are walking around with the stuff. Would you know where to get it if you wanted some?"

I shook my head no. "But Agatha Christie's killers never had any trouble finding it."

"Who?"

"Never mind," I said. "Was there any evidence that someone broke into the place?"

"Nope, none." He gave me an unsympathetic look. "Those Weinsteins, one or both, had the motive, and it looks like they had the means, too. That's pretty strong evidence."

"What was the motive?"

"Myrna Weinstein was a rich woman and had a big insurance policy on herself. Manny and Kevin won't ever have to work again if they don't want to."

Kevin didn't work now, I thought. "Which of them do you think did it?

"That's a good question. I don't know. Maybe they were in cahoots. We tried to take them to the station for questioning, but the son freaked. He said he'd be eaten by wild animals if he went outside. Can you believe that? Anyway, the father called the son's psychiatrist, who said we'd destroy him if we tried to take him from the apartment now. Is little Kevin putting on an act?"

"I don't know," I said, getting up from my seat. I made a production out of washing and drying my cup and returning it to the cabinet. "At least you'll have one clean cup," I said, clearly being sarcastic.

I should have known I was wasting my effort. "Gee, yeah, thanks," he said. He sounded sincere.

I said, "I'm going to the Weinsteins' to take another shot at them. I'm also going to look at Meredith's computer files. I'll let you know if I learn anything important."

"You won't," he said. "We already did that. But come back anyway when you've finished. You can wash the rest of the cups."

I won't repeat what I said to him.

Returning to the Weinstein home was *déjà vu* all over again, as Yogi Berra put it, except that, this time, Joanne Koppel wasn't there. Mr. Weinstein still looked as though his world was coming to an end; from Kevin's expression, his already had. "They're going to arrest me for murdering my mother," Kevin said.

"Why's that?"

"Because they found my cyanide."

"That's a good reason," I said.

Manny Weinstein stood. He ran his hands down the outsides of his thighs, then up, then down. "It's no reason," he said. "It's natural he'd have it. He worked with the stuff."

"Why would he have it here?"

"Why not?" Mr. Weinstein sounded belligerent. "We get mice sometimes."

"In this expensive penthouse apartment? And you're supposed to get rid of them yourselves?" I shook my head in disbelief.

"We take care of our own problems," he said, then turned bright red, afraid, I guess, that I'd think Myrna was one of the problems they'd handled. It was difficult not to feel his words fit the scenario. I let it go. Slowly, his color receded.

I turned to Kevin. "Did you stash it in the computer paper?"

He looked surprised. "No."

"So somebody else put it there? Who knew you had it?"

"My father . . ." His voice trailed off. "He didn't do it," he said, his voice rising. "He wouldn't. He's kind, not like my . . ." Again, he didn't end his sentence.

"Mother," I said, finishing it for him.

"That's right," Manny said, twisting his hands together. "She couldn't understand, or couldn't accept, that my son has some problems right now. But we're working on them, aren't we, Kevin?"

As a nonfiction writer and sometimes sleuth, I try to keep my feelings out of it so I can stay objective. Not this time. *Please don't let it be Manny,* I said to myself. It wasn't just because his obvious attachment to his child was touching. What would Kevin do if his father was taken from him?

For that matter, what would the father do if his son was convicted of murder? What a mess. I found myself wishing that some romance writer, as nasty and undeserving as Meredith, if that were possible, would turn out to be the killer. I didn't have high hopes, however.

With Mr. Weinstein's reluctant permission, I went through Meredith's correspondence. I learned two things: her fans practically worshipped her, and she was a bitch. I already knew those things, but now they were confirmed.

I learned another thing, too. I'll come to that.

To whom was she a bitch? From her letters, which I found on her computer, she wasn't nice to other writers, especially those asking any sort of favor, such as a back cover blurb. And she was nasty to just plain folks who wrote her to give her story ideas. Her general comment went along the lines of, "What makes you think I need your help?"—only in harsher language. If I'd been a recipient of one of her letters, I might have considered killing her myself.

What was I supposed to do with all of this information? Even if I excluded people who didn't live nearby, that didn't mean one of them wasn't guilty. Any correspondent could have hopped on a plane or train, gone to her house, and done her in. It would have been worth it as pay back for her insults.

I decided to let the police work on her correspondents. At least Messrs. Weinstein and Ms. Koppel were easily accessible.

What was the third thing I'd found? It was some love notes to a man named Saul Behringer; they were buried in chapters of her last novel, which was still on her computer. It looked as though Myrna had had an affair with Behringer. I wondered if he was the man she'd been waiting for at the Lakeside Hotel the first time I met her.

As soon as I got home, I looked Behringer up in the phone book. He was a stockbroker with an office in the Muldoon Building, which was close to Meredith's apartment. I told his receptionist I needed an immediate appointment to invest a large sum of money I'd just received. I got one.

Saul Behringer didn't remind me of Manny Weinstein in any way. He was tall and good-looking and very debonair in a gray, European-cut suit. "What can I do for you, Ms. Crowne?" he said after shaking my hand and conducting me to a chair.

It was a nice chair. The whole office was nice: lots of rich burgundy leather, even on top of the ornately carved desk, forest green walls, and feathery Kentia palms. Mr. Behringer appeared to be doing okay.

I said, "I'm afraid I tricked your secretary. I don't have money to invest. I'm employed as a detective by the estate of the late Myrna Weinstein."

He had been sitting back in his chair, looking alert but relaxed. I watched him stiffen. Slowly, he leaned over his desk. "What's she have to do with me?" he said.

"That's what I want to know. I was going through Ms. Weinstein's correspondence that she'd put on her computer and found her letters to you."

"The fool," he said in an angry voice.

"You could say that. Anyway, I'd like to know what the story was with you two?"

He glared at me. "There wasn't any story. We had a little fling, that's all. I think she was going through a mid-life crisis and was using me to cushion it; that sort of thing happens all the time."

"Did it end?"

"You bet it ended. She wanted us to get divorced and marry each other. I told her I'd never do that because I love my wife."

"You have an interesting way of showing it."

"Listen, you little vampire, I don't have to take that from you. It's none of your damn business, and you can just get out of here."

"I guess I will," I said. "Oh, one more thing. Were you the man she was waiting for at the Lakeside Hotel a few days ago?"

"I don't know what you're talking about."

I had a strong feeling he was lying.

He said, "Are you going to tell the police about me?"

"What do you think?"

"You'll be sorry," he said grimly. "You'll be damned sorry."

Joanne and the Weinsteins agreed to meet again at the Weinstein home, that is, Manny agreed for himself and Kevin, who, he said, was sleeping. When I went there the next morning around ten, Kevin was still, or again, sleeping. I said I'd go on without him.

As she had the previous time, Joanne came in after me, gave Manny's arm a squeeze, and sat down near him. Was she a huggy-kissy type who naturally touched even people she'd newly met or—just perhaps—had she and Manny been acquainted before after all? Maybe, as the Bible put it, they had even "known" each other. What was sauce for the goose and all that.

"I want to ask you something," I said to Joanne.

"Sure." She gave a tug to her minuscule red skirt, which she was having difficulty keeping over her lower parts. A jeans and sweatshirt type myself, I never had such problems.

"Am I wrong to think that you and Manny have been close? Is there something going on between you?"

Joanne laughed. "You really are a detective, aren't you, Rachel? You're right."

She turned to Manny who'd been making protesting noises. "What's the difference, hon? Meredith is gone now, so we don't have to keep our relationship a secret any longer, especially since we didn't kill her."

He said, "What relationship? It was a momentary weakness on my part."

At least he hadn't tried to put the blame on Joanne.

He glanced over at me. "Believe me, Rachel, I would never have killed Meredith because of her."

"What's that supposed to mean?" she said.

"You're too much like her."

Joanne burst into tears. "Like her? That's the meanest thing anyone's ever said to me, Manny. I hope you rot for that."

He looked gloomy. "I'm sure I will."

I don't know how much longer this would have gone on, or what it would have led to, if Kevin, who'd come into the room without any of us seeing him, hadn't started sobbing. "Stop it," he said. "Stop. Or I'll do it for you."

I didn't try to find out what he had in mind. Even if he could have taken part in a coherent conversation, there was too much general hysteria for us to have one. I said goodbye shortly after that.

Something woke me during the early morning hours. At first I thought it was some kids in a souped-up car. I looked at the clock. Four A.M. was a little late for hotrodding, even among the future-hope-of-the-world set.

I heard it again. A skunk, I thought, messing with the trash can, or maybe a raccoon. We still had plenty of those around from the days when Fairfield had been farms and woodland. Then I heard cursing. Peering out of the window, I saw that someone was righting the metal can, which, apparently, had been knocked over. I lifted the sash. "What are you doing?" I hollered.

Whoever it was threw something in the can, placed the lid back on, and ran like hell. Moments later, I heard a car start off and zoom away. Silence, then noise—a lot of noise. I've never fought in a war, but that's what the sound made me think of—bombs, flying bullets, shrapnel.

I threw on some clothes and rushed outside to see what was going on. Tom and most of my neighbors were already there.

"Some small explosive device," he said when he saw me. "I've called the bomb squad and the fire department. Do you have any idea who might have done this, Rachel?"

"Sure—Manny Weinstein, Joanne Koppel, or Saul Behringer."

"Who?"

"I didn't tell you about him yet, did I? I got his name from a letter on Meredith's computer. The two of them were having an affair. I interviewed Behringer yesterday, and he threatened me."

"Enough to explode your garbage can?"

"I think so."

"I'll check him out."

"Ask him about sending Meredith flowers, too."

He looked puzzled, but agreed. "How come you didn't mention Kevin Weinstein?" he said.

"Because he's afraid to go out of his house. Do you think he'd leave his safe haven for the streets of Fairfield after dark? There really are all sorts of animals out then."

"Unless he's putting on an act," Tom said.

"Yes, unless that."

In fact, I didn't think he was, nor did I think he was a killer. I had a pretty strong hunch who was, though. I needed to talk to the Weinsteins again. There were still some things to straighten out.

On this occasion, the doorman was on duty. He was about to buzz the Weinstein apartment when Manny appeared in the lobby, saw me, and came over to greet me. He was wearing a dark green jacket over his blue blazer. He gave me a little hug, affording me the opportunity to smell his pleasantly musky aftershave, and said, "Go on up and let yourself in; I left the door unlocked. I'm on my way to get some bagels. Kevin's awake, for a pleasant change."

"That's good," I said, pleased that he seemed less depressed than previously. "See you soon."

I took the elevator up to the eighth floor penthouse, calling Kevin's name as I walked in the door. I didn't want to spook him. When I got no answer, I thought he might have gone back to bed. Then I spotted him on the balcony, one foot on the rail, the other on a none-too-steady stool. It was obvious he was planning to take a header.

I screamed for him to stop. He looked over his shoulder at me. "Don't come closer," he said.

Truthfully, I didn't want to because of my paralyzing fear of heights. I couldn't let Kevin Weinstein jump, but I couldn't stand the thought of getting near the edge of a balcony, either. Suppose he pushed me over, too. I imagined the sickening speed, the impact as I hit the street.

"Kevin, please get down and come away from the rail. You don't need to jump. Even if you killed your mom, it's not the end of the world, not like committing suicide. I'll get you help. I promise." He kept looking at me. "Think of your father. Don't do this to him."

He lowered his left foot onto the stool and made a shaky turn so that he faced me. He was still up against the rail. "It's my fault. None of this would have happened if it weren't for me."

"You mean the cyanide?"

"I mean everything, the health insurance, everything."

"I don't know what you're talking about," I said. "Tell me."

"No." He turned back toward the rail and raised his foot again. He was going to go over.

I did maybe the bravest thing of my life. I rushed toward the edge of the balcony, which by now he was half over, grabbed his arm, and pulled him to the floor.

Then I flopped on top of him, in case he decided to give dying another try. Kevin yelled that I was killing him. That's irony for you. His arms were going like fan blades, and he got in a few punches.

Suddenly I was grabbed around the neck. "What are you doing to my son?" Manny screamed at me. I was afraid he was going to slug me. "Leave him alone."

"Are you crazy? He's trying to kill himself. He was going to jump."

I heard Manny groan, then the three of us were on the floor of the balcony, a mass of arms and legs. I managed to extricate myself and roll toward the safety of the living room. Let Manny handle Kevin. I had barely enough strength to stand.

I slumped into a chair, watching Manny haul his son onto the Persian carpet, then slam shut the sliding doors and lock them. I noticed that both father and son were trembling violently.

When both men were finally seated across from me, I took a deep breath, and said, "Okay, let's sort this out."

Manny glared at me. "I leave him alone with you for two minutes, and when I come back he's trying to kill himself."

"Listen," I yelled, "I saved his life. Without me, he would have taken a nose dive, maybe timed just right to hit you on your bagels."

Manny stared at his right shoe, which had a big scuff mark across the toe. He probably acquired it when we were rolling around on the balcony floor. I don't know what his fine footwear had represented in his life, but that scrape apparently shattered any remaining equilibrium. "Look at that." Tears filled his eyes.

"Dad, don't," Kevin said, reaching a hand toward his father. "I'm not worth it. Everything's my fault."

"Nothing is," Manny said. "Do you hear me? Nothing."

"He's right, Kevin," I said. "Now what's this about health insurance?"

Manny sighed. "I suppose there's no use going on with this masquerade. Everything is falling apart, which is just what I didn't want to happen."

He looked ready to talk. I wasn't about to divert him with questions. "Go on," I said.

"Myrna told me she was thinking of divorcing me. What would I have done then?" His voice took on a desperate note. "I can't afford to live on my salary. I certainly can't afford to take care of my son on it. The health insurance was the last straw."

I leaned forward in my seat. "What do you mean?"

"Kevin can't survive without it, yet Myrna was saying that she was going to drop his coverage. Mine, too. His medicines cost a phenomenal amount.

Without Meredith, there was no way I could pay Kevin's bills, unless she were to die before she could leave me for good. In that case, I'd inherit all her money and a very large life insurance payment. Then Kevin would be safe." He looked lovingly at his son.

"I see," I said. "I'm sorry."

He sat across from me, the most dejected person I'd ever seen. But suddenly he seemed to gain strength. "You know what, Kevin can still inherit. He didn't kill anyone. So he'll be okay, won't he?"

"As far as I know," I said.

Manny put his head down and wept. "Thank God."

I let a few moments go by before I said, "Manny, you didn't confess anything to me except your desires. Desires don't equal murder."

He looked up at me with red-rimmed eyes. "I don't know what you're getting at."

"Don't confess to me," I said. "Don't confess to anyone, especially not the police. Get yourself a good lawyer. That's the person you want to talk to."

"But . . ."

"Don't say anything else. Trust me, okay? Even your wife did."

I left their apartment and went home. I figured those two weren't going to go anywhere.

As I was climbing the steps to my townhouse, I heard the phone ring. I got inside fast, wondering what was going down now. Maybe Kevin had tried to kill himself again. Maybe this time he'd succeeded. Or maybe Manny had spilled his guts to the cops after all. The person on the other end of the line was Tom. My voice shaky, I said, "What's up?"

"I talked to Behringer. He admits having had an affair with Whitney, admits sending her flowers, denies having killed her, and absolutely denies that he blew up your trash bin. I figure he did it, though, and I think we'll be able to get him for it."

"That's good," I said. "Listen, I just came from the Weinsteins'."

"Yeah? Did you find out anything else? We still can't pin it on anybody without a confession. I'm starting to feel frustrated."

When I didn't answer, he said, "Well?"

"Nobody confessed to me, either. You know, Tom, without that confession, or any real evidence, this thing is up for grabs. Suppose none of them killed her—I mean not her husband or son or the ex-agent, either. Maybe . . . maybe she committed suicide because Behringer rejected her. It wouldn't surprise me if a woman with her kind of ego couldn't take that. She could have turned her hatred and frustration on herself and her family."

This was the kind of psychologizing based on nothing that I didn't have patience with, but I was shamelessly willing to use it now. I said, "Don't forget, she was a really vindictive woman. She would have enjoyed causing them grief."

"I can't believe she'd have done that to her son. Her own kid?"

"I think she'd do it."

"I don't know. There's no proof that she wasted herself. She didn't even leave a suicide note."

"So? And, keep in mind, she was a real expert on poison."

"What are you talking about?"

"I mean the *lashon* herring kind," I said. "It's not only stuff like cyanide that's deadly. Think about it."

I hoped he would.

SHELLEY SINGER lives in Northern California and writes books about the private investigators Barrett Lake and Jake Samson. In this story, she decided to have Barrett return to her hometown for a school reunion. Strange events occur that bring out the best in the one-time school teacher turned private investigator.

Lost Polars

▾   ▾   ▾   ▾   ▾   ▾   ▾

SHELLEY SINGER

OVERWHELMING. SHE SURVEYED THE BALLROOM, searching for a familiar face, the face of someone, anyone, she'd seen or talked to recently, like maybe in the past decade.

The stage along the back wall was decorated with stuffed polar bears, blue and white paper chains, and a big sign that said, "Welcome North High class of 1967! Go Polars!"

She shouldn't have come to Minneapolis. Why had she thought she could escape indecision in San Francisco by running to the old familiar confusion in Minnesota? Stupid.

Tito had finally made the offer she'd been nagging him to make for two years—partnership in Tito Broz Private Investigators. Full time, he'd said. Quit teaching, he'd said. A big change. A pivotal decision. Pushing for it was one thing: getting it was something else. She needed time to think, she'd told him. But Tito was Tito. What for? he wanted to know. What do you need to think about? Put up or shut up.

I have to go to my reunion first, she'd said. Reconnect with my roots. Put up or shut up? No. There's always a third choice: run like a bunny.

So here she was, 2,000 miles away from the office in a big room with 300 middle-aged people who remembered her with pimples, if they remembered her at all. And they were all with their spouses. She aimed for the bar at the back of the room and ordered a glass of Merlot.

"Barrett!" A cheery voice from behind her.

Thank God. A face that belonged to the present even more than the past. Franny Kaplan. A member of the Plymouth Avenue Expatriates dinner group, North Side natives all living in the San Francisco Bay area. Franny's eyes were glittering, possibly with social gluttony, possibly from more than one glass of the white wine she'd just taken from the barman. She'd pinned her polar bear name tag haphazardly, crookedly, to the . . . silk? . . . over her left breast. The yearbook picture glued to the bear was a grainy copy, but Franny hadn't changed much. Always seemed happy, youthful, and ready to party. Even standing inches from Barrett, her gaze fluttered and slid through the crowd. She couldn't look at enough faces at once.

"Did you just get in? I thought you were coming in earlier, but the desk said . . ." distracted by a loud laugh, Franny let her sentence trail off while they both searched out the source. The explosively humorous Polar was a big man Barrett couldn't place. He was just slapping another man's shoulder.

Franny asked. "Would you believe that's Joe Levinson?"

"Which . . . ?"

"The fat one. He's gotten so . . . big. And gray. Quite a few of us have." She patted her own dyed, dark-brown hair ruefully.

"I thought he was on the Lost Polar list." They'd gotten several newsletters over the past year or so, full of various bits of information about the graduates and the reunion, to prepare them for this weekend.

"Well, I guess he got found. Actually, I thought he was dead, but we heard that about Daisy Bjorn, too. And they say she showed up at the 25th. So! Did you just get in?"

"I spent the afternoon visiting the old neighborhood. The schools, Plymouth Avenue, the shops. What's left of things." Once in town, she'd been drawn, like a lemming, a salmon, a football fan, to the North Side, where, if you listened really hard for the ghosts, you could still hear immigrants telling Yiddish jokes.

"Glad you didn't get shot. Well, I'm off to collect gossip. After all, I can talk to you anytime. See you!" Franny drifted off to find some local news.

Shot? The old home hadn't looked quite that bad, not in daylight. Her parents' store was long gone, of course, just like they were. The little corner grocery they'd seen as their ticket into the middle class. They'd managed to create a modest security for themselves and their child by working long hard hours, until the late sixties when a mob burned down the store, and the deli on the corner, and the . . . oh, hell, forget about that part.

Standing on Plymouth Avenue in front of the boarded up storefront that used to be Goldberg's Variety, she had remembered faces and houses and old yellow streetcars, squinting until the scene shimmered and melted enough to resemble its past. She was there again, with the others, the citizen of a voluntary ghetto, a transplanted *shtetl*. In her case, not by blood. Her genes were a scattering of Chippewa, French, Swedish. But her adoptive parents were passionately Jewish, and she was theirs.

Did that make her Jewish? That all depended on what "Jewish" was. Religion? Her folks were not religious. Genes? Racial memory? Shared history? Home base? Even when she'd dared to ask the question, there didn't seem to be an answer. She was part of the neighborhood, like a cell in a Jewish body, absorbing a sense of history and wounded justice that had led her first to teaching and then, in middle age, to a more dangerous way of trying to tip the scales. Sometimes, an eye for an eye.

A short, dark-haired woman was waving at her, smiling, hurrying to meet her. Judy Garbman. Wearing a very brief yellow dress. She brought with her a faint scent of lemons, a perfume to match her outfit.

"Well you certainly are a familiar face after all these years—and don't tell me, let me guess!" Much to Barrett's amazement, Judy clamped her hand over Barrett's nametag. "Barrett Lake!" She laughed and took her hand away. "See, I didn't even need to read it. You haven't changed a bit."

She remembered that about Judy. Full of irritatingly cute games. But she'd take the "you haven't changed a bit" and pretend it was so.

"Neither have you." In Judy's case, the pleasantry was true. She looked good. And prosperous. That rock on her finger looked like a real ruby, bigger than the diamond on her left hand.

"Thanks. I was so glad to hear you were coming. First time, right?"

Barrett nodded. For decades, she'd been too busy stumbling over her own life to even think about going back, although she'd kept thin threads of connection to some of the old crowd. It was those threads that had brought her together with the Plymouth Avenue Expatriates after more than twenty years of thinking she had the Bay area to herself.

Judy continued to natter on. "I haven't been to one in years. The fifth? The tenth? I don't remember. I think the fifth."

Barrett shrugged expansively, implying that life was like that, always other things to do, life to lead. Destiny . . . fate . . . years passing. Sigh.

"You know," Judy said, looking around the room, "I can't recognize some of them at all, and others just seem vaguely familiar. 'Course, it's been so many years . . . Oh, there's Mick." She grimaced. "We had a little tiff. It's make-up time. See you later." She watched Judy dash toward the man who, she assumed, was her husband. Expensive suit, unhappy face.

Barrett was halfway to a group of long-lost pals when the large man walked directly into her path and stood there, blocking her way, standing too close, smiling, showing his teeth. Wearing too much aftershave. Something cheap and heavily sweet. Joe Levinson. His name tag showed a young shaggy-haired, skinny boy she remembered only slightly. He glanced at her own name tag, trying not to be obvious.

"Good to see you, Barrett." He stuck his hands into the pockets of his well-pressed gray suitpants. "How ya doin'?"

"Good. And you?"

"Great. Real estate. Out of Chicago. And I don't mean selling little houses in Skokie." He chuckled.

"Oh?" She hadn't known him well in high school, hadn't particularly wanted to. She was beginning to see why. She'd asked him how he was, not what he did. And, she thought, he was bound to elaborate.

He did. "Yeah. Land. Canada. Very big right now. Great hunting. Got a buck once, rack like this." He held his hands wide apart. "And how do you spend your time?"

She spent some of it despising people who killed animals for no good reason. "I'm a teacher." She wasn't about to tell this guy she was also a P.I. He'd get all excited, and she'd never get rid of him.

"Well, darned nice to see you again, Barrett!" And he was gone, zip, just like that. Fine with her, certainly, but his instant departure had been startling. Even insulting. Oh, well. Maybe he hated teachers.

She moved quickly into the safe circle of friends. Semi-safe. Always that small raw edge of separation, a sense of difference, even if she was the only one who felt it. And how could she? She stood with the three Bobbies, all of whom spelled it differently, the two Annalees, Franny of the Expatriates.

Franny suddenly sucked in her breath, staring to their right. "Oh, God, this isn't going to be pretty."

Barrett followed her gaze. Judy Garbman, a man, and a blonde woman she couldn't quite place. The man was holding the blonde's arm, and she was snapping and snarling at Judy. Judy stood there like a tree. A small, dark, scowling tree in a yellow miniskirt. Alone. Hadn't she made up with her husband? Only a few words sifted across the distance and through the crowd.

"Nervy bitch . . . can't believe . . ."

"Now come on, honey, let's get a cup of coffee." The man was tugging at her with one hand and patting her back with the other. She didn't move.

"Showing up here like a piece of old trash . . ." Not much of a simile, Barrett thought. A bad penny. Clichéd, but at least apt. The man was pulling the blonde woman harder, now, and she seemed to be leaning toward him. She started crying. He grabbed both shoulders, turned her around, and marched her off. Like a soap opera, Barrett thought. Or a made-for-TV movie.

She set her now-empty wineglass on a nearby table and turned to Franny, the hunter and gatherer.

"What was that about?"

"You really don't know, Barrett? Well, honey, you've been out of touch too long. That's Helen Peterson. Way back, oh, maybe twenty-five years ago, Judy had a long, long affair with Helen's husband, Billy. Almost broke up the marriage. I'd love to know what he was thinking during all that carrying on just now." If she ever found out, so would everyone else.

Definitely a soap opera. Not much of a plot.

Franny continued. "And then Judy took off for a couple years. She was a lost Polar for a while. Went to Cincinnati? Cleveland?" She looked at one of the Annalees, who thought a minute.

"Chicago." The closest *big* big city. "Barrett was in Cleveland."

How did they know that? She'd been there for a year and hadn't told anyone. Her surprise must have showed. Annalee smiled.

"We always knew where you were, Barrett."

They had? Always? She'd think about that later.

A waiter came by and offered them a tray of white crackers topped with little pompadours of processed yellow cheese. Only three of the women accepted. One or two mumbled something about never eating cheese. Barrett, tempted by the junk food, turned away from the tray and noticed Judy, shaky but still game, checking out the crowd and arrowing toward Joe Levinson. She stopped in front of him and clapped her hand over the nametag on his chest. He stared at her as if she'd lost her mind, exchanged a few words, and escaped.

Barrett's attention shifted from Judy to Joe. The man really worked a room, shaking hands, slapping backs. He began a conversation with Mick Garbman and—*that* had to be Randy Blue! She'd dated him for a few months in tenth grade. He played the trombone, or did then. She'd heard he was making a lot of money in computers or something like that. Modems? Faxes? Joe scribbled something down, passed on a card, got Randy's. They shook hands. Joe did a be-right-back-gotta-go-talk-to-whatsis shuffle and took off after Billy Peterson who was standing, alone, in the middle of the room, sipping at a cup of coffee.

A real type, Joe. But the hunting? That was weird.

Franny was now chatting cheerfully about Helen's drinking problem. The dark Bobbie, never much of a gossip, turned the conversation to Barrett's work.

"We're so proud of you . . ."

"I can't believe how brave . . ."

"I could never . . ."

"Tell us about some of your cases, please! Any murders?"

A few. Killers, kidnappers, embezzlers, extortionists. Prostitutes and street kids and victims. They seemed to want to hear about it, but she avoided details. She didn't know why. Maybe it was better to keep it glossy? After ten minutes or so, they returned almost seamlessly to gossip, this time of a milder sort.

They talked about how some of "the girls" in the crowd hadn't made it this time for one reason or another. A bad tooth, a bad back, a job loss, a weight gain. Walter had gotten rich and lost it all. Billy Peterson had parlayed his family's money into a major wholesaling something-or-other. Tom wasn't as handsome now as he'd been at the 25th. Oh, my God. Carla Helstrom. Was that a granny dress she was wearing? Barrett looked. A granny dress all right. And beads. Looks like she fell asleep on prom night and woke up thirty years later. Was she wearing patchouli oil, too? Barrett decided she would make a point of not finding out.

A loud scream silenced them. It started somewhere outside the room and flared to a howl, materializing in the doorway in the person of one of the Saarinen triplets—Jill Saarinen, Barrett thought. Everyone froze, until Dale Sequist, the editor of the school paper their senior year, ran toward Jill, gripping her shoulders, talking to her, listening closely to her gasped and mumbled words. Barrett didn't stop to think or say a word to her friends. Like a race horse or a heavyweight at the bell, she moved. Before she was halfway there, Dale had put Jill in her sister's care and had dashed through the door, followed by several nearby men and a couple of women.

Decision time. Talk to Jill or follow the posse? Jill first.

By the time Barrett reached the wailing triplet, both her sisters were comforting her. It took a second to get her attention.

"What's happened?"

"I think she's dead."

"Who? Where?"

"Judy Garbman. In the toilet."

Dead? No. Maybe she'd fainted. Better find out. Follow the posse.

As Barrett approached the women's room, the group she was pursuing was already on its way out. She tried to thread her way through their oncoming bodies to get to the door and have a look, but Dale stopped her.

"You don't want to see it."

"Yes." She shoved him out of her way. "I do."

The stall door was open. Judy was sitting on the toilet, but she hadn't been using it. Her clothing was more or less in order; her face was not. Her tongue protruded, her dead eyes bulged, and Barrett thought she could see a mark on the throat. No, she had not fainted. Barrett felt a quick burn of tears, a spasm in her throat. She had to close her eyes to regroup, wanting to lean against the wall but knowing she should touch nothing. When she opened her eyes again, she glanced at Judy's hands. The rings were still on her fingers. Not a robbery. Random violence or something personal.

She returned to the ballroom, searching until she again found the quivering triplet.

"Tell me exactly what you saw when you went into the restroom."

Jill sobbed, staring at Barrett in horror.

"Please. Tell me."

She shook her head in quick tiny jerks. More like a tremble than a shake. "They're calling the cops. I'll have to tell them, too. I don't want to say it twice."

"Please."

She sighed and looked to one of her sisters for support. The sister shrugged. Jill gave in. "Okay. I walked into the bathroom. I saw this stall door open about an inch. I pushed it and . . . " she gagged, "she was sitting there."

"Did you touch her?"

"God, no!"

More questions got no more answers. Jill tried, but the only other part she remembered was Judy's tongue, "Way out of her mouth. It looked so big."

Barrett found Dale and asked him the same questions. He hesitated.

"Maybe we should wait for the police."

She'd be shunted out of the way for sure, then. She showed Dale her P.I. license. That seemed to make it all right for him to talk to her.

"Oh, yeah, I heard you were doing that."

He was too preoccupied with the real excitement to work up a lot of enthusiasm about her wonderful job. Unfortunately he didn't have much to say about the death, either. The stall door had been open, the posse saw Judy, they touched nothing.

Barrett wandered away from Dale, trying to put some quick impressions in order. She noticed that their class president, the emcee for the night, was at his post on the stage, but his tall thin body was slumped into a folding chair and he held a glass of something brown in his hand. Poor thing. He hadn't had a chance to tell a single joke or make fun of a single classmate.

Barrett sat down in a corner, wondering how to put the puzzle together. What to do next and how fast to do it. Judy had just had a fight with Helen. Where was she? She'd also had a fight with her own husband. Where was he now? And Billy. Helen's husband. Had she missed something? Had Billy made a brand new pass at Judy or had she greeted him too lingeringly?

Just as she was plucking at those thoughts, Randy of the trombone and the faxes brought Judy's husband, Mick, into the ballroom. He was wearing pajamas. His hair was sticking up in cowlicks at the crown. He was crying, his teary eyes darting around the room.

"Where is she!"

Was his agony real? Randy murmured to him and kept his arm tight around his shoulders.

The police would arrive any second. Maybe she had time to get in a few questions.

She touched his arm. "Mick, I'm so sorry." He tried to focus on her, but it was obvious he had no idea who she was or why she was standing in front of him. Randy smiled sadly at her. Their first greeting.

"I'm glad you two had time to resolve your spat before, um . . ." Great opening, Lake, she told herself. She was hurrying too much. Randy wasn't smiling any more.

"Spat? We didn't . . ." But Judy had said they did.

"Well, good, Mick. I hope you can take some comfort in the dignified way she handled that scene with Helen and Billy. They were all friends once, isn't that right?"

"Huh?" Mick articulated. Randy, scowling at her, rose with silent indignation and placed his tall body between Barrett and Mick. She wasn't behaving the way he thought she should. She felt an old familiar stab of doubt. People who really belonged didn't . . . fill in the blank.

Barrett glanced back toward where she'd last seen that cluster of her old friends. Several of them were still standing together, and one or two more had joined them. Those who weren't whispering in each others' ears were watching her. One of the Bobbies made a thumb-and-forefinger circle, nodding energetically. Go get 'em, Barrett. Solve the case.

Well, all right, then.

At that moment, the first wave of cops arrived. Four uniformed police clomped through the door, two by two, glancing at the man in pajamas suspiciously. Dale hurried to meet them. One of them muttered something to him, and he ran to the stage, where the class president still sat, slouched and drinking. Dale spoke to him. The president dragged himself to the mike, cleared his throat, took a sip of the brown stuff, and gripped the mike stand.

"Nobody leave this room," he yelled. He sat down again.

Two of the cops stationed themselves at the two exits from the ballroom. One of the other cops had a ring of keys. He closed and locked one set of double doors.

Dale took cop number four out the other door, the one closer to the women's room and Judy's body, and cop number three locked that door after them. The combination of movements seemed practiced, almost artful, like a complicated dance. Cop number three then marched to the stage, glanced once at the class president—as if he were wondering what he was doing up there—and took hold of the mike.

"Everybody needs to sit down." He waited. "I said, *everybody* sit down."

They began to find seats.

"What about the hotel staff?" The bartender yelled from the back of the room. "We're not supposed to be sitting. The waiters aren't supposed to be sitting. Or the bussers."

The cop glared at him. "You are now. Sit. And don't talk to each other. Sit and be quiet."

"What if there aren't enough chairs?" The bartender again. The cop looked disgusted, shook his head, and left the stage.

Barrett knew that the police didn't want the witnesses, suspects, and innocent bystanders talking to each other, colluding, or contaminating their own memories. The detectives would come and interview everyone. Barrett could only hope they'd get there soon and eliminate some of the people quickly, or the reunion would last all night and part of the next day. And this whole ballet could be a fat waste of time. The killer might very well have done the deed and run from the hotel before the body was found. Or could still be in the hotel, but waiting for a good time to leave.

Who was missing from the ballroom? How would she ever know? And were all the hotel exits being covered, too? There was no way to know how many police were in the building. Were they checking out everybody?

Mick, Judy's husband, was now sitting with his elbows on his knees, his hands covering his face. A cop stood over him like a sentry. Of course. Everyone knows that the spouse is always the most likely suspect. Another good reason, she had always thought, not to marry.

But while the bleary Mick might be the best suspect, Barrett was just as interested in Helen, who stood beside her husband, Billy. They weren't talking. She looked nervous; he looked calm. Both of them blonde, both handsome. Billy looked better than Helen. Maybe he didn't drink as much as she did. As Barrett watched them, Helen spoke to Billy and walked toward the door, where she said something to the fourth cop. He nodded and took her outside. Probably a trip to the women's room. Maybe she wanted to revisit the scene of her crime. Could a woman hold a grudge that many years? Judging by her verbal attack on Judy, this one could. And the murder had been committed in the women's toilet, after all. It would take a desperate man to go in there. Of course, killers do tend to be desperate . . .

Someone was pounding on the ballroom door. The cop left Mick where he sat and let in two more uniformed officers. One of them exchanged a few words with the cop just inside the door and, leaving the door open now, stationed himself outside, looking as immovable and focused as a Beefeater.

More ballet.

Helen's husband Billy was standing near the coffeemaker, holding his cup, sipping, looking as if none of this chaos applied to him at all. Barrett wanted to talk to him. What about the rule of silence? What about the rule of chair-sitting? Well, the hell with all that. She wanted a cup of coffee.

She sidled up to the coffeemaker, pouring some into a cardboard cup, and strolled the three steps to Billy's side.

She spoke very softly, out of the side of her mouth.

"You must have felt pretty uncomfortable when your wife and Judy—"

A shrug, a whisper: "Why should I?"

"Because it was about you, I suppose."

"Bygones are bygones. It was a lot of years ago. Helen just overreacted."

Aha. "To what?"

"To nothing. To old news." He said it loudly enough to attract a glare from one of the cops and walked away, presumably to find a chair.

Helen returned. Should she try to talk to her? Oh, good. She was coming Barrett's way. This was the perfect time. Billy—yes, he'd parked himself in a chair, still sipping coffee—was making no move to rejoin his wife. Did he think she was a killer?

Two detectives, one tall and blond and one stocky and dark, were now huddled with the uniformed officers who'd been the first to arrive in the ballroom. The tall blond one went immediately to Judy's husband, Mick, and took him out of the room.

Barrett intersected Helen's path.

She opened. "Terrible, huh? A murder here . . ."

Helen nodded. She looked stunned and her eyes were red. Alcohol? Fear?

"I was just talking to your husband—" a cop glanced at her. She clamped her lips shut and waited for him to look away. "He seems quite shocked by all this."

"Billy? Shocked? I doubt that. Son of a bitch."

"What's wrong? Did you have a fight?"

"Just look what he's gotten me into." The cop came over, asked them to stop talking, told them to go sit down. They did. Together.

"Gotten you into?" This was promising.

"Sure. They probably think I offed the bitch. But I guess I'm not the only one who hated her."

Around the room, people were whispering to each other, restless, tense. The cops couldn't keep after all of them.

"Have any ideas about the killer?"

"Didn't I hear you were a detective? Am I some kind of suspect?" Everybody watched television.

"The police are bound to be interested in that fight you had with her. Maybe if you explain to me—"

"They're interested and so are you. Anyone could have done it. And I don't know who did. So forget it."

That was what Barrett had to do. Forget it. At least for the time being. The stocky detective was walking their way. The tall detective was still missing with Mick Garbman.

"Miz Peterson?" Barrett moved a short distance away, slowly, hoping to hear something of the detective's conversation with Helen. That was a washout. He only asked her to go with him "for a talk."

Too bad. The best suspects were gone for the moment.

One of the Annalees swooped past, stage-whispering a tip: "I just heard they arrested Mick."

Gossip or reality? She'd have to find out. The Annalee continued in a wide circle, a word here, a word there, heading for the door to the hallway and the women's room.

"Barrett." The soft voice came from beside her. Randy. They nodded to each other.

"Really good to see you again, Barrett." She smiled. "But what the hell was all that about, that thing with Mick? How could you? The man just lost his wife, for God's sake." Huh. Hell with you, Randy. This is what I do. And couldn't the police do a better job of keeping people in their chairs?

"Sorry, but I had to. Do you still play trombone?"

"Yeah. But you really shouldn't have—"

"I know." Change the subject again. "Saw you talking to Joe Levinson a while ago. Shaking hands."

That did it. Randy grinned and shook his head, distracted from her social error.

"Yeah. What a guy." Did he mean it or was he joking?

"Sounds like he makes big deals."

Randy nodded enthusiastically. "You bet. And a few of us are getting in on one of them."

He wasn't joking.

"Really? Have you given him any money?" Randy shrugged and looked sly. She wasn't much interested in the big deal, but she was interested in some of the people who were in on it. "I noticed him talking to you and Mick. Billy, too. What's it about?"

"Very big. Canada. Big money in, bigger money out. You should look into it." This hardly seemed like the Randy she'd known. Joe had swept him away. Barrett was remembering the boy and his band. No lead guitar for him. A sweet rebel who loved and played the music that was old even then. Glenn Miller. "String of Pearls." Maybe his excitement over Levinson's deal was okay. Part of the innocence she'd loved in him then.

Both detectives were back in the room, now, and a few more uniforms had arrived. She thought she'd better sit down for a while, maybe next to someone who could tell her something.

"Really good to see you again, Randy."

"Me, too." They hugged, murmured the usual "talk to you more later" stuff, and parted.

Joe Levinson was sitting near the bar, looking sulky, a vacant chair next to him. She looked around the ballroom. The two detectives and some of the cops seemed to have disappeared again. Maybe she could find out a little more about Mick and Billy. She already knew both of them had money, which could explain Joe's interest in them.

She planted herself beside him. "Horrible, huh?"

"We're not supposed to talk." A rule-follower? He didn't seem like one.

"It's okay. The detectives are gone and the uniforms are busy keeping an eye on this crowd just to make sure no one jumps through a window."

"There aren't any windows." He didn't even have to look. He knew. He'd scoped out the room for escape routes. She thought this said a lot about his career—or his love life.

"Noticed you talking to Randy. And Mick and Billy. How well do you know those guys?"

"Not well. Just doing business. I think we should be quiet now."

She didn't feel like being quiet, and she already knew he wasn't interested in doing business with her. But he wanted to do business with the men she was beginning to think of as "the two husbands," and he might have seen or heard something while he was courting their cash. Maybe she could get him chatting.

"So sad about Judy. I knew her pretty well in school. We used to talk about how we could be related. Our grandparents all came from the same town in, well, it's Belarus now. Kobrin."

He gave her a blank stare. She asked a question anyway. "Where are your people from?"

He looked, as her mother used to say, like he'd just found half a worm in an apple. "Moscow, maybe. Yeah. Moscow." Well, that was always possible. Not Minsk, not Pinsk, not Brest-Litovsk. But he didn't really seem to know. Or care. And then there was the hunting.

The detectives came back into the room. She dropped her voice, wanting to continue, interested in his answers. "The old neighborhood has changed a lot, hasn't it?"

He turned on a semi-sweet good ol' boy smile. "Yeah. 'Fraid so. Too bad."

"Even the theater's gone. What was it called again? It's been so long."

"Yeah. Been so long. I don't remember, either. Think I need a cup of—" Unbelievable. "And the deli—was it on Newton? What was it called . . . ?"

He shrugged and smiled again. He didn't know. Compared to him, she was made of North Side clay. She was the primordial Lake—née Lakoff—retracing her ancestral steps past Ellis Island, through Russia, around the Black Sea, south through Turkey. Hiking across the Red Sea with Pharoah in doomed pursuit.

"So you were in Chicago and so was Judy. Ever see her there?"

Not a flicker of what she was looking for now. He laughed easily. "Big town, honey." True. "I gotta ask those cops if I can take a leak. See you later."

Once again, he fled from her. He approached a uniform and spoke a few words. The cop went out the door with him.

Barrett got up, too, but she went to the tall blond detective. Good looking. Hazel eyes, long, straight nose. Full lips.

"I have to make an important phone call. Can I do that? If one of your guys comes along and watches me, or listens in or whatever you want? It's really urgent and . . ." She hesitated. Maybe it would be better not to say the call was connected to the case. "And important."

He studied her suspiciously before he nodded, slowly, and called over one of the uniforms. Not good looking. A bad-stomach expression on his face. He followed her sourly out to a phone booth.

She dialed the agency number. Eight o'clock here, six o'clock there. Tito was frequently still in the office at that hour. Three rings and her partner picked up. Partner? Was she already thinking of him that way? Did that mean she'd made up her mind? No. Maybe.

"Tito. This is Barrett. We've got a murder at the reunion." He cracked up, laughing that donkey laugh of his. "For God's sake, stop hee-hawing. I mean it."

He hiccuped once and stopped. "Too bad. It's a great joke"

"Glad you like my material. Listen, I need some quick data. You didn't miss a payment on the search service, did you?" He assured her that he hadn't. Or at least he didn't think so. She told him what she wanted, and he said he'd get back to her within an hour. She turned to the cop, who was looking at her curiously, now. Piqued, too. What was she doing talking about their murder?

"He's going to call me back."

Grudgingly: "Make an appointment." It took her a minute to understand what he meant.

"Oh. Okay. Tito, I'll come back to this phone—" she gave him the number, "at exactly . . ." She looked at her watch. "At exactly 9:05 Central. I'll call you then."

"Seven-o-five here. Got it. But let me call you in case it takes me another ten minutes." And he was gone.

The cop was trying to seem unconcerned. Officer Cool. But he was almost dancing in place. He couldn't wait to get back and tell the boss.

"Done?" She nodded. "Then let's move it, okay, ma'am? One of us'll bring you back here at nine."

"Thanks."

He hustled her toward the ballroom, never actually touching her but hovering at her back. "You some kind of lawyer?"

"No."

"Well, I thought, what with the search service. Pricey. Not everybody . . . That's on-line public information, right?"

She told him it was. He might just do well in his chosen career.

He took her back into the ballroom and headed straight for the tall blond detective. It's about this phone call she made, he would be saying. She told the guy about the murder. She told him to check out a search service, and she's not even a lawyer. You know what those things cost. He'd tell the detective what kind of information she'd asked for. The detective would be in her face in seconds.

Barrett decided to make the first move. Talk to him before he had to come to her. Be a pal, friendly, helpful.

The detective met her halfway. "What's this about? This search thing?"

"There's someone here who may be running a scam, and I was checking on it."

"Running a scam?" One corner of his mouth quirked. She decided he was a punk.

She pulled her I.D. out of her bag.

"Oh, boy! A private eye! And from California, too." A smart-ass punk. "So what makes you think we should call in bunko?" He spat the word like a noir movie hero. Humphrey Bogart, maybe. Very funny.

"I know you've got a lot of good suspects. Helen Peterson. Her husband Billy. Mick. I heard you arrested Mick." He raised his eyebrows but said nothing. "But there's someone here who just doesn't fit."

"Fit? Cut to the chase, Nancy Drew."

Sure, Dick Tracy. "Okay, for starters, this guy said he hunted. Jewish men don't hunt."

The detective rolled his eyes. She went on.

"He says he's Joe Levinson but he didn't know what town in the old country his people came from. Most of us do. Our grandparents talked constantly about where they or their families came from and who else came from there." The cop looked skeptical.

She fired the big guns. "He didn't know the name of either the movie theater or the deli on the old North Side and that's impossible." No North Side Jew would ever forget. It was their history, their identity. Part of their souls. Certainly part of hers. She knew an outsider when she met one.

The cop sighed. "People do forget."

"Hey," she shot back, "are you Jewish?" The cop stared at her, silent. Then he shook his head.

"Well, I'm telling you, he can't be Joe Levinson."

"Point him out." She did. He laughed. "The big guy? Bet he's put on a hundred pounds since high school. You gonna tell me he's not this Joe guy because he doesn't look the same? This is not exactly a young crowd." She wanted to punch him in the stomach. "I'm sure most of them don't look the same."

"Matter of fact, most of them do. Let's see what I get back from my partner, okay?"

"Sure. Why not. But we're working a murder case, not confidence."

"There's someone here who isn't who he says he is, I guarantee it. And someone's been killed. He's from Chicago, and the victim spent a few years there in the seventies. She still looks like she did in High School. Or looked, anyway. Easily recognizable. He's impersonating someone from our class. Wheeling and dealing. Couldn't there be a connection?"

Not to mention that Judy had been playing her little nametag game, telling all her classmates that they looked familiar. Maybe he thought she had already spotted him as someone other than Joe Levinson, someone she'd once met and was now remembering as Harvey Green or Stan Olson or Jack the Ripper. He'd looked pretty upset when Judy had accosted him. He had to do something or he had to get out, fast. And he wouldn't want to leave, since his scam seemed to be working so well.

"There could be. There always can be. This Jewish angle . . . sounds like you're stretching things. But I have to admit you'd know more about that than me."

That's right. She would. He was bending, trying to be ethnically sensitive. Good.

"I don't care if you believe me now. Maybe he is Joe, and he had an accident and can't remember anything. But let's try the search, please. All you have to do is not let him go until we hear from my partner." That felt right, too. Partner. She could handle it.

The detective didn't answer at first. Then his expression shifted to neutral. "I'll take you back to the phone when it's time."

Barrett spent the next hour waiting with her friends. At first they'd shot her full of questions, hurried, whispered interrogations, but she'd only told them she thought she had a suspect, and she wouldn't name him. She couldn't take a chance, she said, on someone inadvertently tipping him off. Franny was the only one who came right out and said she hated her for keeping the secret, and swore she'd "get" her somehow.

Barrett watched the police interview one person after another, some very briefly. One by one, with excruciating slowness, her classmates were leaving the room. The crowd didn't look much smaller, and the ones who weren't fascinated by the tedium of police procedure were getting sullen. A few had tried to push the cops to take them through first. The room seemed to be getting warmer, and a lot of the women were fanning themselves with their programs. One held a little pink battery-operated fan two inches from her neck. There was a lot of muttering, and she heard someone crying. The class president was asleep in his chair on the stage.

The lucky ones who'd already left, Barrett was thinking, were probably sitting in the bar talking about their interviews and speculating about the killer.

Barrett noticed the police did not talk to the Joe Levinson impostor. He was still waiting. Sulking. Because she'd asked the detective not to let him go? Was he really doing what she'd asked? It was always possible, she supposed.

At nine o'clock, that same detective came to get her and escorted her to the phone. Tito called five minutes later and this was what he had: Three reunion real estate scams in the past four years. There was always a guy who turned out not to be the real classmate. He took money from investors and disappeared. All three of the real classmates had lived in Chicago. At one of the reunions, the one in Madison, Wisconsin, a classmate had been murdered. The search had also provided a description of the impostor, and it worked fine for "Joe Levinson."

But Tito had said the real classmates "had lived" in Chicago. Was that what he really meant?

"Tito, what about the people this man was impersonating?"

"All three dead. One questionable, two natural causes."

The detective made Tito repeat the whole spiel for him. Then he led Barrett back to the ballroom, sat her in a chair, and told her to stay there.

Before he got away she stopped him with a question. "What about Mick Garbman?"

He smiled at her. A friendly smile. "What about him? We called a doctor. He's in bed."

Again, Barrett's eyes searched the room for "the girls." Half a dozen were still there. They were watching her. She gave them a quick nod. They tried, and mostly failed, to conceal their excitement. Things were about to start happening.

The cop talked to his partner, who glanced at her twice during their conversation. The partner nodded and left the room. They couldn't possibly tell her what they were doing. That would be uncop-like. She could only guess, and hope, that they were checking out Tito's information and even following some lines of their own that would lead them in the same direction.

Two hours later, she was still waiting, "Joe" was still waiting, and the cops were still talking to the ballroom's inmates. About a third had by now been allowed to leave. Maybe they'd be finished by breakfast time. She wanted to stay where she was, right there in that room, for as long as it took.

The stocky detective, who had been in and out of the ballroom several times, came back in, moving uncharacteristically fast. He glanced at Barrett again, only now his expression held more wonder than wariness. He looked stunned. Barrett thought that was probably a very good sign.

He and his partner talked. The stocky guy walked over to where "Joe Levinson" sat, not far from Barrett, took his arm, and led him toward the door.

But good old Joe didn't get it yet or, at least, was going to pretend for as long as he could. He was complaining, "I been waiting here all damned night! It's about time you talked to me. I'm a busy guy. This whole thing is an outrage." He pulled his arm away from the detective and, trying for dignity, straightened his tie. When the cop took his arm again, began softly reading him his rights, and signaled several uniforms to join the party, Joe's indignation and dignity failed him. He looked around, desperate, eyes wide, breath coming hard through his open mouth, searching for some way out.

No windows, Joe.

Except for Barrett's friends—two of them were still in the room—the hundred or so classmates who were still waiting mostly looked confused. They didn't quite get it, either, not yet. Someone yelled, "You don't have to wait anymore!" And a few people who desperately needed to break their own tension laughed. Then word began circulating: They're reading him his rights. She even heard her own name mentioned a few times and realized that people were beginning to stare at her. She caught sight of Randy. Poor Randy. His face was all screwed up in pain and disbelief. No big Canada deal for him. Barrett sent him a mental message: think about it this way, Randy—at least he didn't get away with a pile of your money. She hoped he'd figure it out once the shock passed and feel a whole lot better.

The blond detective approached her. "You earned this, Barrett, so I'll tell you—the Joe Levinson you guys went to school with fell off a bridge six months ago."

"In Chicago."

"You betcha. Good job, Lake. Hate to say it, though." He smiled and walked away. You betcha. Minnesota talk.

Now, Barrett knew, the investigation would get complicated. The police would have to begin tracing relationships and connections. They'd find out who the fake Joe really was. They'd start looking into his link to the real Joe, his friends, his death. Maybe, if they were lucky, they'd find ties to one of the other guys he'd impersonated. Or the classmate in Madison. To people who knew Judy, and to Judy Garbman herself. The Judy that was. Way back. Twenty-five years ago, young, and as wild as everyone else was then.

Doing things. Meeting people. And maybe remembering one of them tonight. Or maybe not.

BOB SLOAN teaches high school drama in New York City and is the author of *Bliss Jumps the Gun,* the second book in his series about New York Policeman Lenny Bliss. Here the mystery revolves around the character and experiences of a self-absorbed rabbi. This story originally appeared in *Reform Judaism Magazine*.

The Good Rabbi

▼   ▼   ▼   ▼   ▼   ▼   ▼   ▼

BOB SLOAN

THE RABBI WROTE NEATLY. It was something he'd been chided for in high school, the boys had been suspicious that his handwriting was too perfect to be a boy's, and the girls had been wary of him, thinking he might be some kind of spy. He ignored their ridicule and worked diligently at his desk, the act of writing sometimes overshadowing his subject. Lee's strategy at Vicksburg or Holden Caulfield's neurosis were secondary to the thrill of shaping the letters, controlling their symmetry, aligning the apex of their curves to imaginary ceilings, sending each small "p" and "g" diving below the surface at exactly the same depth. And his sentences lining up on the page with the precision of a well-drilled marching band.

The rabbi was writing to a member of his congregation that afternoon. He was known for these letters and took great pride in them: his thoughts and advice. No—his counsel. The rabbi sat in his office in his distinctive bow tie and V-neck sweater, and assiduously composed letters in response to the troubles and concerns his congregants brought to him. He listened, asked questions, and then bid them take their leave, which disconcerted those who, like at the counter, required that their needs be instantly met. But they were used to it now, waiting patiently for him to compose his thoughts and the few extra days it took for them to arrive in the mail. He'd been told that even before reading his letters, the mere act of gazing at his handwriting, of taking in the exquisitely shaped letters, instantly began to calm whatever trouble was in their soul. The rabbi took this as a compliment.

His inspiration for the letters came from the Book of Job. After God dumped his slop bucket of pain and torment on him, Job sat silently for seven days with his friends. They sat with him on the ground for seven days and seven nights, and no one spoke a word. . . .

What did he do in those seven days but organize his thoughts. And in the ensuing argument, Job is the more rational. It's God who seems to be improvising like a second-rate comic, Who speaks from anger, Who sounds wounded. The rabbi sought to emulate Job's patience. If Job could wait in pain to answer, his body a moonscape of sores and boils, then the rabbi, sitting behind his grand oak desk in his plush leather chair, could certainly do the same.

Sometimes he allowed himself the pleasure of imagining his letters collected in a large volume. He saw people reading it just before bed, placing it on their night stand, turning out the light, their last thoughts before sleep being how wise he was.

He already had a book proposal of letters he'd written to his daughter, addressing the many challenges and anxieties she would face growing up. They were filled with wisdom and humor, though one editor suggested that it might help if his humor were actually humorous. His daughter was only six now. In a few more years, he would let her read the letters, unless they were accepted by a publisher sooner than that.

He was finishing up a letter now to Mrs. Zipkin, who spoke to him yesterday at length about her fears that her daughter might be a lesbian. He remembered the girl from confirmation class. She didn't seem lesbianesque then, but the rabbi had to admit that if she wasn't in the act of passionately kissing another woman, he wasn't sure exactly what a lesbian looked like.

Lesbian is as lesbian does, the rabbi wrote to Mrs. Zipkin. You must not allow this to influence the love you have for your daughter. The barest seedling of an idea, but his weight as rabbi would, like Jack's magic beans, make it grow into a giant stalk of insight in Mrs. Zipkin's mind. I confess, Mrs. Zipkin, I would have just as hard a time imagining my daughter having sex with a man as I would with a woman. He wondered if he was revealing too much, but he was approaching the end of this letter, and he had three more to work on before leaving the office for the day. Her happiness is your primary concern, Mrs. Zipkin. Put aside your expectations and embrace hers. But invite her back to temple with you. These days, I believe a strong spiritual foundation takes precedent over one's sexual preference.

It was not one of his most inspired efforts, like his poetic thoughts to griev-ing widows or the sage counseling he passed on to troubled couples. Fast-balls of grief and angst he hit over the fence. It was the existential curves, like those thrown by Mrs. Zipkin, that he grounded weakly back to the pitcher. He might leave this one out of the collected works.

The intercom buzzed. His secretary spoke.

"Fred Siegel is here," she said.

"Yes."

"He doesn't have an appointment, but he says he's very distressed. He says . . ."

Then the rabbi heard what must have been Fred's voice both in the back-ground on the phone and, at the same time, through the door, which gave the rabbi the eerie feeling that Fred was in two places at once.

"It's a matter of life and death," Fred said.

The rabbi had never actually heard anyone utter that phrase. It sent a tiny shudder through him, and at the same time he felt excited.

"Show him in," the rabbi said.

Though he didn't remember speaking to Fred before, he recognized him at once. He owned a fancy wine and liquor store in town that did quite well. Fred himself was an unassuming man, handsome in a gruff kind of way, well-dressed, his blazer cut smartly and his pants of a thick, textured wool. His hands were clean, his nails polished. Fred didn't seem overly distressed. His firm handshake did not belie any nervousness.

"Sit down, please," the rabbi said.

Fred sat, not sinking back into the chair, but not sitting on the edge of it either. He was a tough one to read.

"You enjoyed that Chablis, Rabbi?" Fred asked in a calm voice, referring to a kosher wine from a small French vineyard he had suggested the rabbi try.

"It was quite nice," the rabbi replied. He had later ordered a case.

"That's good."

Fred folded his hands in his lap and sat silently. He seemed in no partic-ular rush. What happened to the matter of life and death, the rabbi thought.

"Working on one of your letters?" Fred asked, casually eyeing the paper on the rabbi's desk.

"Yes, in fact." He casually turned the letter over; not that Fred could see from where he was, but he had to protect it. He nervously adjusted his bow tie.

"You said it was urgent, your needing to see me."

"Life and death, Rabbi," Fred said.

"Tell me what's on your mind." After a steady dose of marriages in free fall, of bar mitzvah consultations, of meetings with prospective brides and grooms who were more likely to inquire about a good florist than what psalms to read at the ceremony, the rabbi was keenly curious about what Fred had to say. Here was something that piqued his curiosity, that exuded a bit of danger. After all, the rabbi was only human.

"Everything's confidential here," Fred said, gesturing to the letter. "Isn't that right, Rabbi?"

"Yes," the rabbi said, leaning forward, sensing it was about to start.

"So anything I say to you will not leave this room."

"Absolutely."

"Good."

"Life and death, you said."

"Yes, Rabbi, I did," Fred said. "And I'll get right to the point. I very much want to kill someone."

"Oh."

The rabbi froze. He wants to kill, he thought. He'd never dealt with anything like this before.

"You mean," the rabbi said, "that you're very angry with someone and you . . . want to kill them—rhetorically. In a manner of speaking."

"No, I want to kill them in a manner of strangling, Rabbi. In a manner so their eyeballs pop out of their pissant head. I want to kill them so they are aware, in the entire last minute of their life, that they are about to die and that they can do nothing about it. I want them to feel helpless. Above all, that's what I want."

"You're serious," the rabbi said.

"Definitely."

"Dead serious."

Fred flashed with anger.

"Is that supposed to be a joke?"

And suddenly the rabbi saw how broad Fred's chest was, and that the wine merchant's shoulders were quite wide, and that his hands, on which he'd earlier noticed only the manicured nails, now seemed terribly thick and strong, used to lifting large cases of liquor. The rabbi swallowed hard. Someone in his congregation had murder in his heart, he thought, and he had come to him, in a way, to confess, to ask for help. And the rabbi thought that he had to say something because he sensed from Fred that this murder was imminent. He had to say something now.

"You didn't eat, honey," his wife said after dinner. "If it wasn't kugel, I might not have noticed. But you always eat your kugel."

All through dinner he'd been preoccupied with his pitiful performance that afternoon—his hands fluttering around his desk, stuttering, his words and thoughts half-formed, convoluted, sounding like George Bush, sounding like a teenager, while Fred sat calmly in his seat. Then Fred asked him directly, "Rabbi, what should I do?" And all he could come up with was a few generic answers—Fred should see a therapist, or try talking to the person he was so angry with; pray. Or could write him a letter. It sounded like another joke.

He needed time to consult his texts, time to reason things through. But Fred couldn't wait: "It's all I think about, Rabbi. It's like a cancer." The rabbi wasn't used to this. He liked the mushy world of sorrow, where his advice brought solace and eased pain. Fred was a time bomb ticking away. Fred was May Day, May Day—We're going down!

He asked Fred what the man had done to him.

Who says it's a man?

All right, what did the person do to you?

I can't tell you.

Why?

Because you'll know who it is.

And then the rabbi would do what? Warn them? Drop a subtle hint? Call them up and say lock your door. Why, Rabbi? He would say never mind why! Do it! Get a bodyguard. A gun.

Look! Look where this had led to. Now he was talking about guns. Besides, he couldn't warn anyone. He was bound to silence. To Fred's silence. He was practically an accomplice. They were handcuffed together. When Fred's hands were around the man's throat, the rabbi's would be there too. Moving in unison, like old dancing partners.

Because you'll know who it is. In three more days, the rabbi would stand in front of his congregation leading Shabbat services and look out and wonder who it was that Fred had marked for death. Fred could be sitting right next to them, looking on in their prayer book, toasting them at the kiddush, touching glasses—*l'chaim.* How ironic. And if they turned up dead in their bed the next day, their eyes popping out of their head like Fred said, how would he feel then?

He wanted to tell someone. He should tell someone. The police. But what would he say?

A man came to me and said he wanted to kill someone.

Kill who, Rabbi?

He didn't say.

Why?

He didn't say.

How?

Strangling. His hands around his throat.

Then it's a man he wants to kill.

Who said it's a man?

"Are you okay, Daddy?"

It was his daughter, Abby, staring up at him with great consternation. He was annoyed with himself for bringing such creases of worry to her young brow.

"Yes, sweetie," he said. "I'm okay." But he was not okay. He was upset. Fred had upset him.

"Then can I pull your tie?"

She started to move toward him, but his arm shot out and held her back.

"No," he said.

She started to whimper. All she had wanted was to pull the knot from his bow tie, their special after-dinner ritual. It was supposed to be fun. His wife came in from the kitchen.

"What's wrong?" she asked.

Fred Siegel of Siegel's Wines and Liquors wants to strangle someone until their eyes pop out of their head! That's what's wrong! This was what he wanted to say. But he didn't. Instead he got up from the table.

"I have to make a phone call," he said. He gently stroked his daughter's head. "I'm sorry, Abby."

He went into his study and closed the door. He called Fred Siegel at work, but they said he'd gone home. He called there, but got an answering machine. The rabbi left a message.

"Fred, I want you to come and see me again tomorrow," he said. "And together we'll go to the police and talk to them. As your rabbi, this is what I am strongly urging you to do." Then he added, "I have maintained your confidentiality."

He hung up and instantly felt better. They were just words, after all. Fred hadn't done anything yet. And while Spinoza might argue our thoughts and our deeds are all extensions of God, there was still an empirical difference. The desire is not the act. So he'd done the right thing. For now.

He made up with Abby and read her a story. Later, when his wife tried to find out what happened, he told her it was not as serious as he'd made out. She seemed to believe him, though he was sure she had her doubts.

He went to sleep that night with a sense of accomplishment quite different than usual. Though his initial response to Fred had been less than stalwart, he was pleased with its resolution. He felt something new opening up for him.

The next morning his wife greeted him at the breakfast table with an envelope.

"I found this at the front door," she said, "when Abby was going to the school bus. It's addressed to you. I guess they left it last night."

The rabbi opened it up. Inside was a plain white piece of paper. In the center were two handwritten words that had been cut out and pasted on. He recognized the handwriting immediately. After all, it had been the same for the last thirty years. Neat. Perfect. His own words, but in someone else's voice—a dark, menacing voice.

The beautifully shaped letters read: IT'S YOU.

As Fred Siegel stacked cases of a Spanish red wine—he was running a sale—thoughts of the Inquisition ran through his head. He imagined his nemesis being burnt at the stake, torn apart by horses, tied to a post as a hulking hooded flogger lashed him to death. But there was no satisfaction for Fred, because the bastard didn't cry out in agony and beg for mercy. Even in his very own fantasy, Fred couldn't get revenge. It wasn't fair.

Fred knew the Spanish red wasn't going to move. Kefalidis could sell it easily, but he would have to mark it down to just above cost. People didn't know from Spanish red. Maybe to them it meant blood—from civil wars, from wounded, dying bulls. But Fred knew one person who would snatch it up—Epstein, high priest of the loss leaders, *shamus* to the buys of the week. With frightening kabalistic intuition, Epstein would arrive, wine guide under his arm, and circle the display like a shark, demand a discount off the markdown, load up the trunk, silently gloating. Epstein's profit was Fred's loss. Fred fastened Epstein to the flogging post and waited for the torturer to catch his breath.

And what would the rabbi say about that? What gems of Hebraic liturgy would he invoke to make Fred feel better about losing money when his competitor was flourishing? What pearls of wisdom would the rabbi intone—look for a smaller store with cheaper rent? Maybe he'd get a letter full of sage advice. Fred could show it to the landlord.

And then there was the missing bottle of Margaux '61. Fred had discovered the loss last week. The empty place in the locked cabinet once housed a hundred-and-forty-three-dollar bottle. Marcia didn't remember selling it. Neither did José. One of them took it. He knew. He should have fired them both. But the next help might steal even more.

And what was the cost of fancy wine compared with the thousands he'd just thrown away trying to get his wife pregnant? They'd tried every scientific breakthrough, medications, stimulants, antibiotics, torture in the name of creating a life. For the last few years, her ovulation was the center of their lives, the way the Egyptians waited for the Nile to flood. Month after month, Fred came into test tubes behind a curtain. Good thing you have strong hands, one doctor said jokingly. It would help if you were ambidextrous, said another. He grew to desire the naked women in the magazines he used for stimulation. *Aurora's very serious about riding her horses, but she still knows how to have fun.* Fred wanted fun. *Dawn's a chem major pulling down straight A's, but that doesn't keep her off her surfboard.* Fred wanted to surf, too. It wasn't sex but freedom he craved. Fred wanted to help Aurora buckle her saddle, to tie Dawn's surfboard to the top of the car and get lost on the way to the next beach. But then he'd snap out of his reverie and remember his purpose, why he was sitting in the clinic. And as the sound of hooves and the spray of the ocean disappeared, his litany of sorrows would return: his wife's despondency, their shared futility, his store's sagging sales, his lackluster life.

"So what am I supposed to do with this?" the detective asked the rabbi, holding the piece of paper. "*It's you,*" it says, "*It's you* what?"

"A man tells me he's going to strangle someone. The next morning my wife finds *this* message under our door. It seems logical to me."

"What does?"

"That this is his attempt to convey his intention to do me harm."

"A threat."

"Yes."

"Mmmm hmmm."

The detective was treating this as a joke. His name was Harry. The rabbi knew him from Little League. Fathers in his congregation periodically complained that Harry stacked his sons' teams, wondering if it was fair or morally defensible for Harry to scout the junior high playgrounds, parking his cruiser by the ballfield and recruiting eleven-year-old pitching prospects. Couldn't the rabbi do something about it, speak to him, get him to play by the rules?

"Is it possible the guy's having fun?" Detective Harry said.

"I seriously doubt it!" the rabbi answered vehemently.

"Hey, easy there, Rabbi. Maybe he's just pulling your chain."

The rabbi didn't know he had a chain to pull.

"So who is it?" Detective Harry asked.

He knew he shouldn't say, shouldn't reveal what had been shared with him in confidence. But this was no time for Talmudic hairsplitting. It was a matter of life and death. Fred had said so himself.

"Fred Siegel," the rabbi said.

"Fred the wine guy?"

"Yes."

"I know him. He's got himself a nice shop. Great markdowns. The only person *he* should want to kill is Kefalidis, who just opened that huge store out in the mall. Wine, cheese, those rotisserie chickens. It's some operation."

"But the note was left at *my* doorstep, Detective! And found by *my wife*," the rabbi's voice so full of anger he hardly recognized it. "I'd like to know what you're going to do about it."

"What do you want me to do?"

The rabbi didn't understand. The detective should know what to do. He should have a standard procedure for situations like this. There should be steps to take. A process.

"I feel you should talk with him," the rabbi said.

Harry mulled this over, leaned back in his chair, clasped his hands behind his neck. The rabbi could see the nicotine patch on his arm.

"Isn't that what you do, Rabbi? Talk to people?"

Why was he being so patronizing? He and Harry were equals—figures of authority, respected members of the community. But the detective was treating him like a petulant child.

"Yes," the rabbi said. "I often talk to people."

Actually, in the last few years, the rabbi had been avoiding direct contact.

He was relying more and more on the missives he composed in his office sanctuary.

"I'll have to think about it," Harry said. "But right now I've got to get to practice. We're 3 and 0 this season. Got a couple of boys from your temple on my team. A girl, too. Dynamite shortstop. She can really pick it, Rabbi. You should stop by and watch a game some time."

Harry headed to the door, then stopped and turned back.

"You're the one who should really talk to him, Rabbi," the detective said. "Maybe he broke some kind of Jewish law. Hold him accountable for what is in his heart. I can't do that, but you can."

The rabbi parked down the street from Siegel's Wines and Liquors. He watched the front door. No one entered, no one left. Business seemed dead.

Why him? Just two words—"IT'S YOU"—had changed everything. They had been cut from one of his letters, but the rabbi didn't remember sending Fred a letter. Of course, he'd written so many, he could have forgotten. Maybe Fred drank. That's it. He'd probably sat in the back room, consumed his samples, and conceived this scheme in a drunken haze. No. Fred didn't look like a drinker.

The door opened. Fred was leaving the store, walking toward him. He had to hide his face. He looked around—all he had was a prayer book, a dead giveaway. (Dead!) He sank down in the seat, ducked, and held his breath. His heart kept racing long after Fred had passed. What was happening? It was as if *he* was the criminal.

He looked up just in time to see Fred enter the bank. Was all this a mistake? Maybe he wasn't the one who Fred wanted dead. Maybe Fred had someone else in mind altogether. Perhaps he should meet with Fred, talk to him—man to man. But not alone. He'd get Mikhail, the Romanian trainer from the Jewish Center, sit outside the office, pretend he had an appointment. Reassured, the rabbi drove back to the synagogue.

Mrs. Gort and her son Zach were just walking out of his office when he arrived. Penny, his secretary, her hands fluttering helplessly at her side, was in obvious panic.

"I didn't know what to do, Rabbi," Penny said. She flustered easily.

Mrs. Gort, her face already pulled taut by unseen knots, managed to stretch it into an even tighter grimace.

"I'm sorry," the rabbi said.

"We can't stay," she replied. "Zach has a Little League game."

"I usually lead off," the boy said, glaring at him. "I'll miss my first at bat."

"I can assure you it was very important, Mrs. Gort. A matter of life and death."

"I'd expect nothing less from my rabbi," she said. "We'll see you next week. I hope."

He couldn't remember the last time he'd missed an appointment. What was going on? F-R-E-D. He needed to put an end to it. But first he would finish up the letters he had to write.

He heard a voice speaking to him from far away, then realized it was Penny, standing in his office doorway.

"What did you say, Penny?"

"I'm sorry that they were rude," she said. "I mean, they were, weren't they?"

"Yes, Penny, but it wasn't your fault."

"Oh, thank you, Rabbi. Thank you."

She was so grateful it was like he had just rescued her from the deep end of the pool.

"I have to work now," the rabbi said.

"Writing your letters?"

"Yes."

The woman needed something more in her life than her job and the latest weight-loss fix. She wasn't close to being overweight. For Penny, this was more like a hobby. She collected diets like his nephew collected stamps.

"You can go if you want to," he said.

"Umm . . . I just have a few things to finish up. You want some coffee, Rabbi?"

"No."

At last she closed the door. He opened his desk drawer and removed his special pen. He took out a piece of stationery and started thinking about Mr. Rappaport, a sixty-eight-year-old widower who was conflicted about meeting someone new.

It's only been a year, but you're lonely. Would Carol have wanted you to be lonely?

In his letter to Mr. Rappaport, he wanted to relate a tale from the Baal Shem Tov, but the thoughts weren't coming. He stared at the page. His handwriting was appalling. The salutation was jittery, letters misshapen, the words dipped and angled downward like he had washed down that entire case of Fred's Chablis. Fred had done this to him. Fred had taken away his skill, his gift. He dialed Fred's store without thinking, knowing that if he paused to reflect he'd hang up. A woman's voice answered.

"Is Fred there?" the rabbi asked.

"Sorry, he just left."

"Do you know where?"

"Who's this?"

"His rabbi."

"Oh. Sorry. No, I'm not sure. Maybe home. He didn't say. Can *I* help you? We're having a special on Spanish red, if you like that sort of thing."

"No. I just needed to speak with Fred. I'll try him at home."

But Fred wasn't home either. The rabbi put his pen back in the drawer. He put the paper back in the box. He would find Fred, and he would talk to him.

Fred shoved the rag into the plastic milk container filled with gasoline. He had siphoned it out of his tank, sucking on the tube to get the flow started. The petrol taste lingered in his mouth. He then put the milk container in a heavy cardboard box, making sure it was not a wine case. His plan was to drive by the temple first. If the rabbi wasn't there, he would go to his house. The fear made Fred tremble, but there was also a sense of liberation, of impending freedom. But first he wanted to see the rabbi, hear what he had to say. With the right words he might talk Fred out of it. He really hoped the rabbi was at the temple. It would be harder for Fred with the rabbi's wife and daughter around.

The gas was starting to soak into the cloth and the fumes were permeating the car. Fred opened the window, just enough.

The temple secretary told him the rabbi wasn't there, but Fred brushed past her and barged into the office. She was staring at him, a mousy thing with stringy blond hair, wringing her hands. She could be cute if she fixed herself up, Fred thought, as he slammed the door in her face.

The rabbi was halfway home when he decided to drive back to his office for his stationery and pen. He would work at home tonight, basking in the love of his wife and daughter. He would read to Abby, tuck her in, reassure her all was right with the world.

The rabbi walked into the synagogue office. Penny's eyes were nearly bugging out of her head.

"He was here," she said.

"Who?"

"That man. The one who upset you so much yesterday. Mr. Siegel."

"Fred Siegel?"

"He barged in, right past me. I tried to stop him, Rabbi. I did."

He turned and rushed into his office. There on his desk was another note. Four words this time, each cut with surgical precision from one of the rabbi's letters.

It's you I want.

"Did he say where he was going?" the rabbi asked, his heart racing.

"To your house, Rabbi."

"Call my wife. Tell her to lock the door. No! Tell her to take Abby and go to Mrs. Klein's house down the street. Now!"

"Mrs. Klein's?"

"Yes, you idiot!" He was running out the door, to his car. "And tell her not to ask why. To just do it! And then call the police and tell them to meet me at my house!"

He tore out of the lot, squealing his tires and almost losing control. He accelerated down the long tree-lined synagogue driveway and merged onto the main road, nearly sideswiping another car.

It's you I want.

"Well, you're going to get me," he said aloud to himself. The good rabbi, tearing at his bow tie, yanking out the knot, whipping the tie from his collar as he swore oaths of malediction. "But you're going to get more than you bargained for."

Racing home, the rabbi imagined Fred at the screen door, ripping off its hinges and tossing it onto the front lawn. Then he saw Fred kicking down the front door, and the rabbi's wife and daughter were inside. The rabbi had told them to go next door, to be safe, to wait until the police got there. But they didn't. Why? Why were they still inside? They were hiding in an upstairs closet, his wife's hand over his daughter's mouth to keep her from crying out. Fred was downstairs shouting, throwing lamps and vases, Shabbat candlesticks, framed family pictures, all smashed on the floor. Next to go was the rabbi's sacred letter collection. Ripping open the strap of the soft leatherbound folder, Fred was tearing the letters, chucking them in the air, mashing them into the carpet.

It's you, Rabbi! It's you!

The rabbi drove like a maniac. He had to get home before Fred headed up the stairs, before his daughter's whimpering led Fred to their closet and certain catastrophe.

Now he imagined his wife on her knees, pleading for Fred's mercy, hoping, somehow, to snap him out of it, to make him see reason.

Just don't hurt my daughter! Please, do what you want to me, but please, please, please . . .

The tires squealed as he turned onto his street. He accelerated, careening down the block, driving to save his daughter.

There were three police cars in front of his house. He slammed on his brakes and skidded to a halt, narrowly missing a hydrant and a telephone pole.

He recognized Detective Harry standing on his front porch, talking to his wife, her arm wrapped protectively over their daughter's shoulder as Abby hugged her stuffed animal. A group of uniformed cops stood by their cruisers, chatting. No one seemed in any particular distress.

"Rabbi," Harry called.

"Daddy," Abby shouted. She ran down the path and jumped into his arms. He held her close. The uniformed cops quieted down, watching the scene.

"Honey, we were so worried about you." His wife kissed him on the cheek and held his arm with startling strength. "When Penny called from the office, we didn't know what to think. Fortunately the police got here right away."

"Any sign of Fred?" the rabbi asked Harry.

"His wife said he's not home from work. She hasn't heard from him. I have a car out looking."

"Thanks," the rabbi said.

He felt emboldened, almost like a warrior, standing shoulder to shoulder with the detective. He had responded bravely, decisively, to protect his family. He hadn't stopped to analyze the situation, to judge the philosophic merits of several different perspectives. He had *acted*.

It was a cool, pleasant evening. The large trees lining the street were blowing gently in the breeze. Neighbors stood on their lawns and gathered on the sidewalk in small clusters. In a moment the rabbi would walk over and tell them everything was under control.

Then he saw a car parked two houses down, partially hidden behind some hedges. A sinister place for a car. The rabbi could make out a shadow in the driver's seat, watching intently. Spying. He could feel it.

"There!" he shouted, thrusting out his arm and pointing directly at the car.

Immediately the taillights came on, the engine started, and the car rushed away.

"Who was it?" his wife asked.

"I didn't see."

"We'll check it out," Harry said. He barked out a few crisp instructions on his walkie-talkie. Almost instantly, a cruiser's lights flooded the front yard. Then it sped off.

"Do you think it was him?" the rabbi's wife asked. "Do you?"

"I couldn't tell."

"We'll know soon," Harry said. "Best get inside now."

Suddenly exhausted, the rabbi let the detective usher him and his family into the safety of home.

Fred was parked behind Kefalidis' liquor store, in the shadow of a dumpster. He'd been there for the past hour, just sitting, thinking, weighing the possibilities of setting the store on fire, thinking how there were probably dozens of clues he'd left already, plus the chemical traces, tire impressions, fibers too minuscule to wipe away, all the tracks would lead the police to his door.

And of course there was the most obvious clue. Who would most want the new liquor store burnt down but the man who owned the *old* liquor store?

But mostly Fred just sat and felt sorry for himself. Here he was, an honest man who worked hard and loved his wife, who went to services and donated money to the temple. So why was he so loaded with misery? His business was failing, he couldn't have any children, his faith was crumbling, he was on the verge of becoming a criminal.

He'd gone to the rabbi for counsel and for what? To get the same advice you'd get from any stranger on the street?

On the other hand, perhaps the rabbi didn't know what to say because he really believed that Fred was going to kill someone. How would the rabbi know that he was just trying the idea on for size, seeing how the words sounded, hoping that just by wanting Kefalidis dead the bright red neon above his shiny liquor store door would never come on again.

But now, in the car, the matches in his lap, the rag stuck in the milk jug topped with gas, Fred realized the rabbi's advice was more profound than he'd first suspected. The rabbi was doing him a favor by taking him seriously. Because, after all, what *do* you tell someone who says they want to kill another human being?

Fred heard the rabbi's voice in his head: *Don't do it. I want you to talk to the police.*

Then something clicked and Fred realized he didn't want to go to jail. He wanted to sell wine. He liked it. He liked the idea of people making toasts with glasses filled with a Merlot he'd suggested, gracing a picnic with a Chardonnay he'd recommended. He was no killer. His performance in the rabbi's office was just that—a performance. And pretending to be an assassin was really an act of cowardice. He dropped the milk container, still reeking of gasoline, in a garbage can in front of an all-night deli, not worried if his fingerprints covered it since he'd done nothing wrong.

The rabbi's wife had made hot chocolate for Abby and coffee for Harry. The four of them were sitting at the kitchen table, not really saying anything when the front doorbell rang. The rabbi got up to answer it, but Harry put a heavy hand on his shoulder.

"You wait here," Harry said. "Let me see how volatile he is."

From the kitchen, the rabbi heard the muffled, excited voices of Harry and the officer. Then the door closed. Silence. The rabbi looked at his wife.

"I'm sorry this all had to happen to you, sweetie," she said, echoing his earlier thoughts about *her*. But now the rabbi had to question, what exactly *was* happening? And he was still troubled by his nightmare of Fred invading his home. Why? It wasn't fear; he felt safe now with the police there.

He was disturbed by the climax, the decimation of his precious letters, his legacy. Then it hit him: his letter collection had become his congregation; he was more concerned with his words than the people to whom they were addressed. He remembered a story about a wise rabbi, a *tzaddik*, who, while walking home at night through his village, sees a man who had recently died. *"Why are you here?" the rabbi asks. "You were such a good man in your life; there was no need for you to come back." The man replies, "Rabbi, a few nights*

*ago I was sitting in my room thinking about what a good person I was, flush
with the many good deeds I had done in my life. And in that glow of celebrating my goodness, I died. That's why I have come back."*

The front door opened.

"Could you come here a moment, Rabbi?" Harry called.

The rabbi glanced at his wife; she nodded encouragement. Steeling himself, the rabbi headed toward the front hall.

Standing there, dwarfed by the uniformed officer, was his secretary,
Penny, hands fluttering helplessly, a sorry, lopsided smile stuck on her face.
At the sight of the rabbi, she burst into tears, blubbering something that
sounded like *"I'm sorry."*

"This was the person in the car," the trooper said.

"And she's confessed," Harry added, the slightest touch of irony in his
voice.

"Confessed to what?" the rabbi said.

"She said something about some notes she left on your front door. On
your desk. Some kind of love notes, I gather."

Penny buried her head in her hands and turned toward the trooper, who
had no choice but to drape a long, muscular arm over her bony shoulder.

The police cruiser was parked in front of his house when Fred pulled into
the driveway. What were they doing here? How could they know? A thought
flashed in his mind—take off—but he knew the cops would easily track him
down before he got far. Besides, Fred had a problem with backing up quickly—he got confused and inevitably started steering the wrong way. He'd
almost backed into his neighbor's shrubbery that time he was in a hurry to
pick up a pizza with mushrooms and extra cheese. Imagine what he'd do
fleeing the law.

"Fred Siegel," the trooper said, getting out of his car.

"Yes."

"I need to have a word with you."

Just then the front light went on and Fred's wife came running out of
the house.

"I was so worried," she said. "The police have been looking all over for
you. They wouldn't tell me why. Did you do something, Fred? Did you do
something you shouldn't have?"

The trooper jogged across the lawn and faced the Siegels.

"We just seeded that grass," his wife said.

"Sorry, ma'am. If you could both just wait here a moment."

He turned away and spoke rapidly into his walkie-talkie. Listening to the garbled response, he turned back to the Siegels.

"Sorry, sir. False alarm I guess. Call Detective Harry Klavan at the station in the morning." He handed Fred a card.

"Sure," Fred said.

"And he wants you to call the rabbi, too."

"Okay," Fred said.

"You people take care now. Sorry about the inconvenience."

"Sure."

The trooper walked back to his car, careful this time to stay on the path. He started the engine and drove away quietly into the night.

"What was all that about?" Fred's wife asked him.

"I'm not exactly sure," he said. "I guess the rabbi will clue me in tomorrow."

He slipped his hand into hers and together they walked up the steps into the house. There was a lightness to his step Fred hadn't felt for a while. How odd it is, Fred thought, that though he hadn't really come close to burning down Kefalidis' store, the fact that he stopped himself, that he gained control of himself, probably helped him more than if he'd gone through with it. Maybe he'd try to explain that to the rabbi tomorrow, right before he made him the offer on the wine.

The rabbi sat alone in his basement next to the furnace, his collection of letters piled on his lap. He wanted to shove them into the fire. But he'd forgotten that the furnace had been off for the past few weeks, and besides, he wasn't sure how to open it.

His letters. They were the culprit in this whole ridiculous, embarrassing mess. He'd been hiding behind them for so long, he'd forgotten how to deal with real people. His congregants had become his readership, and like many writers, he'd fallen into the bad habit of writing for himself, infatuated with the sound of his own words.

The good rabbi stood on a chair and stored his box of letters on a shelf above the workbench. They'd no doubt be laughing about this down at the police station for weeks: how the rabbi confused a secretary's love notes for death threats and mobilized the entire force. The story could become legendary, retold to each new group of rookie cops, becoming more fantastic from year to year.

Still, it was the safety of his family he had defended, and men had been doing whatever it took to protect their homesteads since the beginning of civilization.

He sat for a moment at his workbench and thought about poor Penny. He never believed he was the type of man women had crushes on. He would need to talk to her. For his own piece of mind. And hers. She was probably embarrassed, humiliated even. No doubt there was an emptiness in her life. He would try to help her find some kind of peace. He felt sorry for her.

But not for Fred. The rabbi was angry with the wine merchant and would tell him so. Tomorrow he would call Fred and insist he come down to the office. Then he would question him and chastise him, persisting until the rabbi got to the bottom of this mystery. Who did Fred want to kill and most importantly, *why?* Then he would get Fred to seek professional help. Or alert the police. It was time for action. He was through with philosophizing. Enough with the letters. It was fitting that his own words would come back to haunt him. He just wondered why it had taken so long.

He turned off the basement light, leaving behind in darkness a part of his life that would be better tucked away until he could understand it more fully.

"I'm coming up," he called to his daughter. "I'm coming up to tuck you in."

JANICE STEINBERG'S mystery novels feature public
radio reporter Margo Simon. The first four mysteries
take place in San Diego. Her latest novel, *Death in a
City of Mystics,* transports the reader to Safed, Israel,
which for centuries has been a center for the study of
Kabbalah, a form of Jewish mysticism. Writing her
latest book turned out to be a transformative experience for the author and drew her closer to Judaism.
She is now studying for her adult bat mitzvah.

Wailing Reed

▼   ▼   ▼   ▼   ▼   ▼   ▼   ▼

JANICE STEINBERG

JUST BECAUSE KLEZMER MUSIC MADE HER CRY and just because she'd done
a public radio story on Klezmania, a local band reviving the musical style of
eastern European Jews . . .

Still, who was she to track down a missing clarinetist, a man who made
that reed instrument wail as if it had a soul capable of experiencing the most
profound suffering and joy?

The first time Margo Simon had heard the clarinetist play, tears filled her
eyes. Unexpected, embarrassing, until Ira Nadler, a white-haired dealer of
rare music, discreetly handed her an immaculate handkerchief. Nadler's
Old World grace had soothed her embarrassment—that and the fact that he
was crying, too.

Maybe that was why, when she'd received the music dealer's vague
request for her help in "a delicate matter," she had immediately agreed to
meet with him. Leaving the radio station early, she'd gone to his elegantly
furnished apartment in one of the older parts of San Diego.

Nadler had insisted on making tea before divulging a word about why
he'd called her. Watching him prepare the tea, pre-warming the china pot
and measuring Assam leaves—did he even own a Lipton teabag?—Margo
had wondered what the meticulous older man *wouldn't* consider delicate. A
trip to the supermarket? Or was that a precarious balancing act between his

need for sustenance and the esthetic assault of bright lights and modern packaging? Surely, she decided, Nadler had summoned her over some minor concern. Any irritation she felt was compensated by relief that, whatever was troubling him, she could possibly set his mind at rest.

The matter *was* delicate, however, and more than that. Although he spoke as articulately as when she'd interviewed him about klezmer for the radio, Margo sensed something wildly at variance with the highly civilized, antique-filled surroundings and the smoky tea in cups that were so fine they were nearly transparent.

Ira Nadler was afraid.

He waited until he'd poured the tea, offered a plate full of Pepperidge Farm cookies, and introduced her to his Siamese cats, Heifetz and Perlman. But then, with what from Nadler seemed like rough abruptness, he launched into his story.

"I gave a dinner party two nights ago. A small party. Only four guests. What can you do in an apartment that doesn't have a proper dining room?" he said, as if apologizing for not inviting Margo. "After dinner, we went into my study. I wanted to play for them a record I'd just discovered. I can't be one hundred percent certain, but it may be the only record in existence of Zig Wolinsky when he was just starting out, playing with a band in Ozorow, Poland, in the early 1920s. Wolinsky went on to be one of the great klezmer violinists. There are quite a few records of him playing with his group in Warsaw. But the Ozorow record! I'm not aware of any collection that includes it."

For a moment, excitement over his "find" filled Nadler's eyes. Then fear returned.

"I played the record," he said, "and we came back into this room for dessert. Except for Jeffrey Holland."

"Jeffrey Holland," Margo repeated. The name rang a bell, and when Nadler said, "The clarinetist with Klezmania," she pictured the skinny young man who played like a demented angel.

"Jeff wanted to look at some sheet music I'd acquired along with the record," Nadler continued.

"He rejoined us ten or fifteen minutes later. I went back into the study after my guests left. I couldn't listen to the Ozorow record again—something so old, you need to let it rest after you play it. I just wanted to look at it, to imagine the world in which it was made." He sighed, stared into his hands. "The record was gone."

"Do you think Jeff Holland took it?"

"I asked myself if anyone other than Jeff left my sight after I played the record for them." The answer, according to his eloquent shrug, was no. "And I searched the study from top to bottom, of course."

"Could I see your study?"

"Certainly." If Nadler was insulted that she thought an old man's eyes might have simply overlooked his precious record, he was too polite to show it. He led her down the hallway and opened a door.

Margo felt as dismayed as Nadler to think the gifted young musician could be a thief. She hoped the music dealer's office would be a rabbit warren where the record could be hidden in plain sight. But even though records filled floor-to-ceiling shelves on every wall, the study was the headquarters of Nadler's mail order business; and if he had prepared tea with strict attention to detail, it was nothing compared to how he maintained the records that were his livelihood. Each was neatly labeled and alphabetized. Amid the decades-old 78's, a very modern computer kept a detailed inventory.

Choosing a record at random, Nadler walked through everything he remembered doing when he'd played the Ozorow record the other night. As a tear-drenched Yiddish ballad filled the room, he explained that the old 78 rpm discs were made of shellac instead of vinyl, which made them highly breakable. It was another reason he was concerned about the purloined record. If broken, it would be lost forever.

The ballad ended and Nadler reshelved the record immediately; it was what he did with every record, he insisted. Together—and without success—he and Margo examined each of the records in the "O" section for "Ozorow" as well as "W" for Wolinsky, as he had already done several times. He'd searched the adjacent shelves as well.

The Ozorow record might still be misfiled. But it seemed more and more likely that Nadler's suspicion of Jeff Holland was on the mark.

"The dinner party was two nights ago, right?" Margo said, when they returned to the living room. "Have you talked to Jeff since then?" Though she couldn't imagine Ira Nadler even obliquely asking one of his dinner guests if said guest had made off with the equivalent of the family silver.

"He's missing."

"What do you mean, missing?"

"I've tried calling him. I reached his roommate this afternoon. The roommate hasn't seen him since he left for my party."

"If they keep different schedules . . ." Margo had had roommates she'd barely glimpsed for a week at a time.

"They do. The roommate goes to work early. Jeff is in a rock band as well as Klezmania, so he comes home late and sleeps until ten or eleven. I suppose I shouldn't worry. But . . ." He reached for a pipe from the table beside him, then paused. "I'm sorry, do you object to the smell of pipe smoke?"

"I love it. My father smoked a pipe."

Nadler occupied himself with the ritual of pipe-lighting. His fingers trembled.

"Jeff didn't touch his mail yesterday or today," he said. "Or open the *New York Times*. He subscribes to the *Times* and the roommate never looks at it, just brings it inside in the morning."

"Is he in a relationship? Maybe that's where he's been."

"He split up with his girlfriend last month."

Maybe he got lucky, Margo thought but didn't say. Not that Nadler seemed innocent of the realities of modern romance and its one-night stands. Still, the phrase seemed too vulgar.

"Do you think he sold the record and took off someplace?" she asked. "How much is it worth?"

"Not enough to finance an extended trip." Nadler smiled ruefully. "If there were that kind of money in archival klezmer records, I could move to La Jolla and stop having nightmares about living in the gutter in my old age.

"What I think happened," he said, "is that Jeff took the record—it was so beautiful, I of all people can understand how he felt he had to possess it. Then he got scared. Maybe he's hiding now because he's afraid I've gone to the police. But I have no wish to press charges. How could I send to jail a man who already plays with such passion? A year in jail, and his music would break your heart, you couldn't even bear to listen. The only thing I want is for him to return the record to me. That's why I'm asking for your help. He'll be frightened if he hears I'm looking for him. But if you could act as an intermediary . . ."

Why did I say yes? Margo asked herself the instant the word left her mouth. She continued to wonder about this as she went from Nadler's to her next destination, her stepson's soccer game.

A "delicate" matter? That was an understatement. How about "volatile," as in something that would blow up in her face when she accused Jeff Holland of theft? And how was she supposed to find a clarinetist on the lam? Nadler had reluctantly parted with the names and phone numbers of the members of Klezmania, as well as those of the three other guests at his dinner party—as long as she promised not to breathe a word to any of them that would hint at Jeff's crime. He couldn't forgive himself if he cast a blemish on such a promising career. All he wanted from the young musician was the return of the record and a vow never to steal again. That was the highest form of repentance in Judaism, he said, for the sinner not to repeat the sin.

He doesn't need a reporter. He needs a rabbi.

Margo decided that, barring some sign from the universe, she would call Nadler when she got home from the soccer game and tell him she wasn't the woman for this job.

During a timeout in the game, she picked up a copy of the local entertainment weekly that someone had left in the bleachers. The paper was open to ads for clubs, touting their featured bands. She was about to turn the page when a garish ad jumped out at her: Fingernails on a Blackboard had a gig tonight. It was the one other piece of information Nadler had given her—the name of Jeff's rock band.

As a sign from the universe, it lacked spiritual resonance. But it solved the problem of locating the missing clarinetist. And Margo figured she'd be more comfortable than a rabbi going to the Voodoo Club.

Three hours later, she was reconsidering. There must be one or two hip rabbis, some at least a decade younger than she, who'd feel less out of place amid the pierced and tattooed denizens of the Voodoo Club.

She felt as if she'd walked into the song, "Something is happening here and you don't know what it is, do you, Mr. Jones?" Except that Dylan had written the song before any of these people were born, and Margo used to see herself as the smug insider who did know what was happening. Now she was the pathetically square Jones. It consoled her a little to think that Dylan might feel the same.

A band was playing. She scanned the group, looking over a small sea of multicolored heads. Not spotting Jeff Holland, she pressed through the crowd to the bar.

"When does Fingernails on a Blackboard come on?" she asked the bartender as he mixed her gin and tonic.

"Nine," he said, placing her drink in front of her.

"But it's nine-twenty now."

"Duh." He glanced toward the stage.

Die, punk scum, she thought. She said, "I thought they had a clarinetist."

He turned to take another order, acting as if he hadn't heard.

"Politeness greases the wheels of civilization," she muttered, picking up the change she would have left as a tip.

She edged toward the stage. When she'd first glanced at the band, she had looked for a clarinetist, hadn't seen one, and assumed Jeff wasn't there. But Nadler hadn't mentioned whether Jeff played his clarinet in the rock band. Probably, like many musicians, he was adept on half a dozen instruments. Fingernails on a Blackboard had two guitarists, a keyboard player, and a drummer, a standard rock band lineup. But there were also a sax player and a percussionist whose intriguing array of instruments sounded South American. Margo actually liked the band's music: they played an interesting if sometimes weird hybrid of rock and jazz, just as Klezmania's music combined traditional and modern influences. It seemed like the perfect rock band for Jeff Holland. So where was he?

"Didn't show up," the saxophonist told her during the band's break.

"Did he call and say he couldn't make it?"

"Didn't call. Didn't show. I'll be right there!" he said to the drummer, who was telling him to move his ass.

"Has he ever done that before?"

"Are you kidding? Mr. Professional? He's the one who's down on the rest of us if we're two minutes late for rehearsal."

"Aren't you worried about him?"

"Right now, the main thing I'm worried about is how do we do our songs without him? Gotta go. We're changing some of our arrangements. You want to talk to somebody who knows Jeff, Scott's a good friend of his."

"Scott?"

"The bartender."

Oh, hell.

She stalled by dialing Jeff's number. She got his roommate, who still hadn't seen Jeff since he'd left for Ira Nadler's party two nights ago. Gritting her teeth, she headed back to the bar.

Customers were two- and three-deep, and when she got the bartender's attention, she talked fast.

"Jeff Holland is missing. Can I talk to you about him?"

"Not now. Things quiet down here around eleven, eleven-thirty."

Which is when this early-rising soccer mom turns into a pumpkin. She complained to herself. She ordered a cup of coffee, leaving a generous tip this time, and found a place to sit during the Fingernails' next set.

The band was good—clearly serious musicians—and Margo was increasingly troubled by Jeff's non-appearance. Musicians were like radio people. No matter what was happening in your life, if you were scheduled to perform, you smiled in the mirror, said "Show time!" and went on. Or you sure as hell let someone know you weren't going to make it. She thought of the fear she'd sensed in Ira Nadler. Was there something the music dealer hadn't told her, some reason he was concerned about Jeff's state of mind? If Nadler had held something back, could Scott complete the picture?

The bar was still busy during the next break, but once the band returned to the stage the crowd divided into serious fans who pressed up close and folks who took off after having one for the road. (This crowd didn't seem to have heard of designated drivers.)

Margo asked for another cup of coffee, decaf this time.

"What did you say about Jeff being missing?" Scott said.

She explained about Jeff's apparent absence from his apartment for two days, followed by his not showing up tonight to play in the band.

"You some kind of cop?"

"A reporter. But I'm not working on a story, just helping a friend who hasn't been able to get in touch with Jeff and is worried about him."

Was Scott just suspicious by nature or had he had real-life bad experiences with authorities? Margo wondered, gazing at the red and black snake tattooed on his left arm. The reptile's head and flicking tongue crept up the bartender's bicep to just below the edge of his sleeveless T-shirt; its body coiled around the entire length of his arm to the wrist. Beautiful if sinister, the tattoo was a common fashion statement in certain twenty-something circles. It was also the kind of emblem one might acquire in prison. What did it say about Jeff Holland that Scott was a good friend of his?

What it said, she found out after she'd spent five minutes convincing Scott that her intentions were benign, was that Jeff and Scott were boyhood buddies and their families were still neighbors in a suburb of Los Angeles. The two boys had started taking clarinet lessons together and they both still played.

"I just do it for fun. Jeff's the one with all the talent," Scott said.

Once he started talking, he was as worried about Jeff as Ira Nadler had been.

"Jeff would never blow off a gig." He fingered his snake tattoo as if it were worry beads. "One time in grade school, he talked his mom into letting him play in a concert when he had a fever of a hundred and one. Minute the concert ended, he passed out. The most exciting thing that happened in fourth grade. Hang on." He went to draw a beer for a customer.

"Does he do drugs or alcohol?"

"Jeff? No way."

"Any idea where he'd be, if he hasn't been at his apartment for the last two days?"

He took care of another customer, then came back with the decaf coffee pot and poured Margo another cup. "On the house," he said. "What did you want to know?"

"Where Jeff might be, if he's not at his apartment. Does he have a new girlfriend?"

"Dunno, but like I said, he wouldn't blow off a gig. All I can figure, there's some kind of family emergency. How 'bout I call my folks—not tonight, it's too late, but first thing in the morning? They'll know if anything happened to the Hollands. Give me your number. I'll let you know." He rubbed the tattoo. "Hey, what about calling hospitals in case Jeff was in an accident? I could do that when I get off work tonight. Always takes me a while to wind down, and hospitals are open all night."

Maybe Scott's wariness was catching. The more he offered to help, the more Margo suspected he was jiving her. And the more concerned she got about Jeff Holland.

It felt absurdly cloak-and-dagger, but she found a place to park on the street, out of range of the floodlights in the club parking lot, and waited. By one-thirty, when the bartender left the Voodoo Club, she'd gained an exquisite appreciation of why no one should use a little Mazda Miata for a stakeout. The car she followed, an older Honda Civic, was what she would have expected Scott to own, as was the apartment to which she tailed him; he lived in a slightly down-at-the-heels neighborhood not far from San Diego State University. Whatever might be fishy about the bartender, he wasn't conspicuously living beyond his means. Nor did he go home and then furtively reemerge to lead her to Jeff's lair. Despite what he'd said about needing time to unwind after work, his lights went out in fifteen minutes. Another fifteen minutes and Margo left, not sure whether her body was screaming more for a warm bed or a chance to stretch at last.

"Show time!" she told her reflection at seven-thirty the next morning. She'd slept in as long as she could, but she was scheduled to cover a mayoral news conference at nine.

Her reflection growled back. She applied significant amounts of makeup to the circles under her eyes and kicked herself for not getting Scott's phone number. She didn't even know his last name! Assuming he followed through on calling his folks, what did he consider "first thing in the morning?"

There was no word from the bartender when she arrived at the radio station after the news conference. She decided to give him until noon—and then what? Call the police? Would the police be seriously concerned about the less-than-three-day absence of an adult man? Maybe if she brought up the theft of Ira Nadler's rare record . . . except Nadler would probably refuse to substantiate the charge.

While she dubbed the mayor's remarks from a cassette tape to reel-to-reel for editing, she looked at the lists she'd gotten from Nadler of the members of Klezmania and the people who'd attended his dinner party. One name appeared on both lists—Mike Appel, Klezmania's violinist.

She called Appel and told him she'd heard about the Ozorow record and thought it would make a great story. (Not a lie. Once the record was found, she'd love to do a feature on it.) Since Appel was a violinist himself, what did he think of the great Zig Wolinsky's violin style? And wasn't he, rather than a clarinetist, more likely to covet the record? Nadler had insisted that no one but Jeff had the opportunity to steal it, but could he be absolutely certain? Appel sputtered excitedly about the record and Ira Nadler's contributions to klezmer musicology. She remembered from interviewing Appel that his conversation always sounded as if he'd just drunk five cups of espresso—the fiddler was as high strung as his fiddle.

"It must have been an amazing evening," she said, "with Ira playing the record and you and Jeff Holland listening. Do you know how I can get in touch with Jeff? I tried his apartment, but he's not there."

"We've got a rehearsal in an hour. I'll tell him to call you," Appel said.

Absorbed in editing her story, she didn't look at a clock until she got a phone call at twelve-thirty. It was Mike Appel, saying Jeff was an hour late for the Klezmania rehearsal.

"Could he have gotten the time wrong? Or gotten stuck in traffic?" she asked but didn't believe it.

"That's what the other guys keep telling me," the nervous violinist replied. "But Jeff's never screwed up the time of a rehearsal. And if he's in traffic, why isn't he calling on his cell phone? It happened one time and he was like, 'I'm on the 805 at Balboa, how about you guys work on this or that until I get there?' He called every five minutes with some other idea about how we should be playing."

Margo brought her story on the mayor to an acceptable if slapdash finish that would have made a perfectionist like Jeff Holland wince. If she didn't have his friend's phone number, at least she'd made note of the address.

Following Scott in the wee hours, she hadn't noticed that he lived only a few blocks from Ira Nadler. The bartender's neighborhood was a bit scruffy, the cheap stucco apartment buildings in need of paint; some of them were marred by graffiti, the first but probably not the last incursions of East San Diego gangs. It struck her that, for all the genteel ambiance Nadler created in his apartment, his street was declining as well. He'd mentioned nightmares of ending up in the gutter; maybe it wasn't just a melodramatic turn of phrase. On the trail of Jeff Holland's boyhood pal, Margo found herself thinking about the music dealer: Was there ever a Mrs. Nadler? Any kids? How well could one do in rare records? Not well enough to retire in Rio on the proceeds, he had told her. But he made a living. Still, what happened if he became ill and couldn't keep his business going? Did he have any savings?

Scott's building was a standard California four-plex, with the apartment entrances along one side. A metal gate opened onto a skinny paved walk edged by a long-forsaken attempt at landscaping; one desiccated jade plant clung to life. When she'd followed him home, she'd seen a light go on in the unit on the top front. She took the stairs to that one and knocked.

She heard a whisper of movement inside, then nothing.

She knocked again.

"Yeah, all right." His voice sounded slurred. When he opened the door, she smelled why.

Threaded through the foggy reek of cigarettes, she picked up a sweeter odor, a pleasant smell she associated with younger times and usually evening hours. Marijuana.

"Oh, it's you," Scott mumbled.

"Did you call your folks?"

"Uh . . ."

"You were going to ask if Jeff had a family emergency," she prompted.

"Yeah. I called, I said I would. He's not there. I'm worried about him."

"You look worried." Damn, why hadn't he called her?

"Hey, somebody like you takes a Valium. I smoke a joint." Although the hostility seemed habitual, his voice was soft, as if the marijuana had taken the edge off his attitude.

"Sorry." Why antagonize him? One more question, and she never had to see the bartender again.

"Can you think of anyplace Jeff might go if he felt like he needed to get away for a few days?"

"If he needed to get away and I knew where he might be, then why would I tell you?"

"Because maybe there's something wrong. He missed a gig last night and a rehearsal today."

"A rehearsal, too?"

She could almost see him trying to stack his thoughts, like a kid laboriously assembling a pile of blocks.

She gave the blocks a push.

"If you know where he is, can't we check and make sure he's okay?" she said.

"I don't know, I haven't talked to him. But there's this place in the Cuyamaca Mountains, maybe an hour and a half from here."

"A house?"

"Somebody's cabin that they let him use. I went there with him once."

"Whose cabin? Is there a phone?"

"Can't remember. Here's what. I'll go up there, see if he's there, and let you know if he's all right."

Scott shuffled toward the sofa, which was piled with clothes. "Just have to find my car keys."

"I'll go, if you tell me how to get there." It would be criminal to let Scott get behind the wheel of a car. Besides, if Jeff Holland was hiding because he was scared about having stolen the record, she wanted to find him herself before he heard that a reporter was trying to track him down.

"Uh uh. I can find it but it's like, I won't know until I see it."

"Look. Friends shouldn't let friends drive stoned. Why don't you navigate and I'll drive?"

He must have been really wasted because he didn't even put up a *pro forma* argument. "Sure. Okay." He shoved his feet into a pair of flipflops and followed her to her car.

In a movie, it would have been the start of a great romance: He and she detest each other on sight, then fate throws them into a car together for a trip to a beautiful mountain hideaway . . . Except in the movies, *she* wouldn't have been married and *he* would have turned out to be profound, witty, or both. Instead he was marginally coherent, only opening his mouth to sing along with Counting Crows, the one tape she had that met his approval. (She planned to give it to him. After listening to the tape twice, accompanied by Scott's raspy baritone, she never wanted to hear it again.) And after forty minutes of trying different roads that *looked* like the road he'd taken with Jeff to the cabin, she was ready to dump him at the nearest Greyhound station and tell Ira Nadler he'd just have to wait until Jeff resurfaced on his own. If Jeff had a mountain hideout, surely that's where he was, and the fear she had felt from Nadler—the fear she'd begun to feel herself—was utterly groundless.

"I've got, like, a terrible case of the munchies," Scott said.

"Look in the glove compartment."

"What is this, twenty-year-old trail mix? Hey, try here. I think I recognize that signpost."

She'd have more faith if he hadn't already recognized six other signposts. Nevertheless, she turned down a dirt road that looked like every other dirt road they'd taken, edged with a sprinkling of vacation homes.

"That's it!" he said.

"You remember the cabin?" A rustic wood-and-stone building with a bright blue door, it was set prettily among the trees.

"That's Jeff's car."

She and Scott went up to the door and knocked. No answer.

"Jeff! Hey, it's me," Scott called.

Margo tried the knob. The door was unlocked.

As if it had been crouched waiting to attack, the smell flung itself at them.

"Jesus Christ." Scott, swifter than she, crossed the hooked rug to the man sprawled before a stone fireplace.

"Don't touch any—" she started, but already Scott was examining the man like a professional, barely disturbing the body, even though slow tears dripped down his face.

"It's Jeff," he said. "Goddamn! Somebody shot him in the chest."

Somebody! Or Jeff himself? But the dead musician's hands were visible—and empty. So was the rug around his body.

"There's no phone in this room," Scott said. "Wait outside and I'll check the rest of the house." Jeff's stoned friend had metamorphosed into Mr. Take-Charge.

Gratefully, Margo nodded. She was dying to breathe some fresh air. Still, she took a moment to scan the room. The cabin was sparsely furnished except for an expensive-looking stereo system. She checked the turntable, in case Jeff had come here to listen to his stolen prize. But the turntable was empty.

Nor did she spot the Ozorow record through the windows of Jeff's car. Had he asked someone to meet him here to buy the record—someone who'd killed him rather than pay the price? Hard to imagine a collector of klezmer music pulling a gun, rather than writing a check. Maybe, if Jeff was the kind of person who'd steal the record, he was involved in other criminal activities as well? Had he called anyone on his way to the cabin? she wondered, remembering his cell phone.

"Hey, what are you doing?" Scott said as she reached for the door handle. She explained about the cell phone.

"Damn. We probably shouldn't touch the car. Let's at least try the neighbors."

"You've done this before, haven't you?" she said, as they trudged down the dirt road.

"Not exactly. But I was in the Army, in Bosnia. I've seen dead bodies."

They didn't have far to go. A few houses away, a retired couple had turned their weekend getaway into their permanent residence. They made Margo and Scott stand outside while they called the sheriff's office. "Sorry to be so suspicious. We lived in L.A. for forty years," the husband said through the locked screen door.

"Whose cabin is that?" Margo asked.

"You're talking about the place three houses down? The blue door?"

She nodded.

"Belongs to a gentleman from San Diego. He does something in the music business. Mr. Nadler. The kind of man who likes everything just-so. He'll be upset that somebody sneaked into his place and got himself killed there."

"Sorry, I'm going to be sick." Margo ran into the trees, toward the road.

She kept going until she got to her car. By the time she stuck around to give a statement to the sheriff, police in San Diego would be contacting the owner of the cabin to inform him a man had died there and ask if he knew anything about it.

She wanted to break the news to Ira Nadler herself. And to demand that he tell her . . . what? She only knew something felt terribly wrong and the wrongness centered around the music dealer.

"Hey, what the—" Scott had followed her. He jumped into the passenger seat.

She gunned the motor. "The man who owns the cabin, he's the one who called yesterday and asked me to look for Jeff." She hurtled past the retirees' house. Scott didn't try to wrestle the steering wheel from her, and she sighed in relief. If she could get him on her side, she'd actually welcome his company. She realized she didn't want to enter Nadler's apartment alone.

She told Scott about her meeting with Nadler and the story of the stolen record. Except, why the hell would Jeff steal from Nadler and then go to Nadler's cabin?

"Did Jeff have his own key to the cabin, so he could use it whenever he wanted?" she asked Scott. "Or did he have to get it from Ira Nadler?" If Jeff had a key, maybe he figured the cabin would be the last place Nadler would think to look for him.

"Dunno. But I can tell you, Jeff would never steal anything. When we were kids, everyone tried shoplifting from this one store in the neighborhood. Except Jeff."

They stopped talking. The Miata might be a lousy stakeout car, but it was swell for fleeing the scene of a crime. Margo took the mountain curves as fast as she could, glancing behind her for pursuit vehicles. And she thought about Ira Nadler.

Mike Appel, when they'd talked that morning, had told her more about the music dealer than she'd known before. "Ira came from a family of fiddlers, did you know that?" Klezmania's violinist had said. "The first time he picked up a violin, he was five, living in a tenement on the lower East Side. He could have been one of the great klezmer fiddlers. That's what he learned from his father—it's in his blood. But who was listening to klezmer back then? Ira wasn't going to waste himself playing in some moldy bar mitzvah band. And he didn't really have the technique for classical or the licks for jazz. Some guys made the transition—Benny Goodman, Artie Shaw. But Ira came along just a little too late for the big bands."

The frustrated violinist had hung around the business, getting into rare music through his own passion as a collector of klezmer records. He'd dealt in classical, jazz, rock, folk, whatever he could find a market for. When the klezmer revival came along, he was perfectly situated not only to provide records to collectors but to satisfy the hunger for information about the musical form that had virtually been rescued from the grave. Margo had known Nadler was an expert, but she hadn't realized he was considered one of the pre-eminent klezmer musicologists in the world. And he was making sure his knowledge wasn't lost, Mike Appel said. He'd recently taken an apprentice.

"Who?" she'd asked.

"Jeff. I thought you knew."

How much was the Ozorow record *really* worth? Margo wondered, reaching the straight slab of the freeway and pushing the car up to eighty-five. Nadler had brushed off her question about the record's value, but could it make the difference between a comfortable retirement and the poverty he feared?

Had Jeff Holland, musicologist-in-training, understood the record's value as well?

But that brought her back to Jeff stealing the record, a story she was finding harder and harder to believe. During the remainder of the drive to Nadler's apartment, she began to imagine what might have really happened after the dinner party. Only one part of the story eluded her completely—

Why?

Ira Nadler greeted her and Scott with his usual charm. For a moment, she was sure that everything she'd been thinking must be wrong. Still, she turned down a cup of tea and he didn't offer twice.

"We've been to the mountains. To your cabin," she said.

Sitting erect in an armchair, wearing the sport jacket and tie that were his daily attire, Nadler displayed tremendous dignity—and absolutely no surprise.

"We found Jeff there. Ira, I'm sorry. He's dead."

"Yes," Nadler said.

She could sense Scott, beside her, ready to jump at the white-haired man. But Scott had promised to let her take the lead, and he kept quiet as she continued.

"You knew." She paused for Nadler to respond. He didn't. She said, "You asked him to go there with you after the dinner party."

"In separate cars, yes."

She had to lean close to hear him. Resting palm-down on his thighs were the elegant hands of the violinist he might have been. And his fingernails, she noticed, were chewed ragged.

"Do you own a gun?" she asked.

"In these times, an older person living in this neighborhood . . . You have to be able to defend yourself. You can't count on the police to protect you."

"Ira, what happened? Did you and Jeff fight over the Ozorow record?"

"Let me play you something." He stood and motioned them to follow him.

"Wait," Scott said.

"Ah. The bodyguard speaks."

"Where's the gun?" Scott asked him.

"In the drawer, top right." He nodded toward a cherrywood sideboard.

Not taking his eyes off Nadler, Scott opened the drawer. He used a handkerchief to pick up the gun he found there and emptied it of bullets. He put the bullets in his pocket.

"You want to search me, in case I have another one? Maybe an AK-47 in my pocket and a knife strapped to my leg?" Nadler said with a wry smile.

"Yeah." Scott handed Margo the gun he'd found and subjected Nadler to a quick, efficient search. The music dealer's lack of protest confirmed Margo's theory—and made her heart ache.

Once Scott had completed his search, Nadler led them into his study and put a record on the turntable. It was a klezmer group, the song dominated by a colorful violin solo.

"Zig Wolinsky?" Margo asked.

Nadler held up a finger. He didn't answer her until the last wailing strains ended and—carefully, holding it by the edges—he removed the record from the turntable.

"No, it's not Wolinsky." As he spoke, however, he held up the record for her to see. Neatly lettered on the label, above the original Yiddish characters, was the word *Ozorow*.

"But it's the Ozorow record?"

"That's right."

With a movement as shocking as it was slight, he released his hold on

the record and let it drop onto the floor. Margo gasped, expecting the fragile shellac disc to shatter. The carpet saved it, however. She stooped and
picked it up. She thought she knew why Nadler had risked breaking the
record, and why he and his apprentice had argued about it.

"You were sure the violinist was Zig Wolinsky, and Jeff proved you were
wrong," she said.

"Jeff knew the violinist wasn't Wolinsky," Nadler replied.

Something in his tone teased her, suggesting she was missing something
important. Damn, what was it? And why was he playing games with her? She
felt claustrophobic in the study, her mind crowded by all of the music made
decades earlier.

"You don't kill someone because they caught you in a mistake," she said,
thinking out loud.

"I didn't make a mistake about the identity of the violinist." He spoke
gently, as if prompting a slow student.

"Jeff wasn't telling you anything new. You already knew the violinist
wasn't Wolinsky."

"Very good, my dear."

"But you were going to sell the record as a Wolinsky record?"

He nodded.

"And Jeff objected? Ira, how much was the record worth? Would it really make such a difference?"

"Money? A few thousand, at most. It had nothing to do with the value
of the record. Jeff didn't just threaten to keep me from making this sale.
He intended to destroy my reputation."

"How could he, over one record?" As Margo spoke, she understood. "It
wasn't just one record, was it? You've sold other records the same way, saying they had historical value they didn't?"

Nadler mumbled something.

"What?" she asked.

"What was the harm? In the neighborhood where I grew up, you learned
to work every angle. You had to, to survive. If you were more clever than the
next man, you won. You made a few dollars. If someone else was more clever
than you, they won—and you swore you'd be smarter the next time. What
was the harm?"

"I'm calling the police," Scott said.

"Of course." Nadler handed him the telephone receiver.

After Scott made the call, Nadler suggested they return to the living room. "So much more comfortable, we can all sit."

He took his place in the armchair and lit his pipe. The fragrant pipe tobacco reminded Margo of her father. In spite of herself, she felt fondness for Ira Nadler.

What he had given the world was so precious. He had helped save from extinction the musical expression of a culture that was virtually annihilated.

What he had taken from the world, however, was so much greater.

She leaned forward and fixed her eyes on his. "When you asked Jeff to go to the cabin, were you planning to kill him?" she asked.

"Was I planning? Consciously, I don't think so. Did I take the gun? Yes. Of course, I always took the gun to the cabin. A habit. But then you have to ask, don't you, why did I ask Jeff to meet me there?"

"Was it an accident?"

"Does it really matter?"

"Why didn't you just turn yourself in?"

"I couldn't."

"But you meant for me to find out what happened."

"Not at all. I meant to put the matter in God's hands. If you were more clever than I, you'd win. If I was more clever . . . well, the metaphors from the old neighborhood only go so far. Could you get me a glass of whisky, dear? There's a bottle in the sideboard, just below where your friend found my gun."

While Margo poured him a drink, he selected a compact disc and put it on the modern sound system he kept in the living room. Jeffrey Holland's clarinet burst forth—passionate, playful, lost forever.

Tears stung Margo's eyes. She looked at Ira Nadler. He was weeping, too.

JAMES YAFFE is the author of many novels and stage plays. He began writing "Mom" stories for *Ellery Queen's Mystery Magazine* as a teenager in 1943. He is now professor of literature at Colorado College in Colorado Springs. This story was originally published in *Ellery Queen* in 1968 and reprinted in *My Mother, The Detective* (Crippen & Landru, 1997).

Mom Remembers

▼   ▼   ▼   ▼   ▼   ▼   ▼   ▼   ▼

JAMES YAFFE

"ONE THING I'VE ALWAYS WANTED TO ASK YOU," said Inspector Millner to my mother. "How did you ever get interested in crime detection in the first place?"

Mom laughed and said, "From Mama, naturally. She taught me all I know."

This was a surprise to me. Mom never talked much about her parents or her childhood days.

"Nothing on earth is more boring," she used to say, "than an old lady looking backwards." So I put down my knife and fork and said, "Your mother had a talent for solving crimes, Mom?"

"A talent, he says! Did Einstein have a talent for adding up numbers? Does Van Cliburn have a talent for playing the piano? All right, Mama never went to a college maybe, but as a detective she was a regular P, H and D! If you're interested, I'll tell you about the first murder I ever ran up against. It was Mama who solved it—I only stood by and watched and learned—"

But before I go ahead, I'd better explain what led up to these reminiscences from Mom.

It was the fourth of May, a Wednesday night. Ordinarily, Shirley and I go up to the Bronx to have dinner with Mom on Friday nights—but the fourth of May is a special date in Mom's life. It's the anniversary of her wedding to Papa. Shirley and I don't like her to be alone for that.

Forty-five years ago Mom and Papa were married. She was eighteen, and he was just twenty-one. They had gone to school together and lived in the same tenement building on the Lower East Side; their families had come originally from the same little village in the old country. For a long time, their parents had agreed—because that was how things were done in the old country—that the children would get married someday. It was not part of the arrangement that they had to be in love with each other—but strangely enough, they were in love with each other.

For over thirty years they lived together happily. They left the lower East Side and moved to the Bronx. They brought me, their only child, into the world. They saved enough money to send me to medical school. (I dashed their hopes by deciding, after I got out of college, to become a policeman.) Shortly afterward, while he was in his early fifties, my father died suddenly, his heart weakened by too many bills and too much night work and an inexhaustible capacity for worrying about other people's troubles. I'll never forget the look in Mom's eyes—though she struggled hard to keep me from noticing it. Even today, on the anniversary of their wedding, the shadow of that old pain flickers across her face.

Last May fourth, Shirley and I brought Inspector Millner up to the Bronx with us. Inspector Millner is my boss at the Homicide Squad. He's a tall man with a bald head and bulldog features. His scowl can strike terror into the hearts of murderers, but sitting across the table from an unattached middle-aged lady with a coy look on her face, he becomes as shy and tongue-tied as an adolescent boy.

Anyway, Shirley and I have been trying for a few years now to get something going between Mom and him, and though there haven't been any serious developments yet, Mom always seems glad to see him. We thought it might cheer her up to see him on May fourth.

Sure enough, she gave him a big hug in the foyer. "It's a pleasure to welcome you! Tonight is pot roast, your favorite! If you don't make a glutton of yourself, I'll be insulted!"

A good beginning, I thought. Maybe Mom could get through the whole evening without any flickers of that old pain.

A little later, while we were eating her soup at the dining-room table, she said, "You like my matzoh balls, Inspector? It was the same with my Mendel. He used to tell me he could eat a hundred of them, and even the heartburn was worth it." Her voice began to shake a little. "Such a big appetite he had, for such a little, sensitive-looking man—"

This was dangerous ground. Shirley and I spoke up at exactly the same moment.

"I saw a lovely coat at Macy's, Mother," Shirley said. "It was you all over."

"A new murder case broke this week, Mom," I said. "Inspector, why don't you tell her about it?"

"Coats can wait, darling," Mom said to Shirley, and then turned to Inspector Millner. "I'd be happy to hear about your new murder case, if you wouldn't mind taking the trouble."

The familiar glint of eagerness was in her eye. For a while, anyway, she would forget to be sad.

"I don't know why David bothered to mention it," the Inspector said. "It's a perfectly routine case. Nothing in it that could interest you."

"Mom's interested in all our cases," I put in quickly.

"Well then—" Inspector Millner scratched his ear, a nervous habit whenever he had to make a speech in public. "This eighteen-year-old kid, his name is Rafael Ortiz, mugged and knifed a cab driver last night. It's the usual story. The kid's been hanging around with a bad crowd lately, staying out late at night, fighting with his parents. Sure enough, he's finally got himself into serious trouble. Same damn things happening every day, all over the city—getting worse every year—"

"You're positive this boy is the guilty party?"

"Open-and-shut case. The man he knifed came to in the hospital and identified the kid just before he died. And there was an eyewitness, too—a completely reliable witness. So you see, any ordinary cop could crack this case. It's a waste of your talents."

Mom blushed. I don't know anybody besides Inspector Millner who can make her blush. Shirley says it's a very hopeful sign.

So the conversation moved on to other things, and a little later— right after Mom served the pot roast—Inspector Millner asked his question about how Mom ever got interested in crime detection. And she gave her answer— and we were back on dangerous ground again.

"I'll tell you about the first murder I ever ran up against," she said. "As I said, it was Mama who solved it. It was your Papa, Davie, who got Mama and me mixed up in it. My poor Mendel—"

That shake was in Mom's voice again. But I couldn't figure out how to break in and change the subject.

"When I tell you that Mama was a regular genius at solving crimes," Mom went on, "I don't mean she ever solved an actual murder—until the one that happened the day before our wedding. On the Lower East Side in those days, people didn't murder other people so much. In her imagination maybe, Mrs. Horowitz would wish that Mrs. Shapiro should drop dead because Mrs. Shapiro is always bragging about her rich relatives uptown and acting like she's better than other people. But the minute after Mrs. Horowitz has such a terrible thought, she feels ashamed of herself, she begs God's pardon in *schul,* and she makes some chicken soup for the Shapiro girl who's got the grippe.

"The point I'm making is, Mama didn't have any sons in the Homicide Squad or any sons at all—and they would've become lawyers or gone in for some other *normal* type of work. So the only crimes Mama got a chance to solve were the kind that don't get reported to the police or get written up in the newspapers.

"I'll give you a for instance. Mrs. Kinski from the third floor sells her husband's old Hebrew books while he's uptown working in the hat factory. She puts the money in a sugar can in her kitchen, and the next day it's gone. Nobody's been in that kitchen except the janitor's son to fix the water faucet—which is hopeless, because it's such an old faucet, what's left of it to fix? So everybody in the building is talking how the janitor has a son who's a thief.

"Then Mama steps in and asks a few questions and digs up a few pieces of information and remembers something that happened when she was a girl in the *shtetl* in Russia—and out comes the truth. Poor Mr. Kinski stole the money himself so he could buy back his Hebrew books, which he loved more than anything on earth, including his wife.

"And another time—the little Glogauer girl, age nine, faints in school, and the doctor says it's from hunger, even though her mother gives her a dime every day to buy a sandwich and an apple and a milk. The girl won't tell anybody what she's been doing with the money, and she cries if her mother asks her any questions.

"So Mama does a little poking here and a little poking there, and before the end of the week she uncovers a regular organized Chicago-gangster protection racket, which is collecting dimes from all the little kids in the school—and who's running it? A half dozen eleven-year-old Al Caponies!

"This is the kind of crime that Mama was solving since I was a little baby, since as long as I could remember. The mind she had on her! If her opportunities had been better—if she could've been born in the lap of luxury and had a college education—if only she wasn't a widow with four daughters to bring up and living in a slum tenement and nothing but *tsoris* from the landlord! That wonderful mind, wasted on Delancey Street, to think of it sometimes it makes me almost cry!"

Mom trembled a little. Then she gave a shrug. "On the other hand, if life wasn't hard for Mama, maybe she never would have developed her wonderful mind in the first place. She *had* to be smart and think faster and see more than other people—because how *else,* with no rich relatives, do you keep four daughters from starving and turning into old maids? When it's a matter of life and death to read the butcher's mind, believe me you learn how to be a mindreader!

"So anyway, all the time I was growing up from a little girl I am watching Mama and listening to her when she put that mind of hers to work. And also, you should know, I wasn't such a dope myself—so pretty soon, from picking up a few of her tricks, I got the idea I could do what *she* could do, I could be just as smart as *she* was.

"All right, I wouldn't try to hide from you—I got a swell head. And what excuse did I have? Only the excuse that I was eighteen years old. It's a bad disease, but thank God everybody grows out of it—except my sister Jennie who stayed eighteen till the day she died at sixty-three.

"Excuse me, I'll get back to that murder case forty-five years ago, when I finally got the swell head knocked out of me, and found once and for all that I couldn't be another Mama if I worked at it 'til I was a hundred."

Mom stopped, a little out of breath. When she went on talking, her voice was much softer.

"Forty-five years ago—the day before my wedding. When I think what a close call it was—if it wasn't for Mama and her brains, would my wedding ever have happened? Would I be sitting here in the Bronx today? Davie, would *you* be sitting here, today? And the thirty-two years I had with my Mendel, those thirty-two happy years—"

A mist was coming over Mom's eyes—exactly what I had been afraid of. On May fourth, you don't encourage Mom to reminisce. On May fourth, you keep her as far away as possible from her memories.

So I broke in loudly. "Old murders don't interest me, Mom. It's *new* murders I care about. That's what the city pays me for after all. This Ortiz kid, the one who knifed the cab driver—I'm not sure it *is* an open-and-shut case, so I'd like to hear your opinion. Why don't you fill Mom in on the details, Inspector!"

"But the story about her wedding day—"

"You'll save it for later, won't you, Mom? We need your expert advice right now—we have to take advantage of this opportunity. Otherwise we wouldn't be doing our duty to the taxpayer."

I knew this strategy would work. The Taxpayer is a concept that always has a powerful effect on Inspector Millner's conscience.

He fidgeted a little and said, "Well, since David seems to think it's important—" He turned to Mom. "I'll tell you more about the Ortiz case. If it wouldn't bore you, that is."

Mom swallowed a piece of pot roast and leaned forward politely. "When did it ever bore me?" she said.

"This Ortiz kid lives on the West Side in the Eighties," Inspector Millner began. "His parents came from Puerto Rico ten years ago, when Rafael was seven and his sister Inez was eight. Since then, there have been two more kids, two little boys. The whole family lives in a run-down old firetrap off Amsterdam Avenue. Except the older sister, Inez Ortiz—she moved into a hotel room downtown a year ago because she and her father used to fight all the time."

"He's an easy man to fight with, Mr. Ortiz?" Mom said.

"He's an insignificant-looking little man. In his forties, but you'd think he was ten years older. He talks in a soft mumbling sort of voice, but all the neighbors say he's got a violent temper, particularly on Saturday nights when he does his drinking. He works in a shipping room down in the garment district, and the mother goes out five days a week as a cleaning woman, leaving her kids with the janitor's wife. In other words, it's no wonder that a kid growing up in a home like that gets himself into trouble."

"Plenty of them manage to stay out of trouble," Shirley said. "The emphasis in psychology today is far less on environmental factors and far more on old-fashioned willpower and individual effort—"

I could see Mom's nose twitching with annoyance. But she never let herself fight with Shirley when she had a guest at her table. So she smiled at Inspector Millner and said, "You mentioned, I think, that it's only recently the boy started getting in trouble?"

"It began six months ago, when he got out of high school. Up 'til then he was a pretty decent kid, got good marks, held a job in the afternoons as a grocery delivery boy. His parents tell us he was never in a jam, and his teachers and the neighbors confirm that. Also there's no record on him down at Juvenile Court. He lives in a pretty tough neighborhood—there's a gang on the next block that we've been watching—but as far as we can tell, Rafael never had anything to do with them."

"So what changed him?"

"What changes every one of them? They lose hope, that's what. Sooner or later, they get the message—high school, hard work, staying inside the law, where's it going to get them? The odds are a thousand to one they'll end up in a shipping room in the garment center, or washing dishes in a restaurant, or sorting mail for some city department. They get the message, and it caves them in.

"Some of them turn into robots, like Rafael's father—nice, quiet, obedient machines all day long, then they take it out on their wives and kids at night. Some of them turn into vegetables—they float along on welfare, never hold a job more than a few months, drink too much, and blot out all thoughts of tomorrow. And some of them—the tough ones—try to hit back. Only how much damage can one Puerto Rican boy do to the System? Generally he lands himself in jail—or in the morgue.

"That's the direction Rafael's been taking since last winter. First he complained that his job at the grocery store wasn't good enough for him—he had a right to be more than a delivery boy. So he quit and tried looking for something better—and it took him a month to realize he was hitting his head against a stone wall. He couldn't go back to the grocery store, though, or to anything like it—so he started hanging around the apartment.

"His father kept yelling at him and called him a bum. He yelled back and called his father a failure. His mother cried. So he stopped hanging around the apartment. Pretty soon he was showing up only for meals and staying out every night 'til after midnight, and when his father asked him where he'd been, he told the old man it was none of his business."

"He was spending his nights," Mom said, "with that gang you mentioned?"

"That's what his father thought. But the gang swears they had nothing to do with Rafael, and we can't find anybody who ever saw him with them. Whoever he's been hanging around with, it's somebody out of the neighborhood. Which makes it even worse."

"Could it be a girl maybe? Boys eighteen occasionally take an interest in the opposite sex."

"He has a girl all right. Her name is Rosa Melendez, and she lives half a block away from the Ortizes. Rafael is with her every Saturday and Sunday night, but on weekday nights she never sees him. She's asked him plenty of times where he goes, but all he ever tells her is that he's working on some kind of a 'big deal' and as soon as he pulls it off they'll have enough money to get married. Whenever she pushes him for more details, he gets mad at her and tells her that no man wants to marry a nagging woman."

"It sounds to me as if he's got another girl somewhere," Shirley said, "and he doesn't want Rosa to know about her."

"It's possible," the Inspector said. "But for what it's worth, Rosa doesn't think so. She's been worried sick about him, she admits she's suspected all sorts of awful things—but not once, she says, has she thought he was two-timing her. And I believe her. Besides, the 'mystery girl' theory doesn't fit with a certain crazy story the boy's father told us."

"What story?" Mom said.

"About a week ago the boy's mother got sick—a bad case of this virus that's going around—and she had to stay in bed for a couple of days. Well, in the middle of the afternoon her TV set went on the blink—"

"These people are poverty-stricken," Shirley said, "but they can still afford to have a television set?"

"If you're poverty-stricken," Mom said, "you can't afford *not* to have television. How else can you forget for a while that you're poverty-stricken?"

"Anyway, Rafael fooled around the back of the set with a screwdriver," the Inspector said, "and managed to get it working again. That night he went out after dinner the same as usual—after the usual fight with his father because he wouldn't say where he was going—and around ten o'clock he called up from outside to find out if the TV was still working.

"He talked to his father, who asked him where he was calling from. This started another argument—but while it was going on, Ortiz heard voices in the background, from his son's end of the line. They were very low at first, and Ortiz couldn't make out what they were saying. Then one of the voices, a man's voice, got louder, and kind of angry. Ortiz heard very clearly what he said. 'Who's scared of the dicks? If any copper gets in my way, I'll mow him down!' A moment later Rafael hung up the phone."

"And his father told you all this?" Shirley said. "Voluntarily—knowing how incriminating it was?"

"I'm afraid he did. Old Ortiz is very bitter about the boy. 'He killed a man, let him take his punishment.' The mother, of course, is just the opposite. She won't hear a word said against the boy. 'My Rafael wouldn't hurt anybody,' she keeps saying. And for her sake—I admit it—I wish our case wasn't so strong . . ."

The Inspector's voice trailed off mournfully. After a moment Mom said, "What about Mrs. Ortiz's television set? Was it working all right when the boy called up?"

"Good heavens, Mother," Shirley said, "what on earth does that matter?"

"Still I'd like to know."

"The TV was working fine," Inspector Millner said. "The boy's always had a knack for mechanical things. It's a shame he'll never be able to do anything with it now."

"Now?" Mom said.

The Inspector's face tightened. "Two nights ago, he threw away his whole life. Around eleven, a cab driver named Dominic Palazzo—a little fellow in his sixties, five times a grandfather—let off a fare at Broadway and Eighty-Sixth Street, then started east. At Amsterdam Avenue he was hailed by a kid—short, thin, dark hair, which was almost as long as a girl's—that was Palazzo's description. Sounds like most of these crazy kids nowadays, I admit it. The kid got in the cab and told Palazzo to take him downtown—and spoke with a Spanish accent.

"Well, after a couple of blocks, when they came to a dark empty stretch, the kid pulled a knife, held it against Palazzo's neck, and ordered him to stop the cab and hand over his cash. It seems Palazzo had been hit by robbers twice in the last year, and he couldn't afford to take another loss. So he slammed down on the brakes, hoping to knock the kid off balance and grab his knife away from him. But before Palazzo could even turn his head, the kid stabbed that knife into the back of his neck. Then he jumped out of the cab, ran down the street, and disappeared around the corner. Palazzo was bleeding badly, but didn't die 'til two hours later in the hospital. He had time to make a positive identification."

"You brought the Ortiz boy to the hospital?" Mom said.

"Not the boy himself. We went to his home to pick him up—but he'd left after dinner as usual, and he wasn't back yet. We got a photograph of him from his mother—his high school graduation picture, and Palazzo took one look it and said, 'That's him!'"

"Something is puzzling me a little," Mom said. "How come you went to the boy's home to pick him up such a short time after the stabbing? What made you suspect him?"

"There was an eyewitness. He came out of an all-night hamburger joint on the far corner just after Palazzo started yelling. He saw the boy running down the street and recognized him."

"In the dark, from a block away, with the boy's back turned?"

"It's true this witness didn't actually see the boy's face. But he recognized the general build and coloring—and especially what the boy was wearing. A few months ago, the boy bought a leather jacket—bright red, with a black dragon's head on the back—and a black leather motorcycle cap, and he's been wearing this crazy outfit as often as possible ever since. His father told him he looked like a hoodlum in it—so naturally that encouraged him to keep on wearing it.

"Anyway, his parents and some others say that he had this jacket and this cap on when he left his home after dinner on the night of the murder—and our witness clearly saw this same jacket and cap on the boy running away from Palazzo's cab. That, plus Palazzo's identification of the photograph, clinched the case as far as we were concerned. We waited in front of the boy's building 'til twelve-thirty, when he came walking down the street, whistling to himself as if he didn't have a care in the world. Sure enough, he was wearing the red jacket and the black cap. So we pulled him in."

"And he confessed to the crime?" Mom said.

"He *still* hasn't confessed. He swears he wasn't anywhere near Amsterdam Avenue and the Eighties all night long. We asked him where he *had* been, and he said he'd been to the movies with his sister Inez. He picked her up downtown—she works as a waitress in a Times Square restaurant, and her hotel is a couple of blocks away—and they went to see a Western double bill together.

"We contacted her and asked her if she'd been to the movies with him that night. She said she had. Then we got a little tricky—we asked her to describe the two science-fiction pictures they had seen. She started talking about monsters and spaceships—well, the upshot was, they both admitted the alibi was a phony. But Rafael still won't admit he killed the cab driver—and he still won't tell us where he spent the night, or where he's been spending most of his nights in the last few months. Well, under the circumstances, what are we supposed to think?"

The Inspector spread his hands helplessly. There was no missing the look of misery on his face.

Then, in a gentle voice, Mom said, "But this evidence against the boy—is it really so open-and-shut? The cab driver picked up a boy on a dark street, and two minutes later this boy stabbed him from behind—so how positive could the poor man's identification be?"

"Palazzo had a good eye and a good memory, Mom," I said. "A year ago, when he was robbed the first time, he didn't get any better look at the thief—but he picked him out two weeks later from the line-up."

"Besides," the Inspector said, "our other witness saw the red jacket and the black cap."

"Couldn't more than one boy in New York have a red jacket with a dragon on it? Maybe this Ortiz belongs to a gang, and this jacket and cap are their uniform."

"No gang in Rafael's neighborhood wears such a uniform," the Inspector said. "Or anywhere else in the city, as far as we can discover. If there *was* such a gang, we'd be bound to know about it. That's why these kids wear these crazy outfits in the first place—so they can show them off in public."

Mom frowned. Then she said, "And this witness who claims he saw the boy's jacket running away from the crime? Can you trust him, this witness? Maybe he killed the cab driver himself, and he's trying to put the blame on an innocent party. Maybe it's a framing-up."

"Our witness is above suspicion," Inspector Millner said.

"Excuse me—" Mom gave a little smile, with just a touch of condescension in it, "when you've seen some of the things I've seen in my life, you stop believing that any flesh-and-blood human being is above suspicion. The richest member of our synagogue before the war—a man who gave thousands of dollars to charity, a man with white hair and double-breasted suits—but when five hundred dollars were missing from the Building Fund—"

"Mom," I broke in, "even *you* will have to believe this witness." I took a breath. "The fact is, *I'm* the witness."

Not many times in my life have I seen Mom look surprised. This was one of those times.

"Davie—you're making a joke?"

"I wish I were. Last week, a man in the Ortizes' building beat his wife to death. He confessed right afterwards, but I had to get statements from the other tenants. When I talked to the Ortiz couple, Rafael was in the room all the time. Heckling me, making cracks about cops—nothing I'm not used to, you understand, but the incident helped me to remember the boy. And to remember the jacket he was wearing.

"Two nights ago, around eleven, I finished my questioning and went across the street for a hamburger and a cup of coffee. I heard yells from the street and went out to see what was up—and I saw the boy running away from the cab. I didn't go after him because it looked as if the cab driver needed help right away. Besides, I knew I could always pick up the kid later on. Take my word for it, Mom—I would've recognized that red jacket any-where."

Mom frowned harder. Finally she said, "So I believe you, Davie. Natu-rally. What else? Only—something about this case keeps itching at me—"

A gleam of hope lighted up Inspector Millner's face. "The boy didn't do it? If I could tell that to his mother—if you had some proof—"

"Proof I don't have. Only an idea. Not even an idea—a comparison."

"A comparison with what?"

"With what?" Suddenly that shadow, that flicker of pain, was on Mom's face. "This murder—it's like the first murder case I ever ran up against. This Ortiz boy—like Mendel he is. Like my poor Mendel, forty-five years ago—"

My God, we were on dangerous ground again! I didn't know exactly how we had got there, but I certainly intended to get us off. "Forget about that old murder, Mom," I said. "Please keep your mind on *this* murder, will you?"

"What else am I doing?" Mom said. "Don't you follow me, Davie? This murder right now, that murder forty-five years ago—they could almost be the *same* murder. I couldn't solve the new one if I wouldn't think about the old one."

I saw that I was beaten and had no choice but to give up gracefully. "All right, Mom, if that's how you want it," I said. "Tell us about that old mur-der."

Mom folded her hands in her lap and smiled around at us all. "Since you're asking me, I'll tell you," she said. "Only don't let the pot roast get cold, please. Eat, Inspector. Eat, Shirley darling. You, Davie, I don't have to encourage, you'll eat no matter what. And while you're all eating, I'll talk."

"First I have to tell you about my Mendel," Mom said. "Your Papa, Davie, was a wonderful man. But maybe most people nowadays wouldn't agree with me. The things in him which were wonderful aren't so fashionable no more. And come to think of it, who knows when they ever were? A big business brain he wasn't. A big personality that told jokes and slapped peo-ple on the back he wasn't. A face like Rudolph Valentino and a body like Tarzan he didn't have. You only had to give one look at him, and you knew the day would never come when he'd make a million dollars. So phooey with him! Who cares about such a *schlimazl*? But this *schlimazl* was kindhearted and considerate, and he never got mad at people and never said insulting things, and the way he bounced you on his knee, Davie, when you were a little baby—the look of happiness on his face! Plenty millionaires, believe me, live for eighty years and never get such a happy look on their faces, not even when they're adding up their bank books. So for all these things I fell in love with this *schlimazl*, which, in the opinion of a lot of people, including my sister Jennie with the empty head, made me a *schlimazl*, too.

"At the age of fifteen, Mendel was brought by his father and mother to America from the old country. His father was a rabbi. Such a fine-looking man, with a long black beard and eyes that caught on fire when he got angry at somebody and a deep voice that could fill a whole synagogue and also a couple of blocks outside! Into the same building he moved as Mama and my sisters and me—two floors above us—and pretty soon he was made the rabbi of our *schul*. And I have to admit it, everybody respected and admired Mendel's Papa, but also everybody was a little bit afraid of him. Because nobody was as strict as he was for keeping the old ways, obeying the old laws.

"For instance, maybe one of the women—strictly accidental, you understand—would get a milk dish mixed up with a meat dish, and she wouldn't find out about it 'til just before dinnertime. So instead of throwing everything out and starting the dinner all over again, maybe she would say a little apology to God and serve the food to her family and forget to mention her mistake. All right, was this such a big sin? Did she do it to save herself trouble?

"No, she did it to keep her loved ones from going hungry. So wouldn't God forgive one little accident when it's a question of a hard-working husband and growing children who need their nourishment? Yes, God would forgive but not Mendel's Papa! At *schul* on Friday night this poor woman would stay as far away from him as she could. If he once looked her straight in the face with those black fiery eyes, she was positive he could see right through to the terrible secret in her heart.

"Mendel, when he got off the boat in New York City, didn't know one word from English. Yiddish and Hebrew were all he knew. His first year in this country, 'til he learned the language, wasn't easy for him. And I wouldn't lie to you, his English never *was* exactly from Harvard College. He could say what was on his mind and understand what others said, but all his life, 'til the day he died, he spoke with an accent—and his last day on this earth, in the hospital bed, he forgot all the English he had learned, and all his words were Yiddish.

"Just the same, he went to school at P.S. 84 'til he was seventeen, and then he went to work for Friedman & Son, Men's Underwear. He was a cutter in the shop. Not exactly the type of work his father had in mind for him. His father wanted him to be a rabbi, a scholar, and follow in the family tradition.

"But first of all, Mendel wasn't the scholarly type—his pleasure was from people, not from books. And second of all, America isn't like the old country. Back in the *shtetl*, a young man that spent all his days studying the Talmud was a hero. He gave pride to everybody, and if he needed food to eat and clothes on his back, who wouldn't be glad to contribute?

"But here in America, on Delancey Street, it was hard enough finding the food and clothes for your own children—and who needed scholars anyway? Did the American newspapers ever print stories about any scholars? Did you ever read where a scholar won a prize or made a speech or got elected to anything? To be a success in America you had to be a businessman or a professional man or a star in the movies. So who was going to make contributions for Mendel to spend his life with his nose in the Talmud?

"His own father couldn't do it because let's face it, a rabbi on the Lower East Side in those days wasn't getting the type of salary, with bonuses and a house and complimentary trips to Israel, that these famous important rabbis with vests and no hair on their faces are getting today. So Mendel went to work as a cutter in Friedman & Son's shop, and not even his Papa, no matter how angry he got, could do anything about it.

"Three years he worked in Friedman's shop. He was a good cutter, my Mendel, and also he had bigger ambitions. And all the time I was in love with him, and he was in love with me. So you're asking, what were we waiting for? For two things only—that I should be eighteen years old, and that Mendel should save enough money so he could quit his job, set up a tailor shop on his own. And since he didn't drink or smoke, or strut around in fancy clothes, or go out with no-good women, with Jezebels, that only show an interest in a man if he spends a lot of money on them—since his idea of a happy evening was to come down two floors and play three-handed pinochle with Mama and me—his savings in the bank were growing very nicely, even though Friedman & Son were, God knows, not exactly showering him with riches. Finally, when I had my eighteenth birthday, Mendel said that the time was come to look around for a store to rent—and he talked to my Mama, and I talked to his Papa, and the wedding day was set for the fourth of May. Which only goes to show—people can make their plans, but God might have a plan of His own up His sleeve."

Mom stopped for a moment and gave a little shudder. "God's plan was to play on Mendel and me a little joke. Not such a funny joke, in my opinion—but since when are we supposed to appreciate God's sense of humor? The joke went like this—the trouble that suddenly came to my Mendel, and nearly stopped him from having a wedding or anything else in his life, was brought on his head by one of those no-good women, those Jezebels that he never would have anything to do with.

"Jezebel, naturally, wasn't her name. Sadie Katz was her name. All right, it don't sound so glamorous. In the movies you never saw a vamp named Sadie Katz. In the history books you never read how any Sadie Katz was a king's girlfriend and changed the fate of a nation. Well, it's like William Shakespeare said in one of those plays that they made into a movie. 'What's in a name? A girl could be called Rosie or any other name and still she wouldn't smell so sweet.' Hundreds of years ago he wrote those words, and he could've been talking about Sadie Katz!

"She worked at Friedman & Son the same as Mendel. She was on the sewing machines, so she wasn't even on the same floor with Mendel. But she liked to walk around the shop a lot and give a look-over at everybody that happened to be wearing pants. Half the time her sewing machine was turned off, and she was wandering here and there, wiggling her hips and blinking her long eyelashes at anybody who enjoyed such spectacles. And plenty enjoyed, believe me—including Grossfeld the foreman—a man in his forties with five children and a sick wife! But how else, if it wasn't for Grossfeld, did Sadie Katz produce such a small amount of work and still not get fired?

"She was a dark-haired girl, except occasionally when she felt like being a blonde, and originally she was from Lithuania. A Litvak—so what could you expect? No, excuse me, I shouldn't have made such a stupid remark. The Litvaks are the same as anybody else—prejudices I haven't got, believe me. It's only that something comes over me when I think of that Sadie Katz. Even after all these years.

"Anyway, she was working in the shop for six, seven months when finally she met my Mendel. And after that there practically wasn't a day she didn't throw herself at him. She went up behind him while he was cutting and she mussed his hair. She told him how good-looking he was. She left the shop when he did, brushed against him in the doorway, and walked along the street with him. She dropped hints—they were as big as atom bombs, those hints—that any time he wanted to he could call her up and take her out.

"No, don't interrupt—I can see the question on your faces. Didn't I just get through saying that Mendel was no Rudolph Valentino, and no John D. Rockefeller either? So why should this Sadie Jezebel, this Delilah Katz, take such an interest in him? For such a girl, what was the attraction of a homely little man that got his fun from playing pinochle with his fiancée and his future mother-in-law?

"The answer is that Mendel had one attraction for Sadie Katz, which none of the other men in the shop had—Mendel wouldn't pay any attention to her. To her charms and her beauty, though frankly I could never see that she was so beautiful, he was positively a blind man. When she mussed his hair, he squirmed—but from embarrassment, not from excitement. When she told him she wanted to go out with him, he thanked her—politely because Mendel could never hurt anybody's feelings—but explained he was engaged to get married, so he didn't go out with any girls except me.

"Well, the truth was, Sadie Katz never ran up against anything like this before. She was used to the men hanging out their tongues for her, throwing themselves under her feet, hopping up and down when she told them to hop. That some poor little cutter, some nobody without a penny to his name, should be able to do without her so nicely—this was a blow to her pride. She couldn't sleep peaceful again 'til she got Mendel to hang out his tongue for her like everybody else.

"Meanwhile, naturally, she didn't give up her social life from aggravation over Mendel. At the rooming house where she lived, the landlady said she went out practically every night of the week with some man or other. Sometimes he'd come and pick her up, and sometimes she'd get all dressed up and go out alone, without telling anybody who she was going to, and at two o'clock in the morning she'd come waltzing in, still alone but singing to herself. And that same morning she'd get to the shop an hour late or even more—only you can take three guesses if that *noodnick* Grossfeld ever bawled her out!

"Well, this is how it went until the night before my wedding. May third, forty-five years ago—when all of a sudden Sadie Katz ended up the way so many Jezebels and Delilahs end up. She got herself murdered."

Mom gave one of her dramatic pauses. Then she looked around the table, "What's the matter?" she asked. "Why isn't anybody eating? The pot roast isn't up to the usual standard?"

We all assured Mom that the pot roast was delicious, and we started eating again. She relaxed and went on with her story.

"On May third, at six in the evening, there was a party in Mendel's honor. A bachelor party, with jokes and speeches and drinking toasts to say goodbye to Mendel being an unmarried man. Ten or twelve people were at this party—Mendel's closest friends from the shop, and also Grossfeld the foreman, who wasn't such a close friend actually but how do you tell the foreman you don't want him at your party? Everybody chipped in with a little money to buy Mendel a wedding present—a fountain pen with a gold clip and his initials on it. Right then and there Mendel took it out and wrote with it, and then he cried a little—from pleasure, you understand.

"This party was held on the first floor of the shop, which had Mr. Friedman's private office and the showroom for the out-of-town buyers. Mr. Friedman, from respect and liking for Mendel, let them use the showroom— and he himself made an appearance at the party near the end. He made a speech, calling Mendel a fine human being and a first-class cutter. Just between us, I think Friedman still had hopes he could keep Mendel from quitting his job and opening up a tailor shop—because even in those days, with sweatshops and no unions, a good cutter wasn't so easy to find.

"But excuse me, I don't want to do Friedman any injustice. He was a man with his heart in the right place. Being the 'Son' in Friedman & Son—the old man died years before—he had an idea the employees didn't respect him like they used to respect his father. So to make up for this he wore those expensive suits, he lived uptown on Park Avenue, he played golf, he made long-winded speeches, and sometimes he was a little highhanded in his business methods.

"But deep down underneath, this wasn't the real Friedman. Didn't he give Mendel a whole two days off for his honeymoon? Didn't he tell his wife—she used to be Stella Plotkin from Stanton Street when she worked for him as his secretary, but now she was Stella Friedman with two mink coats— to tell their cook to bake a small-size chocolate cake for Mendel's party? Didn't he provide the champagne himself, at his own expense? Imported French champagne it wasn't, if I remember correctly, it was champagne from Newark, New Jersey, but still it was a nice gesture on Friedman's part.

"How many times afterwards did I wish that this champagne had been nothing but grape juice! If it wasn't for this champagne, Mendel never would have had this trouble. The fact is, he wasn't used to drinking alcohol. A little wine on the Sabbath, this was his limit. And if he took more than one glass, he was dizzy for the rest of the night.

"But at the party, with everybody drinking toasts and wishing him luck, how could he sit there and not drink back at them? So by the time the party was over—and it only lasted an hour—Mendel had five glasses of champagne in him, and the world was doing flip-flops in front of his eyes, and he was talking a lot louder than usual. Without beating around the bushel, Mendel was drunk.

"He was so drunk that he couldn't walk home all by himself. So Grossfeld the foreman and a couple other fellows had to help him walk along the street. They did a lot of singing and shouting on the way, and Mendel did as much as anybody else. A block or two from home it suddenly came into his head that it wouldn't be such a good idea if his Papa smelled champagne on his breath. I told you already that Mendel's Papa thought the Orthodox ways and traditions were more important than anything on earth. And one of the oldest traditions is that a Jewish boy shouldn't get drunk. He shouldn't be a Prohibitionist either, you understand—he can take a schnapps or two for relaxation—but he never goes overboard and loses his head and makes a fool of himself. If Mendel's Papa, a rabbi, found out that his own son was drunk, what a *megilla* there'd be!

"So Mendel stopped at a candy store and bought a roll of peppermints for a nickel—his idea was to chew the peppermints and take the champagne smell off his breath. But he was in such a condition that he couldn't stick to this idea. He put the peppermints in his pocket, along with the change from his dollar bill, and he forgot all about them.

"Anyhow, Mendel and his friends and Grossfeld reached our building, and Mendel walked up the stoop, and then he turns to say goodbye to his friends. He not only says goodbye, he makes a speech. His voice is so loud and his gestures are so funny that children come running to look at him and people stick their heads out of windows up and down the block. Mendel waves his arms and shouts at them, 'I'm a happy man! I'm in love, and I'm getting married! Look at the beautiful fountain pen my friends gave me! Also they gave me five glasses of champagne!'

"And at this moment, like she was dropped there in a whirlwind, Sadie Katz is suddenly standing next to Mendel. From the shop she followed him, and now she can't resist the temptation—she puts her arms around him, gives him a big kiss on the mouth, and says to him so everybody can hear, 'You're a free man until tomorrow, Mendel. So why don't you drop in tonight and visit me?' And she runs off.

"Then Mendel goes upstairs to his apartment, and his papa is waiting for him at the door. Right away, as soon as he got a look at his papa's expression,

Mendel was sober again. From the window Mendel's papa had seen what was going on in the street, and now he was angrier than Mendel could ever remember him—and Mendel's papa was a man who got angry two or three times every day. So for half an hour Mendel's papa called him terrible names—a drunkard, and worse than that—and then, like a miracle out of the sky, Mendel did something he never did before in his life.

"He answered his papa back. He argued, he contradicted. He said he wasn't a drunkard, he said his papa was old-fashioned and narrow-minded, he said he had a right to live his own life. He didn't say these things maybe with the eloquence of a Jeremiah, a Franklin D. Roosevelt, a Rabbi Stephen Wise—but he said them, this is what counts. After twenty-one years, where did he get the courage? Maybe it was the champagne. Or maybe, on the day before his wedding, a man stops being afraid of things, because he don't think anything worse could happen to him.

"So the argument got louder and angrier, and finally Mendel's papa called him a sinner and a transgressor and ordered him into his room. And Mendel said, 'Why should I go into my room? It's early yet, the night hasn't even begun—I have to go out and do some more sinning and transgressing!' Then, while his papa shook a fist at him and his poor mama moaned and squeezed her hands, Mendel went marching out of the apartment.

"It was eight o'clock at night when he left. It was after midnight when he got back. His mama heard him closing the front door, then going to the bathroom, then making noises like he was being sick in the sink. Then she heard him going to bed. A little later she sneaked into his room and saw him fast asleep, with his clothes thrown all over the furniture. So she emptied the pockets and hung up his suit, and sneaked out of his room again.

"The next morning, the police came and arrested Mendel for strangling Sadie Katz to death, some time between nine thirty and eleven the night before."

Mom gave another one of her pauses. She has a genius for knowing when to make her listeners wait.

She ate a piece of pot roast, washed it down with a mouthful of water, and went on. "Sadie Katz lived in Mrs. Spiegel's rooming house on Avenue A. It was a five-story building, and if it ever saw better days, they must have been before the American Revolutionary War. Sadie Katz had a room on the second floor, which was just about big enough for a bed and a basin. Mrs. Spiegel lived on the first floor, with Mr. Spiegel, who went out every day and sold old clothes from his pushcart while Mrs. Spiegel took care of the rooming house. They came from Germany five years before, the Spiegels, and looked down their noses at anybody who came from Russia or Poland. They pretended to be cultured and intellectual. Spiegel was always reading German books, and the two of them went three or four times a year to the theater.

"On May third, according to the Spiegels, Sadie Katz got back to the rooming house at seven o'clock—which must have been a few minutes after she made such a spectacle of herself in front of our building. She went up to her room, and they could smell a piece of meat cooking on her hot plate. In Mrs. Spiegel's rooming house there was only one telephone—it was on the wall in the ground-floor hallway, and the roomers had to put a nickel in if they wanted to make a call. Sometimes people from outside would call this phone, which happened at ten minutes after eight on the night of May third. Mrs. Spiegel answered the ring, and a voice—a low whispering kind of voice, like somebody with a cold—asked to speak with Sadie Katz. Mrs. Spiegel yelled upstairs for Sadie, and went back to her apartment where she was giving Spiegel a knockwurst dinner.

"She closed her apartment door, naturally, but not all the way—maybe by accident. The Spiegels could hear every word Sadie Katz was saying on the phone. 'What a surprise to hear from you!' she said. 'You want to see me tonight? I'm flattered,' she said. 'No, I won't meet you outside. I'm tired, and I want to spend a nice evening at home. So why don't you come over here?'

"There was a long pause, and then Sadie sounded a little angry. 'Why should anybody see you?' she said. 'You'll ring the front doorbell, I'll come down and let you in myself. And what if somebody does see you? Am I a social outcast or something? Is it a crime to pay me a visit?' Then she gave a laugh and said, 'What are you afraid of? You're still a free man, aren't you? You can do what you like!'

"And then she said, 'All right, I'll expect you in about an hour.' Then she hung up the phone, knocked on the Spiegels' door, and told them she was expecting a visitor tonight, and she'd appreciate it if they let her open the front door when the bell rang. Then she went upstairs to her room.

"It was nearly nine-thirty when the front doorbell rang. Mrs. Spiegel opened her door and started out to the lobby—but Sadie Katz appeared on the stairs at the same time. 'I'll get it, thank you,' she said, and she deliberately waited 'til Mrs. Spiegel went back into her apartment. A few seconds later, the Spiegels heard the front door opening, then they heard Sadie's voice, loud and cheerful, and another voice, very low and muffled. And then they heard two pairs of feet climbing the stairs. But they never even caught a glimpse at Sadie's visitor.

"A little later the Spiegels went to bed, because Spiegel had to get up at the cracking of dawn and go out with his pushcart, if he expected to compete with the other old clothes peddlers from the neighborhood. So they slept all night and woke up at five o'clock. At six o'clock, Mrs. Spiegel saw Spiegel out the front, then she went upstairs to give a knock on Sadie's door—she did this every morning, so Sadie would wake up in time for work. Only this morning there was no answer to the knock.

"Mrs. Spiegel tried the door, and it wasn't locked. She went into the room and saw Sadie Katz lying on the floor. Sadie was wearing her fanciest clothes—what she'd been wearing at nine-thirty the night before—but her make-up was smeared, her sleeve was torn, and her tongue was sticking out. So Mrs. Spiegel started screaming.

"May fourth this was. The morning of my wedding day. Only before this morning was over it looked like there wouldn't be any wedding.

"The police came to Sadie Katz's room and examined the body and heard from the Spiegels about the phone call and the visitor. Especially they were interested in one part of that phone conversation: 'You're still a free man, aren't you? You can do what you like.'

"Who could Sadie have said these words to, except somebody who pretty soon would stop being a free man—in fact, somebody who was on the verge of getting married? So the police went to Delancey Street, got Mendel out of bed, and arrested him."

"The evidence seems pretty flimsy," I said. "We wouldn't arrest a man on evidence like that today."

"Excuse me, I forgot to mention," Mom said. "There was one other piece evidence. On the floor of Sadie's room was a big mess, things that fell there from the struggle with the murderer. Part of this mess was a new fountain pen, with a gold clip, and with Mendel's initials on it."

Inspector Millner sucked in his breath. There was a look of concern on his face, as if he were Papa's closest friend, and the murder had happened only yesterday.

"But it was even worse than that," Mom went on. "The police asked Mendel where he was between eight o'clock, when he left his apartment, and after midnight, when he came home again. Mendel said he didn't know. He got on the subway and stayed on it 'til he felt like getting off—he didn't even notice what stop. Then he walked along the street for a while, only he couldn't say what street. Some people passed by him and laughed at him for having his hat on. Then he sat on a bench in a little park—he couldn't say what park, he couldn't say how long. Finally he got up and went back to the subway, but it turned out he didn't have any money in his pockets—so he walked all the way home.

"Then the police showed him his fountain pen, and he admitted it was his and looked surprised that it wasn't still in his pocket. The police told him they weren't satisfied with his story—who would be?—but Mendel wouldn't change it.

"And then Mendel did something that made his case practically hopeless. 'I'm guilty,' he said. 'I broke the law. I deserve to be punished.' And he went up to his papa and got down on his knees. 'Forgive me, Papa, I'm a sinner and a transgressor, just like you called me!'

"Naturally the police pounced on this. 'Are you confessing the murder?' they said to him. 'You're admitting you went to the girl's room and tried to make love to her. And when she rejected you, you flew into a rage and killed her?'

"But Mendel just blinked at them and said, 'I didn't kill anybody,' and went on saying how guilty he was. He went on saying it all the way to jail."

Mom broke off with a sad little smile. "An hour later, while I was trying on my wedding dress, they broke the news to me. I started shouting that I had to get to the jail, and see my Mendel and comfort him in his time of trouble.

"Mama tried to calm me down. 'Don't be in such a hurry taking off your wedding dress,' she said. 'If you're not careful, you'll tear it.' But she didn't insist very hard on this. Because the same thought was in her head and mine—the chances were that this dress would never be needed."

Through the window, we heard a woman yelling. "Herbie, get up here right this minute, or you're in bad trouble! You hear me, Herbie?"

It broke the spell. It pulled us out of the Lower East Side of forty-five years ago, with its ramshackle tenements and narrow streets, back to the Grand Concourse and the TV antennas and the faint humming of air conditioners.

"For heaven's sake, Mother," Shirley said, "what happened?"

"What happened?" The sadness went out of Mom's smile. Some of the old tartness came back to her voice. "We're all here tonight, aren't we? So that's pretty good proof that the wedding dress was used."

"You cleared your husband of suspicion?" Inspector Millner said. "You solved the murder?"

"How could I be in any condition to solve anything? At eighteen years old, even under ordinary circumstances—even if the man you love hasn't been put in jail—you're slightly hysterical. So it wasn't me who did the solving. It was Mama.

"Right away, as soon as I was out of my wedding dress and back in my normal clothes, Mama made me sit quiet on the sofa and gave me a glass of seltzer water and took hold of my hand.

"'All right,' she said, 'let's take one minute to talk over this situation. You wouldn't do Mendel any good by running down to the jail and crying over him. All you'll do is get him wet. What's needed now is figuring out some way to prove he's innocent.'

"'Mama, you believe he's innocent?' I said, and if somebody gave me a million dollars I couldn't have been more grateful.

"'Naturally I believe,' Mama said. 'A nice boy like Mendel that wouldn't even cheat in a pinochle game. If he drank all the champagne in New York, he couldn't play around with another girl behind your back. And murder? With his kind heart and his weak stomach, he couldn't murder a cockroach in the sink.' Then Mama looked at me very hard. 'And you, baby? You don't believe he's innocent? You love him, and you've got doubts?'

"I swore to Mama that I had no doubts. This was the truth—but let's face it, it was still a relief to find out that Mama agreed with me. All by itself my opinion was strictly from the emotions of a girl in love. With Mama behind it this opinion suddenly had some sense in it—there was even a possibility we could make other people believe it, too.

"'So let's go over the facts,' Mama said, rubbing her hands together exactly like she did before she 'went over the facts' about Mrs. Kinski's sugar can. So for the next half hour, Mama and I told each other three or four times what the police and the neighbors and Mendel's mother had told us. I concentrated hard on every bit of it, trying to see it with Mama's eyes and think about it with Mama's mind. How many times had I said to myself that I could solve problems just as good as Mama solved them! So here was my chance, with my Mendel's life at stake. Now was the time to prove I wasn't strictly a bag of talk.

"After half an hour, I didn't have an idea in my head. But suddenly Mama gave a big smile and nodded her head a couple times. 'Good, good, I'm beginning to get a thought,' she said. 'Now you can run down to the jail and cry over Mendel, baby. But also don't forget to ask him a certain question I've got in mind. And then you should drop in on Grossfeld, the foreman at the shop, and ask him a question. And another question you should ask the Spiegels at the rooming house. And in the meantime I'll go upstairs and give a little sympathy to Mendel's poor mama and papa and while I'm there, I'll ask them a question, too.'

"Then Mama told me what her questions were, and none of them made any sense to me. But I agreed to ask them anyway, because in those days when a mother told a child to do something, you did it, and you didn't put up any argument.

"Down at the jail they let me talk to Mendel in a long room with a table between us. First I told him I loved him and believed in him. Then I begged him he should tell me the truth where he was between eight o'clock and midnight last night, and if he had any witnesses he should give their names to the police. But Mendel just shook his head and told me he wasn't any murderer but he couldn't say no more than that. And anyway what did it matter, since a no-good like him deserved only the worst?

"So when I saw I couldn't make him act sensible, I changed the subject and asked him Mama's question. 'After your fight with your papa last night, did you change your clothes before you ran out of the apartment?'

"'When did I have time to change my clothes?' Mendel said. 'I got home, Papa and I yelled at each other, I ran out. I wore the clothes I was wearing all day long. And why, please, do you want to know?'

"But how could I tell him why? I didn't *know* why I wanted to know. So I kissed him across the table and told him he shouldn't lose hope, then I went away to ask the rest of Mama's questions. On account of the murder, Friedman had closed the shop this morning, so I went to the building where Grossfeld lived. He had four rooms on the top floor—and his wife was lying in the bed smelling like medicine, and his kids, all five of them, were making enough noise for a hundred.

"It wasn't easy to make my voice shout above the racket. But I finally asked Grossfeld, 'Can you tell me please, before Mendel left the party yesterday, was he sick maybe from the champagne? Did he go to the men's room to be sick?'

"This was another question I couldn't make any sense out of. What did it matter if Mendel was sick or well? If a man commits a murder, they wouldn't let him go because he had an upset stomach at the time. 'As a matter of fact,' Grossfeld answered me, 'Mendel did get sick. It came over him just as he was getting ready to leave. He went running to the men's room and stayed there ten minutes, and when he came out he was looking a little green in the face.' I thanked Grossfeld, and then I headed for the rooming house where Sadie Katz was killed.

"The police were standing in front of it, and I had to convince them I had important business inside. Finally I got into the Spiegel apartment, where Mrs. Spiegel was lying on the sofa, still being in a state of shock from finding a dead body, and Mr. Spiegel was fanning her head. But underneath the shock I could see in Mrs. Spiegel's eye a pleased look, from being the center of attention.

"I apologized for disturbing her at such a time, which was enough encouragement for her to tell me the whole story of her terrible experience. But finally I managed to ask Mama's question, which was even crazier than the other two. 'The two of you are lovers of the theater, I understand. Which do you prefer, the American plays or the Yiddish plays?'

"When I asked this, they looked puzzled—not half as puzzled as I was, though! They answered me that they went most of the time to the Yiddish theater. 'The American actors talk so fast,' said Mrs. Spiegel, 'you couldn't follow the story.' 'Or understand the jokes,' said Mr. Spiegel.

"So I thanked them kindly and went back home and told Mama what answers I had got. And right away she rubbed her hands together, and said, 'Good! In fact, perfect! I also asked a question and got an answer. With all the wailing that's going on upstairs, it wasn't easy to put a word in edgewise, but finally I took Mendel's mama aside and asked her if she wouldn't tell me, please—when she emptied out her son's pockets at midnight last night, did she happen to notice how many peppermints were left in the roll? And she answered me that she didn't find any peppermints in his pockets at all. So what do you think of that, baby?'

"I said to her, 'I think I'm going to start crying in two seconds, Mama. They're accusing my Mendel of killing a woman and you're worrying that he's eating too much candy!'

"But Mama didn't get annoyed or upset at me. A woman who, at the age of thirteen, hid in a closet for two hours while a pogrom was going on outside don't get ruffled so easy. 'Baby, baby,' she said, 'use already the brains God gave you. You know all the facts from the murder, you heard the answers to my questions—so now you should be able to prove who is the murderer.'

"That's what Mama said to me on May fourth, at eleven o'clock in the morning, forty-five years ago. And that's what I'm saying to you now."

Mom stopped talking and gazed around at all of us. On her face was that look of satisfaction which is always there at a moment like this. She knows perfectly well that we're going to admit our stupidity and beg her for an explanation.

"I don't see it," Inspector Millner said. "The case against Mendel, your husband, looks awfully strong to me."

"The case was strong," Mom said, "as long as Mendel wouldn't come up with an alibi, with a witness who saw him where he was at the time of the murder. What Mama had to do was figure out for herself where Mendel was, so the police could find his witness even without his cooperation—"

"But if there was such a witness," Shirley said, "why on earth didn't he say so? Surely an innocent man wouldn't deliberately let people think he was a murderer!"

"Wouldn't he?" Mom's voice was very quiet. "Suppose there was something which, in his opinion, was worse than being a murderer." These words filled the room for a moment.

Then the Inspector said, "What could be worse?"

"It's a question of how a person was brought up," Mom said. "What was he taught to care about and have respect for and be frightened of? But I'll show you what I mean, step by step, the way Mama showed it to me.

"'Where did Mendel go between eight o'clock and midnight?' Mama said to me. 'He went someplace where people laughed at him for wearing his hat. So what does this mean to you, baby?'

"I answered her, 'It means he went to a neighborhood where there aren't any Jews. A Jewish boy is supposed to wear his hat all the time, cold or hot, inside or outside. It's part of the religion, it shows his respect for God. In a Jewish neighborhood, nobody would be surprised at seeing a boy with his hat on.'

"'This is true,' Mama said, 'but you didn't go far enough. How many times did I tell you? Half an answer is as bad as no answer at all. Even in a neighborhood without any Jews, what's so peculiar about a boy walking along the street with his hat on? It's early in May yet, it's not so hot that hats are ridiculous."

"'You're saying, Mama, that Mendel lied about the people laughing at him?'

"'About that he told the truth. Why make up such a story? But the minute he mentioned those people laughing, he remembered he couldn't tell the whole truth about them, because if he did he'd have to explain certain things he didn't want to explain. He wasn't walking on the street when these people laughed at his hat. He was inside—he was indoors someplace where you're supposed to take off your hat. He didn't take it off, and to the other people this was funny.'

"I was a little annoyed at myself, I admit it, for not figuring this out too. So I pretended I didn't think it was important. 'Indoors or outdoors, what's the difference?' I said. 'Maybe the people laughed at Mendel in the subway. He already told us he rode in the subway last night.'

"'If the laughing happened in the subway,' Mama said, 'why should he lie about it and say it happened on the street? And anyway, what man ever takes off his hat in the subway? So only believe me, baby—Mendel was inside someplace last night. Now tell me, please, what kind of place?'

"I couldn't tell her. My mind wasn't working. So Mama said, 'Think, baby, think. What about the money in Mendel's pocket?'

"'Wait a second, wait a second,' I said—and my mind was showing signs of life again. 'On the way home from the shop last night, Mendel went into a candy store and bought a roll of peppermints.'

"I could see from Mama's excited look that I was on the right track. 'So, so? What about those peppermints, baby?'

"'He paid for them with a dollar bill and put the change in his pocket. Then he got home, had a fight with his Papa, and ran out again without changing his clothes. He took a subway, stayed out for a few hours, then decided it was time to go home. But when he went back to the subway station there wasn't any money in his pockets! What happened to his change from the dollar bill? A nickel for peppermints, a nickel for one subway ride— he should have ninety cents left. Did he get his pocket picked? Foolishness. A boy like Mendel, who isn't exactly the rich-looking type, don't attract pick-pockets. He spent this ninety cents, Mama! This place where he went indoors, where he wouldn't take off his hat—it was some kind of store where he bought something for ninety cents.'

"'Good, good,' Mama said. 'But what kind of store is it where you're usually expected to take off your hat?'

"I couldn't say a word. All of a sudden my mind had run down again. Mama shook her head and said, 'You made such a good start with the peppermints, baby. Why don't you finish with them already? On the way home from the shop yesterday, Mendel bought peppermints. But he didn't eat them, he put them in his pocket and forgot about them. And after midnight, when he was finally asleep in his bed, his Mama went through his pockets and what did she find? No peppermints. Sometime in those four hours while he was out, he ate all the peppermints. So why?'

"'He was hungry,' I said. 'Didn't he miss his dinner?'

"'Does a growing young man make a dinner on a roll of peppermints? There's another reason for eating peppermints, no? The reason why he bought them in the first place—'

"'To hide the champagne on his breath from his Papa,' I said. 'But Mama, this was no reason any more, because Mendel's Papa already found out about the drinking.'

"'Naturally, that's the point I'm making,' Mama said. 'He ate those peppermints to cover up something else on his breath. Maybe to cover up—'

"I broke in on her because now, as clear as daylight, I saw the truth. 'To cover up something he was eating! Isn't that it, Mama? The store he went to in that non-Jewish neighborhood was a restaurant! In what other kind of place are you supposed to take off your hat? He was hungry, he went in there, he sat at a table, and ordered something which cost him ninety cents. It must have been something awful, Mama—because he swallowed a whole roll of peppermints to cover up the smell of it—and when he got home at midnight, he went straight to the bathroom and got sick!'

"'Very smart thinking,' Mama said, 'but you're sure it wasn't the champagne from the party that made him get sick in the bathroom?'

"'No, it couldn't have been,' I said. 'He already got sick from the champagne, earlier in the evening just before he left the shop. So at midnight it was something else that made him sick—something he ate at that restaurant—'

"'*Mazel tov*!' Mama said, and she looked prouder of me than I ever saw her look before. 'So tell me, baby, what was this food which gave Mendel such a sickness? What was it that he felt so ashamed of he had to cover it up with peppermints, and it upset him so much it made him sick?'

"'Mama, I don't know!' I said, and to tell you the truth I was practically in tears. 'I don't know what he ate in that restaurant, and even if I did, how is it going to get him out of jail?'

"Mama took me in her arms and patted me on the shoulder. 'Baby, it's so simple,' she said. 'If you wasn't so worried, you'd see how simple it is. A boy like Mendel, a quiet shy boy who don't stick up for himself—last night he finally stuck up for himself, he finally told his papa he was going to live his own life. And naturally, when he ran out of the apartment he was mad—a lot madder than some other boy would be, because Mendel's been saving up this madness for twenty-one years.'

"'I'll show Papa,' he said to himself. 'I'll do something desperate already! He'll see that I'm not under his thumb no more!' Then Mendel got off the subway and walked for a while and saw this restaurant and decided to do the positively most desperate thing he could think of. He went into the restaurant and ordered—'

"'Pork!' I blurted out, between sobbings and gulpings.

"'What else?' Mama said. 'Pork or ham or bacon—the forbidden food, the food that no orthodox Jewish boy who was brought up like Mendel can eat without giving God a slap in the face. He ate the *trefe* pork, and for maybe five minutes he felt like he just did a brave wonderful thing.'

"'But twenty-one years don't go down the drain in one night. All of a sudden, the brave feeling went away, and Mendel was hating himself, he was full of shame, he was expecting any minute that God would bring the thunder and lightning down on his head. And worst of all, he was imagining what his papa would say if he ever found out. Whatever happened, he couldn't let his papa find out!'

"'So he ran out of the restaurant and he stuffed his mouth with all the peppermints so there shouldn't be any smell of pork on his breath. Then he went home, and the idea of this forbidden food in his stomach was finally too much for him, so he got sick in the bathroom. And in the morning, when the police came and accused him of killing Sadie Katz, what a terrible pickle he was in! To clear himself he had to tell them what he was doing at the time of the murder, but this is the thing he can't tell anybody. Better the whole world should think he's a murderer than his papa should find out he ate *trefe* food.'

"When Mama finished, I was relieved and happy and mad, all at the same time. 'This is why he keeps saying how guilty he is, Mama? This is why he calls himself a sinner and a transgressor and admits he broke the law? That Mendel—how could he be so crazy?'

"'When you're twenty-one, it's easy,' Mama said. 'So we'll save him from his own craziness, baby. We'll tell our idea to the police, and they'll check up on restaurants, and it won't be long, believe me, that somebody remembers the skinny boy who wouldn't take off his hat.'

"And Mama was right, like always. The police found that restaurant by three o'clock in the afternoon and my Mendel was out of jail by four—and at five o'clock, exactly on schedule, Mendel and I got married. And we lived happy ever after—for thirty-two years."

We were silent for a moment, and then we all talked at once.

"If your husband didn't kill the girl," Shirley said, "who on earth did?"

"What was Papa's fountain pen doing on the floor of Sadie Katz's room?" I said. "And how do you explain the phone call she got on the night she was killed?"

"And why," Inspector Millner said, "did you tell us that this old case reminds you of the case we're working on now? What's the comparison between your Mendel and the Ortiz boy?"

Mom chose to answer this last question first. "I'll tell you the comparison," she said, "as soon as you answer me two questions." Then she raised a finger. "One. In the last few months, since the Ortiz boy started staying out late at night, is he spending more money than usual—wearing expensive clothes maybe, or buying fancy presents for his girlfriend?"

"Evidently not. Neither his sister nor his mother has seen him in any new clothes in the last four months. And his girl, Rosa Melendez, claims he doesn't even take her out to the movies as much as he used to."

"Two," Mom said. "When he was in high school, what classes did he have in learning how to put things together and take them apart?"

"Vocational training, you mean? He never had any. He always refused to take those courses at school, maybe because his father was always telling him he should take them."

Mom gave a nod. "Thank you. It's what I expected. Like you said—it's an open-and-shut case."

Inspector Millner got that look of misery on his face again. "You mean, you can't help the boy? You agree with us that he's guilty?"

"I was sure you'd feel that way, Mother," Shirley said. "If ever anybody's guilt was perfectly obvious—"

"Obvious?" Mom shook her head. "Like Mama told me years ago—jumping to conclusions is the best way there is to fall flat on your face. For months this Ortiz boy goes out after dinner at night and don't come back till midnight and wouldn't tell nobody where he's been, so everybody jumps to the conclusion he's doing something crooked."

Inspector Millner said, "What *other* conclusion—"

"These robbings and killings," Mom said, "which he's supposed to be doing every night—he only does them on weekdays. On weekends, on Saturday and Sunday nights, he goes out with his girlfriend like always. This don't seem funny to you? A gang of robbers that takes vacations on weekends, especially on Saturday nights, when more people are likely to be drunk and walking late on the streets and carrying a lot of money?

"And another funny thing: for months this boy is doing all these robberies but instead of spending more money than usual he's spending less. So what's happening to his profits? And one answer is coming to me, maybe there aren't any profits, maybe there isn't any gang of robbers."

"But Mom," I said, "that voice the boy's father heard over the phone when the boy called up his home a week ago—"

"This voice, it's the funniest thing of all. You remember what it said, this voice? 'Who's scared of the dicks? If any copper gets in my way, I'll mow him down!' An expert on gangsters I'm not, but occasionally I read the newspapers and look at the television and listen to the kids in this neighborhood talking. Tell me if I'm wrong, but it's my opinion a young tough guy nowadays wouldn't say something like 'dicks' and 'mow him down' if his life depended on it. The popular word today is 'fuzz'—no? And if you're going to shoot somebody, maybe you'll 'blast' him or 'cool' him. But 'dicks' and 'mow him down'—this is what they used to say twenty-five years ago. In fact, this is what they're always saying in those old movies with Humphrey Bogart and Edward G. Robinson."

Inspector Millner slapped his hand down on the table. "You aren't implying—"

"'You're right, I'm implying," Mom said. "That the voice talked like one of those old mobsters? Why not, if that's what it was? And where are they nowadays, those old movies? On television, am I right? When Mr. Ortiz talked to his son on the phone last week, what he heard in background was an old movie on the television."

"I don't see what that proves," Shirley said. "The boy and his hoodlum friends happened to be watching TV that night—"

"Look a little harder at that phone call," Mom said. "Like Mama used to tell me—half an answer is as bad as no answer at all. Why did the Ortiz boy make that call? Because he fixed his mother's television set early in the afternoon and he wanted to find out if it was still working. But who can fix a television set just by fooling around inside it with a screwdriver? Some knowledge and experience it takes. But this boy never had any classes in vocational training at his high school. So I'm asking myself where did he learn how to fix television sets? And I'm answering by putting two and two together.

"For months he's been staying out four hours every night—he never goes out like this on Saturday or Sunday nights—he's been spending not more but less money than usual during these months—the place where he goes has a television set playing—and suddenly, out of nowhere, he's got a talent for fixing television sets.

"Does this sound to you like a boy who's robbing and killing with a gang? Or does it sound like a boy who's taking a night course in how to be a television repairman so he can get a good job and marry the girl he loves?"

Looking half encouraged and half worried, Inspector Millner started shaking his head. "But if that's what he's been doing all these months, if that's what he was doing the night of the murder, why didn't he tell us? Why didn't he ever tell his parents?"

A sad little smile was on Mom's face again. "The younger generation," she said. "You think maybe it's changed after forty-five years? A Jewish boy on the East Side, a Puerto Rican boy on the West Side—but still they're two boys, with the same feelings and hurts and foolishness inside of them. For this little Ortiz boy, like for my Mendel, some things are worse than being arrested for murder. For both these boys the most important thing is, Papa shouldn't find out their secret."

"You're being illogical, Mother," Shirley said. "Your fiancé did something that his father would've disapproved of. Naturally he didn't want to be found out. But this Ortiz boy, if your theory is correct, has been doing something his father would approve of. So why should he try to hide it?"

"You answered your own question. Because his father would approve of it. In fact, when he was in high school his father told him to do something like this. The boy positively refused—but a few months ago he decided, all by himself, that his father was right. He signed up for the night course, he's been working at it hard and steady—but how could he admit this to his father, to such a father? How could he give his father the satisfaction of saying 'I told you so'? A boy's pride—is there anything stronger and crazier?

"And after a while, naturally, this turned into a vicious circle—the boy wouldn't say where he went at night, and this made his father call him a bum, and this made the boy even more stubborn about keeping his mouth shut. Until finally, even when the police arrested him, he couldn't back down from his pride and confess the truth. Sure it's not logical—unless you happen to be an eighteen-year-old boy."

Inspector Millner was beaming all over. "First thing tomorrow," he said, "I'll start checking all the schools for TV repairmen! That boy's mother—she's going to be so happy—"

A shadow came over Mom's face. "I wouldn't count on that," she said.

The Inspector looked up at her uncertainly. "I don't follow—"

"The boy didn't kill the cab driver," Mom said. "But just the same, his red leather jacket and his black motorcycle cap were at the scene of the crime. You saw them running away from the cab, Davie, and your eyesight I wouldn't doubt. So if the boy wasn't wearing those things, who was?"

"He was wearing them when he went out that night, Mom. His mother and father both say so."

"Absolutely. Every night, when he went out, he wore them. Because his father didn't want him to. But what about when he got to his repairman school? He couldn't show up there in such a crazy outfit. He had to wear a neat clean suit there, like any other serious hard-working student. So before he reached the school every night, there had to be someplace where he could take off the red jacket and put on the nice suit. And when school was over for the night, he had to go back to this place and change into the jacket again, and leave the suit for the next night.

"Where could he find such a place? A hotel room? But how could he afford it? A friend's place? But who could he trust with such a secret? One person only. His sister—what's-her-name?—Inez. She's a year older than him, she has a room in a hotel downtown, she hates their father even worse than he does. The night of the murder, he left his red jacket and his black cap with her, the way he's been doing for months. And after he left for his school, she put on his jacket and his cap, the way *she's* been doing for months, and she went out to rob cab drivers. With a pair of pants, it's a perfect disguise for her—because the cab driver would swear to the police that he was robbed by a boy, not a girl."

"And Rafael is a small thin boy!" I said. "He wears his hair long, like all these kids nowadays. In that red jacket and that motorcycle cap—not to mention the family resemblance—it's no wonder Palazzo identified him as the killer!"

"And it's no wonder," Mom said, "you thought you saw him running away from the scene of the crime."

There was a silence. Then a soft sigh came out of Inspector Millner. "I'll have her picked up tonight," he said. "And I guess I'll call her mother—"

Another silence, and then Shirley couldn't contain herself any longer. "That's all very well, Mother," she burst out, "but what about the old murder, the Sadie Katz murder? Did they ever find out who killed her?"

Mom turned to Shirley, smiled at her a moment, then said, "Did I forget to tell you? Excuse me, my mistake. Mama found out who killed her—naturally."

"Your mother was able to explain the fountain pen?" Shirley said. "And the phone call, when Sadie Katz seemed to be talking to your fiancé and inviting him up to her room?"

"The phone call was Mama's best clue to the real murderer," Mom said. "Why did the police think it was Mendel who made that call? Why was Mendel supposed to be the man Sadie Katz invited up to her room? She had plenty of men on the string—including somebody who never came for her at the rooming house, but always made her meet him outside—so why should the police pick on Mendel?

"Well, like Mama pointed out, it all boiled down to one thing that Sadie said to that man on the phone, 'What are you afraid of? You're still a free man, aren't you? You can do what you like.' Who could Sadie have meant by these words except a single man who was about to get married? And except for Mendel there was no such man in her acquaintance.

"But Mendel had an alibi for the murder, so Sadie wasn't talking to him on the phone. So, like Mama told me, 'Maybe those words didn't mean what everybody thinks. After all, who heard Sadie saying those words? Mr. and Mrs. Spiegel—two old people that just came over from Germany five years ago, that never learned English so good, that prefer Yiddish plays to American plays because they can't understand what the American actors are saying. Isn't there a good chance these two people maybe didn't hear so clearly what Sadie Katz said on the phone?'

"Mama didn't have to go on. In a flash I saw what she was getting at. 'Mama, that's the answer! The Spiegels thought that Sadie Katz said, You're still a free man, aren't you? You can do what you like. But what she really said was, You're Friedman, aren't you? You can do what you like. It was Mr. Friedman, her boss, that she was talking to on the phone. She'd been having an affair with him, and he's the man who never picked her up at the rooming house, who'd been meeting her outside. He called her up that night and wanted to see her. She insisted he should come to her place—and when he said he was afraid somebody might see him, she laughed and said that a big shot like him could do what he liked.

"'So he came to the rooming house and went upstairs with her—and maybe he told her he wanted to break off their affair—and maybe she got mad and threatened to tell his wife. So he strangled her. And as for the fountain pen, Mama—well, when Mendel got home from the shop yesterday, didn't he stand on the stoop and wave at people and show them the fountain pen? And didn't Sadie Katz run up to him at that moment and throw her arms around him and kiss him? So maybe, in his surprise, he dropped the pen, and maybe Sadie picked it up—automatically, absentminded, the way people do—and that explains what it was doing in her room.'

"I stopped talking and waited for Mama to tell me what a detective genius I was. But she only shook her head."

"'Half answers, always half answers,' she said. 'Out of "you're still a free man, aren't you?" how could you get "you're Friedman, aren't you?" Where's the *still*, and where's the *a*? Even if you didn't understand English so good, you'd notice that certain sounds were left over. What Sadie really said on the phone had to be a lot closer to what the Spiegels thought they heard.'

"'But what was it, Mama?'

"'Baby,' Mama said, 'it's a well-known fact that embarrassed husbands commit a lot less murders than jealous wives.'

"'Mrs. Friedman? She's the one—'

"'Why not?' Mama said. 'She found out about her husband's affair, and she called up Sadie Katz on the phone and demanded to see her that night. She wanted to meet Sadie uptown, but Sadie liked the idea of making this ritzy rich woman come down to her. "What are you afraid of?" Sadie said to her. "You're Stella Friedman, aren't you? You can do what you like." And sure enough, an hour or so later, Stella Friedman did what she liked— she strangled Sadie to death!'"

Mom stopped for a breath, then went on quietly, "At the trial, incidentally, the jury found her not guilty, on the grounds of temporary insanity."

That was the end of Mom's story. I breathed a sigh of relief. What I feared hadn't happened. She had gone through all that reminiscing about the old days, about her wedding day, but she looked as cheerful as ever.

And then my heart sank. Suddenly there were tears filling Mom's eyes.

"What's the matter?" Inspector Millner cried. "Is there anything I can do?"

"I'm all right, I'm all right," Mom said. "I was only thinking—the younger generation today, the younger generation in the old days, maybe there is a difference after all. Poor Mendel—he was ready to die so he shouldn't make his father ashamed of him. And this Ortiz boy—he was ready to die so he shouldn't make his father *proud* of him."

Slowly Mom began to shake her head. "It's a funny world we're living in these days. Mama wouldn't like it much, I think. It's a good thing maybe that she never lived to see it."

Mom lowered her eyes. A moment later she took out a handkerchief and blew her nose. When she looked up, she was smiling again. "So now for dessert," she said. "In your honor, Inspector, I baked an angel food!"

Then Mom got to her feet, and like a general at the head of his victorious army she marched out to the kitchen.

BATYA SWIFT YASGUR has been publishing short stories regularly in such magazines as *Ellery Queen* and
Midstream for a number of years. She has written
non-fiction books as well as three young adult mystery books. In this story, Yasgur sensitively deals with
a troubling problem that is uncovered in the process
of solving the mystery. "Kaddish" originally appeared
in *Ellery Queen Magazine*.

Kaddish

▼   ▼   ▼   ▼   ▼   ▼   ▼

BATYA SWIFT YASGUR

"WHY ME?"

"A nice Jewish question," MacAllister answered. "Why you? Because
you're of their faith, that's why."

"But I haven't been a practicing Jew for years—"

MacAllister shrugged. "Jews will probably open up more to another Jew
than to an outsider." He smiled his toothy smile and clapped me on the
shoulder. "Go on, Schwartz. Here's the file. Find out who murdered the
rabbi."

But you don't understand, I wanted to shout at his fleshy back as it
retreated from my little cubicle. I'm worse than an outsider. Worse than a
goy. I'm an *apikores,* an apostate, my own parents won't have me in the
house. You don't understand, MacAllister. I don't want to prowl around
the study of some dead rabbi any more than I want to sit at the feet of some
living rabbi. Can't I slosh through the mud and investigate that body that
washed up on the banks of the Hudson last week? Or risk my neck in Harlem
dredging up information on that missing baby? I'd gladly take a gunshot or
two, but keep me away from ghosts with *yarmulkes,* keep me away from the
shadowy echoes of Hebrew prayers and Talmudic chants.

But there's no arguing with MacAllister once he's made up his mind, once
his red face creases into its smug folds, once he thinks he knows. You do as
you're told, like a child in religious school.

So here I was, uncomfortably edging my way into the *shiva,* the room where the mourners, family of the deceased Rabbi Weissman were receiving guests to comfort them.

A hushed room, covered mirrors, a buxom woman in a formless dress, torn at the collar in memory of the dead, her head modestly draped in a scarf, dabbing red eyes. The rebbitzen, I guessed. Mrs. Weissman. Two young men, Rabbi Weissman's sons, on either side, one with earlocks and a Hebrew book open on his lap, the other looking more modern, with *The Jewish Way in Death and Mourning* in his hand. A bevy of people, men with *yarmulkes,* women with wigs or scarves, long skirts, long sleeves. Murmured snatches reached my ears:

"Yes, he was a *tzaddik,* a holy man . . ."

"To think, such a tragedy!"

"A murder—in our community—what next—"

I elbowed my way gingerly to the front. Conversation ceased, as a dozen Orthodox eyes turned to look at me. A stranger in their midst. A stranger who should belong.

"Rebbitzen Weissman? I'm sorry to intrude, I know what a difficult time this is for you, but I need to ask you some questions. I'm Jack Schwartz." I displayed my badge.

"Oy, more questions?" She turned her red eyes toward me. "I thought I'd answered them already and *genug schoin,* enough, let me be."

I shrugged, feeling worse than ever. "I'm sorry, really, but I've been assigned to the case, and I always ascertain the facts for myself." (Indeed, that had been my undoing in the religion: take nobody's word for things, not the rabbis, not the Talmud, and trust nothing that I haven't experienced. A bad idea for a religion that relies upon the testimony of others.)

I glanced at all the open-mouthed visitors, glaring at me. "Is there someplace where we can talk privately?"

Of course not, I realized. Stupid of me. No Orthodox woman would converse alone in a room with a man. I was about to apologize yet again, when, as if on cue, the guests all rose, muttered the obligatory Hebrew words of consolation, "May God comfort you among the mourners of Zion and Jerusalem," and filed out, leaving Rebbitzen Weissman and her two sons.

An awkward silence, punctuated by sobs. I opened with the usual questions.

"Where was your husband when he was killed?"

"In his study at the *shul*—at the synagogue," she translated for my benefit.

"Why was he there?"

She shrugged, a look of disbelief on her face. (You mean, you don't know, what kind of detective—and worse, what kind of Jew—are you anyway? it said.) "He always saw congregants in his study. They came to him in droves, especially at night. After evening services and his evening Talmud class. He rarely came home before ten o'clock at night. I always said to him—'Levi, you work too hard. You should take better care of yourself.' But he was such a devoted man, always doing *chesed*, acts of kindness and charity. He always put the congregation before himself." And she began to cry again.

"Mama, don't," said the earlocked son, handing her a tissue.

"Father was like that," said the second son, the modern one. "And such an exponent of the faith! I wasn't always religious—I strayed away from the Torah—but he brought me back with his love."

I didn't want to hear this, the eulogies, the paroxysm of posthumous worship. "So who came to see him that night?"

"I don't know. Levi never talked about who came with *shailos*—you know, religious questions—or for counseling. It was personal."

"But he had a diary," Modern Son added quickly. "You should find it in the top right hand corner of his desk."

I wrote that down. "Any enemies?"

The three began talking at once, a hubbub of denials. I held my hand up.

"No one, especially a rabbi, is universally loved. Come on, tell me the truth."

Exchanges of glances, a few "hm's" and "er's." Then a big sigh from the rebbitzen. "All right, yes, there were a few. But you can't seriously suspect someone within the *shul*? Surely it was an outsider, maybe a hit-and-run driver who shot him through the window of the study as he drove by on the street, maybe some anti-Semite, a neo-Nazi, there's a whole bunch of them in the next town over—"

"We're investigating all that. A neighbor thought she might have heard a car, we're looking into that, but we can't rule anything out."

"Even other Jews—I can't believe that, that another Jew would—"

The familiar irritation rose to the surface like a rash. "Jews aren't immune. They're—we're—as prone to pettiness and crime as anyone else." My voice was sharp, I realized I'd have to tone it down or these people would never open up and trust me. "Just tell me, please. Was there anyone in the *shul* who disliked your husband?"

"Well. There were a few people who made *tsoris* for him, tried to block his contract renewal. Reuben and Rachel Glassner. They've hated my husband because he didn't visit Reuben's father in the hospital. He couldn't help it," she burst out, "nobody told him old Mr. Glassner was sick till it was too late. But they won't believe that. And Simon Siden, he thinks my husband's sermons were too long." A pause, the rebbitzen's knuckles pressed to her eyes. "Oh, and Judah Mackler. He thought my husband's religious rulings were too lenient. Oy, was he angry that my husband allowed Kosher-Taste Caterers to cater in our *shul,* because there was that scandal about rabbinic supervision there a few years ago, and lots of Orthodox Jews won't eat their food."

I scribbled busily. "Anyone else?"

Another pause, more glances exchanged, more sighs. "No, but you'll check the neo-Nazis? My husband, he was a Holocaust survivor."

"I'll check everything."

The rebbitzen nodded, grasped her sons' hands. "Anything else you can tell me?"

She shook her head, her eyes welling again.

"Anything about your husband? How did he spend his time? Did he have any hobbies, involvements, something which could help me to—"

The babble of praise broke out. Hospital visits, charitable acts, hours spent over Talmudic tomes.

"He loved to read mysteries," the Modern Son mentioned diffidently.

"Ssh." It was a sort of hiss from the earlocked son. "It doesn't honor our father's memory to have people know that."

I swallowed the bile that had risen bitterly to my throat. "What kind of mysteries?"

"Sherlock Holmes," the young man said, glancing apologetically at his brother. "Whenever Father wanted to relax, he used to read Sherlock Holmes. He had a copy here, and one in his study at *shul.*"

Thank God. It made the late unfortunate Rabbi Levi Weissman a *bissel* more human.

I put my notebook away and turned to leave. "I'll let you know as soon as I find anything out."

"Wait." It was the rebbitzen, holding out a tremulous hand, which she almost put on my arm. Then, remembering the religious restriction against touching men, she dropped it. "You are Jewish, aren't you."

I nodded, a lump suddenly blocking my throat.

"Orthodox?"

"No, I'm not Orthodox."

She shook her head. "My husband would have fixed that. If you had met him—"

Fixed that. Fixed me. I muttered something, not the prayer of comfort and consolation—and fled.

Interviews, interviews, establishing alibis. Nothing. The Glassners had been at a bar mitzvah (plenty of witnesses). Simon Siden had been resting in bed, his wife shrilly and indignantly protested. Judah Mackler had travelled to New York to attend a Talmud class. (He wouldn't set foot in Rabbi Weissman's, he informed me, enunciating every syllable as if I were an infant or mentally retarded, because the rabbi was far too lenient in his religious rulings, and so even his Talmudic scholarship couldn't be trusted.) The synagogue's neighbor mentioned something about a car, but she couldn't be sure. She'd heard the gunshot and called the police, but was it really a car she'd heard first? It had been so late at night, and she had been so deeply asleep, and her boiler often made noises that sounded like an engine.

All blank. The study had better hold more promise.

And so, timid and trembling, I pushed open the door to Rabbi Weissman's study.

And found myself, after years of running, face to face with the angels and demons of my childhood: the volumes of Torah and Talmud, commentaries and sages, titles of gold gleaming seductively and wickedly at me from their maroon covers. Rashi. Nachmanides. Maimonides. *The Code of Jewish Law.* And there, dimpling like an old friend, *The Complete Sherlock Holmes,* as well-thumbed as any Talmudic tractate, sitting on the desk.

I nosed around the office, prowled like a caged lion, glancing out of the window. The front window looked out onto the street. Sitting at his desk, where he was shot in the head, Rabbi Weissman could have easily been targeted by the hypothetical neo-Nazi in a car. It had been a warm night, the windows were open . . .

No one could have come through the back window. A small stream ran muddily under the window. Anyone shooting through that window would have had to slosh through the murky water and would have alerted the rabbi to his presence. But the rabbi had been found, slumped over his desk, facing away from the back window, facing the front. That would be well and good except that the shot was to his left temple. Anyone shooting from the street couldn't have hit his temple unless—

Unless it wasn't someone shooting from the street.

I shook my head. The old dicta of childhood rose, rumbled, warned: "Never suspect another Jew." It would be easy, too easy, to drown the appointment book, to look no further, to gloss the whole thing over and the hell with MacAllister.

But no, there was also a commitment to the truth, to justice. (And more phrases from childhood rose, unbidden: "God's first word is Truth and His Justice is eternal.") Slowly, reluctantly, I opened the desk drawers. And, sure enough, the appointment book was where the young man had said it would be: in the top right-hand desk drawer. Feeling like an intruder, as I always did when going through the personal effects of someone else—living or dead—I opened it to the date of his death.

Appointments: Mrs. Faige Cohen, 9:00, Mr. David Brown, 9:30, Mr. and Mrs. Hyman Nahmanson, 10:00.

And then a new round of interviews, as I trudged from door to door.

Faige Cohen, a diminutive, white-haired, shriveled up old lady, had come to see the rabbi regarding a confusion of pots and pans. She had cooked a chicken in her dairy pan, and had her grandchildren coming tomorrow. Was the chicken kosher, since dairy could not be mixed with meat? Could she serve the chicken? Her voice shook as she recounted the rabbi's remarks. "I—I was so upset, you know, since my husband Joseph died, may he rest in peace, I don't have much money, just my little pension, and I didn't know how I would replace a whole chicken. And the rabbi, may he rest in peace, said I should just go ahead and use the chicken." No, she knew no one who could wish him ill, she was home by 9:25, and the bus driver on the #155 line could identify her if necessary.

David Brown was a young man, barely out of his teens, a *yarmulke* resting unevenly on a shock of red hair. "It was a weird situation I went to see the rabbi about. A religious question, you know, and I was sure the rabbi would say, no, no way." He shook his head and folded his arms. "But he said yes."

"Yes to what?"

"Well, I'm in college, you know. And, like, most professors usually don't schedule exams on Saturdays because of *Shabbos*, the Sabbath. They're usually pretty considerate of the Orthodox students, and they know our rules. See, we don't write on Sabbath, you know."

I nodded. I knew.

"Well, I couldn't get Microeconomics rescheduled. A bitch of a professor, she's real nasty and I'm sure she's anti-Semitic. You know. And she had to go and schedule our big final right on Saturday. I couldn't get out of it, I would've failed, you know, and, like, I didn't know what to do. But Rabbi Weissman threw me for a loop. He said yes, I should go take the exam, I could write if I needed to."

To write on Saturday? This was bizarre. To violate Sabbath? The chicken was possible, even though my own training told me that a chicken cooked in dairy utensils was *treif,* unkosher, and had to be discarded. But maybe the rabbi, with his learning and his expertise, knew of some loophole, some leniency that I wasn't aware of. But Sabbath was inviolable, except in life-threatening situations. Something was odd, incongruous. It was with a strange, queasy feeling (not dissimilar to the squishing in my stomach the first time I ate pork) that I proceeded to the Nahmansons.

The door was opened by a thin, bearded, bespectacled young man, obviously in the middle of dinner (he was still holding his fork, and a napkin was tucked in his pants). A petite, kerchiefed woman peeked out shyly from the kitchen.

Greetings, apologies about the interrupted dinner, then on to business. "Why did you come to see Rabbi Weissman the night of his death?"

A glance passed between them, frightened, tremulous. "How did you know? This was a—a very private matter, nobody was supposed to know we came."

"And nobody did." I tried to make my voice as soothing as possible. "Your names were in his diary. That's how I found out."

The news didn't seem to relieve them. "I'm sorry," said Hyman. "But it's too private to talk about."

"In a murder investigation, I'm afraid nothing can be kept private."

Again, the frightened glances. "Please believe me when I say that nothing we talked to the rabbi about could have possibly been connected with this horrible tragedy. It was—it was a highly personal matter."

God, how I hated this part of it. The pushing, the prying. "I'm sorry, really I am, but a man is dead, and these are questions I have to ask."

The petite woman burst into tears and ran out of the room.

Hyman glared. "Well, if you must know—" he thrust out his lip belligerently. "We're newlyweds. Married three months ago. Rabbi Weissman performed the ceremony." He paused, licked his lips, his beard trembling. "I—we—I mean, my wife—are you familiar with the Orthodox marriage laws?" Before I could nod, he plunged on. "A man can't touch his wife—

make love, even hand her a plate—during her menstrual period, and for seven days afterward. My wife has had something which Jewish law sees as a long period. She just won't stop staining. The doctor says that's normal during times of stress and transition. But it's been hell." His voice broke, he covered his face. "A tease, a miserable tease, to share a room with your new bride, a woman you can't even touch. Your wife. We couldn't stand it any more, we went to Rabbi Weissman hoping there was some leniency he could find. And he studied the holy books and, well, he found a way." A tiny smile creased the tormented face. "Even when she's staining, we can still hug, hold hands and—" his face reddened and he looked at the floor, "well, you know."

I knew. I knew. I knew the torment, I knew the liberation, and I knew so much more.

I knew before I re-entered the study, before I opened the holy books that were strewn across the desk, that the rabbi had consulted (or pretend-ed to consult), I knew before I unearthed my rusty Hebrew, cleaned it and oiled it and used it to delve into those ancient tomes. There was no way, not within Jewish law, that Hyman could be allowed to touch his wife while she was staining. Not during her period. It was a cardinal sin, a violation of all the tenets and codes, tantamount to eating on Yom Kippur, and worse, far worse, than eating pork, worse than violating the Sabbath, the penalty for which is death.

The rabbi was cutting corners. No, that was an understatement. Rabbi Weissman had completely dumped Jewish law—at least any law that made life inconvenient, difficult, or painful for its followers.

And, sitting in his chair, I thought I understood. "You do not under-stand a man until you've stood in his shoes," so say the rabbis. Sitting in Rabbi Weissman's chair was enough.

The stream, the endless stream of sorrows and pleas, the burden of being spokesman for a God of dread and restriction, of rules and penalties, when inside, it was all crumbling, the demon of doubt growing, consuming, chas-ing him from pulpit to lectern to podium to sing the praises of the faith in flawless Hebrew and propound its mystery and its wonder. To sing to him-self, to that part of himself that held the memory of swastikas and babies' blood, still raw, still screaming from within the void.

Yes, I knew. I knew the demon and I knew its devil's pact: escape. As I had escaped into the world of the goy, the non-Jew, into the police force, into the arms of women and into restaurants that served pork and milk together, and my parents had mourned me as dead—as I had so escaped, so had he. He had taken a more courageous step, mourned as dead because he was dead. Dead, I was now sure, by his own hand.

But how? No suicide note, no murder weapon. How could someone shoot himself in the head and conceal the murder weapon with such skill?

The answer lay in this study, it had to. This was his home, his abode, his haven and his prison. Someplace here, there was a clue, there had to be. I searched again, crawled along the floor, peered in every corner. Nothing.

Desk drawers: nothing. Floor: nothing. Bookshelves: nothing.

I sat down again, moving things around on the desk. If I were Rabbi Weissman, and I was tense, beleaguered, strung out, what would I do? Where would I turn? Not to prayer, God had abandoned me, had abandoned six million of my brethren. Not to the holy books. They held nothing but torment.

Then I remembered what the Modern Son had said. Whenever his father needed to relax, he read Sherlock Holmes.

There was a bookmark in Sherlock Holmes, and I opened to the story "The Problem at Thor Bridge."

And there, in the story, was the answer. No suicide note needed. The story was enough. A suicide plan right there, all laid out.

Like the woman in the story, Rabbi Weissman had a gun. Who knows where he got it? It really didn't matter. He had tied a string to the gun, weighed it down with a rock which he hung out of the window. Immediately after shooting, he let go and the gun was whisked out of the window, away, away, into the muddy pond below.

So I went. Schwartz the desanctified Jew who knew exactly what to do. I went there.

And saw the pond yield its muddy evidence, then, as I dragged it, and that terrible testimony surfacing.

The gun, complete with string and rock.

Suicide.

But, oh, the shame and stigma of a suicide in the Orthodox community. The rabbi's grave would have to be dug up so he could be buried outside the cemetery, outside the community, a sign of his sin, that he had disposed of himself, damaged a life and a body not his own but God's. His secret wrenched and paraded before the congregation, the merciless light of truth glaring upon his remains, upon the remains of his widow, his children, upon the ruins of their temple of memory and faith.

But that is not what happened because it was not what I decided I would tell them.

Instead, this: let this crime be filed as unsolved (another rabbinic dictum rising to the surface, evidence muddy but unmistakable: "One can alter the truth for the sake of peace."). Let MacAllister grumble, let the rebbitzen mutter about police incompetence, but let the dead remain buried intact, let the living hold onto their illusions.

And so I entered that house of mourning, that *shiva,* again, the mourners flanked by congregants who parted as the waters of the Red Sea to let me through.

"No answers," I told them, the sobbing rebbitzen, the somber sons, the murmuring congregants. "Hit and run driver makes the most sense. We'll never know."

She nodded, they all nodded, then shook their heads, a swell of Yiddish and Hebrew and Aramaic growing louder, louder, until the earlocked son glanced at his watch. He stood up. "*Mincha*!" he announced. "Time for afternoon prayer."

The women took off like frightened rabbits, while the earlocked son did a count. "Seven, eight, nine . . . not enough for a *minyan.*" He turned to me. "Can you be the tenth man?"

Me? *Apikores,* apostate, sinner. Me?

Me, a Jew. Still a Jew, always a Jew.

I took the prayer book, opened it to the correct page, memory casting aside disuse, words ancient and terrible rising, arcing from my throat, words I swore I'd never recite again.

But this was right. Somehow, this was right, to participate in this one last act of prayer. I could do it, I had to do it. A memorial to the dead. Not to the dead rabbi, no, he was beyond memorials, beyond tributes, he was someplace where none of that mattered. No, this was a memorial to his faith, now dead, shattered, dissolved in a blast of gunpowder and blood. A memorial to his faith, that broken vessel of light, its sparks scattered and lost.

And to mine.

Yisgadal v'yiskadash sh'mei rabboh.

May I be comforted among the mourners of Zion and Jerusalem.

Continuation of Copyright Page

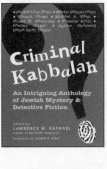

Spirituality

HOW TO BE A PERFECT STRANGER, In 2 Volumes
A Guide to Etiquette in Other People's Religious Ceremonies
Edited by *Stuart M. Matlins & Arthur J. Magida*

"A book that belongs in every living room, library and office!"

BEST REFERENCE BOOK OF THE YEAR

Explains the rituals and celebrations of America's major religions/denominations, helping an interested guest to feel comfortable, participate to the fullest extent possible, and avoid violating anyone's religious principles.

•AWARD WINNER• Answers practical questions from the perspective of *any* other faith.

VOL. 1: America's Largest Faiths

VOL. 1 COVERS: Assemblies of God • Baptist • Buddhist • Christian Science • Churches of Christ • Disciples of Christ • Episcopalian • Greek Orthodox • Hindu • Islam • Jehovah's Witnesses • Jewish • Lutheran • Methodist • Mormon • Presbyterian • Quaker • Roman Catholic • Seventh-day Adventist • United Church of Christ

6" x 9", 432 pp. HC, ISBN 1-879045-39-7 **$24.95**

VOL. 2: Other Faiths in America

VOL. 2 COVERS: African American Methodist Churches • Baha'i • Christian and Missionary Alliance • Christian Congregation • Church of the Brethren • Church of the Nazarene • Evangelical Free Church of America • International Church of the Foursquare Gospel • International Pentecostal Holiness Church • Mennonite/Amish • Native American • Orthodox Churches • Pentecostal Church of God • Reformed Church of America • Sikh • Unitarian Universalist • Wesleyan

6" x 9", 416 pp. HC, ISBN 1-879045-63-X **$24.95**

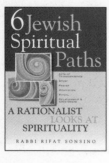

SIX JEWISH SPIRITUAL PATHS
A Rationalist Looks at Spirituality
by *Rabbi Rifat Sonsino*

The quest for spirituality is universal, but which path to spirituality is right *for you?* A straightforward, objective discussion of the many ways—each valid and authentic—for seekers to gain a richer spiritual life within Judaism.

6" x 9", 208 pp. HC, ISBN 1-58023-095-4 **$21.95**

THESE ARE THE WORDS
A Vocabulary of Jewish Spiritual Life
by *Arthur Green*

What are the most essential ideas, concepts and terms that an educated person needs to know about Judaism? From *Adonai* (My Lord) to *zekhut* (merit), this enlightening and entertaining journey through Judaism teaches us the 149 core Hebrew words that constitute the basic vocabulary of Jewish spiritual life.

6" x 9", 304 pp. Quality Paperback, ISBN 1-58023-107-1 **$18.95**